The Catnap Ramblers

book 3

Aurora and the Guardian

J.B. Thwaite

Ebook: ISBN 978-952-65297-9-0

Paperback: ISBN 978-952-65297-7-6

Hardcover: ISBN 978-952-65297-8-3

Book cover and illustrations: J.B. Thwaite aka Napukettu.

Publisher: Napuke, Finland (http://books.napuke.com)

Content information

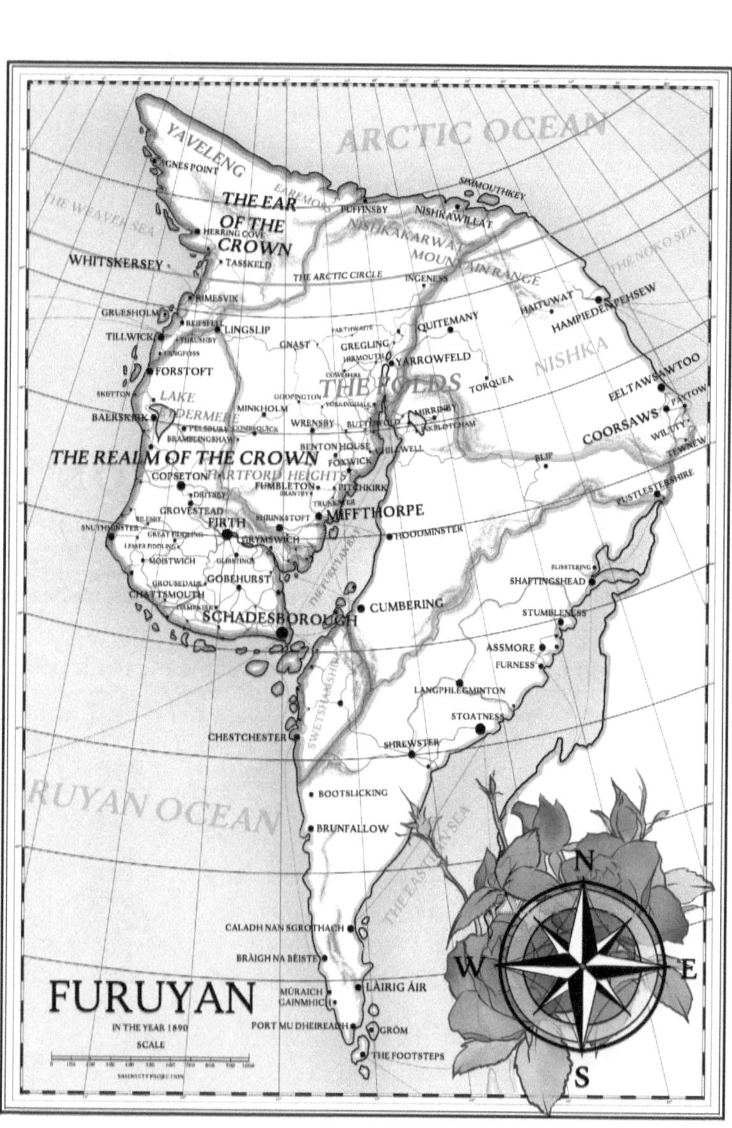

ARCTIC OCEAN
YAVELENG
AGNES POINT
EAREMOU
THE EAR
OF THE
CROWN
SAMMOUTHKEY
PUFFINSBY
NISHKAWILLAT
THE WEAVER SEA
HERRING COVE
NISHKAKARWAY
MOUNTAIN RANGE
THE NOKO SEA
WHITSKERSEY
TASSKELD
THE ARCTIC CIRCLE
INGENESS
HAITUWAT
HAMPIEDEN PEHSEW
RIMESVIK
GRUESHOLM
REIFSFELL
LINGSLIP
FARTHWAITE
QUITEMANY
NISHKA
TILLWICK
THRUSHBY
GNAST
GREGLING
YARROWFELD
LANGFOSS
HIRMOUTH
FORSTOFT
COWEMIRE
THE FOLDS
TORQUEA
EELTAWSAWTOO
SKIFTON
LAKE
GOOPINGTON
PAYTOW
BALRSKIRK
UPPERMERE
MINKHOLM
YOSKINGDALE
COORSAWS
WILUTY
PELSBURG
COMBQUICK
WRENSBY
BUTTERGOLD
MIRRINBY
TEWNEW
BRAMBLINGSHAW
BENTON HOUSE
CHILLWELL
BAKBLOTOHAM
THE REALM OF THE CROWN
FOXWICK
BLIP
HARTFORD HEIGHTS
COPSETON
FUMBLETON
PITCHKIRK
PUSTLESTERSHIRE
DRITSEY
BRANTBY
GROVESTEAD
FIRTH
SHRINKSTOFT
TRUNKSTER
MIFFTHORPE
BILESBY
DRYMSWICH
SNUTHMINSTER
GREAT FIDDLING
HOODMINSTER
LESSER FIDDLING
BLISSTERING
MOISTWICH
GLIBSTING
SHAFTINGSHEAD
GROUSEDALE
GOBEHURST
STUMBLENESS
CHATTSMOUTH
HAMPAIRK
CUMBERING
ASSMORE
SCHADESBOROUGH
THE FURRY AKEWAY
FURNESS
LANGPHLEGMINTON
SWETSHAMSHIRE
STOATNESS
CHESTCHESTER
SHREWSTER
RUYAN OCEAN
BOOTSLICKING
BRUNFALLOW
THE EAST CORN SEA
CALADH NAN SGROTHACH
BRÀIGH NA BÈISTE
N
MÙRAICH GAINMHICH
LÀIRIG ÁIR
W
E
FURUYAN
PORT MU DHEIREADH
GRÒM
IN THE YEAR 1890
THE FOOTSTEPS
SCALE
S
BASSNETT PROJECTION

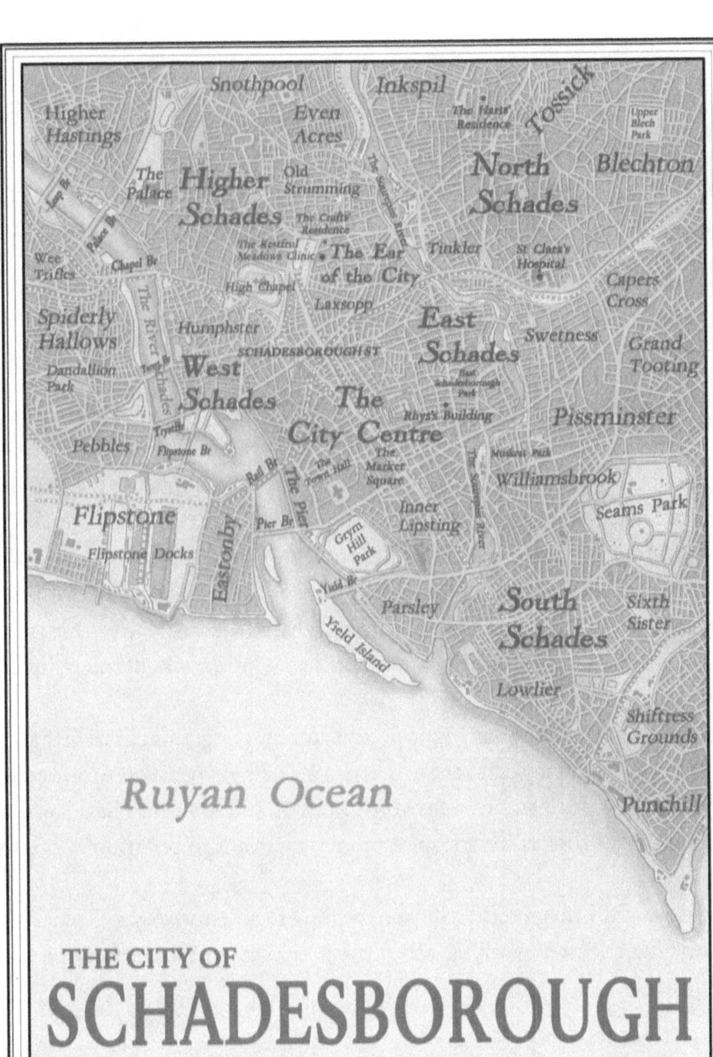

THE CITY OF
SCHADESBOROUGH

Note from the Author

This book is written in British English. Here is a bucket of z's for my American readers to take along and add where you see fit. Take the whole bucket with you, so you can collect all the extra letters (mainly u's) into it. You can return it at the end of your read, and I will take care of the recycling. I ~~apologise~~ apologize for the inconvenience!

Because this story has fairly many points of view and a couple of time jumps, I've added character-specific dinkuses (the decorative thingam-abobs) at the start of every chapter and scene break (where the point of view changes) to clue you in.

I am deeply sorry for any typos, extra commas or grammatical mistakes in this book. I and my editor have been on a lengthy expedition to hunt and catch the pesky things, but we are only human, and some may have slipped through. My inbox is always open should you want to point them out to me.

And lastly, I am grateful to anyone willing to give my story a chance. It's something I've been working on for over a decade, so I sincerely hope you enjoy it!

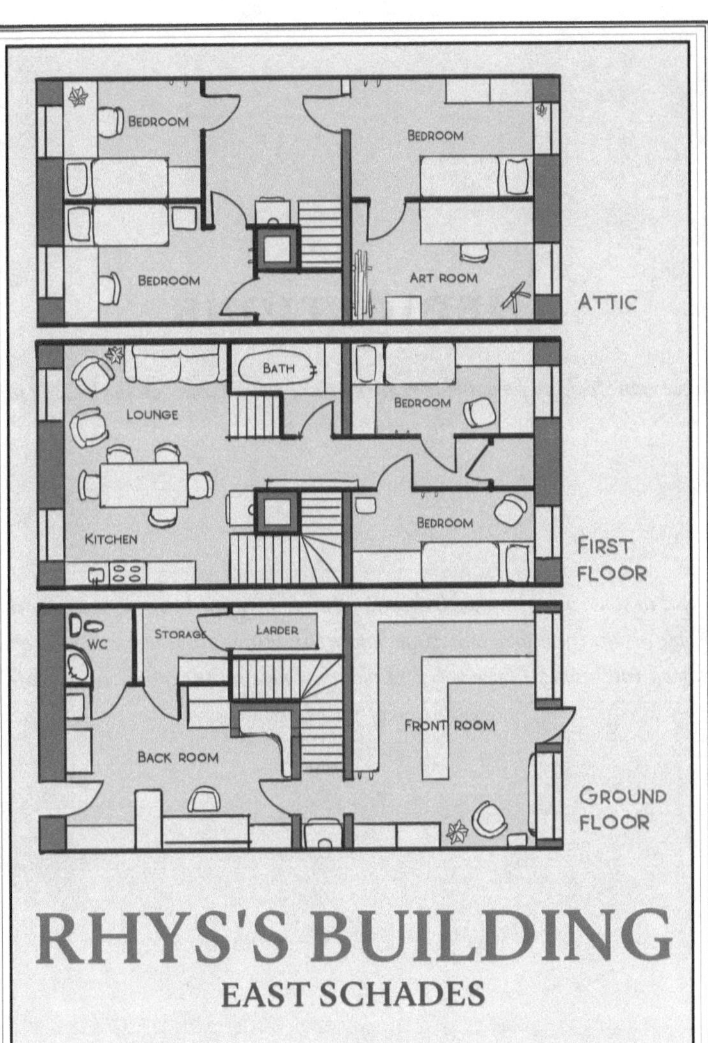

RHYS'S BUILDING

EAST SCHADES

DEDICATIONS

To everyone looking forward to reading this book. Thank you for having faith in me and the story.

And to you, struggling with chronic illness: may you have patience for the people around you who sometimes end up making things worse despite their good intentions. I hope you find plenty of joy and meaning in your life regardless of your hardships.

CHAPTER 1

D r Vesper set down the piece of paper after reading the message typed on it for the second time. She reached for Theodore, took a sip and let the lukewarm tea linger for a moment on her tongue. Then she grabbed Florence and scribbled something on the side of another piece of paper and tried to gather herself.

No, it was no good. A short whistling sound slipped through her nose, and she glanced at her office door, wondering whether it was robust enough to thwart such sounds.

She hurried to read the paper for a third time, her chest tight, fearing she'd somehow misunderstood. This was a promotion, wasn't it? This was an invitation to come work with the research team at the Restful Meadows sleep disorder research clinic in Schadesborough with the best of the best, all fully funded.

Dr Vesper took a deep breath and bit her lip but couldn't keep her smile from widening. The nervous excitement was begging to burst out, but she was at work, and having to deal with her male colleagues was already a handful. She peeked out into the lobby to make sure no one but Ms Larkspur was within earshot.

Ms Larkspur looked up, so Dr Vesper waved her in.

"What is it, doctor?"

"Look at this and tell me..." Dr Vesper showed her the message. "It is what I think it is, right?"

Ms Larkspur's eyes widened as she confirmed Dr Vesper's assessment.

"Oh, dear. Finally!" The head secretary shook Dr Vesper's hands, and she could no longer restrain herself.

"I'm getting a cat!" Dr Vesper yelped with tears in her eyes.

"Congratulations!" Ms Larkspur also started to cry and gave Dr Vesper a tight hug.

Dr Vesper was cleaning out her office when Ms Larkspur dropped off a parcel for her. It was relatively large and heavy and looked to contain some of the sleep research data and relevant patient files that they had collected at the Sleepy Leighs Treatment Centre during its first few years of operation.

Ms Larkspur knocked on the door again and wheeled in a cart with another, somewhat larger and older-looking box.

"This is from the old storage at the back. Dr Barffmouth said to bring you everything marked H4C-RSS to assess whether you need it at your new post. Just pack what you need and leave the rest in this room. I'll retrieve it later." Ms Larkspur gave Dr Vesper the key to the box. She looked apologetic when she retreated from the room, and no wonder because it was a lot to go through when there was already much to pack.

Dr Vesper finished emptying her desk drawers. She had separated personal items into a crate and stacked the miscellaneous papers into a neat stack on the desk. It was getting late, and she had another half left. Perhaps if she bit the bullet and stayed for the rest of the evening, she might have time to sift through everything and not have to pop back in the next morning.

Ah, darn. What was this doing here? She'd meant to return Vincent's file to the archive weeks ago. It probably wasn't urgent since they'd already discharged him, and no one had reminded her about it when she'd forgotten. She flicked it open and read through the mundane cover page details. There was something fascinating about this set of tests and test results, but because he wasn't strictly speaking her patient, she had avoided involving herself deeper.

With results like this, maybe... maybe...

No, she'd better not finish that thought. It was not right to pin those expectations on anyone, and Vincent was not a test subject to prod and poke.

Dr Vesper closed the file, browsed through the files in the new parcel she'd received and started the daunting task of going through the H4C Restorative State Study archives.

They were held back from the pioneering sleep research done roughly three decades ago, back when this field of study was in its infancy. Some of the key tenets were still questioned by the scientific community, no doubt largely because the lead scientist had been a woman.

It had taken most of the old beards three decades to forget her gender and start accepting some of the merits. A lot of it had to do with countless men riding on her coattails, publishing their follow-up studies without acknowledging where they had pulled their revolutionary ideas from. They would criticise and discredit her relentlessly, yet steal her ideas without shame and claim them as their own.

It was no wonder the bulk of this research had gone underground to be worked on by the carefully vetted team Dr Vesper was now going to be a part of. She was most excited about the prospect of a new apartment that would allow her to keep a cat, but this was an incredible opportunity she was grateful for in more ways than one.

The bulk of the dusty, yellowing paper did not fill her with any particular joy, but since trust in her judgement had earned her this privilege, she started the arduous task of going through it all. Data output sheets, non-standard numerical values, obscure scribbles on the edges of the papers... There was something endearing about the oldest layer of research notes. Dr Vesper lifted those aside. They must have been instrumental in forming some of the relevant hypotheses at the time but no longer served much purpose.

The original data were not standardised, but there might be a chance to reorganise and revise them to a satisfactory degree to increase the sample size where it was less than optimal. New test subjects weren't easy to come by these days.

Dr Vesper gathered up some of the patient files and their respective data stacks to move them over into the large trunk of papers she was taking with her. A few of the folders slipped from her grasp and fell to the floor. Typical. She scooped them up and shuffled them back into a neater stack.

"Subject one. Displays an abnormal type seven pattern after being exposed to treatment. Restorative impact negligible. Temperature twenty points above average on the Basenyett scale," Dr Vesper read aloud under her breath. Type seven. She spun around to scramble through Vincent's file to the page of his test results. "Type seven... mild fever."

It could have been a coincidence. A little unusual, but a perfectly valid coincidence. What was the RI index? It hadn't been that much below average, had it? Dr Vesper skimmed through the list and cringed. It was worse than she'd remembered. These had been taken shortly after a substantial injury, so some deterioration was to be expected. She hadn't thought much of it at the time.

What if this was normal and had nothing to do with the injury?

Dr Vesper turned back to the old research file. The characteristics described looked eerily similar. It must have been a freakish coincidence. Even had Vincent been subject one, why would his results be this similar three decades later? Type seven characteristics were far from asymptomatic, so Vincent must have sought help for them long since. There were plenty of treatment options to try. Even without a full cure, the latest therapy should have improved the numbers somewhat.

No, thought Dr Vesper. Subject one must have been an old man by now. Vincent was... Dr Vesper referenced the file. Vincent was only thirty-seven. The research file was from over thirty years ago. Surely, no one would subject a toddler to—

"Evaluate whether cognitive impairment or developmental delay." Dr Vesper felt ill. "Displays ordinary play behaviour." She closed the file and shut her eyes. She was hit with a pang of guilt that she'd, even for a fraction of a second, entertained the thought of studying Vincent.

At least he was getting help for it now. Dr Barffmouth's suggestions were mostly valid, so with the right treatm— Dr Vesper stared at Vincent's files, her focus pinpointed on the last few empty lines. Who were these tests for and who had ordered them? She'd written her evaluation and recommendations, but these had sat in her desk drawer for weeks without anyone inquiring after them. Who was in charge of Vincent's care, and why hadn't they followed up?

The instructions had been to file these. Not deliver them to Doctor So-and-so. If anyone, that responsibility would have fallen on Dr Barffmouth or herself here at Sleepy Leighs, yet Vincent hadn't been assigned to either of them. Did Vincent have his own physician at home? Did he want to keep this extra private? Why? It wasn't something to be ashamed of.

Maybe Ms Larkspur had something that would shed some light on this? Dr Vesper grabbed Vincent's files and headed into the lobby while Ms Larkspur was still working at her desk.

"I need one last favour."

"What is it, doctor?"

"Do you have the signup sheet for Mr Swifty here, or have you taken his papers down to the archive already?"

"I'm not supposed to show those to anyone, doctor."

"I know, but if you were to look away for a moment, might I still find the sheet in your cabinet?"

"I'm sorry. I take them down every third month. I have April through May here currently. I believe he was first admitted at the end of March, but I could check..." Ms Larkspur peeked into her cabinet.

Getting a hold of the signup sheets after they'd been taken into the archives would require a lot more effort, especially since Dr Vesper was due to leave the next day and had little official reason to go poke around.

"Ah, that's right. I do have him here. He's scheduled to return later this week."

"He is?" Dr Vesper cursed her luck. She'd be in Schadesborough in two days.

"Yes." Ms Larkspur checked that they were alone in the lobby before placing the sheet on her desk where Dr Vesper could see it. "Are you looking for his phone number, dear?" Ms Larkspur whispered and tapped that particular row on the sheet knowingly. "He's much taller than I expected. Handsome."

Dr Vesper blushed.

"No, no... I mean, yes, he is handsome, but that's not why I—" Why was she so easily reduced to a babbling fool? This was important!

"Oh, that reminds me. He left a message for you." Ms Larkspur dug through her papers.

"What?" Dr Vesper lost her trail of thought completely.

"Yes, it was something about whether it was all right for the child to stay with you while—" Ms Larkspur stopped looking for the message. "I suppose that's not going to work now that you're leaving tomorrow?"

"This week, you said? Ren is coming? And the cat?"

"Don't you have everything packed up, ready to go?" Ms Larkspur spotted the corner of the message and pulled it out to show Dr Vesper.

"Yes, that's true, but wouldn't it be awful if Ren had nowhere to stay…" Dr Vesper took the piece of paper and read it. It seemed Vincent was indeed coming back for a checkup and asking whether he could bring Ren and Sir Swifty along like last time.

This was not just personal curiosity, she assured herself, failing to assure herself. Regardless, she needed to stop reverting to a giddy teenager and focus on what was important.

Sir Swifty.

No!

"Can you let them know it's fine? I'm moving out of the apartment tomorrow, but I think I shall stay in Dritsby for a few more days to take care of some unfinished business, and I do not mind the company." Dr Vesper eyed Vincent's signup sheet and determined there was no mention of anything other than the physical injuries. Dr Skinpitt had been listed as the doctor in charge of Vincent's care. "You wouldn't happen to know whether Dr Skinpitt is in today and where he might keep his keys?"

Ms Larkspur raised her eyebrows and reached into her desk drawer.

"I do not keep track of Dr Skinpitt's schedule and wouldn't have the slightest idea where he might be wasting his money on hazard on an early Tuesday evening, and I most certainly wouldn't know where he may have misplaced his keys." She set the keys on the corner of her desk. "But I do know he takes his 'tea' in his office at six before heading home an hour later."

"Thank you, Ms Larkspur. You are a treasure." Dr Vesper took the keys and headed downstairs into the basement.

Dr Vesper skimmed through Dr Skinpitt's notes on Vincent's surgery and postoperative care. Dr Skinpitt was not one to skimp on the details, and the first half read more like a tale of horror designed to give misbehaving children nightmares. The latter half was less gruesome but revealed nothing that would put Dr Vesper's mind more at ease.

Nowhere on Dr Skinpitt's notes was there a mention of a request for further testing or treatment for anything outside the knee and the shoulder injuries. Dr Vesper had expected as much, but she'd wanted to be sure Dr Skinpitt hadn't ordered a wrong set of tests by accident. She'd wanted to explain this away as a clerical error.

The H4C could have been ordered by Dr Skinpitt if Vincent had requested privacy or if Dr Skinpitt had decided he was a high-profile client, but there were no H4C markings on these notes, and they hadn't been stored away in a locked cabinet. As far as Dr Skinpitt was concerned, he was treating Vincent as a regular patient.

Dr Vesper put the notes away and exited the office into the dark corridor. She stepped closer to a beam of light shining from a small window near the ceiling and perused the old research notes and Vincent's test results she'd grabbed when she'd left her office.

What the hell had she got herself into? All she could think about was Ren's excited face when she'd told her how Vincent's condition was improving and that peculiar degree of ease in dealing with Vincent when he was clearly not doing well, like she'd seen him in that state many times before.

With an untreated, severe sleep disorder and a potentially chronically low RI index, what sort of life was Vincent leading? And worse, it wasn't a recently discovered condition; someone had known and knowingly chosen not to do anything about it.

And—Dr Vesper squeezed the research notes in her hand—someone had known, knowingly made it worse and left him to wander, helpless, like some sort of free-range science experiment with no say in the matter.

CHAPTER 2

D r Vesper packed Theodore the teacup, Florence the fountain pen, Jarvis the journal and Catherine the croton topmost in the crate on her desk. She turned off the unnamed desk lamp and sat down on the unnamed chair by the desk. There was no sense in naming any of her possessions, much less the things she couldn't take with her.

She'd sorted the contents of the boxes and packed the rest of her things because those were on her list of things to do, but with her excitement depleted, she wasn't sure why she was doing these things. How was she supposed to take this job and continue as she'd planned, knowing what she knew? Since ignoring it and walking away was too painful, what was she supposed to do? How was she supposed to fix this?

Dr Vesper had dealt with her issues on her own for so long, she had no one to turn to for advice or to rely on when she needed help. She'd rinsed Theodore, and it lay empty in the crate. Neither Florence, Jarvis or Catherine were talkative or comforting. Perhaps her mother had been right, and she should have found herself someone to share her life with? That way, she wouldn't have had to face this so alone.

She closed the trunk and set the crate on top of it. There would be someone coming to pick it up in the morning to take it into storage until she had sorted out the details of her new apartment in Schadesborough. Ms Larkspur had probably long since left her desk, and the building was quiet and the lobby empty.

Dr Vesper lifted open the trunk, balancing the crate on top of it, and snatched Vincent's patient file. Catherine fell over but did not spill much of the contents of her pot. A corner of the folder got caught between the lid of the trunk, but it did not break when Dr Vesper pulled it loose. She tucked the folder under her cardigan and exited her office.

She didn't know what she could do, but she knew she couldn't let this go on. She needed to find a way to help Vincent without drawing attention to herself. Once that was done, she'd decide what to do about her new job.

Ren gave Vincent a hug and watched him hobble alongside the doctor until they disappeared behind a corner. She lifted Sir Swifty's box onto Ms Larkspur's desk so that they could both try to poke fingers through the lattice to give him scratches. Ms Larkspur wasn't overly fond of Sir Swifty, but she seemed decent enough to not decline the chance to exchange these greetings.

"Will Dr Vera be here shortly? Is she in her office?" Ren asked.

"She knows about your arrival, so she should be here shortly. Is he hungry? I have some leftovers from my lunch..." Ms Larkspur pulled out a half-eaten sandwich and offered Sir Swifty some of its toppings.

"You're already here? Hello again!" Dr Vera entered the lobby. She was not wearing her work whites but rather a casual summer dress. The weather was much warmer here than it had been up north. It almost never got hot while riding the speeder, but Ren had to admit she was starting to feel slightly overdressed now that she was off it.

"You're not working today?" Ren picked up Sir Swifty's box and walked back to the entrance where Dr Vera was waiting for her.

"No. Have you eaten yet? I'd like to chat with you about a few things, if you don't mind." She knelt to the box and greeted Sir Swifty with a nose boop.

"I haven't had lunch yet." Ren followed Dr Vera out to the front yard. "Vincent said it's all right if I want to take Freya, so long as you ride up with me. Is that all right? She's fast!"

It wasn't an outright fib. Vincent had given this permission for moving the speeder if it got in the way. Ren had driven it plenty enough to be confident she wouldn't crash it on a clear day, so he probably wouldn't be able to tell or even care that she'd driven it into town instead of across the yard.

"Are you sure?" Dr Vera looked doubtful, but the brilliant thing about her was that she also seemed curious and excited about the speeder.

"Yes. It only takes a few minutes to drive into Dritsby. I'll show you where you can brake and steer in case something happens. Nothing's going to happen, but it's fun to know, right?" Ren lifted and pushed the cat box over her head against the side of the sidecar. Standing on her toes, she was now tall enough to shove the box just barely over the side, but Dr Vera helped her by nudging it from the side.

"You can climb up by using this foothold here." Ren demonstrated and climbed up to the cockpit recess. "Sorry, there's some dried mud up here..." She pulled out a leather pad, shook off the loose dust and debris and covered the back of the seat with it.

Dr Vera climbed into the sidecar and looked over the side to where Ren was dusting things off.

"We've been on the road for a while, and I haven't had a chance to clean up."

Ren wondered if messing up the dress would be where the doctor drew the line. To her relief, she climbed up and sat on the pad with no complaints. She said nothing while Ren started the preparations, but when it was time to start the engine, she did eventually open her mouth.

"Are you absolutely sure you can operate Freya on your own? She's such a... large... a large piece of machinery."

"Here's the throttle. Here's the reverse thrust. This is the emergency break. You got that?" Ren showed her the levers and knobs. "If anything happens, all you have to do is twist this, and it will slow down."

"How fast does it go?"

"Very fast." Ren turned to look at the doctor's face to assess whether she was asking out of curiosity or worry.

"Can you show me?" She looked almost coy asking. Ren grinned.

"Of course!" She started the engine and let it warm up. "Oh, almost forgot!" She jumped into the sidecar to strap in Sir Swifty's box. It wouldn't have fallen had she forgotten, but it might have tipped over and caused the cat undue distress.

"Good thinking. Should I also fasten this thing?" Dr Vera asked and pointed at the seatbelt.

"Vincent rarely does, but if it makes you feel better." Ren clambered back into the cockpit.

"I think I will. Maybe you should fasten yours too? Since it's there."

"I guess."

"And perhaps you could persuade him to do that as well? It's for safety, isn't it?"

That was more difficult to arrange. Vincent had his own routine, and he was often halfway to his destination before he realised he'd skipped the step.

"I can try." Ren shrugged.

"He's a little absent-minded, isn't he? I'm sure he'll do it if you remind him." Dr Vera helped Ren fasten her seatbelt. "I think we're ready. Show me what she's got!"

Encouraged by Dr Vera's unreserved enthusiasm, Ren obliged.

Dr Vesper felt refreshed. Riding on Freya was admittedly frightening, but it was also the thing to shake off her lingering anxiety.

Instead of taking Ren to a stuffy restaurant on such a bright summer day, they popped into the bakery for two blueberry pies and purchased a sweet fizzy drink from the local pharmacist. It was perhaps not the healthiest lunch, but it would do until supper.

They parked the speeder at a nearby lake and enjoyed the view, the fresh air and their snack up in the cockpit recess.

"Do you mind if I ask you a few questions?" Dr Vesper handed Ren her pie and took a bite off hers.

"What sort?" Ren took the pie and broke off a piece of the crust. It seemed to pass her taste test.

"About Vincent. I'm sorry if it's too nosey. You don't have to answer them, but if you do, I promise I won't tell a soul."

Ren seemed to take a moment to consider it. She looked back at Dr Vesper with a curious smile.

"Answer me something first."

"Fair enough. What do you want to know?"

"Why are you so interested?"

Oh dear. Was Ren concerned there might be some nefarious motives behind her interest? Dr Vesper didn't want to worry her with the details, so she got ready to assure her it was but a precau—

"Do you have a crush on him?" Ren asked.

Dr Vesper felt her cheeks redden in an instant. It was no use trying to hide it, but she nevertheless covered her face with her hands to buy herself time.

"You do, don't you?"

"No..." Her cheeks were probably as obvious as a pair of ripe tomatoes.

"You're not a very good liar," Ren commented mercilessly.

"I'm sorry..." This was an ambush she'd been wholly unprepared for. It would only make it worse to try to deny it again. "Please don't tell him. I'd rather remain a secret admirer."

"He'd probably like you back, if you gave it a moment. You're really nice, and you like Freya."

The girl's kind compliments were making it a thousand times worse.

"Please don't tell him. I'm only asking because I'm worried about him." Dr Vesper tried to redirect the topic back to what she'd meant to ask, but the words 'he'd probably like you back' were stabbing her heart into a sponge.

"All right, well, what do you want to know?" Ren asked. She'd already nearly finished her pie and took a swig of the fizzy drink. Ah, to be that young and worry-free, Dr Vesper thought.

"You know how I'm not the same kind of doctor as Dr Corkbottom or Dr Skinpitt? People come to me when they have problems with their sleep."

"Right?"

"I think Vincent might have trouble sleeping. Has he mentioned anything about it to you?"

"No. I don't think so." Ren frowned. "He seems like his usual self. How so?"

"But is there anything unusual about his usual self?" The numbers didn't lie. There was definitely something wrong, but Dr Vesper wanted to know just how bad the situation was.

Ren paused for a moment, and her frown twisted further to where her lip started quivering.

"He..." She bit that lip in an attempt to keep it still.

"Does he forget things?" Dr Vesper started with an easy one. Ren nodded slowly. "Does he sometimes seem confused and agitated for no reason?"

"Not usually! Not often... He's mostly not... He says he's fine..."

"It's OK. You can tell me. I'm not going to fault him for it."

"He's really very responsible. He takes really good care of me." Ren's struggle not to cry was heartbreaking to watch.

"I'm sure he does his best."

"He really does. He's really very good. He just..."

"He can't always tell what's real, right?" Everyone was forgetful or irritable sometimes, but such abysmal quality of sleep as Vincent was getting could only translate to severe cognitive difficulties.

"We've been doing fine. I help him out sometimes. It's really not all that often... You're not going to tell anyone, are you? I don't want anyone to think he's unfit to take care of me."

"Have you been worried that he might not be fit?"

Ren looked distinctly frightened but nodded.

"We'll find a way to fix it, I swear." Dr Vesper gave her a hug. This would not do. It was a disaster waiting to happen. "But I will need your help with it."

CHAPTER 3

Things were becoming unreasonably complicated. Ren sat on the hood of the speeder, leaning over the front, stomach pressed on the warm metal. Dr Vera sat on a log bench somewhere below her. They were at the lake again, trying to revise the plan.

The original plan had been to explain things to Vincent and persuade him to cooperate, but despite Ren's best efforts, Vincent had declined and insisted he was fine. They were back at square one.

"I still think he might listen to you." Ren scraped off small pieces of dirt from the hood and tossed them into the lake.

Dr Vera had been scribbling something into her notebook but was now tapping her fountain pen on the side. A few drops of ink had already smudged her fingers and the side of the book without her realising. Sir Swifty was licking himself at her feet.

"You said he has three more days left of the physiotherapy?" Dr Vera looked up.

"Yes. We're heading to Forstoft or Lingslip to pick up some things for Uncle Rhys and then head somewhere up north." Ren was excited to see the Tip of the Ear, but it could take weeks if Vincent got into the mood of doing some sightseeing, and there was the question of how to persuade him to come back to Dritsby afterwards. "I don't know how long that will take. He's mentioned wanting to take me to see Yaveleng while we're up there."

"I can't cure him in three days even if he gave me the chance. The testing alone might take a few nights, and I can't just march in there and hook him up to the monitors. I don't even work at the Leighs anymore." Dr Vera noticed the ink spilling and tried to wipe it with a handkerchief.

"You don't?" Ren hadn't realised.

"No, I was promoted to a research team in Schadesborough. I was supposed to start there two days ago, but I postponed." The ink was not coming off her fingers. She tried to wash her hands in the lake. "If he'd accepted the help, I could have asked nurse Abelia to help with the equipment. I could have done the testing at least and then figured out what to do about the treatment later when you got back from your trip."

"He's such a stubborn ass. He was even saying he might not stay for the rest of his therapy because he feels like they're watching him." Ren dropped a pebble in front of Sir Swifty in the grass. His ears perked, and he aimed his nose at the movement but glanced up at Ren as if he'd sussed her tricks.

"Does that happen often? I mean, that he feels like he's being watched?"

"Sometimes." Ren thought back to the few times Vincent had mentioned it. "Do you think it's possible for someone to be there when he's asleep? In his dream, that is. He said someone told him where Uncle Rhys was, and that turned out to be accurate. And I think he can sometimes hear thoughts when he's feverish." Ren threw another pebble. Sir Swifty did not look amused.

"Type seven," Dr Vera mumbled, wiping her hands dry.

"What?"

"Nothing. Most people would call that paranoia, I suppose." Her handkerchief was never coming clean. "Oh, Florence, you and I make such a troubled duo." She picked up her pen, wiped it and set it aside with her notebook.

"He can be stubborn and suspicious, but I don't think he's paranoid." Ren sat up and pouted. She'd hoped Dr Vera would take her seriously since she'd been so receptive so far.

"Don't worry. I don't think he's paranoid. I'm just worried this might be worse than I thought." Dr Vera turned to look at Ren, expression grave. "I guess I do need to have a talk with him about this myself."

She held the level expression for a few more moments before she dropped down on her haunches and stifled a squeal. "I don't want to!" She hid her face behind her hands and knees and stayed there like a child throwing a tantrum.

Ren leaned over to see better. She'd never seen an adult behave this way. Was she all right? Even Sir Swifty was watching her worriedly.

"You must think I'm silly in the head. I'm sorry." She looked up, face red, but laughing. "I probably am, but I'll get over it in a bit."

"He's really not as exciting as the stories paint him to be. He's mostly a normal person like everyone else." Ren had met many of Vincent's fans, and some of them did get themselves mightily worked up sometimes, but this was a first. Usually they were ecstatic to meet Vincent, but Dr Vera seemed to be doing everything she could to avoid him, and now she'd even confirmed as much out loud. "Or is that what you're afraid of? That he's not as much fun as you expect, and you'll be disappointed?"

"I don't think he could disappoint me, don't worry." She sat back down on the bench and patted Sir Swifty. "But we've got worse things to worry about than my childishness. It could be that he is indeed being watched. If he thinks he's fine enough to travel, and you think the two of you can manage for a while longer, maybe it's a good thing you're heading up north. I'll miss you terribly," she scratched Sir Swifty under the chin, "but it will give me some time to figure this out. We need him to come to Schadesborough when you're done with your trip."

"That could be difficult. He says he doesn't like Schadesborough at all." Ren sighed and lay down on the hood. "How am I supposed to talk him into it?"

"If he absolutely refuses, I might be able to arrange something in Grovestead. Grovestead College has a decent research department with some of the equipment I need, and I know a professor there. Just make sure Vincent takes care of himself until then, and I'll handle the rest."

"I'll do my best, but if he refuses, you're going to have to be the one to talk to him."

R en and Vincent brought a speeder brimming with tools, building supplies and provisions up to Agnes Point. The lighthouse and collection of old, rickety huts were being renovated, and the contrasting new sections against the weathered cladding or exposed timber reminded Ren of Aunt Aster's patched quilts. The round, lichen-covered rocks surrounding these patch quilt huts made them look like gingerbread houses atop a bed of off-coloured cardamom buns. All in all, it was very much to Ren's liking.

Vincent had explained the gist of the situation, but Ren was relieved to confirm Uncle Rhys had not been beaten into pulp by the strange entourage that had brought him here. He did seem somewhat rougher around the edges than she recalled, though.

Uncle Rhys took Ren along on a brisk walk to see an arctic fox den and a litter of fluffy brown kits playing. A few of them were curious and brave enough to watch Ren and Rhys from afar, but when they noticed their uninvited guests, Uncle Rhys said it was time to let them be and return to the lighthouse.

Ren and Vincent stayed for the night before continuing their trip north towards the Tip of the Ear.

The sun did not set once during the following two weeks Ren and Vincent spent exploring Yaveleng and Earemoss, the two expanses of land that made up the cat's ear. Yaveleng was arid and flat, and Earemoss, by comparison, lush, green and mountainous. The two were separated by dozens of kilometres of blotchy palsa mires. None of it posed any trouble for the speeder, but Ren could have lived without the gnats, horse-flies and mosquitos that were abundant around the mires.

Vincent seemed to be in good spirits, but what was there to worry about in such peaceful surroundings, free from the expectations and obligations of the rest of the world? Ren herself had plenty of time to forget her concerns and enjoy the simplicity of fishing, hiking and admiring the rugged, untouched nature.

It was late July when they started to run low on provisions and headed back to Agnes Point. By then, the renovations of the outbuildings had been finished, and the fox kits at the nearest den were getting large and more independent. Uncle Rhys explained they would stay with their family until autumn, but then venture out on their own. Ren was glad she wouldn't be old enough to be pushed out of her nest for a few more years, but this did remind her of the horrible prospect that, one of these days, Vincent's health might deteriorate again, and he might not be able to take care of her.

"What would you do if you knew someone you cared about needed help but refused to get any?" Ren asked Uncle Rhys when the two of them were walking back from revisiting the foxes.

Vincent had been faring well, yes, but the constant daylight was not helping him keep a steady sleep schedule. Now that Ren knew to pay attention to his sleeping habits, she felt bad about not realising there was something wrong sooner. She couldn't fault herself for not noticing it back home, since Vincent slept in his bedroom and she in her own. He was ill so often it was easy to pin everything on that or what Aunt Aster referred to as the winter blues. But now that Ren had spent more than three uninterrupted weeks in Vincent's company on the tundra, she was picking up the patterns.

"Are we talking about Vincent?" Uncle Rhys asked, ruthlessly dispelling any of the vague pretence Ren tried to shield herself with. She nodded but looked away. "What sort of help? Is it the knee thing?"

"No. Not that." Ren wondered whether it was safe to trust Uncle Rhys with all of it or if he'd go straight to Vincent, or worse, report it to Aunt Celandine.

"What is it?" Uncle Rhys stopped walking and turned to face Ren. Faint yellowing bruising stretched between his cheekbone and the corner of his eye, but up close, his features were comfortingly familiar. It made Ren want to trust him. "Is there something wrong with Vincent?" he asked.

"Well, you know how he gets when he's ill…" It was difficult to know where to start, but this seemed like the best bet.

"What do you mean?"

Ren frowned. Had Vincent managed to keep that from Uncle Rhys? Were they not as close as she'd thought?

"Oh, never mind." If he didn't know, she probably wasn't supposed to tell. Maybe she'd be better off making a request to go sightseeing in Grovestead and cry until Vincent relented?

"How does he get when he's ill? Is he ill? I haven't noticed anything, but he's the type to play things down." Uncle Rhys glanced towards where they were going as if he could determine where Vincent was from this distance. The top of the lighthouse was barely visible behind a hill. "Should we take him to a doctor right away? He's not bleeding secretly, is he?"

When it seemed like Uncle Rhys might make a big deal out of it, Ren hurried to correct the misunderstanding.

"No!" she blurted out. "I meant the sleeping thing. He has trouble sleeping. Don't worry about it. Forget I said anything."

"What sleeping thing?"

"Dr Vera said he seems to have trouble sleeping, and I think she might be right—"

"Who is Dr Vera? Someone from the treatment centre?"

"Yes." Ren hadn't decided how much to tell Uncle Rhys, yet, but her answers kept leading to other questions, and she didn't know how to lie convincingly on the spot. "She specialises in sleep, so she knows a lot about these things."

"Did you talk it over with Vincent? And he disagrees? What sort of help does he need? Julian is a pharmacist. He might be able to give Vincent something to help him sleep."

"No, that's not it." Ren had trouble describing the difference. "He falls asleep, but I don't think he's really asleep most of the time." He often had his eyes open and either stared at nothing in silence or mumbled nonsense.

Uncle Rhys sat on a rock and paused to think.

"And you think this Dr Vera might be able to help with that?"

"Yes. She's very smart, and she promised to make him better. But Vincent is being stubborn like he always is. I need to figure out a way to get him to either Schadesborough or Grovestead and convince him to cooperate or find a way to do it without him realising."

"I'm sorry, but are you sure she's not looking to swindle him out of his money with some expensive treatment? How well do you know this doctor? Why does she want him to come to Schadesborough or Grovestead? Why is she so eager to help?"

"She's kind! You'd know if you'd met her. I trust her. Sir Swifty trusts her." Sir Swifty would not tolerate a crook.

"Ah, all right. But I don't know if it's such a good idea to do anything behind his back. Especially if he's said he doesn't want help..."

Uncle Rhys was a jerk. Why was it this hard to get help for Vincent every time? No one seemed to believe he could be in trouble or need help, even though last time he'd really been in peril! Was it all going to be left up to Ren again?

"Oh no, don't cry. I'll help. We'll figure it out." Uncle Rhys gave her an unexpected hug.

"I wasn't going to cry!" Ren didn't mean to but hurried to wipe her face on her sleeve.

"It's that bad? I'll come with you. I've been meaning to ask him to take me to Dritsby, anyway. That's a little closer in the right direction. We'll convince him on the way." Uncle Rhys gave her another hug. "He is a handful, isn't he?"

Ren nodded but felt a bit better. Relieved. Maybe Uncle Rhys would have better luck. He was an adult. Vincent would have to take him seriously.

CHAPTER 4

R hys had trained to the brink of exhaustion with Quin or Julian on most days when he hadn't been helping Victor and the associates with the building work around Agnes Point. In the evenings or the few times it rained, Julian taught Victor sign language in the main house. If he wasn't too tired, and if Quin wasn't in one of his demanding moods, Rhys watched them at it for long enough to pick up a sign or two.

Signing seemed like a good fit for Victor, since, when he occasionally froze unable to speak, he now had something to fall back on. It had made a significant difference to know when he wanted to say something but required more time and space to get to it. Sometimes a single sign was all he needed to say, and he slipped opening his mouth altogether.

Quin, on the other hand, was more than eager to share stories from his and Julian's past. He had to censor most of the details, and none of the stories sparked any memories in Julian or were in any way helpful in solving the mystery of the mummified remains in the attic, but they did help pass the time, even if Julian did not seem to appreciate having to hear them.

With the renovations mostly finished and Rusty set on staying for the winter, Jon-Jon made the decision to stay with him. His decision didn't come as a surprise considering how well—by Jon-Jon's standards—Quin had been getting along with Rhys, Victor and Julian. Evidently Quin had become less of a worry than Rusty making it through the winter out here alone.

That still left six people to fit on the speeder when it was time to head home. Rhys sat on the veranda of his cabin, with a decent view of the speeder parked by the lighthouse, trying to figure out where exactly to fit everyone.

Ren sat next to him, swinging her feet back and forth, visibly anxious. She and Vincent had turned up the day before. Though Rhys had planned to stay here for as long as the weather permitted, the thought of the voiceless and Ren's worry over Vincent were chipping away that resolve.

Vincent was doing what seemed like general maintenance on the speeder. He had one of the cowlings propped open and was cleaning and tightening something. He avoided putting full weight on his other leg but didn't seem bothered by it. Nothing about him screamed abnormal to Rhys, but one glance at Ren's face was enough to make him doubt his judgement.

Vincent, Victor and Ren would fit up there... and then Quin and Julian in the sidecar, but then where would Rhys sit? On either of their laps? Which of them would be less bad? Rhys closed his eyes and tried to purge the mental imagery out of his mind. Maybe he could stay behind with Rusty and Jon-Jon. Maybe the voiceless really didn't need his help. After all, they had specifically told him not to...

Did Vincent dream the same way as everyone else? He'd never mentioned the dreamside, but then again, it hadn't come up. The only time they'd brushed up on anything dream-related was when he was drunk enough to see Rhys stopping by, and those situations were rarely mentioned after the fact.

Most drunkards did not pay any attention to Rhys, and Rhys wasn't aware he'd ever seen anyone doing the same when he was drunk. He'd never heard of anyone dreaming the same way he did but supposed it wasn't impossible. It must have been rare, though, and there was definitely something unusual about Vincent.

Sitting on Quin's lap was probably less bad. Rhys was used to Quin's asshattery, and sitting on Julian—

"Why are you so red? Did you get sunburnt already?" Ren leaned forward for a better look.

"What? No." Rhys tested his cheeks with the back of his hand, and they were indeed warm and presumably then also red. A heat stroke could perhaps help explain these stupid, disjointed thoughts. "Vincent!"

Ren looked further startled, but the mild annoyance was just the thing to push Rhys to get this issue sorted.

"Vincent!" he called again, dropped down from the veranda and started walking toward the speeder. He heard the tiniest, squeaky 'no' behind him but paid it no mind. This was best solved with a proper discussion.

"What is it?" Vincent wiped his hands on the rag he was holding.

"How's your sleep?"

"What do you mean?"

"When you go to sleep, what happens? How would you describe it?"

"I—" Vincent seemed rightly taken aback by the sudden questions, but even with some time to think on it, he was left vaguely gesturing and failing to come up with a decent answer.

"Does it leave you refreshed? What sort of dreams do you have?"

Vincent glanced at Ren, clearly worried about talking about it in front of her, but also because she looked alarmed.

"Ren, I'm sorry, dear. Could you go wait at the veranda there? I promise it'll be fine. I'll call you back in just a moment," Rhys told her. She seemed ready to protest, but when Vincent gave her a gentle nudge, she glowered at the both of them as if gravely slighted but stomped away.

"Why is she so upset now?" Vincent's eyebrows did their confused caterpillar dance. "Did I do something?"

"She's just worried about you."

"Oh, is this about that sleep doctor she's been wanting me to see? I swear it's like she's trying to set me up with her." Vincent deflected with one of his chuckles. "I think they bonded while I was getting this knee put back together, and now she doesn't stop talking about her. I hear even the cat likes her."

"Ah, so you think she's shopping for a new mother?"

Ren sat on the veranda, pouting and casting some potent glares in their general direction. Vincent looked to be taking it in a good stride.

"I'm surprised she's pulled you into this." He was upholding the amused smile. Right. Good effort, sir, but you're laying it on somewhat thick now. Rhys sighed.

"I'd still like you to answer my questions." There was no way Vincent would bother with this level of deflection and show of normalcy if he wasn't self-conscious about something worth concealing.

"What was it that you asked again?" An obvious tactic to buy time.

"There's something to her concern, isn't there? But you don't want to worry her." Rhys waited. Vincent pressed his lips tighter together. "How's your sleep, Vincent?"

The uncomfortable silence persisted for several minutes, but Rhys did not take his eyes off of Vincent's.

"It could be better," he said finally.

"Can you be a bit more specific?"

"I don't know." Vincent wasn't trying to deflect or look away. He seemed to be sincerely trying but drawing a blank. "I don't know what to tell you."

"When you go to sleep, what happens?"

"I don't know."

"You close your eyes and fall asleep and then what? I think you spoke of a bubble once." Rhys tried to help him, but it only made his frown deepen.

"I don't know, Rhys. I can't tell. It's there sometimes, then it's not. Am I ever asleep? Am I ever awake? Well, I suppose I'm not asleep right now... Am I?" He looked about as happy as a drenched dog left out in the field for the night. "How do people usually tell?"

Well, one thing was for sure: he wasn't entering the dreamside like Rhys. It also didn't sound like how most people Rhys had asked described falling asleep. Supposedly, they weren't especially aware when they fell asleep, but they could definitely tell what was what when they woke up.

"You really can't tell whether you're asleep or awake right now?"

"Well, obviously I can tell... Eventually. I pick it up from context most times. But it doesn't feel any different." Vincent put away the rag and cleared his throat. "So, to answer your question, I don't know how I've been sleeping because I'm not exactly sure when or if I've been asleep. But it's always been more or less like this, so I'm fairly used to it. Please don't tell anyone. It would just cause people to worry."

Rhys wanted to respect the request, but this did not seem like something he was supposed to let be. If Vincent wasn't sleeping properly, and if he had trouble discerning such simple things, how was he passing as even a remotely functional human being?

"Ren might be right. If this doctor she's got lined up for you can help, I think you should give that a try—"

"No."

"Don't be so hasty to—"

"No."

"Vincent." The man tended to be a tad on the stubborn side, but Rhys couldn't recall him being this decisive often. "At least tell me why not."

Rhys had to wait for Vincent's response for a few minutes, but once he'd had whatever private debate he was having with himself, he ruled in Rhys's favour.

"I don't trust the place. You know those hands I told you about? I think you called it the voiceless. Your location wasn't the only thing I've heard said in a similar fashion."

"What did they say?"

"It sounded like sobbing."

Rhys was reminded of a certain evening he would have preferred to strike from existence. Out of some deep-seated feeling of unease, he fingered the bird pendant he'd received for his birthday and slipped it inside his shirt, out of sight.

"That might not mean anything..." Who else was the voiceless haunting with those awful sounds? Did they think it was a funny prank? Oh, sweet Guardian, he wanted to burrow into the ground to live with the foxes.

"It only ever happens at the Sleepy Leighs, so I think it has to be in-tentional. There's something about that place. They asked me back for a second checkup, but I think the knee is fine enough. I only agreed to the first one because Ren was so excited to go see Dr Vera, but I think this is the limit of my tolerance. If you asked how I slept at the Leighs, I could say for sure I didn't sleep well."

How could you with the voiceless feeding you a repeating loop of the wails of a blithering drunkard? Rhys felt he might lose sleep from the mere thought of having to listen to himself cry and whinge.

The pendant chafed against his skin, even though it seemed like such a tiny, harmless little thing. Maybe it would be better to carry it in his pocket instead.

"Would you be willing to go if we found you another doctor?" Rhys took off the pendant while Vincent was distracted and put it in his pocket.

"I've been to enough doctors to know they don't know what to do about me. I don't think there's a cure for this."

"I'm afraid Ren is going to pester you about it until you go." If Vincent couldn't be persuaded to do it for his health, then perhaps he'd be willing so as to hear the end of it.

"She might give up..." Vincent watched the girl still glaring at them. "She's not going to give up, is she?"

"You'll probably have to strike a deal with her. If you're worried she's trying to set you up with an ogre, ask for another doctor. What's she like, anyway, this Dr Vera?"

"I don't know. I haven't met her."

"What? Don't you pay any attention to who your daughter spends tim—"

"Ren says she's nice, and if she's charmed the cat, how bad could she be?" Vincent seemed uncharacteristically peeved to be criticised. Knowing Vincent, this was an improvement. "Besides, weren't you there when I was admitted? You must have seen her around. You stand a better chance of remembering her than I do. I was not at my best, and even my best ain't all that great."

"Oh! You mean Dr Vesper? The pretty redhead from the lobby?" When Rhys realised his mind-vomit assessment had reduced the good doctor to a decorative piece, he added, "She seemed smart, kind and competent. I liked her."

"Apparently everybody likes her." Vincent looked like he might start sulking. "You think I should give her a chance, too?"

"Dr Vesper was the one who got them to waive your fees. Ah, this makes sense." No wonder Ren was so fond of the doctor. "Ren! You can come back over now. Vincent will go meet your doctor!" He turned back to Vincent. "Right? We'll come with you if you're scared."

Vincent rolled his eyes but gave up. "Fine. I'll hear what she has to say, but I'm not making any promises."

CHAPTER 5

U nable to bear the thought of sitting on someone's lap, Rhys opted for the questionable pleasure of riding in the luggage compartment. It was cramped and dark but better than having to walk.

He'd had no space to move his legs, and they'd consequently fallen asleep, so Julian and Quin had had to pull him out when they'd stopped to rest for the first time. From then on, they took frequent breaks, but the last stretch before Copseton had been a long one. Rhys shook his legs vigorously after they'd helped him clamber out from the boot.

"We should probably discuss the plan before we jump in," he said when the pins and needles finally subsided. He wasn't particularly excited to confront his father, but with no other living connection to his great aunt, his 'Dear Papa' seemed like the only chance of digging up some of the family secrets and consequently uncovering something new about the building.

"Let's do that over dinner. My treat. I'm starving." Quin helped Ren down from the speeder like a gentleman would a lady, despite her being fully capable of doing it herself and him not being a gentleman. Then he turned back to Rhys. "My worry is that your father sounds like an utter ass of a person. Would he give you the information even if he had it? Does he even have it? Do we have a backup plan for what to do if this yields no clues?"

Quin had been suspiciously invested in the venture, as well as taking care of his travel companions, ever since they'd left Rusty and Jon-Jon behind in Agnes Point. He now guided them towards the nearest restaurant he deemed acceptable in quality, as if an expert tour guide.

"If he turns out to be a complete turd, at least I'll have some closure." Rhys was pretty sure his father was as shitty as fathers came, but he could remember a time when they'd been a happy family. If there was any chance, however unlikely, that his father might get used to having a son, Rhys wanted to give it to him. But he wasn't going to hold his breath. "I could distract him while one of you searches his office. I don't know if he'll have anything useful there though, and he may be inclined to involve the police or seek justice by his own hand, if you are caught poking around."

Rhys tried to recall if he'd ever seen anything worth rummaging through in his father's office, but the man hadn't let anyone in there for very long.

The storage room was another possibility for finding treasure, but it seemed entirely possible all the family memorabilia had been thrown out long ago because ties to most of Rhys's relatives on his father's side had been severed well before they had passed away.

"Sounds exciting." Quin seemed unfazed by the possible consequences. He held the door for the others and paid the head waiter to seat them on some of the best seats in the restaurant. "If you want some guaranteed anonymity for a reconnaissance mission, leave it to me." He waited until everyone else had sat down before taking his seat.

"Speaking of anonymity, I should probably leave you somewhere on the outskirts of Dritsby and avoid drawing attention to myself. Maybe head to Grovestead before anyone spots me or the speeder. You can take the river barge down when you're done." Vincent rubbed his temples.

Now that Rhys was paying attention, the signs of Vincent's close-to-perpetual exhaustion were obvious. It was a relief that Ren was almost always riding up in the cockpit recess and capable of steering should Vincent somehow nod off while driving. Rhys would have had a hard time letting his brother go alone in this condition.

"If we can extract some information from the man before he realises it has anything to do with us, that might be our best bet. It doesn't matter how badly the rest of it goes, we'd have something," Quin said.

"It's possible he doesn't know anything, and we'll be back to where we started." Rhys shrugged.

He hadn't heard any word from the voiceless, but since they had communicated with Vincent at the Sleepy Leighs, they were probably fine and would turn up when they felt like it. When that happened, Rhys would be ready to apologise, work things out and ask for any news.

"I'm still wondering about the remains." Julian browsed the menu as he spoke, so, for a fraction of a moment, Rhys thought he was referring to his dinner choice. "When I spoke with Mr Williams about the samples I took, we never figured out why they were embalmed, or even when. I wonder if he's made any new discoveries since then. Since Vincent is heading straight to Grovestead, and you probably don't need me in Dritsby, perhaps I should tag along with him."

Rhys wouldn't have minded having Julian as moral support but agreed a larger crowd might raise more suspicions. He'd still have Victor if he needed a bodyguard.

"I should probably join you. I left most of my things in Grovestead when we left, and I've yet to take a good look at the records we unearthed at Firth," Victor said.

Ah, fuck. Rhys had forgotten about those. He'd be left with Quin, then. Not exactly ideal, even if the man seemed eerily enthusiastic about the whole thing.

They spent the rest of the evening trying to devise something that resembled a plan, but it did not do much to boost Rhys's confidence.

Quin walked into the Wakefield Inn the following day with 'urgent business' and asked to speak with Mr Wakefield. The woman at the front was reluctant to help him at first, but he was wearing a proper suit, he'd washed up and combed his hair and looked all-in-all very presentable, even important.

As luck had it, Mr Wakefield was in and, after some badgering, agreed to receive Quin in his office. The man looked like an older, more lifeless, soulless mash-up of both Vincent and Rhys, clearly recognisable but different. He wore quite the scowl when Quin stepped into the room.

"Good day to you, sir. My apologies for not announcing my arrival in advance. This matter was sprung on me unexpectedly by an important client." Quin handed Mr Wakefield the business card of one of his associates. Mr Wakefield looked at it briefly and flicked it to his desk. "I am here to discuss with you the property held by one Mr Wakefield, presumably a relative of yours, sir."

"I do not know of any misters Wakefield owning property save for myself and this inn."

"According to my information, it was recently inherited from one Mrs Dahlia Wakefield, who I believe is your late aunt." Quin pressed on as per the plan. "I understand it's a shop of some sort in East Schades. My client is interested in purchasing it."

"You've come to the wrong place. I have nothing to do with it."

With Mr Wakefield so reluctant to engage, Quin would have to present a carrot.

"If I may be frank with you, we have been in contact with the owner, and he seems both highly peculiar and highly suspicious. I need to make sure my client will not be swindled in this transaction. The owner is selling the property well below market value. You wouldn't happen to know why he wants to be rid of the place in such a hurry? Between you and me, I have heard some disturbing rumours about the building. We would appreciate any information you may have." Quin hoped Mr Wakefield's distaste of his son would be enough to loosen his lips.

Mr Wakefield did not look particularly forthcoming but stopped to think. Quin let the man take his time. He was about to give up when Mr Wakefield reached for something in his desk drawer.

"I think I know what this is about." The man gave Quin a tattered business card. "I would advise your client not to buy if he's not looking for trouble. Then again, there might be a business opportunity there if they are shrewd. Under any circumstances, do not mention me. You will not live long enough to regret it." The tone of Mr Wakefield's warning gave Quin the chills. It was difficult to imagine he was a mere small-town innkeeper.

"As you wish. I thank you on my client's behalf. You have undoubtedly saved us from a grave mistake." Quin shook Mr Wakefield's hand, although the man seemed to want to avoid it like the plague and flicked him away after just a brief touch.

"One more thing," the man said. "If your client does decide to buy, tread carefully. These are not the type of people you want to cross."

"Duly noted." Quin gave him a bow before excusing himself.

He stepped out into the corridor, closed the door behind him and checked the card.

> Hosta Therapy Solutions.
> We value your trust.
> Your contact: Harold P. Brown.

This rang no bells, but perhaps the others would know something about it.

Quin was about to move on when he realised he was within earshot of an unexpected one-sided conversation in the room he'd just exited.

"She is out there tarnishing the Wakefield name and making a fool of me. You will finish what you started, do you hear?" A pause. "I do not care—! Fine. But if you cannot deliver, I will take matters into my own hands, and your playtime will be over."

Quin frowned. Finish what? How determined was this man to stop Rhys from supposedly tarnishing the family name? What means would he use? And who was he talking to?

"You have until then, but I'm coming for her, and if she's not presentable like she ought to be, you will be sorry for ever stringing me along. This has been going on for years. Enough is enough!"

One thing was for sure: that man was never going to welcome Rhys home with open arms.

Rhys had never heard of the business named on the card Quin had received, but at least there was a phone number listed below.

"I suppose we'll have to contact them to know more. He warned us to be careful, though. I thought I'd ask around first." Quin took the card back. "What do you want to do now? No offence, but he *really* didn't seem worth seeing."

"I know. I'm not expecting much but, since I'm already here, I might as well..."

"I should probably wait somewhere close by, right?" Quin offered.

"Thanks, but I'll be fine. If there's trouble, I'll use my legs."

"You had better. I'll wait for you at the river, but I'm coming right back for you if you're not there in a half an hour, so don't dally."

R hys was about to enter the inn when he was intercepted and pushed aside to a covered gangway leading to the stalls at the back.

"Are you crazy? Why did you come back?" Rhys's mother looked around hastily. "You should have stayed away!"

"A pleasure to see you too, Mother," Rhys said, irked to be shoved around.

"He can't see you. Especially not today. A shady gentleman came to see him, and he's in one of his moods. It's not safe for you to be here." She squeezed his hand. "You need to leave."

"I'm not afraid of him."

"You should be. He will hurt you." There was unexpected weight and urgency in her words. Had things taken a turn for the worse?

"Are you all right? He's not hurting you, is he?"

"Never mind me. He's been talking about sending you back to that Guardian forsaken place if you ever turn up, and I can't have that happen again!"

"What place?" Rhys frowned. His mother frowned at his frown.

"It's a blessing you don't remember. Trust me, you can't be here. The only way you could, would be to be the daughter he wants. I know that's not what you want." She kept looking over her shoulder and across the yard.

"I can handle myself."

"Please Rhys, you need to leave." It was the first time she'd addressed him as Rhys. He was surprised and glad but also frightened. "He will enlist someone if he can't do it himself."

"I have friends—"

"Will they stay by your side every hour of every day? You need to take this seriously. Don't push your luck, lie low. You don't know what these people are capable of."

"Who? What are you t—?"

"I need you to go and never come back. Not unless he's dead. Promise me." Her hold on Rhys's wrist was painfully tight. She hugged him. "I want you to live true to yourself. Will you do that for me? And please, please take care of yourself. It's a cruel world out there."

"I— ah, you will send word to me if you need help, right?"

"No, Rhys. You need to stay away regardless of what happens to me. Go before he sees you!" She pushed him off.

Rhys had never seen her so serious about anything. She was mouthing "Go, go" when she backed away. He knew he was too confused to make good decisions, so it was probably best to hold off going inside and retreat for now, at least until he'd figured out what all of this meant.

CHAPTER 6

Vincent stopped the speeder in front of the main entrance of the Grovestead College. It wasn't exactly an inviting building with its heavyset dark tile pillars and overshadowing clock tower, but it was better than going back to the Sleepy Leighs.

Mr Craft's professor friend working at the college and Ren arranging her blind date with the sleep doctor at the same location had certainly made the logistics convenient. Mr Hart had no official business here, but he hadn't requested to be dropped off elsewhere and seemed perfectly content following Mr Craft.

"Did she mention how long this might take?" Vincent asked Ren.

"No." Ren hauled the cat box around diligently despite its weight. Vincent could have sworn the cat looked more eager and alert than usual, sniffing the air like he knew where they were going.

"I guess we'll have to play it by ear. If it takes us a while, do you mind waiting here somewhere or should we meet back at the address Mr Quin gave us?" Vincent asked Mr Craft.

"I'm also not entirely sure how long we will be. It's almost noon. We could agree to wait until teatime but, if either of us take longer, meet at Quin's?"

"That sounds reasonable." Hopefully, it wouldn't take that long.

Even after the promise of change of venue, Vincent had found himself dreading having to explain his predicament to a stranger, no matter how affable she reportedly was. He'd spent most of the trip from Agnes Point trying to come up with an excuse to withdraw from this wretched intervention, but something about the long, hot summer days was making his head feel even more sluggish than usual. It might have also been the stress. He hadn't come up with anything decent.

"Let's go. She's probably waiting for us." Ren pulled Vincent along. "Don't worry. We'll fix you in no time."

"I'm fine, though..." Vincent had certainly felt much, much worse before. Things generally hung in a delicate balance, and, from his perspective, this had the potential of tipping the scales either way.

Mr Craft and Mr Hart headed down a different corridor, and Ren led Vincent down another. She seemed to have been briefed with instructions for where to go, since no one had met them at the front entrance and the halls were empty. Considering it was likely lunchtime, it made sense there weren't many people around.

"I think it's this way. She said to knock on a door that says Professor Limpgit."

"Are you sure you're remembering that right?" Vincent had heard a fair share of bizarre names but felt like a line had to be drawn somewhere.

"Oh, you're right! I think it might be this one." Ren pointed at an engraved, gilded sign on the door to their left. It read 'Limpqvist'. That was scarcely better.

She was already knocking on the door before Vincent could request a moment to prepare himself. Not that a moment, or even several, would have made a difference, but he would have appreciated a fighting chance to appear like a reasonably normal human being. Perhaps he should have at least changed into something less travel-worn?

"Hello, is anyone here? Dr Vera?" Ren peeked into the office. Vincent pushed the door open wider so she could carry the cat box inside without bumping into anything.

"Excuse me." He followed Ren into the office.

No amount of preparation could have helped him deal with as absurd a level of confusion as when his head struggled to identify what his eyes were seeing.

"Vincent, this is Dr Vera. Dr Vera, this is Vincent," Ren introduced them. She set the cat box on a chair and waited.

'Pretty redhead', Rhys had said. 'Oh, you mean Dr Vesper.' Vincent's palms were sweating. Vesper. This arrangement of letters was not entirely novel despite his efforts to forget it.

Ren looked worried. He needed to say something.

"Aurora."

"Vincent."

She looked gorgeous.

The situation had turned from uncomfortable to catastrophic in a matter of seconds. This was not what he'd signed up for. What were the odds? Why was she here? Why was it her? Vincent tried to regroup, but after such a long time avoiding anything to do with women, he was disgracefully out of practice and failing.

"You know each other?" Ren asked, now looking both worried and confused. She couldn't have known the trap she'd laid for him, bless her heart.

"I'm sorry, Ren. I should have mentioned..."

The sound of her voice brought chills down his back. It was like the teenage crush had never ended, but this time he was expected to act his age and be able to ignore it.

"Hello again, Sir Swifty." She scratched the cat's chin through the lattice. "I'm sorry, is this awkward? I don't want to waste your time so, if it's fine with you, I'd like to get straight to the point, ask you a few questions and do a few tests."

"Huh?" Vincent tried to process her words while his head was busy browsing through what he'd stored away somewhere in its recesses. "Yes? Right. Sure."

Oh, no. Vincent panicked. If anything was worse than having to share his issues with a stranger, it was having to share them with her.

"Take a seat. This will only take a moment to set up— Is everything all right?" She seemed so calm and composed and not at all upset with him.

She should have been upset, right? Unless it had been a relief when he'd left without a word...

"Uh, yes, I'm fine, I'm fine." He needed to concentrate. Was this actually happening, or was he dreaming again? He hadn't dreamt about her for years, but the situation seemed too coincidental and surreal to be real. "I'm fine." I'm not fine.

"Please take a seat." Aurora gestured at the chair on the opposite side of the desk. Vincent sat down. "Would you prefer if Ren waited in the next room?" she suggested gently.

"Yes." With the very real possibility that he was about to come undone, Vincent was grateful for the offer.

Aurora led Ren and the cat out of the room, and when she returned, she sat down opposite him and waited in silence.

"I'm not fine," he said. He'd been practising, but it remained almost as difficult to say out loud.

"I'm not surprised. I saw your test results." She pushed a sheet of obscure abbreviations and numbers in front of him.

"What is this?"

"These are the standard tests we do for the patients who come to us with sleep-related issues at the Sleepy Leighs. Needless to say, your results aren't great."

"I suppose that's why Ren insisted on dragging me here."

"The good news is, I think I can help you. I need to do some more testing, and it might not be an instant fix, but I'm confident you'll notice a difference." She handed him a pen and another piece of paper. "If you could start by filling this out to the best of your ability, and I'll attach the electrodes, so we can better estimate your current state."

At least he didn't have to answer the questions out loud. Some of them were self-assessments of different aspects of his sleep and mental health; others were problems he was meant to solve to gauge his cognitive capabilities. They were all equally difficult to answer, especially with the added challenge of Aurora's distracting proximity.

"I'm sorry. I can't seem to concentrate..."

"Don't worry about it. Just do the best you can. I'm almost done with these." She was moving aside some hair to attach one of the things.

It had been either Harry or John... or maybe Thomas? It was a little too late to ask her about it, but maybe she was over him by now? Or perhaps they had married... There was no ring on her finger, though.

"This can't be right." She'd turned on the machine but apparently wasn't getting the readings she was expecting. "Maybe it's a connectivity issue. It seems as if you were asleep as we speak."

"How would one know if they were?" Vincent asked in earnest.

"You might not always realise when you're asleep yourself, but I'm awake. I should be able to tell by looking at you."

"Oh."

"This is probably a technical issue. Sometimes these machines malfunction."

"What if it's not?"

She frowned and paused to compare the readings and Vincent's test results. She even looked at the pathetic responses Vincent had had time to scribble down. Her expression grew dark, almost angry.

"I swear to the bloody Guardian—!" She flipped through her papers, looking for something. When she seemed to reach a conclusion, she dropped everything and, face pale, turned to look at Vincent. "I'm so sorry. I'll do my best, but it's definitely worse than I thought."

Aurora had to rethink her strategy. Even from such rudimentary, preliminary tests, she could tell the situation was appalling. Not only had she never seen anything this severe, she'd never run into a case where it was this systematic and deliberate.

She felt desperately under equipped to handle something of this calibre on her own, but if she didn't who would? The only entity with expertise above her own was probably the person responsible for Vincent's injuries.

Aurora wanted to share the load, but neither Vincent nor Ren would be capable of shouldering much of it. One look at Vincent confirmed he was in no state to be helpful. He would struggle to make any sense of it, and the stress was likely to exacerbate the problem. If she could improve his RI index enough, then perhaps... But at present, it would be cruel to expect him to weigh in.

"Where are you staying while in Grovestead? Will you be here for long?" Aurora asked.

"We were invited to stay at an acquaintance's house, but we haven't specified the details yet. Why?"

"I need you to stay put somewhere where I can bring the equipment I need. At least two weeks. Preferably three." That might not be enough, but if he could improve some of his cognitive functions, she might be able to discuss the bulk of it with him and draft a better plan. "Do you have someone here you can trust?"

"Ren?"

"She's a little too young for what I had in mind. Anyone else? Your brother?"

"Yes, I trust Rhys."

"All right. I'd like to meet with him—"

"Sorry. Are you done yet?" Ren peeked in from the door. "Sir Swifty is getting restless in the box. If this takes long, should I take him outside?"

"No, I think we're done for today." Aurora removed the electrodes and started packing away her papers.

"Really?" Vincent frowned.

"This is rude of me, and I apologise, but I'm going to have to invite myself to join you where you're going. You need to relearn how to sleep, and you need to do it as soon as possible. I also need you to arrange a meeting for me and your brother."

"You're coming with us?" Ren bounced from joy, and the cat box bounced along with her. Sir Swifty was riding out the storm but looked just about ready to shred some skin as payment for his hardships. Aurora eased his misery by acquiring the box from its bouncy carrier until the girl calmed down.

"I need to gather some things. Can you take Sir Swifty outside, and we'll be right there?" Aurora re-entrusted Ren with the cat and turned back to Vincent. "And could you carry that for me?" She pointed at a trunk where Professor Limpqvist had placed the equipment she'd requested for loan and gathered Vincent's files back into her bag. The diagnostic machine she left on the table as something not particularly useful for a problem of this magnitude.

"Oh wow, this is heavy," Vincent commented. Aurora glanced at him, worried it might be too heavy, but he'd already lifted it up and was carrying it out the door with no problem.

Damn it. She had to admit there was an annoying, miniscule grain of truth in her mother's words. Maybe men weren't entirely useless after all? Yes, she could have carried that thing herself if she'd needed to, but he'd made it look so easy! If they weren't so gosh-darn-it troublesome, she might have accepted one as a pet.

Chapter 7

"How did it go?" Quin hadn't asked any questions since they'd met up and boarded the ferry. The ferry ride itself had been equally quiet, but he'd found his words by the time they arrived at Grovestead. Rhys appreciated the moment to himself, as well as the polite interest.

"I didn't see him," he said.

"That's good." When Rhys turned to look at him, Quin added, "I had a half a mind to turn back to tell you not to. I'll play dad for you if you need a father figure."

Rhys cringed.

"Thanks but no thanks. I'll be fine without. It's not him I'm worried about. It's my mother."

"Oh?"

"I met her briefly when I was about to enter. She said some things that made me think she might be in danger."

"Do you want us to do something about it?"

"'Us?'" Quin had been extraordinarily kind as of late, so the offer shouldn't have come as a surprise, but Rhys still occasionally had trouble readjusting from the less-than-flattering first impression. "She told me not to get involved, and, with everything else that's going on, I'm tempted to trust her so I can put it out of my mind."

"She's dealt with it thus far... This way." Quin guided Rhys away from the docks. "She's dealt with it for years, so she probably knows how to handle him, but I'll back you up if you want us to rescue her. Did she seem injured?"

"No. I'm a little worried we might end up causing her more grief. But she mentioned a place I've been that I've forgotten, and it's bothering me. She chased me away before I could ask her more about it."

"Could it have something to do with this?" Quin flicked the business card in his hand.

"It's possible. I have nothing to connect it to, nothing rings a bell."

"Let me investigate this first, then. Maybe something turns up, and we'll figure it out ourselves. If not, you can always go ask her later."

"That's probably wise. We've got our hands full as it is. Let's follow this lead and try to sort out Vincent and the remains first. Whatever I've forgotten can stay forgotten for a while longer." Rhys spotted the speeder from afar. "Oh, we're almost there."

They'd walked up the street from the docks toward a sparsely populated, residential area with needlessly vast fenced-off yards rich in exotic, carefully tended greenery. Littered across some of them were intricate statues and ornaments made of various finer quality polished stones, as if just one of them hadn't cost a full year's salary, perhaps more. There were water features ranging from opulent fountains shooting water up to ridiculous heights to more subtle cascading waterfalls designed to blend into a landscape of rocks, ferns and moss.

Vincent's speeder was parked next to a monstrous wrought iron gate typical of the area, but at least the yard the gate opened up to was not quite as garish as the two beside it. Still, against this backdrop, the speeder was reduced to a heap of garbage, and the pitiful sight made Rhys want to wash and polish it or pour some tar on some of the brighter white marble statues.

"You don't have to look like you're being led up to the castle of the Duke of Chattshire. It's not that bad, is it?" Quin interrupted Rhys's moment of imaginary vandalism.

The duke in question was one of the most notorious, obnoxious spendthrifts in the history of the continent, and, according to legend, when he'd lost his fortune and was forced to auction off his property, he'd received no offers as testament to his insurmountable lack of taste.

Quin opened the gate to let Rhys through. By the time they were halfway up to what was more a mansion than a house, a half a dozen members of staff scrambled and scurried to the yard in apparent confusion.

"Did you send for the driver, sir? Was there a miscommunication, sir?" a silver-haired man, presumably the butler, asked Quin when the six of them had formed a more orderly row for the welcome.

"No, there was no miscommunication, Hughes. I have two functioning feet. Have our guests arrived? Have you made sure they are comfortable?"

"Yes, sir." Hughes gestured for the footman to take the small bag Quin was carrying.

The maid offered Quin a cooled, moist towel to wipe his face with. There was another such towel offered to Rhys, who didn't see the point but dabbed himself with it so as not to appear rude.

"Julian?" Quin asked.

"Mr Craft has been escorted to his room, sir. I have seen to the details myself, sir."

"Good. And the others?"

"We have arranged accommodations for Mr Hart, Mr Swifty, the young lady and Ms Vesper, sir—"

"Ms Vesper? Who is that?" Quin walked up the stairs to the front door.

"Oh, that's probably the doctor from Sleepy Leighs I mentioned," Rhys mused.

Curious that she was here. Weren't they supposed to meet at the College?

"She's a doctor, sir? My sincerest apologies, sir. Dr Vesper arrived together with the others, sir." The butler hurried to open the door for them.

"I'm going to need a bath," Quin said. A wave of a hand delegated the task to another member of staff. "Dinner?"

"As per your instructions, sir, it will be served momentarily. Should I inform your guests?"

"Yes, do that. And can you stop hovering around me for a moment? I'm tired." Quin seemed to wave him away not so much like he wanted to be rid of a pesky fly but to get out of an awkward situation.

"Certainly, sir," the butler said and excused himself.

Quin and Rhys were left standing in the grand foyer alone, save for a single young maid trying to blend into a wall in a corner, presumably waiting in case Quin needed something.

"It's big," Rhys said, lacking a better comment.

It was odd how Quin could look both like he belonged here and not. His personality was certainly flamboyant enough, and he usually dressed the part, but, while clearly accustomed to directing the staff, he didn't seem to enjoy being waited on as much as Rhys had expected.

"It was not my choice." Quin faced away and headed for the stairs. "I'm going to freshen up. Ask her if you need something."

The change in mood baffled Rhys only for a moment. He looked around himself, taking in some of the details and feeling the full weight of Quin's words.

"Shit." His quiet comment garnered a wary look from the maid. "Sorry, don't mind me. I'm just annoyed at myself for not knowing when to shut up."

Quin looked like he belonged because he was part of the decor.

A reasonable assumption, perhaps, that Quin might feel a sense of relief upon his return, but this wasn't home. It was more like the forgotten cage of a captive bird.

Regardless, he needed to dust himself off, prune his feathers and entertain his guests tonight, so he washed his face and changed into something more comfortable. Maybe if he could put on enough of a show or prove himself useful, they would not leave him behind.

Julian's room was next to Quin's, of course, and connected with a door. Quin gave the door a wary knock.

"Sorry, are you in?" He wouldn't have dreamed of disturbing in the past, and daring to do it now quickened his pulse beyond comfort.

"Who—? Damn it, Quin, can't I have some privacy?" Julian was clearing away something on the bed. He was dressed but seemed he'd been going through his options to change into something else.

"Your clothes are in the wardrobe. I've had them aired. Pick anything you like. It's yours." Quin entered the room to show him. It had been over a decade, so they probably wouldn't all fit perfectly, but he hadn't changed so much in size that they wouldn't fit altogether.

Julian seemed to be suppressing some annoyance but took a look at what was on offer.

"I'll instruct the staff to take care of your travel wear. If there's anything you need or something is not to your liking, just ask them. Make yourself at home."

"I appreciate the hospitality, but if you're expecting me to move in here with you, you should stop." Julian picked out something to wear and checked that there were no ripped seams or holes made by moth or beetle larvae.

"Of course. Merely hoping you'll be comfortable while you're here." Quin handed him a tie. He reminded himself to snap out of this heavy mood to make the best of the situation.

"Have you always been this much of a kiss-ass?" Julian asked. "It was annoying enough to have your servants hover around when we arrived. Are you going to stick around to watch me undress?"

Quin wouldn't have minded staying for such a treat, but alas, he could tell it wasn't in his cards, and it also wasn't why he'd knocked.

"Dinner will be served downstairs in a moment. I wanted to make sure you were aware. I think they're serving—"

"Don't tell me it's some obscure dish that's supposedly my favourite."

"—food. It's a generic edible substance of no relevance."

Why did he have to be so crabby about it? Quin knew to expect the moods and the temper, but without the other things as counterbalance, they were starting to get on his nerves. None of his usual tricks seemed to be helping, either. Julian had been treating him this way ever since they'd got reacquainted, and when Rhys wasn't around to remind him to behave, he would often become excessively abrasive.

"Thank you for letting me know. I don't know how I would have survived without this information. Now, can you leave? I do not need an audience when I dress myself." Julian was unbuttoning the first two buttons of his shirt. Stupid tease.

"I know you think you're the new and improved version, but I preferred the old Julian." Quin would have preferred it, even if this comment would have earned him a smack in the face.

Actually, especially if it had. It was the stuff after the smack that made it worth it.

"Show yourself out and take your disappointment with you." Julian made no move to engage in anything more interesting.

Quin sighed and retreated from the room. He wasn't ready to give up and admit he'd lost his touch, but he'd been slamming his head to the wall for so long he wasn't sure he had a head or a wall left to slam. How long would he be able to stand this?

But the alternative seemed more frightening.

"Julian?" Rhys knocked on the door. He'd asked the staff for directions and was surprised to find they'd placed Julian at a completely different part of the house than the rest of the guest accommodations.

No one responded to the knock.

Curious about the location, Rhys decided to take a brief look. It was definitely not the same size or style of room as the guest rooms. The furniture was made of dark stained walnut with matching dark upholstery with silver or white details. There was a four-poster bed with heavy black velvet drapes, grey satin sheets and covers with intricate white floral designs. It was too particular not to be someone's specific preference.

While it wasn't what Rhys would have imagined Julian to pick, it did not feel entirely off. This must have been his room. Quin probably hadn't had to instruct the staff to show him here because where else would they take him but his own room?

It felt even worse to be snooping around, but Rhys could not resist making the most out of the opportunity. It was a lovely distraction to pull him away from his heavy thoughts.

He didn't have much time before they would miss him at dinner, so he took a hasty tour around the room, pulled open a few drawers and checked what was in the wardrobe. Quin seemed to have left everything untouched for however long this room had remained empty.

There was a mysterious bag and a bundle of clothes on a bench at the end of the bed with a faint odour coming from them that wasn't the typical sweat and dust from days of travel.

Rhys spotted the envelope that had started this strange journey. He was reminded how little progress they'd made so far.

The voiceless had specifically told him to stop helping, but with such high likelihood they had said it in a fit of anger and not meant it, it felt more like an excuse to not feel guilt over the lack of progress. If the voiceless turned up tonight, he would finally be able to clear any misunderstandings and maybe ask them about the card Quin had received.

Rhys turned the envelope in his hand. It was in a rough shape, crumpled and stained. What on earth had happened to it? He had a faint recollection of seeing it in this state at Agnes Point but hadn't really thought much of it. It smelled about the same as the bag.

The envelope was still empty.

Rhys was about to put it back and leave when something else about it caught his eye. The faint smudges on the inside of the envelope looked like writing. It was not the clearest of handwriting—in fact it looked a lot like Julian's scribbles—but in its defence it was mostly legible despite being so tiny and faint.

Rhys popped open the seams ever so carefully. Most of the inside of the envelope was covered in writing with only some of the beginning missing. It was dated almost exactly fifteen years ago.

> Before I forget, yes, I do love him. It's not so much because of the things he does or doesn't do to accommodate my whims, although I must admit it is refreshing to have someone in my life willing to dedicate themselves so whole-heartedly to me and accept me for who I am. I love him because amidst all this, he's the one person I feel safe with and can always count on. I would trust him with my life.
> When all this has passed, I hope I can do right by him and give him everything he needs because he has given me everything I could ever hope for.

Rhys swallowed. Had he read this letter upon the envelope's discovery, he wouldn't have had a clue who had written it or who its subject was, but having watched Quin's torment from the sidelines for the past month or so, it was now no mystery.

It hadn't been a one-sided, desperate infatuation.

Rhys hadn't meant to doubt Quin's words or his perception of the relationship, but Julian rarely seemed the person Quin described.

"Before I forget..." Julian must have known he was about to forget, so he'd sent this to himself as a reminder of his feelings for Quin.

The way things stood, Rhys had to wonder whether a reminder like this would make a difference. Still, Julian should probably read this since he'd wanted himself to know.

Rhys tucked the envelope into his pocket and hurried downstairs for dinner.

Julian looked to be in a sour mood. It couldn't have been the food or the company, as the food was excellent, and Vincent was gracing them with a hilarious recounting of his adventures defeating the fearsome cauliflower. The conversations that ensued were of various fascinating topics that should have provided plenty of entertainment. Quin, as the gracious host, had even managed to engage Victor in the conversation without resorting to Rhys's usual crude tactics.

Rhys had picked a seat next to Julian for the sole purpose of bringing up the letter as soon as an opportune moment presented itself, but Julian had sat with a pickaxe up his butt all evening, or, at least, his face was fixed to a scowl so deep his bottom must have swallowed one, if not two pickaxes, for him to have reached that depth of displeasure.

Once Victor was in full speed chatting about foreign architecture with Vincent, Quin turned his attention to Dr Vesper to map out half of her working history and research background, her family situation and her interests. For a while, Rhys was preoccupied listening to her explanation on the recent advances in sleep medicine and how they overlapped with some ancient lore about the Guardian.

"I think I read about that somewhere," Julian said, making an effort to retract one of the pickaxes. "Might have even been a book written by you or a relative of yours. Dr Vesper, was it?"

"Yes. I have published a few books, but in hindsight, I probably should have let them mature some before I did."

"No, no. I found it to be excellent, refreshing and helpful in understanding Rhys here." The other pickaxe was almost out.

"Oh? Does he have trouble sleeping? Anything I could help with?" Dr Vesper turned to Rhys, and her aura of accomplishments made Rhys feel like he was shrinking down a size.

"It wholly depends on what Quin's got stashed in his closets," Rhys joked. The mansion did have a nicer feel than a lot of the places they'd passed on their way, but he'd only know for sure once he'd slept in it. His answer made Dr Vesper frown.

"The quality of your sleep is location dependent? That's fascinating."

"Isn't most people's?" People rarely latched onto Rhys's off-handed remarks, so he hadn't expected this one to garner any further interest.

"I think that usually excludes the contents of closets," Dr Vesper noted.

"It's just a little quirk I have."

Rhys trusted most of the people present, and his sleeping issues were not some closely guarded secret, but it did feel a touch too private to share as a light topic of dinner conversation.

"I think you might have guardian potential. If you had been born some thousands of years ago, perhaps you'd have been one of the most highly esteemed members of your community." She'd kindly brought the conversation back to a broader topic but eyed him with keen interest.

"I have too many problems to have the time to guard the dreams of a whole community." Rhys laughed. Even the consultation service he'd provided back in Schadesborough felt too big of a responsibility now that he was busy worrying about his mother, Vincent, Julian and Quin and the whole voiceless situation. "Which reminds me. Does anyone here recognise the name Hosta Therapy Solutions?"

Without needing to be prompted, Quin produced the card from his pocket and sent it around the table, causing a wave of headshaking.

"That's too bad. It's the only lead we got today from Mr Wakefield senior," Quin said. The card returned to him, and he put it back in his pocket.

"A lead? What sort of a puzzle is it?" Dr Vesper asked.

"Not the fun kind," Rhys said. Ren was listening to the conversation in silence but with her eyes aglow with curiosity.

"We found some mummified human remains in the attic of Rhys's building. The two of them," Julian gestured at Rhys and Quin, "went to Dritsby to find out whether Rhys's father knows something about them, but they aren't exactly on good terms because he is, as far as I've come to understand, an absolute prick."

"Julian!" While Julian's summary was accurate, it wasn't how Rhys would have presented it in front of a child. Julian looked at him, glanced at Ren and shoved his pickaxes right back up his keister.

"I can ask around if you'd like. The group I'm working for might be affiliated," Dr Vesper suggested.

"He warned us to be careful, so proceed with caution and at your own risk. We are talking about actual human remains here, and we do not know what happened to them. This Hosta might be extremely dangerous if they're involved somehow," Rhys said.

"Oh, don't pour any more for him." Dr Vesper interrupted the servant about to refill Vincent's glass. They were nearing the end of the meal with not much left on their plates, but there was presumably still dessert left. "Sorry, I need you to sleep well tonight," she told him. When she noticed her interruption had paused the entire conversation, she added, "Contrary to popular belief, a nightcap does not, in fact, improve your sleep."

There were some murmurs as the servant made an effort to refill their glasses but was declined throughout her round. She seemed distressed when she had to leave with a full, freshly opened bottle.

With this pause in the conversation, Rhys handed the letter to Julian discreetly under the table.

"What's this?" Julian lifted it up to read it.

"Later. I meant you should read it later," Rhys whispered, but Julian was already reading it. He glanced at Rhys and then at Quin, and the mining tools in his hindquarters reached new depths. He checked the front of the envelope. The corner of his eye was twitching ominously.

"What is it?" Quin asked innocently enough.

Julian ripped the letter into four pieces, tossed it on the table, thanked for the meal and stormed out of the dining room.

"Jules?" Quin looked like he might go after him.

"You'd better not." Rhys tried to gather and hide what was left of the letter, but Quin snatched the pieces from his hands and from the table. No further words were uttered. Quin read the letter, his face a stony wall. Then he ran after Julian.

"**D**o not talk to me right now!" There was only so much of this Julian could deal with at a time.

"Jules..." Quin's pathetic whine was the exact thing to push him over the edge, and the man was there as if called to do just that.

"Don't call me that!"

"Julian, listen to me—"

"Go away! Stop following me!"

"Please, Julian. That was your handwriting, wasn't it?"

"Do I look like I give a shit?"

The room, the clothes, the food, this whole house and the servants in it were as if catered to him. It was pleasant and inviting, yet at the same time unfamiliar and horrifying: like someone was calling him back to the past, where he was a whole other person he didn't know or recognise. And Quin was taunting him on purpose, always trying to get a rise out of him, despite promising he wouldn't.

"It was your fucking handwriting, wasn't it?!" Quin's tone shifted to an unrecognisable fury to match Julian's.

"So what? What do you expect from me? I'm not that person anymore!" All that was left of him were the empty feeling of disconnect and the dread that he might revert back to a monster at any given moment.

Quin grabbed the collar of Julian's shirt and screamed at his face, "What is so wrong about me trying? Can't you fucking let me have anything?!" The pinkish healed scar at the side of his mouth stretched to its limit.

"You think you want me back, but trust me, you don't." Julian removed Quin's hands off of himself. "Touch me again, and I will truly boil over, and you do not want to be around me when that happens." All this prodding and pushing had to be intentional. They were trying to turn him back into that person without proper understanding of what that entailed.

Perhaps they understood but chose to ignore the warnings? If so, could they push him some more and give him an excuse to prove their stupidity?

"Blow a fucking lid then, why don't you? It's better than having you skirt around the issue." Quin held his ground. "Let's see just how scary you think you are!"

"Do not tempt me. I will snap your neck like a twig." Julian's voice sank to a hoarse whisper as he savoured the threat, ready to let go of his feeble and fast-failing self-restraint at the next excuse.

"What the hell are the two of you doing? Stop!" Rhys's shriek brought him back to reality. Victor was standing behind Rhys, but thankfully the others had stayed in the dining room.

"I'm trying to mind my own business. Keep him the hell away from me!" Julian grabbed the opportunity to retreat into his room. He was so close to losing it. Much too close for comfort. Moments like this reminded him how the world would have been a better place had he kept on walking.

It sounded lovely to have someone accept him for who he was. Maybe Quin was the sort of masochist who could actually pull it off? But no one deserved to be trapped in a relationship like that, no matter how irritating they were. And if there had ever been anything decent about Julian back then, he sure as hell could not remember it now. It was gone. All that were left were the emptiness, dread and inexplicable anger.

"Julian?" It was Rhys's voice from the other side of the door.

"Leave me alone, Rhys."

"I will. I just want to know you're all right."

"I'm fine. I just need a moment."

"You're not going to do anything stupid?"

"No."

"Quin promised to keep away for now. I didn't mean to spring the letter on you like that. I wanted you to check it later. I thought you ought to read it, since you'd thought it important enough to write to yourself about…"

Some rather unsavoury words sprung to mind, so Julian refrained from answering.

"Julian?"

"Yes?"

"Get some rest. We're all tired from the trip."

Ah, shit! Julian hurried to open the door.

"Are you all right for the night? Where are you sleeping? Do you need something?" Rhys hadn't been getting the greatest sleep on the road, and Julian hadn't a clue whether this place was going to be better or worse for him.

"I'll be OK." Rhys was at the door alone with no sign of Quin or Victor. "Probably."

"There's plenty of space in here, if you need to—" Julian was reminded of the peculiar decor of his room and hesitated. Maybe this was the type of stuff Rhys wanted to avoid?

"Thanks. I'll remember the offer if my room starts feeling oppressive. But I think I should get back to dessert. Let the others know no one died. Do you want them to bring you dessert here?"

"No, I don't want any."

"All right. Well. Don't do anything stupid…"

"I won't." Julian hung his head in shame. "I'm sorry."

"Me too. You've got enough on your plate. I'll see what I can do about Quin. Let me know if or when you're ready to work it out with him, but in the meantime, don't worry about it and get some rest."

"Thanks."

"Sleep well."

"You too."

If it happened again, if he forgot everything again, would it end up hurting everyone he cared about, like it had hurt Quin? And how many times could he lose his cool before he truly hurt someone?

If he made no attachments or lofty promises, it would save them from potential heartbreak and disappointment when he inevitably failed to meet their expectations.

He needed to keep them at a safe distance.

CHAPTER 9

Done unpacking his things after dinner, Rhys knocked on the door a few doors over from his room.

"Come in."

He entered a guest room similar to his own—pleasant, but blandly decorated. Vincent sat on the bed with a dozen or so wires running from attachment points on his scalp to a measuring device on a serving cart beside the bed. He was in his pyjamas, waiting for Dr Vesper to finish setting everything up.

"What's all that for?" Rhys asked.

"Oh, this?" Dr Vesper reached for another wire and plugged it into the device. "This is for measuring his brain activity when I begin treatment, so I know the correct dosage and can keep an eye on his sleep."

"Looks complicated."

"This part is not all that refined. I'm hoping to improve his RI index to see if that helps."

"RI index?" Rhys wondered if he could have slept with all those things attached to his head. They looked uncomfortable.

"Restorative Impact index. It measures how well your brain can regenerate and restore its functions during sleep. This is a gross oversimplification, but your brain releases chemicals during sleep that cause a number of different reactions to occur usually in a sequence or sequences. Their job is to flush out what's not needed and to prepare your brain for another day of successful wakefulness. When those reactions do not occur, simply put, your brain will struggle to function properly when you're awake. They are an extremely important part of your physiology." Dr Vesper finished with her preparations and turned on the device.

"Oh, like rest." Rhys watched the device churn out a few squiggly lines onto a strip of paper before it stopped.

"Rest?" Dr Vesper checked the output. "Calibration looks all right, although I think this might be loose." She adjusted one of the wires and hit a switch, and the device spat out another squiggle almost identical to the first. "I guess not." She laughed.

"Another screw loose inside my head, then?" Vincent said, voice softer than usual. For someone so opposed to meeting the doctor before, he seemed awfully taken by her now.

"Could be, but fortunately, this one isn't as essential as the stuff that's still holding up the fort in there." Dr Vesper pulled out a box similar to Julian's medicine kit and prepared a syringe and needle. "What did you say about rest, mister...? Mr Wakefield was it?"

"Call me Rhys. I just thought your explanation matched my experience with rest, that was all."

"All right, Rhys. My name is Vera." She offered him her hand to shake.

"Oh, so that's why Ren calls you Dr Vera. I was wondering what that was about." Rhys shook her hand.

"Yes, I tried to get her to drop the 'doctor', but she's surprisingly persistent."

"Wait." Vincent looked confused. "Your name is Vera? I messed up your name, too?" He shifted from confused to tortured.

"No, don't worry. You didn't mess up anything. My name is Aurora Vesper, but I haven't gone by my first name since my teenage years. Everyone calls me Vera these days, but you're free to use whichever name you'd like." She patted his shoulder, lifted the sleeve and stabbed him with a needle. Rhys gasped. "Oh, sorry. Did I startle you? These old thick needles hurt less when you do it briskly."

Vincent didn't even flinch with the thing deep in his flesh. Vera depressed the plunger slowly and removed the needle much more gently than she'd inserted it.

"That side's been busted since I got roughed up," Vincent said and shrugged.

"I'll need to give this one intravenously, but I haven't actually done this for a while since the nurses usually do them for me. But don't worry, Bernard here won't hurt a bit." Vera took out another syringe and needle and prepared the dose. "Are you ready? You might feel drowsy after this, so you should lie down when I'm done."

Vincent nodded. Vera fastened the tourniquet, wiped the area, inserted the needle, released the tourniquet and depressed the plunger with no indication of her being out of practice or unsure of what she was doing. Rhys was impressed but had to admit he'd hoped she would have shown a genuinely less skilful, less competent side to her by messing it up at least once. She seemed like a wonderful person, but people with no apparent weaknesses or character flaws made Rhys inherently suspicious.

"Now, let's see if we can get you to sleep properly." She helped Vincent lie down and turned on her device so that, instead of spewing a long strip of paper for the output, the needles on the gauges started to flicker. "So far, so good. Let's see the difference between your wake and sleep states..." She sat down on a chair by the bed and gestured for Rhys to take a seat in a chair at the opposite corner of the room.

"Will you stay here all night?" Rhys asked her.

"Yes. I need to keep an eye on this and make sure that when he reaches restorative sleep, he doesn't pop back out of it."

"When will you sleep?" Vincent asked, already sounding groggy.

"Don't worry. I've had all my life to sleep well, and I have the rest of my life to make up for a skipped night or two. It's your turn now."

"Thanks..."

"If you tell me what to look out for, I can take over for you if you need to nap at some point," Rhys suggested.

"Am I supposed to do something?" Vincent asked. He lifted his arms up and watched them like there was something wrong with them. "I feel strange..."

"The readings look promising. Just lay back and close your eyes." Vera guided his arms back down.

"What is this..."

"I can't say for sure whether it feels like it's supposed to, but it's probably the closest you've been to actually falling asleep. The output looks about right."

"I think I like this. So calm. Heavy."

"You can tell me about it tomorrow."

"I love you."

Vera snorted.

"I suppose when, after over three decades of not being able to sleep properly, someone comes and helps you with it, the level of gratitude is easiest expressed with those three words. I think he's out." She turned back to Rhys. "What exactly did you mean when you said 'rest'? And why do I feel like there's something significant about it that I should like to understand?"

After having watched the two of them interact and now hearing this latest exchange of words, Rhys could have sworn he heard an audible click of the pieces slotting together inside his head. They must have known each other at some point in the past. She was making this extra effort to be likeable and impress everyone for a very specific reason.

"Not to put you on the spot, doctor, but why do I get the feeling those weren't just words of gratitude?"

No matter how self-assured and professional she'd seemed all evening, Vera could not disguise the deep crimson blush that reached even her neck and ears.

"Has... has he said something?"

"No, but I know my brother well enough to tell."

Vincent would have professed his love to Dr Corkbottom, Dr Skinpitt or the nurses for the drugs he was given for the pain at Sleepy Leighs if he were the type to say such things in the face of relief alone. Rhys sighed.

"As for your question, when I sleep, I go through the different stages at will. What I've heard, that's not how most people sleep. I understand this probably piques your interest as a doctor and a scientist, but I'd rather not become a test rat. However, if it helps you with your research, I'll answer any questions you have to the best of my abilities."

"I— I'd appreciate that. I do have some, I—" She paused to find her pace but didn't seem to have much luck with it. "He wouldn't have said that in earnest, would he?"

"Why not?" Rhys hadn't seen Vincent express any interest in romantic relationships, so him saying anything to that effect seemed like it would mean something.

"I think I need to adjust the next dose. This looks good for now, but see how this number is below seven? I'd like it to be around ten. At this rate, the next dose is in about three hours. I'll show you what you need to keep an eye out for, and, if you're still up for it, go get some sleep and come back around midnight. I'd appreciate a nap after the next dose." The blush was gone, and she'd regained her earlier composure. Whatever had flipped her switch, she was back in work mode.

What an unfamiliar and baffling sensation, Vincent thought. He had a feeling he hadn't thought about anything for a while. There was a chunk of something missing where he hadn't had to do or think about anything, and things had happened all by themselves.

He was now inside the bubble, but it didn't feel at all as disorienting as before. The edge was crisp and clear, and when he moved his arms, his body on the bed did not respond at all. There was a whole separate him within the bubble, and he could even touch the edge when he reached out for it. He'd never been able to do that before.

"Hey, hands, are you out here? What's your name? Rhys calls you the voiceless, right?"

No response, but the hands were definitely close by. They had been there a lot lately, and Vincent had learned to tell the difference in the atmosphere.

"Are you upset with him? Why are you hanging out with me all the time?"

"Hosta, with me," it responded.

"You know Hosta?" That was the name on that card Mr Quin had passed around the dinner table.

"Yes."

"Do you also know... what was it? Harold P. Brown?"

"No."

"So, is Hosta with you there right now?"

"Yes."

"Where are you? At Rhys's building?" No, wait, wasn't there talk about the remains being moved away? It was so difficult to keep track of the snippets Rhys had told him here and there.

"No. Hosta. Not. At Rhys's building. Right now."

"But they've been there before?" That sounded like something Rhys might want to know. "When?"

"Hosta. Been there before. Time. More words."

"You want words?" How convenient that they knew to request that. All of this had been much more difficult to understand before. "You want time? So, a week, two weeks, or are we talking about years here? Five, ten years? Twenty? Longer?"

"Twenty. Also. Not. Longer. A— Year."

When was it that Rhys had sent that postcard about moving into the city? Autumn last year? So, less than a year ago. Hosta must have been at that address just before Rhys moved in.

"What did they do there? This Hosta." If they were responsible for the remains, then the therapy they provided must have not been great. "Did they hurt you?"

"Hosta. Hurt. Me. Also. You."

"Me? Quin got the card from my father. Why would he have it? Is that what he's used to get back at me somehow?"

"Quin?"

"The owner of this house. He's Rhys's friend."

"Hosta. Not. Friend."

"Are they responsible for your current predicament?"

"Yes."

"Hosta killed you?"

"Yes."

"Embalmed you?"

"Yes."

"And they are where you are, right now?"

"Yes."

Well, that left nothing up to the imagination.

"Where are you?"

"I. Do. Not. Know."

Rhys returned to Vincent's room almost precisely at midnight. Vera was reading a book by the window, the full moon lighting her pages enough for them to be readable without lighting a lamp.

"How is he?" Rhys whispered.

"Fine. I gave him the next dose a minute ago. The readings are stable. They were fluctuating a half an hour ago, but whatever that was, it seems to have passed. Don't be afraid to wake me up if there's anything that worries you." She put down her book, hesitated for only a moment and lay down next to Vincent on the bed.

The bed was wide enough for there to be plenty of separation with her lying on the edge of it. She could have made herself more comfortable but chose to stay as far to the side as possible instead.

Rhys sat down on the chair next to the bed and checked what book she'd been reading. 'The Guardians of Our Sleep', it read on the cover. Seemed like a great distraction.

"Do you mind if I...?"

"No, go ahead."

"Thanks. Sleep well." Rhys opened the book and started reading.

CHAPTER 10

Vincent woke up feeling odd. For one, he could tell he had just woken up and that this state was different from the last one. With nothing to compare this to, he couldn't say exactly what had changed, but he felt better.

"Did I sleep? Was that sleep?" He sat up. A strange, energetic excitement washed over him. Holy hell, was that what that was like? Was it magic? He didn't feel half as achy and tired as the day before. He hadn't much time to marvel at the feeling before he noticed he was not alone in his bed.

Aurora slept next to him fully dressed, on top of the duvet, poor thing. Rhys sat in the chair and yawned. He was awake, if only barely. The two of them had sacrificed their night so that he could have this. They looked exhausted.

"Good morning, Vincent." As he said it, Rhys was caught in a whole series of yawns.

"Did you stay up all night?"

"No, we took turns. Did you sleep well?"

"I think I did. I feel great!" Everything felt sharp and in focus. If one night could do this, what was it like to sleep well every night? "Oh, I need to exchange the 3-millimetre tubing for the next size up. That's closer to the perfect ratio of aeration. The rotor blade angle could also be steeper. If I adjust the whole series, there will be enough space for the insulation. I knew I was missing something! I've got to tell Ren." He plucked off the electrodes attached to his scalp and jumped off the bed to change out of his pyjamas.

"What?"

"Oh, oh, oh, and I chatted with the hands, the voiceless! They said they know Hosta, they're with Hosta, and Hosta is responsible for their death, so you really ought to be careful about how to approach them, if you do. I didn't catch who they were or why they did it, but I'm sure the voiceless will tell us with the right words." Vincent put on his shirt and trousers. "I need some paper and a pen. I think my previous calculations are off..." He rummaged through his travel bags for some fresher socks, his notebook and the pen. The noise apparently woke up Aurora.

"Vincent? Is something wrong? What happened?" Even dishevelled and waking up like this, she looked so wonderful that Vincent wanted to squeeze her.

"I need to fix a few things! Nothing is wrong, everything's perfect. Except for my calculations. They are wrong. It's no wonder the thing stalls. I think I can also fix the temperature issue. It's been under my nose all along!" He put on the socks and hopped over to Aurora on one foot.

"Are you sure you're all right?" She looked at Rhys as if to consult.

"Yes, I'm fine. For real this time. Thank you!" Vincent meant to give her a peck on the cheek, but she turned back to look at him just as he did. He didn't realise what had happened until he was already out the door, on his way to find Ren.

"What the hell is wrong with me," he mumbled, pushed it out of his mind and limped his way to Ren's room, agile like an only-ever-so-slightly-wounded gazelle. He would finally fix the speeder, and it would work well below freezing, but he needed to hurry before this spell was broken, and he turned back into the tired old dullard-Vincent.

Rhys was done with the book about the Guardian. There were only so many times he could mull through the spat between Quin and Julian, or himself and the voiceless, wondering whether there was something he was supposed to do about either, or worry about Vincent's treatment, or the significance of Hosta amidst all of this. His mind kept returning to his mother's words.

He'd longed to hear her acknowledge him for so long it was unreal to think back on it, but every time he did, his heart felt warm. Unfortunately, the rest of the conversation gnawed on his stomach, chilling and sucking out that warmth as soon as he'd thought of it.

Because he had stayed up most of the night, regardless of the rest he'd taken before midnight, Rhys was certainly feeling the extra hours when Vincent bounced up half-past five in the morning, full of energy. After Vera had tottered out of the room in an apparent state of confusion, Rhys decided against returning to his room and crawled instead into Vincent's bed.

A nap for an hour or two would help with the nagging anxiety and the intrusive thoughts of his tired mind, and it didn't really matter where he took it in this house. The guest rooms were all the same.

Even once he'd fallen asleep, Rhys was plagued by the knowledge he'd forgotten something that, no matter how hard he tried to recall, he couldn't. He was worried for his mother's safety, but having something, a place, in his past that he'd forgotten as if it had never existed, was unsettlingly similar to Julian's memory loss, even if not on an equally devastating scale.

No, that wasn't accurate. Now that he was asleep, there was a hint of something at the back of his mind that felt like it might be connected to a memory of sorts: he'd had recurring nightmares as a child.

It was difficult to estimate when—perhaps he'd been six or eight—but he could distinctly remember that his nightmares hadn't had anything to do with his life at the time. He'd been happy at home, doing the normal things kids his age did.

Not only had he been too young to make sense of the events he'd dreamt about, but they had also taken place somewhere he couldn't recall ever being to.

The adults in his life had assured him these were just dreams: mere figments of his imagination that would soon fade away and be forgotten if he let them pass. It was a shame he'd listened and let them pass. It would have been interesting to see them from his current perspective, knowing that none of his dreams were ever just dreams.

Rhys drifted through his thoughts, exploring which dreams he could recall and which not, and the more he brought back, the more he realised there weren't any he couldn't. There seemed to exist a huge catalogue of dreams he could pull up at will, and the extent of it seemed to stretch way past the limits of his brain and memory.

He'd never really considered that the dreamside could hold these things separate from him, but when he thought about it, the book he'd just read and Vera's words on the subject, it did vaguely make sense.

He'd always instinctively understood that the dreamside was another aspect of the same reality he resided in when he was awake: it held the same things, but in an altered manner depending on what processes were going on in his brain as he slept and what capabilities those processes enabled in conjunction with the framework the dreamside provided.

But apparently there was a separate framework and a collection of information here that no longer necessarily existed in his memory. It was like a recorded archive of all of the dreams that had passed through it. If he'd forgotten something, this was where he'd still have it in the form of those nightmares—if he could find the right ones to pull from the bunch and if they weren't too corrupt from an overly active imagination. To think he'd had this potential at his fingertips and not thought to look!

The amount of past dreams was overwhelming, but Rhys could remember the general mood of what he was after and used it to focus his aim. Once he found the right dream, all he had to do was to re-dream it.

Rhys was seven. It was a year or two after he'd realised he didn't dream like the others and that he was always a boy within his dreams. It wasn't something he paid much attention to, but he'd taken notice and started to wonder why things didn't match when he was awake.

When he'd brought this up with his parents, they had at first brushed it off as a silly fancy. The more he'd mentioned it, though, the angrier his father had become, until one night when Rhys had been fast asleep, he'd felt the firm, coarse hands at his throat and seen his father from dreamside strangling him while being unable to wake up or struggle.

Whatever had made the man hesitate enough to not take Rhys's life right then, Rhys didn't know, but he'd stopped when Rhys had finally woken up to fight back. His mother had burst into the room, and his parents had had a massive argument while Rhys had cried, unable to fathom what was happening. There were several occasions of this dream, although Rhys could not remember any of it ever happening.

The dreams blended into images of unfamiliar surroundings, of bleak hospital rooms and corridors that he would trot back and forth in with nothing better to do.

Occasionally, there was an escape to some fantastic location outside—a fragment of a dream within the dream—but the majority were in rooms where he was held or tied to something to keep him from moving, or glimpses of someone smiling at him, but doing things that did not merit a smile in return. He could not describe what was done because his perception of it was lacking, but he could tell how much he'd hated it.

Tied again, he'd managed to wiggle his hand loose, and with that, he was able to free himself from his restraints. The corridor he escaped to was dimly lit, and, though there were only a few small windows above his eye level, he could tell it was late in the evening.

He ran in his ridiculous, lace-trimmed nightgown and ripped off the ribbons they'd used to tie his hair. He had a clear sense of where he was going: he'd scouted the way and knew where to go to get out.

None of what they did would ever convince him that he was a girl. He was frightened but determined, fuelled by the injustice. He was about to dash to freedom when the door in front of him opened without warning.

Rhys jolted and gasped. He'd done this in his original dream, but now for a different, added reason. The figure towering over him was not a stranger, even if it took Rhys a moment to recognise him. It was Julian, only much younger, fourteen at most.

What in the world? Julian looked straight at him. Someone was trailing behind him. Rhys jumped aside and half-flew and half-crawled into whatever room was closest. He hid in a corner behind a cabinet, hoping against hope that he'd been quick enough.

"You can tell him I'm leaving tomorrow," Julian was saying as he entered that same room with a woman behind him. He said nothing about Rhys, even if they'd clearly seen each other.

"You can't leave; I'm not done with you," she said.

"You are done."

"That's not up to you to decide. You are mine."

"I ceased being yours a long time ago!" Julian's voice was cold and his anger abrupt. "Try to stop me, and I'll make you regret you were ever born."

"Don't be stupid. Think of your brother." She sounded much too calm in the face of him.

"What brother? What is left of my brother?! You piece of sh—, I should kill you right now for what you did!" He charged at her throat, but she did nothing, just smiled with his hands around her neck.

"Calm yourself," she said. "You know you can't kill me. Should I up the dosage, is that what you want?" These words seemed eerily effective in dampening Julian's anger.

"You would do that?" He looked conflicted.

"No, silly." She laughed. "That would interfere with the data. But I will let you see your brother if you are nice."

"Really?"

"Yes, but I need you to be a good boy and complete the test first."

"Just this once, but then you have to let me go."

"Yes, sure. I promise." She patted his shoulder.

"Can I have a moment first? I need a moment..." Julian looked tortured as he tried to steel himself.

"Come back in a half an hour, and we'll start in the usual room," she said.

He looked like a half an hour wasn't going to be enough but did not hesitate to leave. The unpleasant woman stayed in the room for a while longer. She wrote something onto a memo on the desk and reached for the phone.

"Dear, I need you to pull the plug on number two again. He's getting difficult. Yes, today, if you can. Good. I'll send him over once we're done." She hung up the phone and checked the time. Rhys did not dare to move. He'd been scared witless of getting caught, but now that he'd had the nerve to listen to what was being said, he was frightened for another reason.

The woman left the room not a moment too soon. Rhys knew it wouldn't have mattered if he was caught—he was safe in his bed, far away from here—but the fear of her presence was still tangible. He had to steady his resolve before he could tiptoe to see what she'd written. It was a schedule spreadsheet.

Justin, 17:59. Pass. Julian, 18:40. Final data. Wipe.

Whatever that meant, it didn't sound good. The door opened again, and Rhys jumped in horror. Was she back? No, it was him.

"Come." Julian grabbed Rhys's hand. Oh yes, right. He was caught, but at least it hadn't been that horrible woman.

Julian pulled him through the corridor and into another room he seemed to deem safer.

"Stop resisting and act like it's working, and they will let you go. Trust me. It'll be easier that way," Julian said. "Be brave, little man."

R hys woke up, confused. What the hell was that? Was it something he'd dreamt up or a real experience he'd forgotten?

He had an intense need to share this with someone, but Julian would probably not be interested in anything to do with his past in his current state of mind. If this wasn't even true, subjecting him to it would serve no purpose.

But what if it was? What if he'd met Julian before, and, whatever had wiped Julian's memory, had happened to him too?

What was worse, it had been no accident! His father's obsession of having a daughter had been even deeper than he'd imagined.

Rhys wondered how much of his self-loathing, dysphoria and cognitive dissonance were due to his condition and what was caused by what they'd done to him at that facility. What part of Julian's discomfort facing any-thing to do with his past was him trying to shield himself from remember-ing and what part was actual memory loss?

Rhys tried to fall asleep again to access more dreams, but he was too anxious and rattled to relax. He wanted to talk to Julian but didn't want to burden him with this frustration. Vincent was busy living it up after his rare night of sleep, so it seemed rude to interrupt. Maybe Victor? Victor wasn't as personally invested and might provide a more objective perspective.

Rhys got up, washed his face and went to look for Victor.

CHAPTER 11

Quin was confident he could pull it off, but it was still a relief when he managed to secure a spot in an investor meeting for the Hosta Group—a company which according to most sources shouldn't have existed—on such a short notice. It had taken layers of staff talking to other layers of staff, a good whiff of money thrown around and a feigned, yet credible, disinterest in the whole affair, for him to get here.

The location of the investor meeting was a mystery even as Quin arrived. A ride had been arranged for him from the station, and they'd brought him to an ordinary-looking office building in midtown Firth.

Not that Quin knew Firth well enough to tell where this was, but he did make a mental note of the street address. Considering the secrecy, the place was probably rented for this specific one-time use with no discernible link to who was renting, but it didn't hurt to pay attention to the details.

Quin was welcomed by a footman of sorts and escorted into one of the rooms. Nothing about the reception or the decor suggested anything clandestine, save for perhaps the drawn curtains. There were a handful of other people waiting for the presentation, enjoying the offered refreshments, and Quin took his spot among them with natural ease and made some light conversation.

Some of them were clearly old money but tolerated Quin not knowing who he was. One could get away with a lot when one had no local reputation, and Quin knew how to play the part of someone with obscene wealth to a sufficiently believable degree. A multitude of inquiries and checks had been made behind the scenes before they'd invited him here, and presumably all of these people had been vetted the same, so it was easy to assume they were peers here of similar wealth and status.

A middle-aged woman dressed in a neat, long coat, practical shoes and a neat updo entered the room with an assistant perhaps half her age. He was carrying a heavy stack of memos and a box of unidentifiable medical equipment. She instructed him where to lay it out and prepared to speak.

"Gentlemen, would you mind taking your seats?" Her voice carried seemingly effortlessly over the casual chatter. A few of the guests took their seats and the rest, like Quin, remained on their feet but gave her their attention.

"We all know why you are here. You have heard what's being whispered in the field—it is certainly exciting news—but you want to know if it's even possible, plausible, to achieve these wonderful achievements, and I am here today to tell you, yes good sirs, it is indeed true. We have the services you are looking for, and we are currently in search of a handful of privileged patrons to join our team." She dropped a heavy stack of papers onto the desk in front of her, presumably for the effect. "Here is the proof. And once I have received your down payment, you will be able to go through it in detail. But first, we need to be sure you are serious about this commitment. Not only do we require your utmost discretion, this agreement will be made for life. Once you are in the know, there is no backing out. I urge you to leave now if that is not to your liking."

She waited a while, and two people did leave the room. She seemed pleased with the ones remaining.

"Good. I will arrange time with each of you to go through the contract and address whatever concerns you may have, but let me first introduce to you what we do here at Hosta Group."

She smiled a bland service smile as she listed the procedures, each more insidious, offensive or even illegal than the next, as if she was merely recounting a shopping list.

Amongst her services were disposing of a person in different ways untraceable by the authorities, manipulating a subject to madness, to submission or to any manner or degree that suited the client's cause, chemically and surgically inducing coma, amnesia, instability, insanity, different medical conditions or more pronounced character traits such as increased physical strength, heightened senses or sharper wits.

The further she got in her litany of deplorable 'treatments', the deeper the pit that formed in Quin's stomach. He admitted he had a relatively lax moral attitude, but the code he'd settled on he maintained quite firmly. He could see the appeal of many of these procedures, but they did not appeal to him. He had to muster a lot of self-control to appear like they did, for now.

"Rest easy, we will deliver without fail. It is not our responsibility to pass judgement, and we do not play the part of your conscience. Your investments go toward the development of our treatments and to cover the expenses for our facilities here in Firth, as well as Copseton, Chattsmouth, Gobeshurst and, of course, the Greater Schades area. This gives you access to our services, as per the terms we negotiate with each of you individually." She signalled for her assistant to hand out a flyer. There was an outline of her presentation with the different treatments and tiers of involvement listed, along with information on how many 'patients' they had already treated successfully, some example-cases included.

If Quin were to gain access to their patient records, would Julian's name pop up? If so, who was responsible for making the order to remove his memory? His family? Was it because he hadn't agreed to take over the business or because of his behavioural issues? Had the situation really been that dire they'd thought he was beyond any conventional help?

Quin had come here as a favour to Rhys but suddenly had considerably less interest in Rhys's father's involvement, the history of the building or the mummified corpse in the attic and much more in whether these treatments were reversible.

If he made a large enough payment, would they ignore past loyalties and do something about Julian? It would be money well spent, Quin thought. He was ready to sign whatever was thrown at him.

Victor was up early after a restless night and another nightmare from the incident years back. When this happened, he would usually get up and paint until the anxiety passed, but he hadn't had anything to paint with for a while now. He gave up on sleep around four in the morning and sat up to stare at the dormer window and the raindrops sliding down across it, forming their usual rivulets.

Faint shadows flickered on his arms and hands when he looked down. He formed the signs for 'fine' and 'calm'. The act of signing and watching himself sign was comforting.

When he was unable to speak, a pen and a paper seemed like the next best thing, but, because a written message was so easy to toss away and dismiss, he was more confident expressing himself with his hands. Moreover, a pen and something to write on weren't always available, but his hands were attached to him—less of a chance he would ever end up somewhere without them. Perhaps with time he'd feel more confident about his options, the nightmares would cease, and he would be able to move on.

"Oh—" He hadn't noticed Rhys coming in, so he wasn't sure how long he'd been there, waiting and watching.

"Sorry. I did knock before I let myself in, but it seemed rude to disturb you whilst you were preoccupied..." Rhys turned a chair toward the bed and sat down. "I was hoping I could speak with you about something."

"What is it?"

"I think I know what might have happened to Julian." Rhys looked somehow unreal, ethereal in this light with the sun not yet over the horizon on an overcast, drizzly morning.

"Oh?"

"Not all of it obviously, just the bits I was there for."

"The two of you go way back?" That was news. It explained why Julian and Rhys were so close—

"We don't. At least, I don't think we do. I don't remember. But while I was asleep tonight, I found that I'd dreamt of Julian long before he moved in last year, and it seemed like something that has happened. Like a nightmare based on real events."

"Oh." Victor weighed this information but needed a little more to go on. "What happened in the dream?"

"I met him as a child at a facility of sorts, possibly to do with Hosta Therapy. I think my father sent me there in hopes they would fix what's wrong with me. I don't know what Julian was there for. It seemed like they were doing experiments on him or trying to get a treatment to stick but failing. And I'm too restless to sleep right now to find out if there's more."

This seemed like the only place to interject before he lost the nerve, so Victor hurried to find the right words.

"I think your great aunt shared your building with someone with connections to Hosta Therapy. The unexplained abbreviations HT, HG or H4C appear on several of the blueprints we got from Firth. Wherever the letters appear, there are deviations from the norms: duct work, utility spaces missing, unexplained storage space, things that don't stand out unless you look for them. I found them all across both Firth and Schadesborough, especially in new-builds or recent repair or restoration projects. There are partial records with the crucial bits missing. Small enough errors to not draw attention. Your whole attic seems to have been in use by Hosta Therapy. I don't know what they used it for, but I'm fairly sure that body had something to do with it."

"That's unsettling. When Vincent woke up this morning, he said the voiceless told him Hosta was responsible for their death. This seems to confirm they're connected, but my great aunt also?" Rhys seemed sad.

"I can't imagine her not knowing. Mr Williams and Julian agreed the remains were about two decades old. That's around the time your great aunt already lived there. I know that wasn't what you wanted to hear..."

"I need to sleep as soon as possible to see if I can find out more. Maybe talk to the voiceless myself if I can find them. If this Hosta is still in business doing shady things, we may not be able to stop them ourselves, but we can try to expose them and find out what happened to Julian and who knows how many others, myself included. My father won't be forthcoming, but I feel like Julian's parents must know something. Julian was in his early teens when I saw him. I don't think he would have gone there unbeknownst to his parents, presumably during the course of several years, and if they sent him there for treatment, they must have had an idea of what was being done to him."

"It sounds like a difficult family matter. Would they be willing to share something like that with anyone? What are you going to tell Julian? Should we let them settle it themselves?"

"They seemed like nice people, but I don't know if I fully trust them. If they sent Julian to Hosta willingly, they're not much better than my father... who knows what they might do, maybe send him back."

"I guess you're right."

"It didn't seem the sort of place anyone should send their child voluntarily, for any reason. I don't care how unmanageable they thought Julian's temper was, it was not justified."

"What do you want to do? Gather more information before we decide?"

"Yes, I need to sleep to see what else I have. Other than that, do you have or can you get more of those blueprints with the abnormalities you mentioned? If there are some here in Grovestead, I could take a look dreamside. Archives, times, dates, procedures, anything that would link them to something illegal that we can get proof to take to the police."

"Rhys."

"What?"

"I hate to say this, but it is far too widespread to be completely covert." Victor had spent some time thinking about it, and the uncomfortable truth was that, while some of it was concealed ingeniously, it was much too extensive. "They probably have connections with someone at the top, with the authorities. I think someone influential is protecting them to keep it all under wraps. I know a lot of building inspectors that could have easily buried those projects six feet under for failing to adhere to building code, yet these spaces and buildings exist." He let that sink in.

"Oh no," Rhys jolted up from his chair and started pacing. "That's what it meant when Vincent said the voiceless is with Hosta! Hosta doesn't want the identity discovered, and they've got connections. Of course they've gone and acquired the remains from the police! I knew we shouldn't have reported it. I was distracted by the Crafts and trying to handle it correctly in front of them. We could have kept the remains until all of this was solved, tried to figure out the identity ourselves. Why didn't I insist they be left where they were for the investigation? We could have overseen it at least to some extent." He looked about ready to panic. "I thought the voiceless was avoiding me because they were upset, but what if something happened to them so they're unable to? Maybe they can barely communicate, maybe that's why they're doing it through Vincent now? What if Hosta decides to completely dispose of the body to cover their tracks, what happens then?"

"Maybe Julian can give you something to help you sleep? If you need to hurry," Victor suggested. Rhys didn't seem keen but nodded.

"I guess I have no choice... unless you want to whack me in the head?"

"That seems unpleasant."

"In any case, there's no time to waste. I need to see if I can still reach them and locate the remains somehow. I just hope I'm not too late."

Rhys barged into Julian's room without knocking. Victor followed close behind.

"I need drugs. Now!" the boy exclaimed.

"What, why?" Julian sat up and tried to make sense of the request. "It's barely eight in the morning." He set his pocket watch back on the table and reached for his glasses.

"I need to sleep, quick, but I can't."

"I can relate to that." Julian had an overwhelming urge to fall back to sleep and ignore them but made an effort to search for what the boy needed.

"Can I sleep here?"

"What?" To Julian's horror, Rhys was already making himself comfortable behind him, in his bed. Had he no self-awareness or sense of self-preservation, still, after all this time?

A shiver raised the hair on the back of Julian's neck, and he tensed up. He glanced at Victor, but he was no help at all. In fact, it looked more like he wanted to cram in the bed as well. "I guess it's time for me to get up." Julian was about to leave but was stopped by a tug at his sleeve.

"No, preferably with you in the room." Rhys was fingering the sleeve. "I need you to guard me while I sleep." It was a mere whisper.

"Right. Do you need him as well?" Julian gestured at Victor, who would thankfully not fit in the bed comfortably, wide as it were.

"Hmm, not right now," Rhys replied. To Victor, he added, "Sorry."

Victor sighed and left the room.

"Here." Julian offered the customary dose. "Do you need me to stay awake, or can you kick me awake if you need me? I didn't sleep well last night." The prospect of waking up to a kick did not sound enjoyable, but at least he'd be able to resume his sleep for an hour or two.

"You can sleep, I think, but I need you to make absolutely sure I don't wake up before ten... or let's make that eleven. I intend to do some scouting, and it's going to be far." Rhys stole most of the duvet.

"All right." Resigned to his fate, Julian reached for a blanket hanging on the back of his chair. He'd give it a try, but he wasn't entirely convinced he would be able to fall back asleep.

Rhys rarely ventured far from where he slept, and with no clue where the remains were other than them likely being somewhere back in Schadesborough, the distance was not going to be healthy to wake up from. There wasn't much risk of anyone waking him prematurely, but with the experience of being woken up by Vincent back in Agnes Point fresh in his mind, he was glad to have Julian in the room as an added safety measure.

"Are you here? Can you hear me? Please answer even if you're mad at me. I need to know where they've taken you. You might be in danger!"

The voiceless must have been somewhere close by to appear for Vincent last night. Rhys checked Quin's mansion for signs of anything unusual, but nothing stood out. It was quiet. There was no sign of Quin either, but Victor was having breakfast alone in his room.

Julian lay in bed, awake, watching the ceiling. Rhys felt bad about having woken him up so early for this, but there was nothing he could do about it right now.

"Please answer me. Are you here?"

They should have appeared by now. Rhys felt awful. He'd assumed the remains were safely tucked away in some storage room while the police investigated their identity. It hadn't occurred to him that they might be in danger. Just as he was losing hope, a hand appeared at his feet and grabbed his ankle softly.

"Ah, thank Guardian! Can't you speak? I can give you lots of words. Do you need more words? Are you mad at me?"

No answer. The hand let go of his ankle. It made a tentative sign.

Had Rhys not seen Julian teach Victor, he wouldn't have recognised it, but it seemed deliberate and familiar now. Rhys felt like an ass when he realised he'd seen them try to sign like this before.

"Help me?" Rhys said. "Yes, I want to help you. What can I do?"

The hands perked up and started signing like mad.

"No, no, wait, I don't know all that. Sign like you would to an idiot, OK?"

The voiceless slowed down, but it was fascinating how nimble their hands were considering how gruesome they looked.

"H-O-S-T-A take you back?" Rhys interpreted out loud to give the voiceless ample chance to correct if he'd misunderstood. "272 M-U-S-K-R-A-T-A-V-E, Muskrat... avenue? Is that the address? Shit, we should have done this sooner!" This would have been so useful back when they would have had more time to go over everything. "Danger? H-O-S... Hosta, yes, I know. Vincent relayed your message. I'm coming to find you. Through here first, but we'll retrieve you later if we can. Are you still... uh, are you still in one piece, or did they do something to you?"

Rhys could not recognise the signs that followed. He beat himself up for not paying more attention to Julian's teaching. Instead, like a fool, he'd been enamoured by the exercise and self-defence routines.

"I'm so sorry, I don't understand. I'm coming over to see for myself. Wait."

Rhys was fairly sure Muskrat Avenue was either near the city centre or on the East side of Schadesborough because those were the only two areas he had some experience of, and he'd heard the name before. Though it was considerably faster to travel through dreamside than by train, it took him some time to get all the way from Grovestead to Schadesborough. He had great luck pinpointing the right area, though.

There were some boat sheds and a few larger buildings along Muskrat Avenue. Two hundred seventy-two referred to a dilapidated office building with a beauty salon on the bottom floor.

Nothing on the outside suggested this was the correct address. Once inside and past the front, it became clear that the beauty salon had been picked for the lingering scents of perfumed soaps, ammonia and various other chemicals that did not seem out of place here but somewhat disguised the rather pungent smell of formaldehyde coming from upstairs.

The smell was nearly undetectable downstairs but obvious on the third floor. Rhys instinctively held his hand over his nose, even though he knew he was breathing air elsewhere.

In a small room down the hall, he found a collection of boxes, jars and vials and a whole host of chemistry paraphernalia he could not recognise. There was also an intriguing folder cabinet, but since he could not open it, and there was no light between the sheets of paper, he could not browse or read what was inside. It wasn't what he was here for anyway, so he tried to spot anything large enough to contain a mummified corpse instead, hoping that the voiceless was still in one piece.

"Are you in here?" Rhys asked. Even though he knew this was a dream, he felt compelled to make no sound louder than a whisper.

"Here." It was the tiniest echo, but hearing anything after the silence was a relief.

Whoever worked here had several sets of body parts—limbs and organs submerged in jars and tubs of liquid—on shelves over the desk. There were also dried-up bones or tissue samples in boxes or on small trays stacked on top of each other. Perhaps some of them belonged to the voiceless? Upon further inspection, Rhys was both relieved and appalled to realise they must have been newer batches, extracted from people or patients likely more recently deceased.

This place was making him increasingly queasy.

Most of the boxes held bottles of chemicals or spare parts, but, packed loosely without padding into a crate in one corner of the room, Rhys finally found what he was looking for. It was safe to say whoever had brought the voiceless here hadn't cared what state they were in upon arrival.

It was close to nine o'clock, and though the upper floors were unoccupied, someone had arrived to work downstairs. The sign in the front indicated that the salon would be open until six in the evening. That limited the access times, regardless of when or if someone turned up to work upstairs.

Even if he'd been able to wake up right away, and they could have caught a hypothetical train departing around the same time, the train ride back to the city would take at least one overnight stay at Firth. The voiceless would have to hang in there for a couple more days. At least the extra night would give Rhys an opportunity to check whether someone was here past the salon's hours and what their schedule might be like, even if that was no guarantee it would be the same the day after.

"I'm going to come for you. I just need to figure out when and how," Rhys promised.

When Rhys got back to Grovestead, he had well over an hour until Julian was scheduled to wake him up. Resting didn't sound appealing when he had such little time left and was feeling this anxious, so he decided to distract himself and make use of the extra time by going through as many of his old dreams as possible.

Julian's scent was a comforting anchor to reality. It also helped to have him so close by to compare while tracking the right dreams. Rhys commended himself for having had the foresight to sleep in this room.

Combined with what he could remember about young Julian's looks, the sound of his voice and the general feel of him, Rhys felt like he had a good chance of spotting something quickly. He also had an inkling of the time period, which narrowed down the search considerably, but there were hundreds of dreams to skim through and not a lot of time left until he would wake up.

Since the dreams seemed to want to follow their own track from start to finish, trying to deviate or abandoning one midway got trickier and more exhausting the more Rhys did it. After a while, they began to feel sticky and muddled from him forcing himself in and out as soon as he could tell they weren't what he was looking for. Maybe there was a limit to what his brain was capable of processing without rest or without waking up in between? He hoped he'd come across something useful soon because he feared he might get stuck on something inconsequential that would waste the rest of what remained of his sleep.

He didn't have time for meaningless childhood dreams, so he amplified his focus, tuned out everything else and concentrated on nothing but the search. The regret from spending too much time waffling around at Agnes Point, indulging in his interests and choosing to forget the voiceless was weighing on Rhys's mind, and he desperately wanted to make up for lost time. The relief of finally stumbling across something relevant was immense.

He recognised the rooms and corridors from before. His senses were on overdrive from his search, and the air was thick with the acrid hospital smell. Deprived of sound, his ears were deafened by a loud hum, until the faint clinks of casters sliding and wobbling across the slightly uneven tiled floor echoed into existence somewhere further away.

The bed was wheeled into one of the rooms, and Rhys realised he was tied to it, again. Him being unconscious explained why he felt like he was floating in the corridor, safe, not having to deal with what was happening to his body.

As long as he was unconscious, he could wander around and pretend like none of it was happening. Being asleep was always safer and superior to being awake. He'd never questioned why he felt so sure of it, even when he'd realised what the voiceless could do to him dreamside.

This was the part where he was forced to wake up. The instant panic was as harsh as the lights, the awful stench of chemicals, the sounds of metal against metal, and leather straps tightening around his wrists as he tried to yank himself off.

No, no, he wanted to go back to sleep, back into the corridor.

The confused, panicked fear of an eight-year-old was sickeningly familiar and not at all what he'd wanted to remember. He was unprepared and unaccustomed to such pain, having never experienced anything like it before and possibly not since. Worse even, it felt like it would never end unless he could go back to sleep. He desperately wanted to go back.

Rhys screamed with the careless disregard of a child until his voice was hoarse, and the sounds coming out of his mouth were not his own. He knew the physical pain wasn't the whole of it. The reason for his predicament was much worse: he saw flickering images of a familiar face distorted in pain and himself helpless to do anything about it.

Who?

Julian?

He hadn't had a name for the face, but this was the only friend he'd had here, and they were killing him.

Rhys had charged at the woman, but she'd grabbed a hold of him and pinned him down without much effort. He'd struggled to get free, the blade in his hands had slipped and sunk down into him, and everything around him had been drowned out by the pain.

He wanted out. Sleep. He needed to sleep.

This dream was a mess. Nothing but random fragments in disarray. Warm and cold sensations, something smooth and sticky against his skin. Every breath was like a fresh stab, but he was forced to gasp for air. His eyes were wide open, but he could not process what he saw. He needed to tap out, it was too much. Who was he, where was he, was he awake or asleep? What was happening? Why?

The corridor.

In a state of utter confused desperation Rhys didn't know what he was supposed to do, but his instincts were all screaming at him to get out of this situation and use all means necessary. Death felt imminent and real. It was no longer an abstract concept: he'd seen it happen right in front of his eyes.

Out, out, out, out... sleep, fall asleep, no, wake up? No, sleep, the corridor, safety. No, he had to wake up. Julian was right there, on the other side of this dream. This was a dream.

There were too many distractions to try to concentrate on anything constructive, so all he could do was to try to withstand the pain and the panic. It had to end at some point.

He was briefly transported back into the corridor. Just as he was about to grasp a coherent thought, he woke up again in pain. This repeated too many times to count. It felt endless. Julian was dead. He'd witnessed it happen himself.

CHAPTER 13

J ulian hesitated. It wasn't eleven o'clock yet, but he'd woken from his nap to Rhys panting, gasping for breaths and even whimpering. The logical thing was to wake him up from his nightmare, but he'd specifically told him not to.

Rhys opened his eyes and stared ahead without blinking. He didn't look like he was awake or aware of what he was seeing. His expression was both frightened and frightening, like he'd seen something disturbing enough to freeze entirely.

He also looked like he was suffocating. Maybe he was trying to wake up, but couldn't? If that was the case, did he want Julian to disregard his earlier instructions and help?

After a few more moments of watching and hesitating, Julian decided to lift Rhys to sit to hold him in his arms and see whether rubbing the boy's back would help him relax and breathe better.

"I'm here, what do you need? Do you want to wake up? No? It's not eleven yet, but maybe it's time. Wake up, Rhys. You're OK, I've got you. Tell me where it hurts. What do I do? Is it another migraine? Rhys? I'll help you if you tell me how..."

Rhys didn't seem to react to any of it, at least not favourably. It now seemed like he no longer wanted to wake up. A few more minutes passed. It was almost eleven o'clock.

That's enough. It's close enough, Julian thought. He shook Rhys.

This must be sleep paralysis, right? Julian had read about it from Dr Vesper's book. It was perfectly harmless, just an unpleasant experience. Rhys would soon snap out of it... probably? If it didn't pass in two more minutes, Julian would rush to go find Dr Vesper to see if she knew what to do.

"It's a temporary malfunction. You'll wake up properly in a bit. What-ever you're seeing is a hallucination. Don't worry." Julian tried to sound reassuring, but when there seemed to be no improvement, he began to lose confidence.

What else was there? Would smelling salts do the trick? He was about to try when Rhys finally showed some signs of waking up.

"Oh my Guardian, Rhys, are you all right?" Julian gave him a tight hug.

Rhys started to sob, but it seemed like the expected thing to do, so Julian was relieved. The absence of curse words seemed a little off, though.

"You were dead, you were dead," Rhys repeated between sobs. "You were—"

"I'm here. I'm fine."

"No, you don't understand! I saw you die."

"You were dreaming. I'm right here."

"It was real! I have no memory of it, but I know it happened. I saw it. I felt it. At Hosta Therapy. You were there almost two decades ago." Rhys looked Julian in the eye, dead serious.

"No, but..." Julian was about to further stress that Rhys had had a dream, and dreams were just dreams, when the thought of the remains in the attic made him reconsider. Rhys had known they were there. Clearly the boy's dreams weren't just dreams.

"It was real, I swear. I'm fuzzy on the details, but I swear!" He looked desperate to have Julian believe him.

"I, uh, I believe you, uh, think it's real, but as you can see, I'm here. I'm healthy. Nothing wrong with me. I don't think I even have scars..." Julian tried to recall if he'd noticed any when Rhys suddenly and frantically unbuttoned his own shirt.

"Shit, see!" For a moment, Julian despaired, not wanting to look at Rhys's bare chest. "Look!" Rhys was visibly trembling as he pointed out an old scar on his abdomen.

"Um, what am I looking at exactly?" There was a whole sea of scars, but yes, the one Rhys was pointing at looked old and not as superficial as the rest.

"This is from what happened when I was there! I didn't even know I'd been until my mother mentioned it, but the nightmares I had as a child are all still there. It was an accident, I think, but it went right through..." Rhys looked ready to gag.

"What about the other ones?" Julian asked before realising he maybe should have kept his mouth shut. Rhys quickly closed his shirt and looked away. Damn it. "I'm sorry. It's none of my business," Julian back-pedalled.

There was a moment of silence as Rhys wiped the remnants of his tears and snot onto his sleeve before Julian could offer him a handkerchief. Definitely not the type to cry gracefully, but at least he was no longer crying...

"I guess I could tell you," the boy mumbled. "Some were my father with the belt. I assume there are a few of those welts on my back as well."

"Some?"

"Most of it was me." Rhys still avoided looking at Julian. "Look, I'm not proud of it, all right?"

Julian didn't know what to say. He hadn't had time to think of anything before Rhys added, "And I may have been intentionally careless just recently, on the way to Agnes Point."

It was probably not an easy thing to admit to.

"Rhys." Julian wanted the boy to look at him, so he set his hand on Rhys's knee. Rhys flinched but turned to look. "Please don't do that anymore."

"I'm trying not to..."

"It's not going to change anything."

"I know. I can't cut them off and risk the—"

"No, I mean, you're still you. That doesn't define you. Besides, if it makes you feel any better, your chest doesn't look that different." Julian opened his shirt in return. He couldn't remember ever being in better shape, but, as far as he was concerned, he was essentially a science nerd with a comfy desk job. He was a little on the lean side due to lucky genes, but by no means particularly muscular.

"Oh," Rhys seemed to be comparing in earnest.

"Granted, I'm hairier, but I'm also not as scarred as you." Julian let Rhys compare as long as he wanted, even if he wasn't particularly comfortable being ogled. It was worth it if it helped Rhys feel even a smidge better about himself.

"There's a scar here, though." Rhys pointed at Julian's side. Julian frowned.

"Oh?" He hadn't bothered to take a good look at himself. There were three little circular marks where Rhys was pointing. "Odd. I don't know what that is."

"I'll bet you they have something to do with Hosta. We were both there. I don't know how you're alive after that, but they did something to you. I don't know where it was, but Victor says they're everywhere. Oh, and the voiceless doesn't seem able to repeat words properly anymore, but they could sign to me! The remains are at 272 Muskrat Avenue, I just don't know how to get in there to retrieve them. Judging by everything I saw, they truly are dangerous!"

Julian tried to piece Rhys's words together but was falling a little short.

"Can you start again? Hosta, that's the thing on the card your father gave Quin? And Victor found something, I suppose from the blueprints? What was that address you mentioned? I thought the police had the remains. And you're saying you've seen things from the past in your dreams. How does that work?"

"What, did I not explain this stuff?"

"No. You usually don't explain much of anything, but I try to piece it together from context."

"Really? You should just ask if I forget. Let's see." Rhys paused to think. "When we were in Dritsby and my father gave Quin the card, I met my mom who mentioned I'd been somewhere I don't remember. When I tried to dig up anything I could remember dreamside, I realised I could bring back all the dreams I've dreamt before. I came across somewhere I'd met you at a facility when I was little. I suspect my father put me there to try to fix me. It seems like it might be the same place as mentioned on the card. Vincent has been chatting with the voiceless, and they told him last night that they were with Hosta and that Hosta is responsible for their death. When I realised the voiceless could be in danger, I wanted to locate the remains in hopes we might be able to save them. Victor has been studying the blueprints and discovered this whole thing seems to span much wider than just one facility or my building. I get the feeling all of it is connected. Does that answer everything?"

"Frankly... No. I'm still hazy on how exactly you communicate with the deceased mummified remains, how you locate them and access your old dreams in your sleep. What exactly is it that you do when you sleep? It sounds a lot busier than when I do it."

"I read a book last night that described it as sleep-roaming. If you recall, Vera explained some of it during dinner yesterday."

"Vera? You mean Dr Vesper?"

"Yes. She told that whole story about the Guardian myth and how ancient tribes used to have guardians sleep-roaming dreamside to keep people's dreams safe."

"I'm sorry, I was a little preoccupied yesterday." Julian had tried to pay attention, but most of the afternoon and evening had been him bumping into things he found pleasant but unnerving. Being bombarded with these things from his past had taken its toll.

"Basically, I'm fully aware of everything around me when I dream. That's why I have so much trouble sleeping. I don't know how the voiceless exists dreamside, but I suspect it's for a similar reason as the dreams do. There's something there that's capable of storing information that doesn't exist in the waking world anymore."

"My memories?" Julian said without thinking. He didn't want his memories back. Discovering his quirks—like that he was really rather shallow, had strange preferences or that he could handle himself in a fist fight—was one thing, finding out his exact crimes and reverting back to who he'd been were another.

"I'm not sure. There might be dreams, but they're dreams, not memories."

"Never mind. I don't really want to know."

"I'd offer to find out, but I..." Blood drained from Rhys's face. "But we should retrieve the voiceless first, before it's too late. And I need you to teach me to sign, so I can communicate with them properly to get to the bottom of this."

"It's OK. If it's as uncomfortable as what happened just now, I really don't need to know."

By noon, Vincent realised it was back. It was not as heavy as usual, but he could definitely feel it. A shroud of weariness settled over him like the muddy sediment covering the bottom of the pond.

He'd just finished putting the filtering system back together and was about to reattach it to the cooler, but the familiar resistance left him staring at the brackets unable to recall what he was supposed to do with them. It took him a moment to organise the washers, nuts and bolts to where they were going.

"Is something wrong?" Ren looked down from the cockpit recess, where she'd been mounting a new fastener for the cat box.

"No. I'm just getting tired." It had given him more than six gloriously lucid hours of creative productivity, so he couldn't be too upset.

"Time for a break?"

"Yes, but I should—" Ah, after his head had responded to what he'd asked from it the whole morning, it was disappointing to feel it resisting even the most basic tasks again.

He looked at what he'd been doing and realised it was mostly backwards. "I guess... not. I should get back to it later."

"Are you hungry? I know I am." Ren climbed down from the speeder. She kindly rearranged the mess in front of Vincent and patted his back. "Don't you dare to be hard on yourself. You've been working for hours calculating and fixing all that," she said and pointed at the dozens of sheets of paper he'd kept in surprisingly fair order next to him, "and you fixed the rudder, the issue with the landing gear jamming *and* you cleared out the luggage compartment, cleaned it and added a small window and some cushioning for Uncle Rhys. I will not have you beat yourself up for not achieving everything on your gargantuan list of things to do."

"Thank you." It was good to be reminded. He'd done it in such a flurry, it hadn't felt like much at all. "You're becoming more and more like your mother every day."

"Oh? Is that bad?"

"No, of course it isn't! Your mother is a kind, considerate and smart lady. She would be very proud—"

"Dr Vera!" Ren noticed Aurora standing behind them. How long had she been there?

"Hello Ren, Vincent. Are the two of you in the middle of something? I was wondering if I could borrow him for a moment."

Vincent realised she may not have appreciated him running off like he had this morning. Thankfully she didn't look too upset.

"We're done here!" Ren collected the papers and handed the stack to Vincent. They were filled with unintelligible scribbles, but they had helped him come to the right conclusions an hour or two earlier. It was strange to think what his brain was capable of when he wasn't tired.

"I'll be right there. I need to clean this stuff away," he said to Aurora.

"I can do that," Ren offered.

"I appreciate that, but I should clean up my own messes." To Aurora, Vincent said, "This will only take a couple of minutes."

"I could help," she suggested.

"No, that's all right. Go on ahead. I'll be right with you." Vincent waved her off. She seemed to hesitate for a moment but returned to the house by herself. Ren punched Vincent in the arm.

"Ouch! What was that for?"

"Why did you send her away, stupid? She wanted to help."

"This stuff is grimy and greasy. I didn't want her to get her hands dirty."

"She wouldn't have offered had she minded. And what about my hands?" Ren thrust them in front of his face.

"Your hands are already dirty. Which reminds me, you should go wash up before we eat. I can finish up here." Vincent picked up some of the tools he'd left lying on the ground. "Oh, and Ren."

"Yes?"

"Maybe we should go see your parents again when we're done with my treatment here. We've only been back to Benton House once since you moved in with me, and they must miss you a lot."

"Yeah, but you need to do as Dr Vera says first. Don't try to use me as an excuse to cut things short."

"I wouldn't—"

"You'd already be calling things off if you hadn't had such a productive morning."

It was true. He'd been working on suitable excuses for weeks, but the brain fog and this morning's unexpected burst of energy had derailed him from the task.

Vincent was curious to see whether Aurora could cure him, but all this attention was disconcerting. And now that it seemed that a couple of hours of wakefulness might cost two people their night's sleep as well as whatever potentially expensive drugs she'd used, he wasn't sure he could ask that amount of dedication for such low rewards.

Maybe if he could sleep well for one more night and direct his energy to improving Aurora's equipment so that it didn't require anyone watching over it...? But he didn't understand what any of it did. How many mornings would it take to study the stuff until he understood enough to make it work? How many sleepless nights for Aurora and Rhys, if they even agreed to it? And what was the cost of those drugs? Were they available in sufficient quantities if he ended up needing to use them every night? Did they have side-effects?

"Vincent."

"What?"

"Stop daydreaming, and let's go. I've finished picking up after us."

"Damn it, Ren..." Vincent groaned but couldn't help but ruffle her hair. "What would I do without you looking after me?"

"You'd be dead in a ditch. Now, let's go. Dr Vera is waiting for you, and I need to get this gunk off my hands."

"It's worse than yesterday. I'd tell you off for overdoing it this morning, but it's not like you did it on purpose." Aurora sighed.

"I'm sorry, did you say something?" Vincent yawned. "Why do I feel like my head is shutting down like a steel mill on strike?"

"Do you feel sleepy?"

"Sleepy? How's that supposed to feel?" Vincent knew the definition but couldn't pinpoint the exact feeling. "I feel like I need to yawn constantly."

"We could test whether you're able to fall asleep on your own if or when you're sufficiently tired."

"Uhhuh." Vincent was sitting on the bed while connected to Aurora's device, and he was tempted to lay back for just a tiny moment.

"Vincent?"

"Hmm?"

"Lay down for me for a bit."

"Oh, I'd love to..." He'd been different degrees of tired before, often or almost always, but this didn't seem the same. As soon as his head had hit the pillow, the feeling eased. Ah. Better.

Oh.

"I'm asleep?" What about lunch? He was supposed to eat. Come to think of it, he'd skipped breakfast.

He watched Aurora brush aside some of his hair and adjust the electrodes now that he was lying down. She looked just as beautiful as she had fifteen or so years ago. Why did she feel so comfortingly familiar? Was it because he'd subconsciously carried her along all these years?

It wasn't realistic to think he'd had the time to get to know her in the handful of weeks they'd been together, and with more than fifteen years apart, she was a whole other person today. For one, she was a doctor. Vincent couldn't even imagine what it must have required from her to become one.

She was watching him.

His eyes were closed, so she was unaware of him watching her back. A slight frown betrayed a hint of worry, but she looked decidedly different than when she was aware of him watching.

Serene.

What a lovely, rare chance to watch her without the pressure of having to think of something smart to say.

Wouldn't it have been wonderful to become a better person and strive to reach her level, though? What a radical thought. Not contend with being intimidated by her accomplishments, hope she'd be somehow less than or merely lament how unattainable she was. Was that possible, or was it his strained brain being overly ambitious?

What if he could be better? What if, instead of struggling to be barely sane or good enough, he had the courage to give this his all? What if he stated his wishes out loud despite them being selfish, regardless of his fear of rejection and abandonment? What if he said he wanted to do and be better?

She was watching him as if listening in on his thoughts. It was an illusion, but it seemed like it could have just as well been real.

Her mouth moved.

"What was that? What did you say?" He'd heard it, but it took him a moment to understand.

"Better not."

Better not, what? Better not be optimistic? Better not say anything? Better not give it a chance? Better not get my hopes up?

"Uh…"

"I'm sorry. Did I wake you?"

"Am I…?" Vincent realised his eyes were open. "How long was I…?"

"Asleep? Seemed like fifteen, maybe twenty minutes." Aurora turned to press something on the device to make it spit out another strip of paper. She compared it with an older strip and turned back to remove the electrodes. "How do you feel? The same?"

"Mostly, yes."

"I think part of the problem is that your brain is not able to sustain the state even if it's capable of reaching it when the conditions are right. It's likely to be hormonal."

"Be what?"

"Hormonal. Hormones are molecules sending signals between your organs and tissues. This is all very new still, but our team has discovered a substance produced by the pineal gland that's responsible for regulating your sleep-wake patterns. But a problem with your pineal gland alone shouldn't cause such drastic symptoms. I wish I could cut you open and see what's there without causing you irreparable harm."

"I'm sorry, what?" Vincent was starting to feel like he'd had a laughable fever-dream where, for a moment, he'd held an outrageous belief that he could come close to Aurora's intellectual level.

"Don't worry about it. We'll figure it out." She switched off the device. "There might still be time to join the others for lunch. Are you hungry?"

"Yes." Better not, indeed. Better not get ahead of ourselves.

CHAPTER 15

Rhys, Julian, Victor, Quin and Ren were sitting at the dining table at varying stages of lunch when Vincent entered with Vera. Vincent stifled a yawn, and in contrast with how he'd been this morning, seemed even worse off than usual.

"I understand if you don't want to participate in this. You don't know the voiceless. I don't know them that well myself," Rhys was saying. He wanted to give the others ample chance to pull out if they were unwilling to break the law for such a vague cause.

Victor looked nervous, but when prompted for input, the man shrugged. Whatever that meant, he did not object or make a move to leave.

"I'm all in for the excitement," Quin said. Julian was doing his utmost to ignore him.

"I don't know if I'll be much help, but you know I'll do my best," Julian said.

Ren looked about to weigh in, but Rhys interrupted her before she could.

"Not you, Ren. You need to stay with Vincent. Make sure he's OK and behaves." Rhys winked at her. She seemed about to object, but a glance at Vincent was enough to get her to sigh and nod.

"What? I'm not that hopeless... Am I?" Vincent, in turn, glanced at Vera.

"I hesitate to ask, but are you able to take us to Schadesborough as soon as possible? You seem... tired." Rhys saved the doctor from answering.

"I'm f—" Vincent yawned. "Today?"

"I guess tomorrow might be better." The speeder would still be faster and more comfortable even if they left the following morning instead of right away by train.

"I can take you, but—" He'd only just yawned but was at it again. "Could you watch Ren while I take them, so Rhys doesn't have to ride in the boot?" he asked Vera. It seemed like a convenient excuse to make sure Ren was well out of harm's way.

"Yes, but I'd like you to come right back, so we can resume the treatment."

"Of course. It shouldn't take more than a day to get there and another one back. Less if I don't stay the night..."

"You should stay the night!" Vera and Ren agreed in unison.

It remained a mystery whether staying overnight would improve Vincent's mental faculties, but Rhys agreed having him drive straight back sounded bad. Especially if he were to do it unsupervised. "Would it be better if all of us returned when we're done?"

Ren, at least, nodded fervently.

"All right. Let's try to make the retrieval as quick as possible." Rhys returned to devising the plan. "There's a salon on the bottom floor. We'll have to break in after they've closed, sometime during the night. Do any of you have experience in something like that?"

In the present company all eyes turned to Quin. Quin eyed them back, exasperated.

"I broke a shop window in my hometown once, but that was *mostly* by accident. It's not the same as breaking and entering."

"I suppose it's obvious, but I wouldn't remember even if I did," Julian said.

"I guess we'll have to try to analyse and anticipate all eventualities, do the best we can and try not to get caught." Quin seemed to be making an exceedingly obvious effort to be supportive, but Julian continued to ignore him.

"We need to figure out how to enter the building," Rhys pressed on, "and retrieve the remains without anyone realising they are gone or noticing we've been there. That means we need something comparable to stuff in the crate. Whoever's packed them didn't seem too interested in what shape they were in, so there's a chance the remains might be heading for disposal soon. There's not a lot of time to find something, but it also doesn't have to be an exact match."

"I might have something." Julian's response garnered some looks all around.

"You happen to have an extra mummified corpse lying around?" Quin eyed him, especially suspicious.

"No, but I know someone who might, and we're conveniently here at his doorstep."

"Then I'll leave that to you," Rhys said to Julian. "We need to figure out how to get inside. Do we stage a robbery, or...?"

"Who would rob a salon? What's there of worth?" Quin was probably right to wonder.

"It's not even a particularly affluent neighbourhood, so probably not much." Rhys sighed.

"Where did you say it was?" Julian asked.

"It's near the river. Not much over there, just boat sheds and such. But I'd imagine it's quiet during the night." Rhys sipped the coffee he was having for dessert, hoping it would give him a kick to help him think. "Maybe I should keep watch dreamside while one of you goes in? I won't be able to warn you if someone turns up, but at least one of you can wake me up to know what happened if something happens."

"I don't mind going." Quin raised his hand. "I've got a business lunch scheduled for tomorrow in Firth, but if you can wait for me for a half an hour on the way, I'd love to help."

"We'll need to eat something at some point anyway, so it's probably fine. The address is 272 Muskrat Avenue. Victor, do you think you could get some blueprints for Quin? I know the layout, but it would be easier to show where to go." Rhys glanced at Victor, who nodded. "Ah, good. But how do we get Quin in? The doors would be open in the daytime, but we can't march in through the salon—" Rhys caught a glimpse of Victor signing.

"Did you want to add something?" Julian had noticed as well. Victor made the same sign again.

"'Wait,'" Julian interpreted. They waited a while, and a few more 'wait' signs later Victor had calmed down enough to get it out.

"I t-think I can get you in without having to break in." He swallowed and signed a few more signs to give himself space to speak. "270-278 Muskrat Avenue, I have the blueprints. I have them on my desk. It's what I was working on before we left. 276 and 278 are being restored with some significant subsidence issues. They're my father's buildings, they're… I have worked on them before." The effort he had to put in to get all that said was tangible. Even his hands were shaking.

"Really? That's great! Better than great!" Rhys was relieved. This might turn out to be more feasible than he'd thought. "So, we have an actual plan for this?"

"I may have to go along with Quin because it's a construction site. It's not safe." Victor sounded strained.

"I don't mind the company." Quin gave him a smile.

Rhys felt better having Victor go with Quin. Between the two of them, they could handle any unexpected difficulties.

"I'm going to see if I can scout the place again tonight to see if there are people there after closing. Would any of you be willing to help Vera with Vincent's treatment for the night? It'd be great to have him reasonably well-rested before we leave."

"I can do that," Julian offered. "I wouldn't mind learning about the treatment if it's not too much trouble, doctor."

"You're interested? It's no trouble at all, I would love to explain it to you!" Vera seemed excited.

"I did say I found your book fascinating. I'm merely a pharmacist, but I wonder if there's anything I can offer from my side of the fence. We could compare notes."

Rhys watched this conversation unfold with a displeased spectator on either side, Vincent looking depressed and Quin irate that Julian and Vera seemed to be getting along. From Rhys's point of view, they were clearly cultivating a professional interest, but even Victor seemed to be interpreting it as something threatening the delicate status quo.

Ren was the only one smart enough to not read too much into it. That, or she was too busy with her dessert to have noticed yet.

"Maybe I could pick your brain after lunch to find out whether there might be some less harsh alternatives for what we're currently using?"

Vera's words appeared to have made Vincent lose his appetite. He was staring emptily at a boiled potato with his fork dangling over his forefinger, ready to fall off. He also looked about to fall asleep where he sat.

"I have been doing some research into some novel compounds extracted from herbs with useful properties with hypnotics in particular in mind. It would be my pleasure to hear your opinions on some of them."

Julian's comment in turn left Quin looking like he'd chewed on a mouthful of raw gooseberries and washed them down with a jug of vinegar. Victor looked about as tortured as he always did, and a mere moment later when Ren had finished her cake, she began to present an increasingly disapproving side-eye.

It was just two like-minded people sharing a reasonably rare mutual interest. What was there to get so worked up about?

Right?

Rhys rubbed his forehead.

Right?

S ir Swifty entered the dining room through the window. Those pesky servants had thought they could keep him away from the room with the most appetising scents of roast, ham and fish, but they had gravely underestimated his ability to climb the outside trellises.

The humans were busy with their inane talk, so Sir Swifty tried his luck, helping himself to a leftover piece of meat on the little human's plate.

"Hey!" Ren shooed him off. Sir Swifty retreated under the table to inspect whether something had been dropped on the floor. The pickings were disappointingly slim. Even the little human had failed to supply him with extra treats.

There was that pleasant smell again, coming from somewhere close by. Sir Swifty sniffed through the various footwear to locate the origin of the smell. He'd expected it to come from the daintier pair of slippers belonging to the good doctor, but the scent was stronger on the feet next to hers. It was coming from the socks?

Sir Swifty did a test push on the feet. A gruff noise came from somewhere above and someone tried to kick him away, though half-heartedly.

"Oh, that's Sir Swifty. Is he bothering you?" Dr Vesper asked.

"No," the gruff-sounding human with the delicious socks said and threw a piece of something under the table. Oooh, it was ham! Lucky day!

"Am I imagining things, or did you throw it a treat? I thought you didn't like cats!" The man beside the one with the delicious socks sounded surprised.

"I don't. They are often useless, filthy and unpredictable. I suppose if it's competent at catching rodents or a pet it's different."

"Don't worry. I've never noticed any mites or fleas on Sir Swifty and he has a very good temperament," Dr Vesper pointed out most perceptively. She stretched her hand down towards Sir Swifty so he could give it a sniff and a nudge for greeting. "I'm almost done with my lunch. Would you like to come sit on my lap, sir?" Dr Vesper made some space for Sir Swifty, who did not mind the prewarmed seat and hopped up.

The gruff man offered him another slice of meat.

"That's only going to encourage it to beg for more treats—"

"Shut up, Quin."

Yeah, shut up, Quin. Sir Swifty glared at the man apparently called Quin and chewed on his deserved treat. He was not a wretched beggar. He was a valued companion and a protector and had more than earned his keep.

"He seems to like you," Dr Vesper said.

"Maybe it recalls me from before when I let it out of the box to stretch its legs. We're fine as long as it keeps a sufficient distance."

Hah. Sir Swifty measured the gruff man from head to toe and decided to test the validity of this statement. He arched his back and stretched to be ready and limber in case he needed to evacuate in a hurry, but then slowly and deliberately relocated from Dr Vesper's lap to the one next to it.

The humans had stopped conversing, no doubt observing with due reverence this marvellous display of dominance. The gruff human was clearly the most prestigious one in the room, and Sir Swifty made himself comfortable on his lap. When no effort was made to push him off, Sir Swifty yawned and started purring.

"I'm sorry, he really seems to like you." Dr Vesper patted Sir Swifty's forehead.

"I suppose... I-It's fine..." The gruff human sounded less gruff than before. See. That was the effect of the Great Sir Swifty. Revered and adored by all.

Dr Vesper leaned a little closer to the gruff human and whispered, "Mr Craft, you're not afraid of cats, are you?" Since the doctor tended to be astute, her missing the mark so royally amused Sir Swifty. The human whose lap Sir Swifty was currently gracing was larger than average and had a no-nonsense oppressive aura he could sense from afar. There was no way this human would fear a creature smaller than himself. The vague smell of fear in this room was proof the others were unnerved by this man's mere presence.

"No, no... of course not."

There, as you heard, you were obviously mistaken. Sir Swifty would have chuckled had cats made such ridiculous sounds. He started pawing on Mr Craft's trousers.

"What is this? What's it doing?" Mr Craft consulted Dr Vesper in a low voice.

"He's kneading. He must really, really like you."

"D-d— ouch, does it have to use its claws like that?" Mr Craft moved his legs making Sir Swifty's seat bounce uncomfortably. "I'll give you the rest of my steak if you stop hurting me," he bargained.

Bah, fine. Apparently this human did not appreciate the full range of Sir Swifty's affection. He retracted his weaponry and resumed with just his paws.

"That's odd. It's as if he understood what I said."

"I think you owe him the rest of your steak."

Wise words, doctor. Sir Swifty turned to look at Mr Craft, who relinquished the last of the meat on his plate.

CHAPTER 16

To not attract attention, Julian, Rhys and Quin followed Victor into 276 Muskrat Avenue one at a time at leisurely intervals at around ten o'clock in the evening of the following day. Rhys and Julian had come on location at Rhys's request so that Julian could wake him up fairly frequently without as many adverse effects.

Although the building wasn't yet restored to full structural safety, it was safer and more secluded than outside. Victor having the keys meant they had no trouble entering without being detected. Once inside, Rhys found himself a suitable corner to sleep, and Victor and Quin continued up the stairs and all the way to the top floor, where there were emergency doors between the adjacent properties.

Rhys had surprisingly little trouble falling asleep despite his nerves. Perhaps it was due to not resting much the previous few nights? Navigating dreamside felt more cumbersome than usual, but it wasn't that much worse than if he'd had a cold or a stomach bug.

Checking the premises, he determined that, while the upper floors were currently completely vacant, there was a person downstairs in the salon. This seemed odd, since no one had been here the night before when he'd done his scouting. If it was the salon owner or an employee, they would probably soon be out the door.

Rhys followed Quin and Victor up the stairs, past some precarious cracks in the wall, over some creaky scaffolding and all the way into 272. Quin looked like he hadn't appreciated the experience, but Victor had managed to assure him of the safety.

After checking that the coast was clear, Quin carried the box of replacement remains into the room Rhys had specified. It took them a while to locate the correct crate with the voiceless in it, but thankfully the remains remained where they'd been.

Quin stayed at the door to keep a look-out while Victor started the careful task of switching the remains. Everything seemed to be going according to plan. Rhys was relieved. Then he was yanked awake.

"Rhys, wake up. I think we might have a problem," Julian whispered.

Rhys was momentarily disoriented, but it wasn't nearly as bad as when he'd been jolted awake mid-search before. It made a big difference to be so close by.

"A problem? What is it?"

"There are people waiting outside. I think they're headed for the salon."

"What? Why? Surely they don't have 24-hour surveillance on this thing?" Rhys had been so preoccupied with the inside of the building he'd missed anything happening outside. He needed to be more careful and more vigilant!

"I don't think they're here for us, or they would have already rushed in. We must have just picked a bad time."

"I need to go back in. Wake me up again in a bit or if something happens."

"Will do." Julian walked over to the window to keep an eye on the street outside. Rhys returned to sleep.

Victor was almost done with the remains. It wouldn't matter that the crew from the street came into the salon, so long as Quin and Victor hurried out in time.

"Are you all right? We came to get you," Rhys told the voiceless to see if they would respond.

For a moment, the floorboards beneath Rhys's feet darkened to pitch black and something tar-like started to ooze from the cracks. A while later, the voiceless seemed to project Julian's hands out of the tar to sign "don't speak, get me". There was something desperate about the way they signed. It made Rhys's stomach twist. He was woken up again.

"They're inside. Are Victor and Quin still at it? Do we need to do something?" Julian asked.

"It's fine for now. They've not left the salon." Rhys tried to jump back to sleep. It was easier if he could avoid waking up completely in between.

He kept an eye on the group of people in the salon. They were discussing business matters, but it didn't seem like salon business. There were eight of them, plus the person who had already been at the salon. All unfamiliar faces.

Victor was done with the remains. He set the crate where he'd found it and picked up the box with the voiceless now inside. Quin held the door for them.

"We've got you," Rhys signed clumsily. The voiceless' advice to not speak hung heavily in his mind. Could someone hear him in his sleep? How was that possible? Wasn't this his realm? He'd never shared it with anyone. Well, except for the voiceless. Did that mean there could be someone else here listening in on him?

Heavy, dark tendrils of smoke dripped down the sides of the box. It was like an octopus expelling its ink upon its escape.

Quin was too intrigued not to take a quick peek into the archives cabinet. The place was quiet, there seemed to be no immediate danger or hurry and, although this did not seem like the place to store patient files, there was no doubt something of interest tucked in there, right at his reach.

The top drawer had a key dangling from it, begging to be turned. Victor was already in the corridor and stairs, heading out with the remains. Staying behind for a couple of minutes was all on him and wouldn't jeopardise their mission.

Quin pulled open the drawer and skimmed through the tabs that seemed to contain descriptive code names for whatever experiments they did at this particular location. Some files were named just 'subject a' or 'b' or 'c'. A few had 'miscellaneous findings' or a mixed set of dates on them. Some of them were old but most from this decade. He pulled some out to see what they contained, but it was mainly just rows of numerical values that he did not understand. Too bad.

But there had to be something useful here. Why had they brought those remains here otherwise? Were they going to do something with them, or were they really headed for disposal? He checked the side of the crate for clues. Surely, if this was an item or a subject of research, it would be labelled.

Indeed, there was a stamp on the side of the crate that read: "A7f-2b".

Rhys was woken up by Julian again. It was taxing, but he was getting better at ignoring the discomfort.

"Are we OK?" Julian asked.

"Victor is heading back with the remains, but I think Quin stayed behind. Wake me again when Victor gets here." Rhys struggled to return to sleep. "Ah, shit. It's too hectic, I need to see..." Rhys closed his eyes, but falling asleep on command, especially repeatedly, was not an easy feat. "It's not working. Quick, can you give me something?"

"This is probably quickest. Trust me…"

The words 'trust me' usually evoked anything but trust.

Julian applied gentle but very deliberate pressure to the sides of Rhys's neck to block the blood flow. It was surprisingly painless and quick. Victor was heading downstairs. The people in the salon were growing restless. There was shouting, but since Quin reacted to none of it on the third floor, he either didn't hear or ignored it. He was going through a cabinet of archives, the blasted fool.

"Fuck!" Rhys was pulled back from dreamside, feeling like he was being sucked backwards. Julian was hovering over him but, more importantly, so was Victor.

"You need to go back. There are people downstairs. Quin stayed behind!" Rhys gasped for air between his words.

"You're OK?" Julian asked.

"Yes, do it again." Rhys did not hesitate. Julian obliged. Where was Quin? What were the people in the salon doing? Uh, he felt dizzy.

Thankfully, it seemed the row in the salon was still ongoing, which meant the people were concentrating on each other rather than anything that was happening above them.

Quin, you stupid fucking ruptured anal gland, what the hell are you doing? Rhys wanted to kick him. He could understand the temptation to poke around, but this was not the time!

Victor was quick on his feet and reached the third floor as Quin seemed to be ready to exit the room. They exchanged quiet words. Quin closed the door carefully and followed Victor. Two people from the downstairs gathering moved to the stairs. There was distance in between, but Victor and Quin were taking their time trying to be quiet and careful around the scaffolding.

The voiceless' hands appeared at Rhys's feet, and he was signing furiously something about the danger they were in. Rhys came to. He felt queasy and light-headed but, more importantly, panicked.

"They're being too slow."

"It's out of our hands. Are you ready? We need to go." Julian had the box of remains next to him. He checked the window to see if the street was empty.

"No, I need to see what's happening!"

"I'm not doing that again. Twice was bad enough, and I can't carry both you and the remains."

"Just once more, I need to know they're coming," Rhys pleaded. If there was a hitch, the least he could do was provide a diversion, or help in some way. He couldn't leave Victor and Quin.

"I'm not, it's not a good idea. What can you even do?" Julian objected.

"Please Julian, just once. To know if we should wait or hurry!"

"Fine." Everything about Julian suggested he was against it, but he applied pressure one more time.

It only took a few seconds. Rhys was in. He searched for Quin and Victor somewhere above. The two people in the stairs were not immediately apparent. Where...? Did they get caught? No one was up at the top floor. Outside? One of the men from downstairs was in the room with the now switched remains. Rhys struggled to locate the other. The crowd in the salon looked to be dispersing, some to a room in the back, others out the door. Exiting the building right now was out of the question. Where the hell were Quin and Victor?

The other man was in the staircase upstairs and looked like he'd perhaps heard something but nothing concerning enough to sound an alarm.

Rhys was running out of time. He knew Julian had already released his hold.

"Shit... shit." He tried to spot either Victor or Quin.

The voiceless spread like a blanket of darkness beneath him. It was a strange chilling sensation. A moment before Rhys was pulled back into reality, the voiceless brought their hands to his neck. Rhys could tell it was Julian's hands the voiceless was copying. Were they trying to help? Rhys felt acutely sick. Whatever this was doing, he was still dreamside and had to put that extra time into good use.

Rhys spotted Quin outside next to a dormer on the roof. It looked precarious but safer than inside where he could get caught. He slowly started to make his way to the other end of the roof where there was a ladder. Good.

What about Victor? The top floor was a mess and difficult to interpret, so Rhys hoped he was just not reading it right. Victor must have hidden for the time being.

Rhys's head hurt. He was preoccupied by the search, but the pain was beginning to demand his attention.

Quin reached the ladder. It was on the opposite side of the building, and fortunately no one was there to see him climb down. He was safe. But Victor?

There were people going up and down the stairs. They were not in a hurry, so it seemed no one had discovered Victor yet.

The darkness beneath Rhys's feet started to spread wider, wide enough to obstruct Rhys's view. He couldn't just leave Victor. Where was he? Everything underneath Rhys's waist was now enveloped in thick, black smoke-like substance.

Cold.

This was... *bad?* Was he dreaming? He wasn't supposed to be dreaming right now. His vision blurred and there were piercing, bright flashes of light. Victor was somewhere above. Rhys could sense it even if he could no longer see. The dreamside was being sucked into darkness. Rhys tried to say something, but nothing came out.

Julian shook Rhys, but Rhys was not responding. This was not supposed to happen. He had waited until the boy passed out, counted to ten and let go. The previous times Rhys had come to in ten, maybe fifteen seconds, as expected. It had now been at least a minute.

"We need to leave, they're everywhere," Victor whispered, having just rushed down the stairs. "Is he all right?"

"I— I don't know, he's not waking up... I let go almost immediately!" Julian fought against the panic, but time was ticking by. What had possessed him to even think of doing something as stupid as this?! Things like brain damage or death were within the realm of possibility.

Victor did not dally. He crouched over Rhys, listened for a breath and started mouth-to-mouth. The following few seconds felt like hours.

When Victor sat up and Julian saw Rhys take a breath, they were both ready to cry. Victor was shaking. Despite this, he scooped Rhys up and headed for the door. Julian grabbed the box of remains and followed. Fortunately, the street was empty, and they made their escape unhindered and without an audience.

Brain damage.

How many minutes had it been? Had it been too long? Was this really worth it, for a box of remains?

Before fully regaining his consciousness, Rhys vomited. He'd heaved over less, and, the way he felt, it was a wonder he didn't expel all of his insides out. He only just missed Victor, who was carrying him, as luck had it, mouth facing down and to the side.

"Victor? Thank god, shit, fuck..." Being able to speak was such a relief.

Victor stopped and signalled to Julian with a whistle. They were no longer at Muskrat Avenue, but it was not an appropriate hour for noise.

"How are you feeling? Do you know who you are, where we are?" Julian was there with the questions. Victor lowered Rhys to stand.

"Can we do this later? I feel like shit." Rhys almost hurled again.

"I can carry him the rest of the way," Julian said to Victor.

"I can walk, thank you." Rhys would not be carried if his legs were working. Victor lent him some support but let him walk on his own even if he was still disoriented. "What happened? Where's Quin?" Rhys had some trouble grasping the situation.

"We were hoping you would know."

"I saw him, he was, uh, on the roof, I think." Thinking hurt. He concentrated on walking and breathing. The cool night air felt good on his face. Ah, air.

"There's a ladder, so, if he hasn't done anything stupid, he should be fine," Victor whispered.

"This was not a good idea. I don't care whose remains these are, I'm not doing that again."

"Shouldn't we be waiting for Quin?" Rhys glanced back at where they'd come but couldn't recognise the street. "Does he know the way?"

"Oh, right." Julian and Victor looked at each other.

"Should I try to look for him?" Rhys suggested. Both Julian and Victor looked worried. Rhys frowned. "What? You don't have to choke me. We're not in that much of a hurry."

"Strangle," Julian corrected.

"What?"

"Choking is when you have a blockage in your airways."

"Were you always this annoying, or is it because my head hurts?" Rhys would have rolled his eyes if he'd thought it was a good idea. Nausea compelled him to make do with a huff.

"This is how I handle stressful situations, so do forgive me for being *annoying*." Julian's jaw was tight and his voice strained. He definitely looked stressed out. Victor wasn't faring much better.

"Sorry. We thought we lost you back there. Do you think it's safe for you to," Victor searched for the right words, "to go back to sleep?"

"Why wouldn't it be? I'm fine." Rhys considered it further. "Maybe. I think. A little headachy and nauseated and tired and uh, what was I saying? Oh yeah, sleep. It's sleep. Sleep is always safe." Rhys sat down on a park bench. "I'm going to try it. You can wake me up in about five minutes."

He lay down on his side with the two of them watching him like he was about to do something incredibly daring and risky.

Falling asleep took a few minutes, but Rhys managed it out of sheer exhaustion. The voiceless had calmed down, and the box that Julian had set next to the bench was looking only ever so slightly charred around the corners.

Rhys was tempted to rest but forced himself to check back to where they'd come. Not keen on going all the way back to Muskrat Avenue, he was glad to see Quin wandering not far behind them.

As he walked, Quin was reading the files in the folder he'd snatched. If they noticed it was gone, they'd realise there had been someone in the room. The whole point had been to try to get in and out without leaving a trace! Rhys had some choice words waiting for Quin as soon as his headache was better and he could be bothered. For right now, he was glad they had all escaped unscathed.

Rhys returned to his body to wait to be woken up but quickly realised neither Julian nor Victor looked inclined to disturb his sleep. They regularly checked he was breathing but signed to each other to avoid making any noise.

When Quin showed up, Julian lifted Rhys up and on his back. Victor took the box of remains. Quin followed them, engrossed in the files he was reading. Rhys didn't have the energy to be mad. He slipped into a deep slumber and let them do as they wished.

CHAPTER 17

Unable to sleep despite feeling tired, Vincent had been reading a book in the upstairs lounge at Rhys's. He heard the others arriving downstairs, so he set the book aside and moseyed to the top of the stairs to see.

Mr Hart carried a box past the staircase and into the back room. Mr Craft appeared in his wake, carrying Rhys in his arms. When he noticed Vincent, he awkwardly lifted a finger closer to his lips to request silence, but he seemed to have no trouble carrying Rhys up the stairs.

"Is he all right?" Vincent whispered and gave way when they reached the top of the stairs. There would have been more of a sense of urgency had something truly been wrong, but Vincent felt compelled to ask.

Mr Craft nodded. Mr Quin and Mr Hart followed him up the stairs right behind him. They headed into the lounge, and Mr Craft lowered Rhys onto the sofa. Vincent reassumed the spot in the armchair he'd occupied before the four of them had arrived.

"Can we wake him up?" Mr Quin requested.

"Why? What's so important?" Mr Craft seemed testy.

"I have something I need to talk to all of you about."

"Can't it wait? He needs the sleep, and I thought I'd go check on the remains."

"No. Especially if you intend to do something with the remains."

Mr Craft eyed Mr Quin but got himself a kitchen chair and sat down to wait.

They woke Rhys up as gently as they could, but it resulted in some grumpy swears and a sharp kick to the shin for Mr Hart who happened to be standing in range.

"Uh, oh, Victor. Sorry! Did I just kick you?" Rhys looked alert for a moment, but when Mr Hart voiced no complaints, he slumped back into a more comfortable position. "I think I was dreaming about something normal for a change. It was lovely... Oh, you! I ought to have kicked *you* for staying behind and mucking about!" Rhys gave Mr Quin a pointed look and garnished it with a not-so-polite hand gesture.

"You can do that later. I have something more important right now." Unruffled, Mr Quin pulled out a thick folder from inside his shirt. "I don't know how to best preface this, so I'm just going to show you."

He took out and showed them a picture of an approximately fifteen-year-old boy. The boy looked like a practically identical miniature version of Mr Craft.

"Meet A7f-2b, or what you call the voiceless." Mr Quin gave the photo to Rhys, and Mr Hart and Mr Craft leaned closer to look.

"That might be who I saw in my dream." Rhys handed the picture to Mr Craft, who took it and stared at it.

"I don't remember."

"His name was Justin Craft," Mr Quin said. "They were researching 'organic espionage' via something called sleep-roaming. The file caught my eye because it's thicker than the rest. There's a chart on how to couple his remains with a machine that takes readings from his 'dream state'. It's said to pull a lot of 'interesting data' from his surroundings even hundreds of kilometres away, if they leave it running for long enough."

Mr Quin spread out some of the papers from the folder for everyone to see but deliberately left some stacked. "This is not the only questionable research the Hosta Group is currently conducting. I was going to spare you the details, but I did find out they are offering services to criminals for profit and possibly also for leverage. I believe they've unearthed a lot of dirt on some higher ups in this city, and, while they assure discretion, I'd be hard pressed to believe that stuff doesn't get used for securing facilities, permits and operating leeway. All that to say, I wouldn't read the details of what they've done to him because it's only going to make you feel enraged and sick to your stomach."

"I don't remember," Mr Craft repeated. He kept on looking at the picture, deep creases forming on his forehead. "I should, at the very least, remember my twin brother, right?"

"They pride themselves in the success rate and effectiveness of their memory erasure services," Mr Quin said. He looked like he might pat Mr Craft on the shoulder but withdrew his hand without the man noticing.

"If you could sleep-roam, I bet you could access some of those memories," Rhys said to Mr Craft. "If the voiceless... if Justin can do it, maybe you can too? My dreams all seemed intact even though I don't remember half of them."

"Is that a naturally occurring trait, or did they do something to facilitate it? I haven't noticed anything unusual about the way I sleep or dream."

"They dabble in a whole range of research." Mr Quin pulled out a flyer and set it on the table for everyone to see. "Wouldn't be altogether surprised if they'd managed something like that."

There was a lengthy silence as the three of them inspected the paper. Vincent could tell even from a distance that a lot of what Mr Quin had mentioned was listed on the flyer in black and white.

"I think it's a naturally occurring trait," Rhys broke the silence. "Unless it's possible they've fed me alternative false memories. As far as I know, I've been like this from birth. I was seven or eight when they put me in that therapy. That's at least a couple of years' worth of memories of me being this way before they had anything to do with me. I can't be completely sure since it may not have been my first time there, but my instinct says they weren't even aware I could do it. They probably would have used me for their research had they known, but all that comes up in my dreams are things related to... to trying to make me better." Rhys swallowed. "If it's hereditary and Justin is your twin, then—"

"I told you I don't sleep-roam. I go to sleep and whatever happens, happens."

"It could be a skill you need to train," Rhys suggested.

"Hypothetically, what if it is? Then what? I go to sleep to have dreams I've had fifteen years ago, for what? How can I tell what's happened and what's just a dream? And considering what we know about the Hosta Group and what you went through trying to re-dream your dreams, do I really want to know? Maybe they wiped me for my own good. Maybe it's better this way." Mr Craft placed the photo face down on the table. They sat in silence until Mr Quin broke it by clearing his throat.

"You may be right in expecting it to be bad, but I'm not sure we have much choice. We need to gather *everything* we can to make sense of this. The more we know, the better. I took the folder because I realised it doesn't matter if we manage to retrieve the remains undetected. We are all in this mess, except maybe Victor here.

"This is not an organisation that would leave anything up to chance. Ever since you turned the remains over to the police, they've known you were involved and need to be watched. With this much history, it's possible they've kept an eye on you even before that. And never mind having the traditional eyes and ears across the city, these people have developed special organic surveillance devices to make sure they don't miss anything! You so much as sneeze, they will know. So, either you live the rest of your lives having to watch your step in case you do something they find suspicious or inconvenient, or you do something about them watching your every step. Or move away somewhere very far off... Coincidentally, I know just the place if you're interested." Mr Quin grinned. "But that's probably not the sort of life you want to lead. That leaves doing something about Hosta and making sure they don't give you grief or at least be prepared when they do."

"I'm not comfortable with you making that decision for me, Quin." Mr Craft's words were cold and his glare stomach turning. "You seem to have a lot of confidence in us going against an established, heavily funded underground organisation that's not shy to use less than reputable methods. In this case, perhaps the smart thing would be to stay under the radar as much as possible, even if it means having to hide."

"You can do that if you want," Mr Quin reminded him. "Them knowing about us poking around doesn't change the options. Staying in the city is going to become unsafe no matter what. Grovestead is nigh better."

"I feel like he has a point. It's only a matter of time before we start drawing attention to ourselves. I would hate to be off guard when that happens." Rhys turned the photo face up again, held it next to Mr Craft for comparison and hummed. "I wouldn't mind avenging your brother while we're at it. I know I'm probably naïve saying that, but I feel like he'd deserve as much after all he's gone through."

Vincent looked at the image now that Rhys was holding it up and wondered why it looked so familiar. Yes, sure, compared to Mr Craft, the resemblance was undeniable, but even outside of that, it was as if he'd met this person or someone very much like him before.

"Odd. Does it smell like rain, or is it just me?" Funny how it seemed like it might not be worth remembering.

CHAPTER 18

R hys went to sleep exhausted. He desperately needed to rest, but, before he could, he had a private theory that he wanted to test out. He was going to try it out and rest after.

Justin's box looked normal: no outward marks of black or smoke oozing or anything of the sort. Rhys approached it, sat next to it and addressed Justin by name for the first time since they'd known each other. Familiar hands appeared through the lid of the box. They didn't look at all as gruesome as they had previously.

"Hello, Justin."

"Hello, Rhys," Justin responded.

"First of all, I'm sorry for yelling at you before. Secondly, I would like to try something, if it's all right with you, but I'm very tired and need to rest, so if something weird happens, I hope you can help me with that, all right?"

"All right. I try, so, do that."

"Let's see if this works. Pull me in like you did before."

Rhys took Justin by the hand, closed his eyes and concentrated. He wasn't at his best, but the feeling was fresh in his memory: the pitch-black, cold void all around him. It was all encompassing like he imagined death would be, but there was something there, albeit a little out of reach. It took a leap of faith. For a moment, he felt like his conscious mind was dissolving into nothingness before it was reconstructed on the other side.

The other side was not dark, thankfully. It was the sort of immaterial state where Rhys could *see*, but at the same time, there was no ambient light or background that he could perceive.

He looked at what he presumed was Justin's dreamside self. The feel was essentially the same as in the picture, only more relaxed. Nothing about him suggested he'd been a corpse for close to two decades; he looked healthy and normal. It wasn't surprising, but what a strange contrast to the gnarly hands and the black tar-like substance Rhys associated with the voiceless.

Rhys wanted to say something but, as expected, couldn't. Since there were no recited words to grab onto on this side, he would have to figure out how to get Justin to see his hands. Thankfully, it wasn't all that hard once he got the gist of it, even if he did spend almost a half an hour experimenting before something materialised.

"Hello," Rhys signed. This startled Justin, who had been sitting in a near-to-catatonic state the whole time.

"Holy shit, what? Who?" Justin jumped up and took steps backwards, surprisingly animated. "Rhys? It's Rhys, right? You're Rhys? You're here? Oh, my fucking Guardian, you're in here? Shit, I can't believe it, wow. What is this? You want something? I'll tell you everything now, shit, Rhys... oh wait, can you hear me?"

Amused by the enthusiasm, Rhys signed yes. Then, since there were words, he tried to figure out how to use them.

"Fucking Guardian shit, shit, right?" Rhys copied. Justin laughed at this like it had been the best joke of the year. To him, it probably was.

"I've been so lonely in here you can't believe! Can you stay a while, please, please? You did say you needed to rest, but I've been stuck here alone for so long, uh..." He started to cry hysterically. "Sorry... sorry, wait..." He tried to get a hold of himself. "I've been stuck here alone for so long, emotions just happen. Who's there to see or care? I haven't had to hold back, so it comes out whenever. Hold on, I need to figure out how to stop this..." He was sobbing, weeping and laughing.

"I, can, wait," Rhys replied.

"Sorry. Oh, you probably want to know about Hosta, right? The whole thing is a mess. You need to be careful, she's mental. If she gets a hold of you, that'll be that... Shit, Rhys, I'm sorry you have to deal with this crap. You and your friends need to get the hell away and not come back. They messed me up so bad I might not remember everything. In fact, I know I don't, but I'll try to answer any questions you have. You probably need words, right? Ah, there has to be a faster way to do this. I wish you could sign a little better."

"I'm sorry you have to deal with this crap," Rhys responded, ruefully. "The whole thing is a mess."

"I suppose we could go back and forth between us, but the between part is rather nasty. I don't want you to get lost in there. That shit's difficult to navigate if you lose your bearings. I was once stuck in there for, I don't know, weeks maybe, until... until..." Justin frowned, trying to recall something. "Someone found me. Who was it? Damn, this is what I mean! There's holes everywhere. I was not alone in here, I swear. Oh, and she can also force her way in with that machine. That feels so fucking rough you can't believe. It's so invasive! She's got everything on the other side, so why can't I have this one thing to myself? I'm an adult right? Or am I? Does it count after you're dead?" Justin continued his monologue almost without pause. Rhys wished he could have responded normally, but at least he was here to listen to all of it.

"Who was it?"

"Well, you know, *her*. The bane of my existence. Makes me wish I'd never been born, you know? She's never satisfied. At least my brother got out. Brother? Yes, I had a brother. No. Several brothers. Which one..." Justin got stuck trying to figure it out.

"J-U-L-I-A-N," Rhys signed.

"Julian? Hmmm... oh, your friend Julian, what about him?"

"You, brother."

"Julian? Really?" He took a moment to consider it. "It's so frustrating to not remember everything. Is Victor also my brother? I know there's more of them, but I can't remember!"

"No," Rhys responded and slowly signed the names of Jonathan, Jacob and Jasmine, even if they were probably all too young to even have met Justin.

"Hah, they all start with a J. How silly of me to think one could start with a V. Are they fine? Did they get out?"

Justin seemed under the impression all of his siblings had met the same fate. Thankfully, things were not as grim as that. The younger ones were with their parents, and they'd appeared to have been doing fine last Midwinter. Mr and Mrs Craft had to have learned something from their mistake with Julian. At least Rhys hoped so.

"Yes. Maybe."

"Good for them. I was worried." Justin frowned and, for a moment, got lost in his thoughts. "You wanted to rest, right? I should let you rest." He seemed sad. Rhys wanted to say it was fine, and that he could stay for longer, but he was admittedly not feeling well, and getting back was a bit of a mystery.

"Yes. I go. But. You. Come. Back. With. Me." Putting together a full sentence out of the fragments was more tedious than he'd expected. Poor Justin to have had to do this all this time.

"Oh, right, hey, that's a good idea. I know the way. You did say you might need help. You're probably tired, so it's not a good time to get lost in the void. Right. OK, where are your hands, hold on, I'll pull you in and push you through to the other side. Here..." Justin pulled Rhys along into the darkness in between.

Rhys was thankful not to have to do any of the work. He was starting to feel like he was only barely holding on to his awareness. Getting back into his own dreamside was a relief.

"Thank you. I don't know if I could have managed that myself." Rhys fell to his back and closed his eyes. "Justin, I meant to say... what was it... oh, right. I think you can probably re-dream the past. That might patch some of those holes in your memory you mentioned. I've also been thinking maybe it's possible for us to tag along with each other when we re-dream. I don't know if that helps with communication, but you might be able to show me things." Something similar had been described in the book Vera had been reading. The context had been different, but, considering Rhys's recent experiences, it seemed like it might work. "In the meanwhile, once I've rested, I'm going to try to learn more sign language. The void in between is indeed unsettling. I'd rather not run back and forth. I've also been wondering what you would like us to do with your remains. If there's anywhere special you would like us to put them, let me know... Now, I think I'll—"

Julian was feeling too jittery to sleep, so he combatted it by being pragmatic and packing an emergency bag in case they needed to leave in a hurry. He finished packing sometime after midnight, but it hadn't done much to alleviate the stress.

Since work usually got his mind off of things, he headed downstairs. Even if he couldn't remember anything about his twin brother, he'd lost the nerve to study the remains, so he needed something else to do.

His desk was a mess. Rhys would probably appreciate him cleaning it up.

The thought of Rhys brought back the gut-wrenching feeling from before. He'd almost lost Rhys. He'd literally almost killed Rhys. He'd always assumed he was rotten to the core, but he'd figured that—if he was careful enough—he wouldn't end up actually killing anyone. His naïve carelessness had almost cost Rhys his life.

Julian could not fathom how he'd ever considered strangling a safe, viable option. His reasoning had been that none of what he had in his kit was fast enough to put Rhys under in mere seconds. The ACE mixture, any of its compounds alone, chloral, opium... none of it was immediate. They took five to ten minutes even for Rhys who was quicker than most to fall under.

At least he'd had the sense to rule out hitting Rhys in the head. But strangling? Why had that felt like such a natural thing to do?

"Can't sleep?" Quin interrupted Julian's private despair. He stood at the stairs and leaned on the railing, no less irritating than usual. Julian regretted not staying in his bedroom. "Or did you have some important work left?"

"Yes," was the easiest, though not the most truthful response. Julian tried to ignore Quin and busied himself with clearing the desk.

"I'm sorry. I think I've been building unfair expectations and making assumptions even after I said I wouldn't. I know I can't have what we had before." Quin sat down on the stairs much the same way Rhys had what seemed like a very long time ago. "I need you to understand you're the most important person in my life. I lost you, and for a moment, I had this dream I could maybe have you back if I played my cards right. I'll gladly settle for a fraction of you in my life because anything is better than not having you at all—"

"I'm not in the mood to talk." Julian would have much rather made this a confrontation to blow off steam, but, since he didn't want to disturb anyone's sleep, he made an effort not to instigate.

"All right." Quin fell silent but stayed to keep watch the whole time Julian was clearing and cleaning the desk.

"Shouldn't you be going to sleep?"

"Shouldn't you?"

Julian looked up at Quin. How was he supposed to maintain this protective distance of anger and resentment when Quin looked like that, like he wanted to be genuinely helpful and supportive? It was inconvenient, unsolicited and made the man that much more difficult to ignore.

"I'll go once I'm done. You don't have to wait."

"I know."

Was he being thick on purpose to rile him up? That would have suited both Julian's inner narrative as well as his perception of Quin. Alas, Quin was not showing any signs of being sarcastic or making fun of him or the situation.

The man stood up and sauntered down to the desk.

"Could I request something from you? Seeing as it's just the two of us here." His voice was soft and almost uncomfortably buttery. Almost. It was at that threshold, like he knew exactly how far to push it before it became gross instead of pleasant.

Julian considered it.

"You can ask, but I'm reserving the right to refuse."

"Of course, but before you refuse, you should know there are no strings attached to this request. You don't have to do anything, and I will not expect anything from you."

"Just spit it out already."

"I'd like to give you a hug." Quin's request was within the few things easily guessed from context, but it still sounded just as ridiculous. Julian sighed.

"But why? And don't tell me some bullshit about love or caring. What are you hoping to gain from it?"

It would have been faster and less of a pain to allow it without the questions, but it seemed like an invitation for more of similar inane requests in the future, regardless of Quin's assurances to the contrary.

Julian wondered if this was really the time and place he'd have to reject all of Quin, once and for all, to make it clear it was not going to lead anywhere, ever. He thought he'd been clear about it before, but since Quin had had his bizarre breakdown, perhaps he'd somehow missed it?

"It's not for me, it's for you." Quin looked serious, but it had to be a joke.

"I don't need—" Julian swallowed mid-sentence. How could a complete stranger, and an insufferable ass to boot, read him so accurately, even when he struggled to do so himself?

"Is it all right?"

Confused, Julian found himself nodding. He received a simple yet firm, no-frills embrace. He'd been despairing over his own stupidity all evening, weighing what drastic measures he needed to take to make sure he wouldn't fuck up again, but all the anxiety and self-loathing melted away when he was suddenly held like this.

"How...?"

"You've looked like you needed a hug for a while now. Today especially. You don't owe me anything. You don't even have to like me back, but if you ever need a hug, I'll give it to you no questions asked."

Quin held Julian for a while longer, and when he let go, Julian felt calm. As his tension eased, he realised how tired he was.

"I need to sleep."

"Good. Me too." Quin pushed him gently toward the stairs. "It's been a long day."

Vincent sat in the corner of the pharmacy, where, for whatever reason, there was a comfortable armchair, a bench, a decorative plant and some convenient lighting for reading. With the September showers and colder winds chasing away the rest of the summer warmth, it was nice and cool near the window and seemed like the perfect spot to keep out of everyone's way.

Vincent had read Mr Craft's copy of Aurora's book but realised he hadn't retained nearly any of it. He'd considered giving it another go, but, a few pages in, it had felt like he hadn't read it at all the first time, and the thought of reading it for the third time as if anew, was too unsettling.

He'd tried to follow the conversations Rhys, Mr Craft, Mr Quin and Mr Hart had had over their mysterious situation with the remains and the organisation called Hosta-something, but he wasn't sure if he'd slept since Grovestead, and his head felt achy. It seemed to be working even worse than usual.

If it was this bad after a single proper night of sleep, then how bad would it get if they persistently tried to fix him for a week or a month? How was he supposed to take care of Ren like this? How was he supposed to take care of himself, even? He could see himself turning into more of a burden for everyone around him when it wasn't even winter yet, and they were already dealing with a lot.

Vincent leaned back in the chair and rubbed his eyes, hoping that would help him feel more alert. It, of course, helped nothing.

Maybe it was for the best that Aurora had other people in her life she could be interested in, and perhaps form relationships with, who could keep up with her and provide her with intellectual companionship.

Mr Hart came in to relight the downstairs log burner. He wasn't the talkative sort, so when he opened his mouth to speak, Vincent flinched.

"Is everything all right, Mr Swifty?" he asked.

"You can call me Vincent..." Vincent mustered the last of his sociable front and tried to form a smile, but even that was more difficult than usual.

"You look tired. Did you not sleep well last night?" Mr Hart probably meant this as a kind, polite question, but it made Vincent want to laugh hysterically.

"Fine, fine. I'm fine. Everything is fine." He could not bring himself to even try to be truthful.

"All right. Let me know if you need anything."

"Yes, sure. Thank you."

Maybe this was the limit, and there was nowhere to go from here. If so, what could he do to cause the least amount of trouble to the people around him?

"R hys."

"Yes? What?" Rhys was taking notes, trying to learn some of the grammatical structure, modulation and non-manual elements of the sign language Victor was teaching him. He hadn't realised it was so complicated and was struggling to put it all together.

Victor was a patient teacher and had a knack for phrasing things in a more tangible manner. Having watched Julian teach Victor, it surprised Rhys how well Victor had processed the raw information Julian had offered him to now serve it to Rhys in such a comprehensive manner.

"Break," Victor signed.

"Really? It's not that late, is it? I thought I was doing a decent job..." Rhys referred back to his notes to see whether he'd made some gross, careless mistake with his last few signs.

"Your signing is fine, but I think you should focus on something else for a moment." Victor had gone downstairs to tend to the log burner and was now adding logs to the burner in the upstairs common area, so it wasn't as if Rhys was keeping him away from other tasks. Rhys had no trouble studying on his own for whenever Victor needed a break, but this time the man had specifically requested one. So, why now?

"Is something wrong? Is it Julian? Quin? Justin?"

Despite the poor weather, Quin had left the house sometime in the morning without mentioning where he was going, and Julian was downstairs in the back room working. It had been a quiet day, which Rhys had appreciated after everything that had happened the past few days.

"Your brother," Victor signed.

"What about my brother?" Rhys signed back awkwardly.

"Go take a look and tell me whether he seems all right to you."

Rhys parsed the signs and frowned.

"He's downstairs, reading, right?"

Victor nodded and didn't seem about to offer more clues, so Rhys stood up and headed for the stairs.

Vincent was stuck reading the first page of the prologue, the noise from the street proving too distracting to aid him in the task. This was the problem with large cities. He almost missed Rhys's words in this noise.

"Hey—*two dozen eggs*—would y—*does he look any different from normal*—like so—*what a buffoon*—tea? I thought—*see, I told you ought to have*—I'd ha—*cats and dogs today*—some."

"Pardon me?"

"Tea, w—*did I not add the flour*—you—*blasted fool! I will*—ke some?"

"Tea?" It was too noisy to make out the words. "I'm sorry, I must be tired."

"*One, please*—Are you—*I don't trust him*—all right? You—*I am so bored, he is so boring, Guardian help me*—n't look so—*my favourite condiment is now ruined forever*—ood."

"It's so noisy."

"What d—*is the matter with him*—you mean—*his cheeks seem red*?" Rhys tested his forehead.

Oh, no. Not this again. Rhys's hand felt cool. Vincent tested himself.

"It's not because I'm sitting right next to the log burner, is it?" He'd been feeling chilly today, but he'd been too tired to pay much attention to it.

"You—*look like a damn tomato*—eem a bit on the warm side—*vandalism! I swear I'll catch those*—how do—*why can't I stop thinking about him*—feel?"

"Do you have a cellar in this house?"

"No, b—*I really would rather hug than strangle p*—there's a storage for—*what does he need a cellar for*—coal around the—*bunnies, I love bunnies*—back. Why?"

"What about a bathtub?" A cold bath might do the trick.

"I think—*Victor was right*—you have a—*stubborn ass of a man*—fever. I'm—*naked and ready*—ing to ask Julian—" Rhys rushed off to the back room.

Vincent leaned back in the chair. It was probably his ears playing tricks on him again, but that last part especially hadn't sounded quite right. He refrained from following, just in case.

Aurora received a phone call from Rhys, informed Ren and started packing. She had delayed accepting her post in Schadesborough for long enough. This seemed like a sign it was time to go.

It was Ren's first time on a train, and she was volubly unimpressed. Having ridden on Freya, Aurora was not surprised.

The night at the hotel proved much more to Ren's liking. Aurora would have slept wherever was most convenient, but Mr Quin had insisted on making the arrangements and paying for everything. Consequently, they had stayed in possibly the best room at the best hotel in Firth, where Ren had been treated and pampered like a princess. She was reminiscing on it when they were bobbing on their train seats heading towards Schadesborough the next day, much less perturbed by the bumpy ride.

Aurora had been to Schadesborough plenty enough times to be used to its characteristic smell and the eclectic collection of sights and sounds, but Ren had understandable difficulty in adjusting as they neared the station.

The smell was partially disguised by the smoke from the train but became substantially more apparent when they gained some distance from the locomotive after exiting the station.

"How do people live here? It's disgusting!"

"You get accustomed to it, I suppose. I hear it used to be worse, and it's much less pervasive when it's cold."

"I didn't think I would ever say this, but I'm glad it's rainy, damp and cold today!" Ren marched a dozen or so steps and stopped. "Where are we heading? Is it far? Are we going to walk?"

"Mr Quin said he would send someone to pick us up. While I would not mind stretching my legs after sitting on the train for hours, I'd rather not stretch my arms." Aurora had carried her luggage from the train to the entrance of the station and that was far enough to know she wouldn't have enjoyed it as a hobby.

"Shouldn't they be here already? Our train was at least a half an hour late." Ren skipped back to where Aurora was standing. "You don't suppose they would have left already?"

"Have some patience," Aurora said, though she'd been thinking those exact thoughts. She opened her umbrella and shared it with Ren, hoping they wouldn't have to wait for long.

"I'm soaked!" Ren removed her coat and shoes as soon as they were in the pharmacy.

"Where is he?" Aurora asked Mr Craft, who sat on a tall stool behind the counter.

"Upstairs. I would advise seeing him alone first." Mr Craft left the counter to help Aurora with her luggage. "Victor?" Mr Craft raised his voice. Mr Hart appeared from the stairs. "Could you carry some of this up there?"

"I'm sorry, they are quite heavy."

"I don't mind," Mr Hart said and lifted the heaviest trunk over his shoulder. Mr Craft handled the suitcases.

"How is he? Any better?" Aurora followed the men to the stairs.

"No. The doctor was here yesterday. He was of the opinion it's not life-threatening, so we've been treating the symptoms as best we can, but he seems to be in an atrocious mood."

"Atrocious?" Aurora frowned. "He's not aggressive, is he?" It was difficult to imagine Vincent in an atrocious or aggressive mood, but sleep deprivation could cause all sorts of symptoms.

"You're not going to let me see him, are you?" Ren, who had been following them, stopped in her tracks mid-staircase. Aurora turned to Mr Craft to confirm whether it was really that bad.

"I wouldn't want to go in there voluntarily myself." The corner of Mr Craft's eye twitched.

Aurora turned to Ren and tried to sound reassuring. "I'll check on him first, all right?"

"That's what Aunt Celandine used to say, and then she wouldn't let me see him!" Ren almost dropped the cat box she was carrying. Aurora decided to help her hold it steady until she calmed down.

"I'm sorry. I'll check on him, but it might be better to wait a while. I will let you see him if he's at all in the condition to do so, but we also don't want you to catch what he's got."

"It's just a cold! I can handle it better than he can!"

"I'm sorry..." Whoever this Aunt Celandine was, she'd probably had good reason to shield Ren from the worst of it.

"I thought you were nice and smart, but you're just like the rest of them! I hate you!" Ren yanked the cat box out of Aurora's hands and nearly lost her balance. She scrambled down, thankfully without injury, but did not stop at the foot of the stairs.

"Ren!" Aurora moved to go after her.

"You need to tend to him. I'll go." Mr Hart set down the trunk at the top of the stairs and swept past her with surprising speed.

She wondered if she would regret leaving it up to Mr Hart, but it was probably for the best. In her state, Ren would run faster at the sight of her than Mr Hart.

"Don't worry. Victor is good with children." Mr Craft left the suitcases in the hallway and carried the trunk the rest of the way into one of the upstairs bedrooms, rightly assuming what Aurora was going to need, perhaps based on the weight. Aurora followed him.

"Do you need me to come in?" Mr Craft seemed dead-serious about not wanting to come in. "I'll be right outside if there's trouble..."

"Yes, that's fine." Aurora had dealt with a wide variety of patients before but had to admit she was nervous not knowing what to expect. Vincent didn't come across as the type to cause problems, but she'd also never seen him in an 'atrocious mood'. "Vincent?"

The room was dark. It was already late afternoon, but the darkness was due to the curtains being drawn shut.

"Go away." Vincent seemed to have burrowed under a blanket.

"It's me." Aurora sat on the side of the bed and set her hand gently on his side. He flinched but remained in his cocoon. "How are you feeling? I came to help..."

He did not respond.

"Vincent?"

"I'm fine. Go away."

"You have a fever, right? It's making it worse, isn't it?"

Again, no response.

"Vincent?"

"What?"

"Your fever. It's making it worse. I'd like to help."

"I don't want to... Where's Ren? I thought I heard her..."

"She came with me. Do you want to see her?"

"No."

If anything, he did seem uncooperative.

"I didn't ask you to come here, did I?" He pulled the blanket tighter around himself. "Stop talking. I don't care. You're too loud. Shut up. Please, shut up..." He sounded distressed and tired as expected. The doctor had probably already done his best to curb the fever, but it didn't require much for the type seven symptoms to emerge according to the test results. It was probably active now, judging by the symptoms.

One solution would be to take him somewhere more isolated until it passed, but Schadesborough was vast and crowded. They would have had to have travelled a fair distance just to get out of the city and somewhere less densely populated.

"I'm not... I'm telling you, I'm not... I'm not possessed... Shut up. Just leave me alone. Leave me," Vincent mumbled. He seemed to be trembling.

"I know something that might help you. Can you sit up for me, please?" Aurora couldn't be sure whether it would, but it had been mentioned in Vincent's file as something that had helped before. "Vincent?"

"What file? I don't want to..."

"Sit up for me for a moment, and if you still want me to leave, I'll leave." At least for a moment, Aurora thought.

"Go and don't come back."

"Fine, but you need to humour me first." It was an uncomfortable gamble but better than leaving him to deal with it alone.

Vincent sat up. He was avoiding looking at Aurora, but his eyes were blood-shot, his face was flustered and he struggled to breathe through his nose. Not as bad as expected but not great.

"What are you going to do about it?" He slumped as he sat.

"Look here." Aurora set her hands to his warm cheeks and guided him to look at her. She pressed her forehead to his and used what she imagined was her loudest inner voice to scream inside her head.

His eyes had been drooping tiredly, but this made them open up wide.

"Aches... Head... My head... Aches..."

She'd wholly grabbed his attention, though.

"Mr Craft will surely have something to help you with that. How do you feel?"

"What?"

"How do you feel?" She enunciated as clearly as she could so he could read her lips.

"I can't hear..." At first, he looked perplexed and worried. "I can't hear... Can you do that again? More?"

Aurora obliged with another scream. The theory was that a loud enough 'sound' would at least temporarily shut off the noise flooding into Vincent's consciousness through whatever gateway that had been jammed open between him and his dream. It seemed to be working. He looked relieved.

"Thank you. I'm sorry... I'm tired. I can't—"

"It's all right. I'll help you sleep. It'll help you fight off this cold. You'll feel better in no time."

"What? I'm sorry, I—"

"It's all right." Aurora unpacked her equipment and made the preparations.

"Is Ren?"

"Don't worry. We'll take care of everything."

Mr Hart had probably caught up to her by now. Vincent might feel well enough the next day to see her, and maybe she would forgive her. Even if Vincent was still ill the next day, he didn't seem so bad they couldn't let Ren visit for a while.

When Victor got back a half an hour later without Ren or the cat, an emergency meeting was held in the lounge to determine what to do about it.

Victor looked crushed to have returned without the girl but said he'd followed her for twenty solid minutes until she'd vanished without a trace a few streets east from the pharmacy. He was drenched, having left without a raincoat, so he hurried upstairs to change. Julian dug out his raincoat from the closet, and Vera searched through her luggage for something appropriate to wear.

"She probably won't have gone too far. She doesn't know the city. Where did Vincent park Freya when you arrived?" Vera asked Rhys.

"Freya? You mean the speeder?" Rhys dug up a map from one of the drawers in the lounge and spread it on the dining table.

"Yes. If she finds it, she might try to drive it out of the city, and that would make things considerably more difficult for us."

"There's an old garage not far from here. We negotiated a fair price with the gentleman who owns it. The speeder is locked up and secure," Rhys assured her. Victor returned wearing a dry set of clothes and his raincoat.

"Ah, Victor, can you take this area?" Rhys circled a chunk on the map. "Julian?"

Julian leaned over to see. Rhys assigned him a similar chunk.

"I don't know the city very well. I'll circle around the block and try not to get lost," Vera suggested.

"That sounds good. I think I might sleep and take a look..." Rhys glanced at her. She raised an eyebrow. "You could come wake me up once you've done a round, and I can let you know if I've found anything."

"How far?" she asked.

"What do you mean?"

"How far can you see?"

"As far as I go, how so?" She looked at him like she wanted a detailed explanation, but this was hardly the time. "Just come wake me up when you've gone around. We can talk about it later."

Julian and Victor had already headed for the stairs. Vera looked tempted to ask more questions but nodded and headed after them. She almost bumped into Quin in the stairs.

"What's going on? Where's everyone going in such a hurry?"

"Ren ran away. We're trying to find her." Rhys was half expecting Quin to be Quin and not care, but the man had been so uncharacteristically involved and attentive lately, it didn't come as too much of a surprise when he looked at the map and offered to help.

"What was she wearing? Where should I look?"

"I'm not sure but probably the green cardigan she always wears. I wasn't there when they arrived and she took off." Rhys pointed out the areas unassigned to anyone. "You could look here. I'm going to sleep and do a quick check."

"All right. This will be a splendid chance for some exercise!" Quin seemed ready to run through the whole city to stretch his legs. Rhys watched him dash off and shook his head.

Where the hell was the Quin who would have suggested the weak should be left behind to take care of themselves or perish? He was now willing to run around after a kid in the freezing rain. What on earth could have caused such a drastic transformation? It didn't seem right.

After scouring through the neighbourhood dreamside, Rhys was stumped. It was getting dark, and the poor weather had emptied the streets. It didn't seem likely that Ren would have knocked on a door to ask for shelter, but, with no sign of her out in the streets, he was forced to consider it a possibility. Where else could she be when she was nowhere out in the open?

Justin's hands popped into existence in front of Rhys while he was taking a break. They were signing enthusiastically, indicating he wanted Rhys to come over to his side through the void.

"I can't now. I'm busy. We're trying to find Ren. She ran away about an hour ago, and I can't find her anywhere."

"Find her," Justin echoed. "Then come," he signed.

"Yes. But there's no sign of h—" Rhys was woken up by Vera.

"Any luck?" she asked.

"No, not yet."

Thankfully, most people in this neighbourhood were kind and decent, so there was very little worry that any of the locals would harm Ren so long as she didn't wander too far. That just left the possibility of Hosta stirring up trouble—

"I'm going back out there," Vera said. She was not wearing anything nearly robust enough for the weather, and what she was wearing was already damp if not soaked through. Never mind an intangible threat of an underground organisation, Rhys sat up and stopped her before she could leave and get herself sick.

"Maybe dry yourself off and check on Vincent first. Julian, Victor and Quin are out there. You've been alerting the neighbours, so everyone knows to keep an eye out. I'm sure they'll find her soon."

"Ah, you're probably right."

"There are towels in the linen closet in the bathroom to your right. Please, help yourself to one." Rhys wondered whether it would only worry her further to mention something about Hosta. It seemed like an obscure concern for the time being, but Quin had sounded serious when he'd spoken up about them. Was it naïve to ignore the warnings and assume there was no immediate danger? This would have been an appalling moment for Hosta to strike back if they'd noticed the missing folder and the switched-up remains.

Maybe Vera needed to know just in case?

Rhys was about to tell her when Vincent emerged from his bedroom.

"Where's Ren?" The man looked and sounded even worse than when they'd sent him in there to rest. He was unsteady on his feet, his nose was running with a force greater than the Grymfors Falls, and he seemed to be at the verge of collapsing into a heap on the floor. "Well, I'm not here to run a race, am I? Where's Ren?"

"You should be resting." Vera had returned with her towel and tried to guide him back into the bedroom.

"What? Why is she out there? What happened?" Vincent grabbed her by the forearm. "Why didn't you tell me earlier?"

She glanced at Rhys, possibly to solicit help. She seemed worried, but surely they could handle a fever-ridden stick of a man with no trouble at all, even if he did get it in his fluffed up brain to go out there to search for Ren in this guardianbysmal weather?

"Can you stop talking all at once, I can't hear anything in this noise!"

"Don't worry about it. Let's get you back in bed." Vera seemed on top of it by herself, so Rhys lay back down on the sofa to wait.

"I trusted you to take care of her..." Vincent sounded rougher than usual.

"We'll find her—"

"I didn't peg you as one to try to take her from me!"

"I'm not. I'll bring her over as soon as we find her. Oh, my. You're still burning up!"

"Don't touch me!"

"Vincent..."

"Why didn't you bring her to me in the first place? No. I don't believe that. Stop screaming at me!" Vincent's gruff retort made Rhys open his eyes again.

Something was definitely off. Was this what Ren had meant by Vincent sometimes acting odd when he was sick? He'd always seemed laid back and unfazed by most things but was now getting borderline aggressive.

"Shut up! I'm not going to hurt anybody!" he yelled. Maybe this would require two sets of hands after all. Rhys got up and joined Vera.

"It's all right, calm down," Rhys tried.

"Get out of my way!" Vincent lifted his cane, looking like he might use it to enforce his order. He wasn't seriously thinking about going out there in that condition, was he? "I will use it. Move aside, Rhys."

"Everyone's already out there looking for her. I'm sure they're bringing her back as we speak." Rhys tried to stand tall and confident, but Vincent was a great deal taller—and suddenly also more intimidating—regardless of his condition.

"Move the fuck aside, Rhys!" The man looked like a crazed, rabid bear with his nose running and face twisted into a snarl. All that was missing was him frothing at the mouth.

Rhys pulled Vera along as he backed away a few steps. Perhaps best to let him go out for just a moment. The cold rain would cool him down a tick, and, once he'd tired himself, Victor and Julian would be able to pick him up with no effort. Hopefully, it wouldn't exacerbate his condition too much.

Vincent glared at him for an uncomfortable moment before he strode past and down the stairs.

"Vincent—" Vera moved to go after him, but Rhys stopped her.

"Let him go for now. I'll sleep and keep an eye on him. Wake me up in a couple of minutes. I'll let you know if he's calmed down and ready to be picked up."

R en sat on the cold cobble floor of a pitch-black coal cellar. The rain tapped on the hatch somewhere above. The cellar was musty and dusty, and she was soaked, but it beat wading out there in the rain. Sir Swifty meowed in the box. He sounded as miserable as Ren was feeling.

"I'm sorry, buddy. I shouldn't have dragged you into this. Are you cold? Wet?" She felt for the lattice in the dark and tried to stick her fingers through to test but couldn't reach. It was too dark to see anything, but she managed to open the latch to insert her hand. The fur felt dry against her fingers. What a relief.

Her relief was short-lived when she felt Sir Swifty squeeze and slide past her hand and out of the box.

"Wait, what? Where are you going?" Once past her grasp it was impossible to tell where the cat had gone. "Sir Swifty?" He wouldn't take off at a moment like this, would he? He was the only support and comfort Ren currently had. "Pss pss pss, Seymeowr? Where are you? Please come back."

There wasn't much space in the cellar, but it was big enough to lose a cat in. Ren started to sob. She wanted to go back to Vincent, but he was sick, and they wouldn't let her see him. She was dreadfully afraid that maybe Vincent wouldn't fight for her anymore. Maybe he wasn't well enough to do it? Maybe he wasn't going to get better this time?

"Please, please get back in the box..." Ren crawled across the cellar but could not find Sir Swifty in the darkness. "Where are you? Don't you leave me, too."

Was it too late to go back? Would Dr Vera be mad at her for lashing out? Would Uncle Rhys take care of her if Vincent was unable? Would they eventually let her see Vincent again?

The problem was she'd run off without paying attention to where she was going, and, even if she did decide to return, she wasn't sure where she was or where to go. And now she'd gone and lost Sir Swifty.

The noise was unbearable. Vincent's face was beaten by gusts of wind and an icy downpour when he lifted his hood to see where he was going.

All the while, dozens of voices babbled over one another in an ear-splitting cacophony. The rain and the wind were almost as loud but did not drown the noise within Vincent's head. The only thing that helped was exposing his forehead to the rain, and it muffled the voices only momentarily until the cold became too painful to bear, and he was forced to cover his head with the hood again.

In a matter of minutes, the legs of Vincent's trousers had soaked water up to his knees. He would have sat in his shit and waded through snow all over again had it saved him from this worry that Ren was out here somewhere, wet and freezing. He needed to find her before the cold made her susceptible to illness or she ran into trouble alone in such a big city.

There was a lamplighter tending to one of the streetlamps ahead.

"Excuse me, sir," Vincent called. "Have you seen a small girl carrying a large wooden box?"

The lamplighter climbed down his ladder and set it aside on the ground next to his stick.

"No—*what a peculiar-looking fellow*—I don't think so." *A girl? Alone? Out here? Is he going to do something to her if he finds her? Looks shifty. A filthy rover? I should call the police.*

"Thank you for your help." Vincent hurried on as fast as he could with having to rely on his cane. His bones ached from the fever and the cold but sticking around to see whether the lamplighter called the police or not did not seem like a good idea.

Coming to crossroads and deciding on routes was a miserable task with all of the random shouts, murmurs and yammering that kept interrupting Vincent's thoughts. There had to be a way to shut all of this off. *Sir Swifty, where are you?*

Vincent stopped.

"Ren? Ren!" That must have been Ren. Where had it come from? The street ahead was empty. There was no one but the lamplighter back where he'd come from. "Ren—!" Vincent's voice cracked. His throat hurt. He tried again but all that came out was a croak.

He hurried—*Seymeowr*—onward. Maybe behind the corner over there? *I'm so alone.* She had to be somewhere close by!

I should scold the blasted fool! Two steps and a half. But why not? Don't I deserve better than this? Sleep, you fool. None of these were her. Vincent looked back but there was no one there. Perhaps a side street? He stopped to cough and tried to see where there might be an alleyway he could follow. The coughing made him feel dizzy. *There's a bloody drifter outside making noise at this hour. Two cups of flour, and where did I put those eggs? Bollocks!*

Vincent ran towards an alleyway, hoping that would lead him closer to Ren, but, after several minutes of wandering, all he could hear was the rambling flow of consciousness of dozens if not hundreds of people preparing to go to bed.

"There—*I must have put them*—you are," a familiar voice blipped through the noise.

"Wh—?" A sharp pain in his throat cut the word short, and he struggled to swallow.

"Down—*need to remember*—ere—*makes absolutely no sense*—dummy." The cat at his feet seemed to assess whether to push against Vincent's legs, but both the legs and the cat were so wet, he settled on a pointed look.

"Ren?"

"In—*six or eight*—the dark—*copper and another*—are you—*I miss him*—ting for?"

Swifty looked annoyed and distressed, probably trying to repeat his words so Vincent could grasp them, but it was much too noisy.

Aurora had done something to make the noise stop, but it had left his ears ringing and him unable to hear anything at all, so nothing like that would be helpful now. There had to be something he could do to make this stop, though. The cat was still trying, but the topmost voice in Vincent's mind was going through a cake recipe. He tried to crouch down to hear better but could still only make out fragments.

Vincent tried to tell the cat to lead him to her but all that came out was a wheeze. Now that he was standing still and the rain was beating his back, his face felt hot and his head was spinning from trying to force the words out through the noise and the pain.

Swifty looked at him and made no move. He seemed too confused by Vincent's lacklustre efforts. This was no good. The cat was useless. But Ren had to be somewhere close by.

"L— Lead!" Vincent croaked. Swifty sat there and tilted his head. The rain became more of a foggy drizzle. Vincent wished the noise could have also become less of a deluge.

I want home.

She seemed so close. If only he could have silenced everyone else to hear where her voice was coming from!

"This way." Swifty headed for the street behind Vincent. It was as empty as it had been some minutes before. But there had to be something for the voice to sound so close and for Swifty to be here.

Vincent closed his eyes and concentrated on her voice. He knew her voice better than any other. It was here. She had to be here. If he could shut these other voices out, it would leave just her.

Daddy, I want home. She sounded like she was crying. Vincent dropped his cane and hurried past Swifty. The sobs and crying echoed in his head as he leapt to a sidestreet he'd missed before.

"I'm here, I'm here!" He yanked open the first coal cellar hatch to see inside. Empty, save for the coal. The next one was the same, but her voice seemed louder, closer. "I'm here!"

He nearly ripped the hatch off its hinges. The sweetest sight, her face turned to look back at him. Tears and coal dust had smeared her cheeks, but she didn't seem injured. He pulled her up by her armpits and gave her a tight hug. She bawled against his chest as he rubbed her back and arms to warm her up.

"I'm sorry. I did a stupid thing," she sobbed. He wanted to tell her it was fine and not to worry, but the last few shouts had stung too sharply for him to even attempt swallowing, much less speaking. He stroked her back to calm her down. "What's wrong? Are you all right?" she stopped her crying to ask.

"Hurts." Vincent pointed at his throat.

"Oh, my dearest Guardian, Vincent." She pulled down his hood and tested his cheek and forehead. "You're not supposed to be out with a fever like this. What would Aunt Celandine say? Or Aunt Aster. We need to get you back inside right now!" She reached back into the coal cellar for the cat box and closed the hatch. "Come, Sir Swifty. We need to go. Which way do we go?" She turned to him for help.

Vincent pointed towards the way he'd come. Now that he'd found her, he was relieved but also felt depleted. He staggered upright but had to momentarily lean on her until the dizziness subsided. It was at this moment he realised that, like an utter arse, he'd yelled at Aurora and Rhys when they had only tried to help him. The state of confusion caused by the noise was no joke.

But it was quiet now.

He tested his forehead. It was definitely still too warm.

He looks so tired. I shouldn't have caused trouble. I'm so stupid.

You and me both, Vincent thought. He squeezed her hand and gave her a smile.

Are you listening in on me?

Vincent nodded.

"Can you walk? Where's your cane?"

Vincent pointed some ways back. She ran to fetch it for him. Swifty jumped on top of the cat box and meowed. Vincent frowned.

How come he could hear Ren but not Swifty? It was so quiet. Surprisingly quiet for such a large city.

"Let's go. We need to get you dried up and into bed," Ren said.

"You too," Vincent mouthed. He lifted the cat box, which was thankfully not as heavy once the cat had jumped off of it. How far was this? He managed a few steps and crumbled to his knees. He got up and walked a couple more steps, but when he fell down again, his knee refused to bear any weight, and his healthier leg was too tired to support all of it.

Ren knelt down in front of him.

"Too tired? Should I fetch help?"

Some rescuer he was. He'd dragged himself out here just to become a useless nuisance, as always.

"Help! Anyone!" Ren yelled and looked around.

"Sorry," Vincent mouthed.

"It's OK. It's my fault you're out here in the first place," she said. "Oh, look! That's Mr Craft, isn't it?" She pointed at the approaching figure not far off.

Vincent sighed. Of course it was Mr Craft. Who else would it be than the wonderful and smart Mr Craft? Vincent gave up the pretence and let himself fall down on his face. He had just enough consciousness left to feel himself be helped up and be carried off by the bloody marvellous man of the hour Mr Craft, but at least after that he was too tired to care.

CHAPTER 21

Seeing as Julian seemed to be bringing both Vincent and Ren home, Rhys had requested Vera to not wake him up for the rest of the night. He grabbed Justin's hands and repeated what they had done the night before. It was easier now that Justin knew what they were doing, but he was a degree too enthusiastic yanking Rhys over to the other side.

"Hi, hello, did you get here all right? Rhys? You won't believe the stuff I found! Wow, I mean, I've been stuck here for so many years, and I didn't think to even try! You seem like such a natural at this, I'm impressed. So how's Julian? How's everyone? Did you find the girl? From this side, it looked like maybe you did, but it's not always easy to tell. I mean, it was much easier when I was alive, and before all that craziness happened, but at least I can still sense my surroundings somewhat. Well, you must have found her since you're here. Oh yes! You wanted my opinion on my remains, right? Forgive me, I'm a little excited, very excited actually. I can't believe you're here again!" Justin was looking around for Rhys's hands, but being yanked through the void had left Rhys too discombobulated to respond right away.

"Look, I don't care what you do with the remains so long as you can keep them still, somewhere safe. I don't know how I'm even connected to them since I'm dead and shouldn't feel anything, but when you haul that stuff around, it feels like I'm losing the last remnants of my sanity. Last week someone rattled the crate for no apparent reason, and I swear I thought my head was about to explode! Which is rather funny because my head's a hardened skin sack with a skull inside. No way that's going to explode by itself. Gross. You don't want to know what's inside the skull." Justin shuddered. "You could put me back in that hole you found me in. Oh, but maybe not. She knows the place. Somewhere less obvious but warm, dry and cosy. I'm not sure it makes much of a difference, but I'd rather not decompose any faster than necessary. It's creepy enough as it is. Oh, and I'd rather not be eaten up too quickly. If it happens slowly enough, it's not as disconcerting. Little bits are carried off somewhere, who knows where. But I suppose it's not all that different from when I was alive. I mean, we lose hair and skin all the time and hardly notice. It just doesn't grow back. One day I'll be completely gone, but luckily it seems that the less of me there is left, the less I care. However, if I could be encased and sealed inside something with as little moisture as possible, that'd be ideal. Does that help? Is it too much trouble? A box is probably fine too. Are you still here? Are you all right?"

"Hello, I'm here."

Justin's raw enthusiasm had provided Rhys with a lot of usable words while he tried to get his hands working.

"Ah, good, I was worried there for a moment. Oh yes, I have something to show you! Should we try it right away? I mean, have you visit my dream. I ran into a lot of shitty stuff not worth showing, but I think you might like this. At least, if I've understood correctly. You inherited this place from the previous owner, right? So, you're probably related to her?"

"Yes," Rhys responded.

"Were you close? I'm sorry for your loss. She seemed like a nice woman, one of my favourite people, really."

Rhys had a few nice memories of his great aunt, but this was the first time he'd heard someone else say something positive about her. His hands still felt a little unwieldy, but he managed to sign "thank you".

Justin smiled. "There you are. I'll take you, hold on." He grabbed Rhys's hands, leaving no time to prepare for what was to come. Rhys winced. For someone so used to traversing his own dreamside, being pulled along with Justin here was surprisingly abrupt and awkward.

J ustin had had a rough day. Most days were stressful, but this one had been downright harsh.

The arrangement was simple: he'd moved up into the attic over the shoe shop. A worker came over twice a day to take the data and give him his medications. He was confined to this room, but this was more freedom than he'd had for a while.

The lady from downstairs, Mrs Hargrave, provided regular meals and took care of the housekeeping, even if that was probably not her job. It was not a bad setup, all things considered. It had just been a rough day.

On top of the usual needles, tubes and electrodes, Justin had had to put up with 'the torture helmet', as he called it. It was never the right size, and it was strapped on with thick leather straps that left deep grooves across his forehead and neck—at least as deep grooves as were possible in those areas.

The drugs often left him confused for a few hours, and he was slowly coming out of one such stupor when she came up with some soup.

"I'm sorry. Not a good day, I see. Do you need anything? I brought soup. Can you sit?"

Her kindness had seemed horribly suspicious and frightening at first, but once Justin had got used to it, she'd become the best part of his day. It felt foreign to be cared for, but next to visitor days and his brother coming by, it was almost as nice. Especially now that his brother hadn't stopped by for a few months.

It must have been in April last, back at the clinic.

He could still sense the connection between them, but it was much fainter than usual. In fact, it was so faint he could barely tell it was there at all. But so long as it was still there, he wasn't too worried. Sometimes it was more worrying when the connection was strong, and he could sense the mood his brother was in.

Mrs Hargrave was an absolute solace. She propped Justin up to sit with a few pillows behind his back and offered him the soup. Then she stayed at the side of the bed to make sure he ate and kept him company until he felt better.

"I thought I might pop by the library tomorrow if you'd like something more to read. I hear they've received a large donation of books recently."

The dream morphed into two dreams as the machine was switched on: pastures somewhere afar and here in the room in the attic. For however long the machine was on, there would be landscapes of rolling hills, clouds, towns, people in meetings, things Justin didn't care about and tried to ignore. What mattered was where they turned it off, and he could only hope it wasn't as far as last time. But until then, Mrs Hargrave would keep him company and be nice to him, and that was all he could ask for.

Snow. Julian's voice downstairs. He rarely got to see Julian these days. They would usually send him away as if Justin didn't exist.

Whatever had happened at the clinic had left Justin confused and out of his mind. He could sense the end was near. Soon he would be out of this body permanently. It was not a happy occasion, but Mrs Hargrave had made things bearable during the embalming preparations. He'd been partially in there while they had done it, but because he hadn't been able to react to anything anymore, they hadn't known how painful it was.

Mrs Hargrave had even been delicate with him after his passing. Once the pain subsided, Justin had experienced peace for the first time in his existence. Too bad it wasn't much of an existence.

There had been people storming in and out looking for him. Little did they realise he was right there, safely tucked away within the floor. Mrs Hargrave kept him company even after he was dead. She'd come in during the night in her dreams much the same way as Rhys did now—just that Justin hadn't known how to cross over to the other side yet. He'd felt her there and assumed it was nothing but a lingering memory or a figment of his imagination.

How long had she been there, trying to keep him company, and he'd only realised once it was too late?

"You saw that, right? That was the best soup I've ever had! I thought you were familiar. It was something around the eyes. She was clearly related to you. And now I can visit her whenever I want. You don't know how happy that makes me! I didn't even know I could dream anymore since I haven't had a new dream since I died. This is so much fun! I've got so many years' worth of dreams to go through again!"

Justin seemed ecstatic over it even when his happy dream had seemed nightmarish to Rhys. All that stuff he'd been attached to, it had felt far from pleasant. Could this have been Rhys's future if he was ever caught by Hosta?

Mrs Hargrave, Rhys's great aunt, had looked older but much as Rhys had remembered her from the few times he'd seen her as a child before his father had severed their ties. It was nice to know that, while she'd been involved with Hosta, she'd still been a positive influence in Justin's life.

"Rhys? I have more, but I don't know if I can show you." Justin hesitated. "I don't know what you'll think of me if I do. I don't want you to hate me. They are painful, or maybe I'm just weak? But they seem painful to me. It can be confusing. Some of it is not real, I don't think. I can sort of tell when it hasn't really happened, but I don't know if you can."

"You... can, tell when, it is not real." Rhys signed to add, "After."

"After? Right. But that can be confusing and frightening when you don't know. Then again, I suppose it's probably not as bad since it hasn't actually happened to you, right? I wonder how much of it translates to you when I dream. Do you feel the same things? Can you hear my thoughts? Is it like in your own dreams? I suppose that's going to be too difficult to explain by signing. Do you want to go back for a while? I don't want to force you to do something you don't want."

"I, want to go back for a while," Rhys agreed.

Justin nodded, took Rhys's hands and pulled him over with ease. He'd had practice going back and forth and was getting the hang of how to take Rhys along. The ride wasn't getting any more pleasant, though.

"Ah, thanks." Rhys stretched out of habit. "It's much easier when you do the bulk of the work. As for your question, it was like when I dream myself, only I had no control over it. It felt strange to be thinking or feeling something different than what I normally would under similar circumstances without all of your experiences as context."

It was uncomfortable but nothing he couldn't handle.

"I think I might be able to tell apart what's distorted because it's a dream and what's pulled straight from your memories. There's a slight difference in flavour so to speak... but we can always have a chat about it afterwards to be sure I didn't misunderstand anything."

Rhys tried to remember what else Justin had asked.

"Ah, I can see how showing me your dreams with all of the details included might feel like an invasion of your privacy, so if you show me something that's private, I promise I'll keep it to myself if you want and won't hold anything against you." He could imagine how uncomfortable he would feel about sharing certain dreams, so he hoped this would alleviate Justin's concerns. "And one more thing." Rhys had been wondering but kept forgetting to ask, "How come you're so good at signing? I can understand Julian having learned for his sister's sake, but she was born after you died."

He waited.

"From, dream. Myself, and. Julian, chat, just. Signing. It's much easier. Privacy." Justin was signing something similar about keeping things secret between him and Julian.

So, they'd learnt it for convenience?

"Can. Switch?" Justin asked.

"Actually, before we do... I think we're going to have to confront Hosta at some point, and it might be sooner rather than later. If there's anything that you could give me that would be useful dealing with them? Any locations that might be worth knowing or anything specific to watch out for. We don't have much to go on since Julian remembers nothing. If there's anything you can think of, let me know, all right?"

"All right," Justin chimed back and offered his hands to Rhys. The jump from here to there was bound to start feeling easier after they'd done it many enough times. Rhys braced himself.

No.

It was not at all better, but at least it didn't take very long.

"Yeah, so I ran across some dreams where I was signing with Julian." Justin smirked. "It used to drive her bonkers not to know what we were chatting about." His smirk turned into a laugh. "To think I'd completely forgotten that, seems so odd, but here we are. I wonder if he would remember if I contacted him in his sleep somehow. I'll have to check if I have any dreams where we do that. If he can, I wonder why he hasn't tried to contact me... Oh, that's right, you said he doesn't remember? At all? It's all those wipes. I don't think they meant to take everything, but I suppose it was bound to happen. Ah, sorry, this must be confusing for you? I'm rambling. I have a hard time keeping my thoughts in order these days. I have a feeling I've been dismantled and put back together a few too many times, and I come undone from time to time. If that happens, just ignore me. I usually recover after a while." Justin paced around, evidently trying to manage the excessive stimuli and mounting confusion. "Right, Hosta. What can I say besides run as far as you can and don't look back? I think my brother had the right idea when he left somewhere for the summer. That was the year I passed. He left every spring after that. All I know is, he found somewhere far enough for her to not reach him. Too bad he couldn't take me with him, but I was already too poorly at the time. Well, obviously since I died. But it would have been fun to see where he went. He sent me letters though. I think Mrs Hargrave was told to confiscate them, but I did find an envelope one time, so I know he was sending them. I think you should pack up and go. If you go, take me with you! Had Julian been able to, he would have done something back then. It's probably beyond him. Maybe he did try something, and it cost him his memory? Anyway, it's complicated. Some of the dreams with him in them, later, after that soup I showed you, weren't fun." Justin paused to think, finally. "What was the question?"

For a moment, he looked extremely frustrated.

"See? I lose track of everything. It's so annoying! Do we still have time? We're not running out of time yet? I'm sorry I'm so useless."

"Not. Useless," Rhys corrected. A little difficult to follow at times, but it was understandable. "Wipes?" Rhys repeated the word to guide Justin back to the spot.

"Oh, yes, right! That's what they used to do, as a protective measure. Having to withstand the experiments was often mentally disturbing, so there was a memory wipe after. It served as a buffer between treatments. Of course, they didn't take into account the link between us, and some of it would trickle through. When it was Julian's turn, he wouldn't recall what they'd done to him, but I did, and vice versa. Or maybe that was part of the point and what they were studying? I'm a little hazy. Mostly they were supposed to protect us from the ill effects of the procedures, though. I think the reason Julian finally snapped was because of all the things they did to me. I don't remember any of it directly, just fragments from my dreams. The things I do remember seem to come and go. Do you know how frustrating that is? Rhys, if I forget Julian again, please remind me! I don't want to forget him again. He's my only family."

"I'll. Remind, you," Rhys wondered if he was supposed to also remind Justin about the rest of his family. It was a little challenging to do right now, so he figured he would do it later if he didn't remember on his own.

"Good. Was there something else I meant to say?"

"Link? Procedures?"

"Yes, the original hypothesis was that twins might share a link from birth, but to me it seemed like it was something that happened gradually because we sleep-roamed so much together. I was always hyper aware of him when we shared a bubble. We couldn't share one unless we slept right next to one another and the bubbles overlapped, so, when it occasionally disrupted her research, she would separate us. But by then I had started to be able to sense Julian from more of a distance and even when we weren't asleep. That seemed to intrigue her all the more, so she'd try different methods and drugs to study our connection." Justin sighed. "I don't even remember a time when there wasn't *something* about us she was wanting to test out. I suspect I didn't know half of it since Julian also kept missing large chunks. We started to keep track of what she did but eventually gave it up as pointless. She seemed passionate about a lot of it, but most of the experiments were unsuccessful, and she'd often complain about funding. I don't know much about that side of it. Do you want to watch some more dreams? I have some that are harmless!"

Justin rejoicing over his less horrible dreams made Rhys want to share all his best childhood bits. Not that he had an abundance, but compared to Justin, there were many, and they were exponentially more fun than a bowl of soup.

"Julian?" Rhys requested, expecting Justin to tell more about Julian, forgetting that he'd just suggested dreams.

"I suppose... Hold on." Justin grabbed Rhys along before he could clarify what he'd wanted.

Chapter 22

It was a dream about Julian being allowed to visit Justin overnight back when they had been around ten. This did not seem like a common occurrence. There was no further context or explanation, but, from what Rhys could gather from the surroundings, it seemed that Justin's health wasn't stable, be it a medical condition or something caused by what they'd done to him. He was being closely monitored and in isolation save for this one instance of being allowed a visitor.

There was a lot of signing, but much of it was non-standard private signs that they'd made up themselves. Rhys had some sense of what was being said, but it was probably because he could feel how Justin was responding to what Julian was saying. The two of them shared a joke, and Rhys laughed, even if he wasn't sure what the punchline was. He just knew it had been funny.

The mood was light all the way up until someone entered the room to interrupt them. It was no one Rhys recognised, but he was angry. The cause of the argument was something that had happened before, so Rhys couldn't follow what was happening. All he knew was that Julian was defending Justin and bit the man in a surprisingly raw and childish move, even for a ten-year-old.

The man struck Julian across the chest, hard enough for Julian to fall on the floor. Rhys could feel Justin's anger as he launched at the man. The pain took Rhys by surprise. There hadn't been any before Justin had tried to move. Before it could go on for longer, Justin abandoned the dream and pulled Rhys out.

"Sorry, sorry. I forgot about that! Would have cut it short sooner, but I mixed this up with the other one. We were signing in this one too. Did you see? Look." Justin showed Rhys some of their secret signs. "This is a warning, could be useful! And these are 'watch', 'OK', 'wait', 'leave' and this one is both our greeting and our farewell. These were probably the ones we used the most. Could be useful for us too if she starts listening in again. I can show you the warning and you know not to speak." Justin seemed pleased.

"Listening in?" Rhys asked, hoping for clarification.

"She has a machine. Don't worry. I don't think she can enter your space whenever she wants. She'd need to calibrate it. I, on the other hand, am not so lucky. She's got so much data on me she probably knows my signature by heart. Oh, also, if I come over to your side, there's a chance the machine may pick up the signal, so it's better to play it safe. It's why I didn't want to risk chatting with you before. Don't ask me over if you've got something private or secret going on unless we're far, far away from here!"

"How far?" Rhys signed.

"I'm not sure. At least away from the Schades. I can't tell where else they keep those machines these days, but they have some in Firth. Maybe Grymswich, Copseton and Grovestead, too."

"Can. They find— you?" Rhys asked.

"They can find my signature here, but they can't trace the remains. If they turn on a machine and I'm within range, it picks up my signal. Nothing I can do. They still sometimes use me for things. Spy on people mostly. The signal isn't as good anymore, but I suppose they're getting something since they keep turning it on from time to time. I wish they'd leave me alone already."

It was a relief that the remains were untraceable, but it also meant Hosta was unlikely to dispose of them as long as their equipment was still working. If Justin's perception of the outside world was limited, there was a chance they were looking for a replacement before they got rid of him. Unless of course they already had one.

"Do, they, know. I'm, here?" Rhys asked.

"I suppose it's possible, but the machine hasn't been on at the same time as I've talked to you. Sometimes it's on, and I have to wait until they turn it off, or, if it's important, I go to subject one and he seems to know to relay the message to you. Oooh, except for when you came to get my remains. The machine was on then, but I had to respond to let you know I was there. It's possible they got a reading out of that, but it could be interpreted as random interference or not enough data to process. I wouldn't be too worried about it, but I guess it doesn't hurt to be careful."

So, good news and bad news. They were already in shady territory with Quin having pilfered Justin's folder, but it would be much worse if Hosta discovered Rhys could sleep-roam. That would make him a prime target to replace Justin.

Moving to Agnes Point seemed more and more inviting, even if that, too, meant having to live his life in isolation. So long as Hosta was out there, Rhys would be in danger of being discovered. And who was this 'subject one' Justin had mentioned? Vincent—?

"Do you suppose we could visit Julian even if he can't sleep-roam?" Justin interrupted Rhys's thoughts. "He's asleep right now, if my senses aren't completely failing me. He feels like he's right there if I just reach over a bit... I don't have very much to lose, do I? I mean, if it goes wrong somehow, and I get lost in the void..."

Rhys could understand why Justin was so eager, but since Julian couldn't remember him, even if it worked, it could turn out less than ideal. Justin might pop over just fine, but if the two of them didn't get along and Justin was stuck there, things could quickly go from bad to worse. Moreover, there might be no one on that side if Julian didn't sleep-roam. Or even worse, Justin might not even reach the other side and would indeed get lost in the void. It didn't seem like a good idea.

"I'm going to try!" Justin declared.

Rhys tried to stop him, but there wasn't much he could do. It occurred to him that his own safety might also be at stake since he had no idea what would happen if he stayed here and Justin left. This wasn't where Rhys was supposed to be. Did this place even exist if Justin wasn't here?

If going through the void was unpleasant being towed through by Justin, it was most certainly not enjoyable when Rhys was sucked in by whatever forces governed this realm.

Thankfully, he soon found himself back where belonged, and while learning this tidbit did ease his mind about going back and forth, his mind was not at ease for long.

Had Justin made it through all right? If this was the end of their friendship, Rhys was grossly under prepared. He knew Justin's remains weren't going to house him forever, but to lose him over this seemed like a cruel joke. Rhys couldn't even wake up to go wake Julian. Then again, what would happen if Julian woke up with Justin still roaming in his bubble? Would Justin return where he belonged like Rhys, or did that not work since he was dead? What if there was nothing to return to, for him?

Rhys wasn't sure how to even enter the void without Justin's hands guiding him in, so all he could do was watch if Julian seemed any different. He realised it was impossible to tell from here. Julian looked to be asleep as normal. Time slowed down to a crawl as he waited.

"Justin, you piece of—"

"Where did you go?" Justin's hands appeared, and he signed his question.

"I was sucked back in here when you left. Don't do stuff like that! You could get hurt or I could get hurt, or…"

"I'm dead," Justin signed.

"It still matters to me!" Rhys took Justin by the wrists and pulled him all the way in. Justin's form on this side was something between himself and his remains—not a pretty sight.

It was gross, but not as bad as Rhys had expected; despite being squeamish, he didn't feel like anything was about to resurface.

"How did it go, did you find anything?" Rhys asked.

"Nothing," Justin signed. His body language suggested he hadn't expected to be pulled all the way through, and he was testing his limbs. Then he shook his hands in a way that suggested he was grossed out.

"Can't find Julian," he signed. "I'm dead," he repeated.

"You suppose I could do it if I tried, is that it? Maybe you'd like me to pull you over?" Rhys asked. Justin hopped a few times excitedly and did an exaggerated praying gesture.

"Look, I don't think it's a good idea. He doesn't remember you. The very least we should do is warn him first. How far did you get? Does it seem like there's even something to go to? How do I go through into the void without you having to pull me in?"

Rhys wasn't eager but wondered if it was something he was morally obliged to try. They were twin brothers, and, though the circumstances weren't great, if it was possible, he felt they deserved to at least meet each other 'in person' again.

"I, pull, in. You find," Justin suggested.

"I need to know how to get back too. I don't want to have to wait until Julian wakes up to see if I'm pulled back. And what if I wake up first? What happens then?"

"Don't, wake up." Justin shrugged.

"I can't decide that!"

"Can't, wake up," Justin corrected.

"Oh, so you think I won't wake up if I'm not here, or?"

"Yes," Justin signed.

"So, if I don't get sucked back in here, I won't ever wake up?" That didn't sound good.

"You, get sucked back in here. You. Not. Dead."

"And here I thought I might get permanently lost in the void if I wasn't careful, and now you're telling me I'll just get sucked back here if something goes wrong?"

"Yes and no," Justin signed. "Mostly yes. Rarely no."

"But it's possible. Is that what this means?" Rhys repeated the signs, a little hazy on the meaning.

"Yes." Justin responded. "Have to wait until, pulled back." He added the sign for 'long'. "Not. Good."

Certainly the thought of having to wait 'long' in the void sounded 'Not. Good' to Rhys, but it was better than being lost for good.

"So, it should be relatively safe to take a look, then? Provided that this 'long' is not hours or days or more."

"Could, be, days. Can't, know, in here." Justin shrugged again.

"I'd like to get some rest before three, four o'clock at the latest, but I believe there's still some hours until then. Maybe I can rest over there if it comes to that. I'd like to try this, but I might not be able to pull you over yet tonight."

Rhys was admittedly intrigued by what he might find if it turned out Julian was capable of sleep-roaming and had his own space dreamside. In any case, it was bad enough that Rhys barged in there unannounced, but dragging a corpse along seemed even worse.

"I'll come pick you up if I can. If it doesn't work out, and I have to wait until morning, I'll take you along the next time. That is, if Julian agrees to it. Does that sound fair?"

"Yes," Justin signed. His shoulders slumped, and he looked unhappy about it. It was difficult to tell since his features were stiff and partially mummified, but the pose was what gave it away.

"All right, what do I do? Can you do it slowly? I'll try to pick it up. Maybe I can do it on my own..." Rhys wasn't optimistic.

Justin sunk into nothingness, slowly but as if effortlessly. Once he was almost all the way gone, Rhys took his hand and was pulled in softly.

The moment Justin let go was what Rhys had dreaded the most. There seemed to be absolutely nothing around him, and somehow he was supposed to navigate and find Julian.

He knew it shouldn't have mattered whether he could breathe here or not—he was safe, asleep in his bed with plenty of air around him—but the darkness and the sensation of pressure encompassing him certainly made him feel like he was suffocating.

What if all it took for him to stop breathing was the belief he couldn't breathe where he was? Was he really going to die if he thought he died here?

He tried to concentrate on Julian. He'd made a mental note of Julian's location, but he now had to make a literal blind estimate. This had been a terrible idea.

CHAPTER 23

Rhys tumbled in with quite the force. He had to take a moment to calm down from the fright, but slow and steady breathing helped, as well as knowing he hadn't actually died in the void.

Once he'd caught his breath, he looked around himself. Justin and Julian's spaces were unsurprisingly similar in atmosphere, but Julian's had a considerably heavier feel to it. The air was thicker here, almost stuffy, though not entirely unpleasant. To Rhys's surprise, all of him had appeared as soon as he'd entered, and thus, he didn't have to spend any extra time trying to make himself visible—another difference between Justin and Julian, or perhaps between someone who was dead and someone still alive?

Rhys spotted Julian in the middle, lying on the ground. A middle suggested there were edges, and indeed the space was like a room-sized bubble that had formed where Julian was sleeping in the real world. Was this the bubble that Justin and Vincent had spoken about?

Rhys had never noticed any edges to his dreamside, so either there were none, they were too far for him to see or they moved along with him. Perhaps these bubbles came in different sizes, and he had got lucky with his? It had never occurred to him that there could be restrictions to how far a person could go, but when he tried to move his hand further than Julian's bubble extended, he was met with vague resistance, even if he couldn't see exactly where the border was.

Julian lay unnaturally motionless, as if encapsulated in or bound by something. Something was definitely amiss here, and it must have prevented him from sleep-roaming when he was presumably capable of it.

Rhys knelt down.

From close up, it was easier to see Julian's features obscured by a mask of some semi-opaque substance. His skin felt cold and wet to touch, though when Rhys rubbed his fingers together, they remained dry. Maybe removing this would help Julian regain awareness?

When he wiped Julian's cheek with a thumb, a fragile film came loose from the corner of his forehead. Rhys pulled it aside, carefully teasing off lace-like sheets until the strange gunk was mostly removed, and he could finally see Julian's features properly.

Julian looked surprisingly youthful, even innocent.

Rhys had grown so used to this face always being at the verge of a scowl that seeing him genuinely calm was like looking at a whole different person. There was no telling how he would react to someone encroaching on his privacy without any prior warning or consultation. Rhys hesitated to rouse him.

He sat in silence. The bubble felt secluded and calm, like in this moment he and Julian were the only people existing in the universe. Once this sense of peace had slowly eased Rhys's nerves, he was ready to give it a try.

Julian was asleep as usual, unaware of anything around him. He'd had a short dream that he wouldn't remember in the morning and was now in deep sleep for the second time. It was at the cusp of his next dream sequence that something interrupted him, and he thought he'd woken up.

"Rhys? What is it? Can't sleep?" He was too tired to open his eyes. He felt heavy, and it took him a moment to shake off the sensation that his body was still asleep, but he eventually sat up as he always did.

"Everything all right? Did you need something?" Julian turned to look. The perspective was off. "Why am I on the floor?" Rhys was sitting next to him.

"You. Did. Something!" Rhys sounded strange but looked excited.

"What? I'm not awake? Is this a dream?" Julian looked around himself. He could make out the bedroom, but he was slightly offset and not where his body was. Peculiar. He glanced at Rhys again. Rhys looked like he always did in Julian's dreams. Fascinating. "So, I'm still dreaming?"

"Not, dreaming, not awake," Rhys said. He signed some letters.

"Justin? Oh, right, the supposed twin brother I have in the box next to my desk. What about him?" He could see where it was when he looked. Funny how detailed this dream was, and his memory, even though he hadn't made a point to memorise.

"Yes," Rhys signed. "Him. Come here. OK?" Rhys wasn't making much sense. This was apparently one of those dreams where he knew he was dreaming. A lucid dream. He didn't have them often, but they were usually pleasant. Maybe this would be as fun as some of the others...

"You, all right?" Rhys leaned closer to look at him.

"I'm fine. You're here. This seems like a good dream." Julian promptly reached forward and kissed Rhys. It felt very real. Hopefully that didn't mean he was about to wake up.

Rhys tried to back away in visible dismay. Julian grabbed him by the arm before he could get too far.

"Come here." He pulled Rhys closer and fell back to lie down with the boy on top of him.

"Not. A dream!" Rhys said, but it wasn't even his voice.

"I don't want to wake up yet. Let me sleep," Julian whined.

Rhys frowned.

"I want you to kiss me, Rhys."

Rhys's frown deepened.

This was a dream, but there was always a hint of realism in his dreams, and Rhys had always seemed to appreciate someone else taking the initiative.

Julian was usually strict about respecting people's boundaries, but the undeniable upside to dreaming was that there would be no consequences for his selfishness if he made an exception and hurried things along a little to save time. He rolled over to pin Rhys down and kissed him. Rhys did fight back a little, but that just made it more interesting.

"I want you," Julian confessed. He'd wanted to do this for so long, it felt only right he'd at least be able to have a taste of it in his dreams. He gave Rhys another, slightly more tender and tentative kiss to see if he was still resisting.

Thankfully, not as much. It was soft and warm. How did it feel so real? Julian opened his eyes and watched Rhys's face close up. The amount of detail was remarkable. Rhys was glaring at him intently.

"What is it?"

"Not. Dreaming," Rhys said, but because it sounded like Julian's own voice, there was no way this could be real. Julian tried to concentrate. Was he missing something?

"Yesterday. Spoke of S-L-E-E-P-R-O-A-M-I-N-G." Rhys signed.

Having only just come out of deep sleep, Julian had a poor grasp of anything outside of the present moment, but this did ring a distant tiny little bell. It was enough to make Julian doubt his judgement.

"Sleep-roaming? I'm not following you. Can you speak up?"

"You. Sleep roaming. NOT. A DREAM," Rhys explained firmly.

"What?" Julian made more of an effort to think. "I don't understand…"

"Oh, for fuck's sake, Julian, you're sleep-roaming! You're doing a poor job of it, but you're doing it nonetheless. You're asleep but you're not dreaming, do I need to spell it out for you?!"

"Finally, you sound like yourself. What was with the charades?"

"Well, I didn't realise it's not the same as with Justin! I was this close," Rhys pressed his fingers tightly against each other, "to kicking you in the fucking groin, but since I was the one to hop into your space unannounced, I'm letting it slide."

"Ah, this sucks," Julian complained out loud. Whatever this state was that he was in, he had trouble keeping his inner and outer voices separate. "I was sure I was having one of those lucid dreams I often have, and now you're telling me I'm roaming? What? This is so frustrating! Also, what's wrong with me? Why am I saying this out loud like I have no filter? What if I say something I meant to stay *private?* You'll know of this tomorrow? Oh, shit!" Julian despaired. "How do I turn this off?"

"I don't know. The same way always do? You don't say it out loud." Rhys shrugged.

"It's not working. You're not supposed to be here to hear all this!" He could keep some of the thoughts in, but he wasn't sure how. More of it bubbled out, and it became tougher by the minute.

"I suppose you'll get the hang of it with practice. This does remind me of your brother, though. He talks a lot, too." Rhys chuckled.

"You're amused? Stop that. It's not funny." While Julian started to grasp the situation better, his output problem was only getting worse.

"Are you always this talkative inside your head?" Rhys was doing a lousy job hiding his amusement.

"I don't know, isn't this a normal amount? Doesn't everyone think all the time? Now you've made me self-conscious about it. I don't like this. It's only a matter of time before I say something *compromising.* I definitely do not want to think *those* thoughts with you here. Some things are supposed to be private." Julian felt cold sweat forming at the back of his neck. "Can you leave? Is this a nightmare?"

"Calm down. I don't think there's much you can say that's *that* bad." Rhys seemed sceptical. The fool. Julian bit his forearm to gag himself. This, again, seemed to amuse Rhys. "That seems to work. Do you still want me to leave? I thought a moment ago you said you wanted me?" He grinned.

"You being such an asshole tells me this is definitely not a dream. You're usually much nicer—" Julian bit his arm again.

"Oh, you dream about me a lot? Interesting."

"I, I... of course I do!" Julian felt his cheeks warm. He hadn't meant to be discussing this, but it wouldn't hurt to make that clear while he was already flustered. At least, it didn't hurt much. He was biting on his arm a touch too forcefully. Rhys seemed to be inspecting and trying something.

"Hmm, there's probably an edge here, but it's hazy, and I can't find where or how to get through it. Looks like I'm stuck here."

"What? Indefinitely?!"

"No, no, I don't think. I presume I'll be sucked back once you wake up. That's what happened with Justin."

"What? He's dead. How does a dead person wake up? That makes no sense."

"No, he left briefly into the void. You waking up should work the same. Or me, but we were wondering if it's possible for me to wake me up when I'm in here. We should test that later." Rhys sat down and made himself comfortable.

"OK, so how do I wake up? No, wait, you said you can't do that. We just wait? For how long? Until morning? What time is it?" Julian looked around for a clock. The pocket watch he'd left on his nightstand showed time, but it looked too obscure to tell.

"It's half past one." This seemed no problem for Rhys.

"That's not good, there's still hours to go! How do I turn this off? I assume I can sleep in here somehow or dream? Are you going to see that? That could be disastrous!"

"Justin had to knowingly pull me with him to show his dreams. I probably won't see your dreams without you wanting me to. Maybe."

"That doesn't exactly assure me. Why did you barge in like this? Didn't you have anything better to do with your time? Perhaps discuss something with Justin? It's not like we have all the time in the world to figure things out. Damn it, can't a man have his sex dreams in peace—" Shit, it was much too tricky to catch himself before he said something he didn't mean to. It was as if he were missing a stopcock where there should have been one.

Rhys was smirking, but at least he didn't seem upset about the kiss anymore.

"So, you're not really worried about wasting time, you're cross with me for interrupting your fun? I like this added layer of honesty. We should do this more often."

"Shit, Rhys. No! You can't march in here whenever you want. I haven't felt this exposed since... since..." He felt like there was something there he was supposed to remember. "It's not there. It's missing again. Not again. I'm so tired of this shit." He bit his lip. His words did wipe Rhys's smirk off his face.

"I'm sorry. I shouldn't laugh. The contrast between you awake and you asleep is just so intriguing. You seem to be even more scatter-brained than Justin, if that's possible. Don't worry, I'll try to be as discreet as I can and ignore the funny bits. You're not yourself here. I'll take that into account." Rhys patted Julian's shoulder.

"Is that meant to be comforting?" Julian groaned. "I mean, I appreciate the gesture, but this has got to be a nightmare. I have too many things I want to keep to myself. The moment something crosses my mind, it's already out there. This can't be how it's supposed to be. There's something wrong with me. Why am I like this?" Julian glanced at his forearm before he bit it again. Something had caught his eye. "What's this...?" He showed Rhys his arm. "Why does it look like that? I didn't bite down that hard." His arm was practically shredded where he'd bitten it, but the marks looked old. "Is this normal, does this happen?"

"I haven't seen it before." Rhys examined Julian's arm. "I don't look the same in my dream as I do awake, but I don't think I have injuries."

"Is it something I should remember? There's always something missing. Have I been here before, done this before? That would make sense. Is the other one the same?" He looked at the other arm, and it had similar marks, though not quite as bad. "Right. I instinctively prefer this side, but I've evidently also used the other one. Who was in here with me then? Why? Why can't I shut up?" Julian tried to make sense of it. "It's intentional...?"

"Is it someone from Hosta?" Rhys suggested.

"Someone's been in here and made a mess. This is not how it's supposed to be!" Julian stood up. He was suddenly overcome by a surge of anger.

There was no filter for that either; it poured out unrestricted. "Shit! I know this. This is not good. Stand back, Rhys. Stay back, I can't—"

He could feel the air grow thick and hot. The space around him started to sizzle and crackle. It reflected the boiling fury inside of him, and there was nothing to hold it back. The intense urge to break everything resurfaced along with the anger.

"I want to ruin everything. I need to destroy everything..."

The reality beyond his dream looked distorted as everything on this side—including what the eye could not see—was cracking and crumbling. He knew he'd done this before, many times, to shield himself from something.

For a moment, he felt clarity. He wanted absolutely everyone and everything to die, as retribution. He wanted to have it all end right now. He bit his arm. He needed to restrain himself, but the urges were stronger here. He couldn't even remember why he was so angry, but it felt intensely justified.

The voice in his head was saying she'd meant to fix this, but it wasn't something she could fix. It was too late for that. Too late to save him, too late to save either of them. It was all broken and too damaged. There was no choice but to seal it away.

"Shut up, you can't fix this!" Julian bellowed. "It's too late!" His words boomed from everywhere at once.

"Julian! JULIAN!" Rhys's voice only barely carried through.

"You're not supposed to be here, you need to leave," Julian thought out loud.

"I can't leave. You need to calm down."

"I don't want to!"

"Please Julian, it's getting painful..."

"I won't, I need this. She doesn't care! She needs to die! I—" Julian bit his arm in desperation. This was bad. He tried to tell himself to calm down, but this always ran its course all the way to the end.

The end? When? Rhys? Rhys was in here. What would happen to Rhys? He didn't want Rhys to die, surely? What was he doing? What was this? He fell into a heap and stared at what was underneath him. Where was this? The distraction helped a little.

CHAPTER 24

"Where am I? Who am I? Why am I like this? Who is she? I know her. I swear I know her." Julian looked confused.

"Shh, shh, she's not here," Rhys soothed him.

"She's not here," Julian repeated until he started to calm down. "I'm sorry, are you hurt?" He looked up to check on Rhys.

"No. I don't know if you can even hurt me here. It was momentarily painful, but that's just a sensation. I'm sleeping in my bed. Safe. Don't worry." This wasn't strictly true, but he wanted Julian to calm down.

"Good. I can still feel something simmering, but if I breathe steadily and concentrate on you, it seems to be waning. Only, I'm still narrating everything out loud. This is so frustrating."

"What the hell was that, Julian?" Rhys asked carefully.

"I don't know what to tell you. It happens a lot when I'm awake, though it's not that bad. I'm broken. It builds up out of nowhere, and I have to fight to not let it out. Did Justin say something? Does he know what happened?"

"He remembers some things, but there are gaps. He said he remembered what they did to you, but I don't know the details. I think I can pull him in here, and you can ask him yourself. Are you sure you're all right? That looked harsh." Rhys checked the arm Julian had been gnawing. The marks looked much less mysterious. It was more of a surprise he still had arms left.

"I'm fine. Just embarrassed and ashamed of myself. I keep putting you in danger."

"What do you mean? I put myself in danger. It's not your fault I'm here."

"I almost strangled you to death."

"No, you didn't. That was Justin. He wanted to help. You've done nothing wrong."

"What? I don't understand. I'm pretty sure that was me."

"No, you let go early. I saw you."

"I'm not entirely convinced, but that's a relief. I keep messing up. I always mess up. I try not to, but it keeps happening. There's something wrong with me." He certainly sounded like he was stuck in a loop.

"Is that what you keep telling yourself?"

"You stopped breathing. If that was Justin, then it's possible to hurt you when you're in here. It's too dangerous. As soon as you're out, don't come back. I don't want to hurt you." Julian bit his lip but added before he could stop himself, "I also don't want you to know my secrets. Damn it."

"Now I'm curious." What a shame Rhys couldn't in good conscience pry them out of Julian. "But we need to figure out how to fix this before your arms fall off. I want you to tell me things because you want to tell me. Not like this. Oh, and I think you need to learn to navigate your dreams. I get the feeling you were at Hosta for a very long time. You might hold information that could give us everything. The location, who is responsible, what their weaknesses are, all of it. Maybe Justin can help you. Maybe you can trust him? He's dead, and he's your brother, so it's not like he can or would want to tell anyone."

"He can tell you," Julian replied drily.

"He probably won't if I don't go over to his side. It's much more difficult to communicate with him when he visits."

"Oh?"

"I don't know why. Maybe because he's dead?" Rhys hadn't really thought about it much.

"Could be because his mouth was sewn shut," Julian pointed out.

"What?" Rhys cringed from the thought.

"It's less disturbing sewn shut, trust me."

"I don't want to know," Rhys decided. "Should I pull him in? He wants to see you."

"Fine. Might as well deal with it right now," Julian said.

"**I**f he comes close enough, maybe I'll be able to see through and grab him..." Rhys was peering at something presumably downstairs, perhaps the box of remains. Julian was getting annoyed of having to bite his arm.

"If you manage to get through, you can leave while you're at it, right?"

"You're really in that much of a hurry to get rid of me? I let you kiss me three times!" Rhys held up three fingers to emphasise the point. "If there's any way I can guide Justin in, he can help me out. But I'm not sure this is any easier than trying to find a way into the void myself."

"What is the void, anyway? Is it that dark space just beyond?" Julian asked.

"You can see it? Really?" Rhys looked incredulous.

Julian stretched out his free hand, and it vanished out of sight. "Uh, it's cold."

"You've been able to see it all this time? I don't know whether to laugh or cry." Rhys hurried over to Julian and slid his fingers through where Julian's hand disappeared.

"Do you need me to do something?" Julian watched Rhys examine the cut-off point. His hand was starting to tingle. "I need to take it out for a bit." He pulled it out and shook it a little before pushing it back in.

"How do you do that? You make it look so easy!" Rhys seemed impressed. "Let's do this."

The boy dove in headfirst. It looked like he was diving into a sack of potatoes. Out of instinct, Julian took a hold of Rhys's wrist to keep him from fully being swallowed into the void. This left him with nothing to bite on, so he both narrated the whole affair and described his frustration over having to do this shit when he could have been having one of his usual dreams.

Rhys's upper body popped back in just as Julian was commenting on how sleep-roaming could have been a useful skill, had he not been so damaged. It seemed to take some effort, but the boy managed to tug Justin into view.

Julian hadn't expected whatever that thing was, and, evidently, neither had Rhys.

"What on earth...?"

"Is that Justin?" It looked more like an animal. The hunched, gaunt figure grew hair all over its body and withdrew into a ball. "What the hell did you pull in?"

"I don't know... It looked like Justin to me. Now I'm not so sure."

The thing morphed into a humanoid shape right under their eyes. As soon as it had formed hands, it was signing.

"Hello! I'm so happy. I heard from Rhys here that you've lost your memory, so maybe you don't remember. I'm Justin. It's been a while!"

"What's he saying? It's a bit too fast for me," Rhys said. "It's Justin though, right? Why does he look like that over here?"

"It was our game. Came in handy too, as a disguise. I thought maybe you might remember if I came in like old times," Justin signed.

"I don't remember." Not only could he not remember, but he was also forced to repeat the fact over and over again.

"I'll help you. There are bound to be dreams with me in them. I can pull you over to my side and show you mine, too. We'll figure it out." Justin's hands were quick but easy to follow. Julian had known sign language for at least the eleven years that he could remember, but it had never felt natural to him. This was fluid and made much more sense.

"More importantly, I need to know why I'm broken. I vocalise every thought, and I can't turn it off. Do you know why? Can I do something?"

Julian asked. Justin paused to think. While he was thinking, he first turned into a more regular-looking human boy then grew up somewhat to mirror Julian.

"Can't be helped, unfortunately. It was to ease calibration, she said. The signal is much stronger this way, she said. I think she was getting tired of us withholding things from her, so she made adjustments so we no longer could. How are the arms? I see you're still chewing them." Justin grabbed Julian's arm to check. "You've been holding back successfully? Did something already happen? I was hoping Rhys would guide me in before anything happened."

"What's he saying?" Rhys sounded impatient and sad to not be included in the conversation.

"He's explaining it's something that was done to me." Julian re-inserted his arm in his mouth to have at least some privacy as he tried to think.

"Maybe I should have warned Rhys, but I figured you wouldn't hurt him. He's *nice*." Justin signed a word that was something more akin to smooth than nice, but Julian could tell exactly what he meant and why he'd thought it mattered.

"It doesn't help if I can't aim my strikes." Julian needed both of his hands to sign, so he bit his lower lip hard enough that all that came out of his mouth was a vague mumble.

"Hey!" Rhys exclaimed. "That's not fair!"

"It's got worse?" Justin frowned. "Was that why she had you retire?"

"I don't know. I don't know anything," Julian was yet again forced to repeat.

"Well, the trouble started when she was testing those mood altering treatments. It wasn't rare that the tests backfired in those early stages, and they'd do frequent wipes to keep you emotionally stable. Something must have stuck regardless. At first she tried to connect you to the machine, but you were too unruly, skewed the data and gave her trouble, so she switched to me. I'm glad it was me and not you. It saved you from this."

"It killed you?"

"She killed me. I think it was unintentional, but when she realised it was happening, she made use of me. She's still making use of me, listening in on people."

"Right now?"

"No. Maybe once or twice a week. She's spying on other, more important people."

"What's she after?"

"Ultimately more funding, I guess. That's what she's always been after, so she can keep doing what she's doing."

"She's doing it for the sake of doing it? Is she a sadist?"

"I don't know. The research always comes first. That's all she ever cared about." Justin seemed bitter about it.

"How do we stop her?" Julian asked.

"I doubt we can, but she's bound to retire eventually. We can only hope she hasn't found anyone to take over after her. The problem is that it's become a lucrative business, and she's too far in it to stop. She might step aside, but we don't know what legacy she'll leave."

"I'm fine now, but before you came in, I had a moment when I was sure I wanted to kill her. I don't even remember her, but I wanted to. What does that say about her, or me for that matter?" Julian signed and did his lip trick to keep it from Rhys. He didn't need more audience for his murderous tendencies. Rhys huffed.

"Sounds about right to me. I can relate. But I'm fairly sure you would have already done it if you could have," Justin signed.

"How can you be so sure about that?"

"I know you."

"Well, great," Julian said out loud. "It seems everybody but me claims to know me. Is that fair? I don't think so. Why can't any of you give me a proper explanation? Frankly, that seems like such vague bullshit. What is it about me that makes you believe this? What makes you think I haven't changed?"

"You're about to throw a fit," Justin interrupted him. "Want help?"

"What? No. Shut up. Don't tell me what I'm going to do. I don't even know what I'm going to do myself!"

"Yes, but it's obvious. I can sense it in the air, and it's so obvious even Rhys is looking alarmed." Justin's signing became softer but more deliberate. Julian glanced at Rhys, who was indeed looking a little pale.

"Well, shit! It feels so uncomfortable, I need to let it out!" The burning sensation was back. He distinctly wanted to bash something.

"All right, I'll help you. Hold on." Justin took him by the hand. "Hold it in, and let me know when you're ready to burst."

"What's happening?" Rhys asked warily.

"Stay clear," Julian snarled between his teeth. The air around them started to flicker. "Now." On Julian's mark, Justin pulled them both into the void.

J ulian woke up in a state of panic. Where was Rhys, was he all right?

After what had seemed like ages in the void, Julian had returned to where he'd come from, alone with neither Rhys nor Justin anywhere to be seen. After all that, he would have thought that waking up would be a relief, but he couldn't enjoy it before making sure Rhys was fine.

He scrambled up from his bed and leapt into the lounge.

"Rhys? Are you all right, Rhys? Shit, wake up. Rhys!" He shook the boy much more forcibly than what he usually did when he needed to wake him up.

"I'm fine, I'm fine," Rhys said before even opening his eyes. "I got back fine. Stop shaking me."

"That was scary..." Julian steadied his breathing, still struggling with the aftermath of his scare.

"Too bad." Rhys leaned over the backrest of the sofa to check the clock on the wall. "There would have been plenty of time left. Maybe I can get back to sleep."

"I'm never going back again, holy shit." Julian was right at the brink of breathing himself dizzy.

"You need to sleep sometime."

"Not sober I won't..." The right dose was sure to render him incomprehensible no matter where, and he would scarcely even have an idea where he was. Nor would anyone understand him if he had to think everything out loud. Hopefully. Maybe. "What a horrible nightmare."

"That's an overstatement. I thought it went better than expected. I just wish you would have let me in on the conversation."

"Well, it was cut short because of my temper. I messed up again—"

Rhys shushed him. Julian was not speaking that loudly, so this was peculiar enough to merit a pause.

"Stop that. You can go back in whenever you want, and we can arrange another opportunity. You didn't mess up anything. It's a minor hiccup," Rhys whispered.

"Twice," Julian pointed out.

"We just need to figure out how to not piss you off in there."

"I don't see how that's even possible. You saw how little it took."

"Is everyone all right? What's the emergency?" Quin rubbed his eyes. He'd been sleeping on a mattress in a corner of the lounge. "You do realise it's three in the morning?" He looked up, unimpressed and irritated.

"Go back to sleep. It's fine," Rhys told him. "Sorry we woke you up."

"Was it at least worth the ruckus?" Quin eyed the both of them, suspicious. Said ruckus was yet to wake Dr Vesper asleep in the armchair, so it couldn't have been that loud.

"We'll tell you in the morning," Rhys promised. Quin waved a hand at them and made himself comfortable facing the other way.

Julian had mostly calmed down.

"It's snowing," he realised.

Rhys turned to look at the window but said nothing.

Aurora had slept most of the night in an armchair in the lounge, so she woke up with a crick in her neck. She massaged it gently while helping herself to some tea. The house was quiet.

Mr Quin lay fast asleep on his mattress, and Vincent's brother was still asleep on the sofa. The clock indicated it was quarter to eight. No wonder then that everyone else was asleep after yesterday's search effort.

Aurora left her teacup on the dining room table and went to check on Vincent. She'd given him his last dose around four in the morning, so he had probably already woken up, but considering his condition, he was unlikely to have left his bed yet.

When she saw the room was empty, and there were no signs of Vincent, Ren, the cat box or their luggage, Aurora's heart sank.

Not again.

This time she had a slightly better understanding of what she'd done wrong, but it still felt unfair. She'd never meant to come between them or insert herself into their family as a self-appointed authority figure. She had no intention of playing a mother. She'd just wanted to guard their precious relationship and make sure there were no unfortunate accidents...

Ah, she could try to defend herself to the moon and back, but the truth was, she'd been cocky assuming she knew what was best for Ren. That was not up to her to decide. And now they'd disappeared and taken Sir Swifty with them without so much as letting her pet him goodbye.

Tears welled in her eyes. Not again. Hadn't she sworn not to get attached? Damn it! She had been doing fine on her own. She didn't need him! It was as if she hadn't learnt anything from the last time.

Angered by her own stupidity, she started packing the equipment. She needed to send it all back to Grovestead and resume her life here. She'd been derailed for way too long when she should have been doing important research at her new job. Guardian help her if she'd blown that opportunity by chasing after a man like a blasted fool!

Twice the fool. Twice! Her tears left blotches where they landed as she packed, but she didn't bother wiping them. There would be no third time, she swore. There was no bloody way she would make this mistake again.

D r Vesper's apartment at the Sleepy Leighs had been modest. She'd assumed she'd have to find a new apartment herself once she got to Schadesborough, but evidently the company had done it all for her as part of her pay. Because the agreed sum was already generous and she was unfamiliar with the neighbourhood, Dr Vesper hadn't expected the luxury she was now tossed into.

She arrived at what was referred to as the Ear of the City: an affluent neighbourhood inhabited by families that had emigrated from the Northern regions of the continent.

They had brought their eccentric building styles along with them, but the exposed tarred timber, steep roofs and pronounced eaves had been masterfully combined with a similar shape language of the prevailing stone architecture around the rest of the city, and so, the buildings meshed seamlessly with their surroundings.

The floor in the hallway was rare green streaked marble from Grymsway on the far side of the mountains. It had been paired with an ornate cedar staircase with copper details, and painted wall panelling decorated by motifs rarely seen anywhere below Lingslip.

Upstairs the house was divided into three apartments on their respective floors, each with a master suite and a spare bedroom for visitors or a maid. There was a common kitchen and laundry room underfoot and staff to take care of such needs for the residents.

Aurora circled around her apartment in a state of shock. Everything was furnished to such high standards that, had it been any better, she wouldn't have been able to tell the difference. There was a note left on the desk in the main room that would serve as her living room and study.

A sincere welcome to our research team, Dr Vesper.

I am most excited and grateful for your willingness to join our sleep research department. I have heard great things about you.

While we have certainly strived to do our utmost to make your adjustment to your new position as smooth as is within our means, there is always the possibility of human oversight. In such an instance, please grace us with your feedback and contact the building manager, Mr Chatbury, who will respond to any needs or questions you may have.

Disclosed are the details of your next assignment, the proposed schedule and the address to our research facility. I look forward to working with you.

With the Grace of the Guardian,
Hosta Aelia

Dr Vesper stared at the piece of paper for a moment before the name at the bottom finally sank in. It wasn't as if she hadn't been aware of who she was going to be working for, but the name on the research papers and books she released was always shortened to H. Aelia and the company mentioned in her contract was called Healia Healthcare.

Somewhere at the back of her mind, Dr Vesper had had a sneaking suspicion that it operated under the same umbrella as Hosta Therapy Solutions, but she hadn't firmly connected the two until this very moment.

It made sense that the person capable of authorising research on a toddler and a sinister entity possibly connected to a dead body would be linked somehow, but what broke her heart was that the scientist she'd looked up to and modelled her career after might really be conducting such damnable research even today.

If only it were a thing of the past, she thought and closed her eyes.

The Restful Meadows sleep disorder research clinic was a tall and imposing building resembling a traditional stave church, nestled at the centre of an enclosed park, much akin to a churchyard.

While it wasn't intended as a room of worship, painted on the vaulted ceilings were similar frescoes of the Guardian as in a church, and the theme continued in the tapestries, carvings and other decorations.

Dr Vesper had expected the unpleasant chemical smells she had grown to associate with the Sleepy Leighs, but a gentle scent of resinous sap and wood mixed with spiced incense greeted her instead.

The staff that passed her spoke in hushed tones, the wooden structures absorbing any harsh, sharp sounds they might have made, leaving only the subtle creaks of the floorboards underfoot. Standing at the entrance to the nave, even in such a large empty space with the ceiling somewhere nearly twenty metres up above her head, Dr Vesper was surprised by the quiet, serene atmosphere.

In all possible ways she could describe, this was more of a church than a medical facility. The only difference was that where the intricate rood screen separated the nave and the chancel, and the layman and the clergy or, as in this case, the layman and the staff, there were stairs heading down underground behind the altar.

When she had done her research into the Guardian lore, Dr Vesper had come across her employer's near-to fanatic interest in the subject, but she hadn't realised its full scale.

"Dr Vesper? Welcome to the ReM Clinic." A member of staff stood by the rood screen, at the foot of a large, gilded statue of the Guardian.

She was replenishing the fragrant blocks of incense burning amongst glowing embers in a large copper bowl attached to the top of the

Guardian's torch. When she was done, she checked Dr Vesper's credentials. "Is this your first time here? It is quite something, isn't it? This way, if you would, doctor." She guided Dr Vesper to the stairs as if leading a sacrificial lamb to slaughter.

Somewhere below, behind a pair of heavy wooden doors, the lamb discovered the research facility spanning across almost the full length and width of the Ear of the City.

CHAPTER 26

After a tour around the facility, Dr Vesper was introduced to the rest of the research team and some of the patients. She was shown to her office: an unexpectedly well-lit room with a large skylight window opening up to the back garden of a townhouse.

"Wait here, please. She will be right with you." The member of staff that had given Dr Vesper the tour excused herself. Dr Vesper was left alone in her new office, wondering whether she would be able to settle here, beautiful though it was.

A kind-looking woman in her approximate fifties peeked in through the open door. She looked much the same as in some of the pictures Dr Vesper had seen, except older.

"Dr Vesper, a pleasure to meet you at last." She offered her hand for a handshake. It was cool but not cold. Her smile seemed genuine. Nothing in her demeanour suggested she was willing to subject an infant to the torturous barrage of tests described in Vincent's file.

"My apologies for taking so long, doctor." Dr Vesper returned the smile with some trouble.

"Please, call me Hosta. I spend so much time working here and at my private lab with some of my assistants that I like to think of my team as my second family."

"In that case, please call me Vera."

"What a lovely nickname." The words were complimentary, but something about her gave off a hint of displeasure. "I hope you like your new office. Did Ms Lobelia already show you our library?"

"Yes, she did."

"Good. Could you be a dear and fetch some of these volumes for me, and meet me in room sixteen?" Hosta handed her a piece of paper with a list of almost a dozen titles of religious texts. "I would like to have a chat with you about a few things before we get started."

The selection seemed curious, but Dr Vesper nodded. A few of them she had already read before. They were among some of the earliest translations available for some of the oldest texts uncovered about the Guardian.

"I'll meet you in about a half an hour, but if I am late, feel free to peruse the texts. This may seem odd to you, but trust me, it will make sense when I explain the context." Hosta smiled and patted the side of Dr Vesper's arm. "Truly, welcome to the team!"

R oom sixteen was a small room with a table and a few chairs, a shelf, a cabinet and some equipment Dr Vesper didn't recognise despite her experience in the field of sleep science.

She skimmed through the first few volumes while waiting for Hosta. The texts were for the most part incomprehensible, as was often the case for texts as old as these. Dr Vesper hoped Hosta's words about the context were true, as she had no clue why the woman had picked these out. She fervently hoped this wasn't a test because if it was she was sure to fail.

Hosta arrived almost an hour later with apologies for being late, as well as two cups of tea. She set up one of the machines on the table and turned it on. It was similar to the diagnostic monitors Dr Vesper was used to using but different enough for her to not recognise what it was for.

Hosta had brought a stack of folders with her and spread a few sheets in front of Dr Vesper. She took the volume Dr Vesper had been reading and turned some pages until she found what she was looking for. Then she turned on the machine.

After a minute of irregular humming noises, the machine gave an output. It was a string of numbers and letters that corresponded quite closely with a paragraph of text on the page she had picked.

"What is this?" Dr Vesper asked.

"This is how we know what substances in a person's brain govern their sleep, whether they are ready to fall asleep and when they are roused from their slumber prematurely. This is how we know about hormones and neural conduit secretions."

Dr Vesper had read about these recent discoveries, but the reports had failed to explain exactly how they had been discovered. She had assumed it had been an oversight or a matter of space in the publications they were published in.

"But these texts must be centuries old..." She hadn't seen this particular volume before, but the ancient language was unmistakable. She could only barely understand it because of her grandfather's insistence that she learn it as a child.

"Our ancestors were much wiser than a lot of us give them credit for. I have compiled a key for some of the terms and structures not commonly taught by the scholars or the priests." Hosta pulled a thin notebook from under her folders. "Go through all of these. That should help you get you up to speed.

"Our ancestors were savvy when it came to the specifics of our sleep. There is a lot we can learn from them, if we know where to look. I have acquired every piece of text I have been able to uncover with any mention of the Guardian. This church and the overt guise of reverence has had its uses, but don't be fooled, we are not a religious organisation." She pointed out another matching passage. "When you're done studying these, I have some recent data I'd like you to look over. I have a feeling we might finally be getting closer to the answer."

She did not specify what she wanted an answer for, and Dr Vesper was too overwhelmed to ask her.

"I'll leave you to it," Hosta said, but Dr Vesper barely heard her, reading, instead, the pages in front of her with renewed interest.

It had never made much sense to her before, but Hosta was right: the context made it all so much clearer and easier to understand. Somewhere on these pages of previously incomprehensible religious gibberish the answer to curing Vincent's condition seemed to be waiting for her.

D r Vesper's head ached. She'd spent several days going through the material Hosta had provided and more that she'd sourced from the vast underground library herself. She'd had to divide her attention between this and the rest of her work, so her days had become exponentially more hectic than they had been before.

She was yet to find what she or Hosta were looking for, though, but one thing was for sure: the people responsible for translating and interpreting the original texts had been grossly incompetent. Not only had they missed the important information screaming at them on these pages, but they had also misunderstood the correct identity and purpose of the Guardian.

Where today, most people believed the Guardian was a deity proverbially watching over people's sleep and scholars had only just proposed the existence of several tribal guardians caring for their communities in the past, it was now clear to Dr Vesper that the Guardian was not a person or a deity at all.

It was an apparatus. It was something interacting with intricate organic machinery within the body, stored in a person's hereditary matter, or genes, as they were referred to in these texts. Its purpose seemed to be to analyse, diagnose, prevent and cure health issues related to, or through, sleep.

It was true that there had been people in charge of overseeing the proper functioning of the Guardian apparatus: individuals who had taken care of it by sleep-roaming to make sure it ran smoothly and that no one misused it.

It was even true that the Guardian was watching over the people connected to it while they slept.

But it was no naturally born entity.

It was a man-made biological machine somehow existing everywhere around the people it served, undetectable by modern technology and accessible only via sleep. The people overseeing its function had received extensive genetic modifications that had allowed them more access, but those modifications had also made them more dependent on the Guardian and more susceptible to its issues.

Accounts of natural mutation over the course of centuries of passing down these genes had been recorded causing significant degeneration to some of those connections. Not only that, but this frightening abomination had become corroded and corrupted by the centuries it had stood neglected without proper maintenance. And there was no one alive in the present day capable of servicing it.

No wonder, then, that so many people were suffering from such complex sleep-related health issues. This thing needed to either be fixed or somehow destroyed in a safe manner!

The more Dr Vesper read, the more she gravitated toward wanting to preserve and fix it. Its capabilities were tremendously beneficial for diagnostics and treatment of a whole host of common issues, and it would have been a shame to lose them entirely. Not only that, but she couldn't be sure if the thing could even be destroyed, as all-encompassing as it was, or that it could be done without causing significant harm to anyone depending on it.

She was determined, now more than ever, to learn and understand everything about the Guardian.

But there was a hitch. The resources that allowed for all of this research weren't free. And to keep the core of this information from falling into the wrong hands, collecting funds was not as straightforward as openly asking the general public to contribute.

Dr Vesper could see the challenges posed, but, because her new boss was tight-lipped about details, she couldn't evaluate whether the means were justified or a necessary evil as the only option available, or whether there could have existed a more ethical alternative. She could only guess that these details were kept under wraps to protect her and the rest of the research team from knowing the morally uncomfortable truth so that they could concentrate on their research.

"You look tired, Vera. How about taking a break?" Hosta looked up, seemingly worried. She had been going through some papers at the other end of the table from where Dr Vesper was sitting, taking notes.

"It's fine. I just haven't been sleeping well." Dr Vesper massaged her neck. "That's ironic, isn't it?"

"Do let me know early on if it becomes troublesome. We can help you with that here, you know." Hosta smiled with motherly warmth.

"Of course. But thank you, I think I'll be fine. I probably just need to turn in a little earlier tonight."

"It's already ten o'clock, dear. I fear that ship has sailed." She poured some more tea into Dr Vesper's cup. "I hope there's nothing weighing on your mind. You know you can always tell me if there is. You're almost like a daughter to me."

As accommodating and kind as she appeared, Dr Vesper could not get Rhys's warnings out of her mind. Perhaps he hadn't meant to implicate her personally but rather the Hosta Group as a whole? It was too early to tell for sure, but she seemed like a genuinely kind person.

"Thank you. I will definitely keep that in mind."

"I mean, if you are still worried about what happened earlier today..."

She was referring to an incident with one of the patients, which, truth be told, had left Dr Vesper feeling at unease for a fair while afterwards.

It hadn't been her first time dealing with a patient in distress. Hallucinations and confusion from lack of sufficient restorative sleep could often make people aggressive, even violent, if they were at all predisposed to it.

"If it ever becomes stressful enough to disturb your sleep, we do have some solutions for that. Some things aren't worth remembering, after all." She set her hand on Dr Vesper's for a moment. "Just say the word, and we will remove it for you."

CHAPTER 27

Julian was in the pharmacy serving the last of the day's customers before closing up. With nothing better to do, Rhys sat at his former consultation corner and watched the thin, light layer of snow being whisked around the streets, settling for a moment when the wind died down, but resuming each time just as restless and chaotic.

The bell rang as the door closed after the last customer. Julian turned the sign and locked the door. His hand was still on the handle when two pairs of mittens banged on the window, and he flinched.

Rhys leaned over to the side to see. There was a familiar face right on the other side of the windowpane, peering in and smiling brightly. Julian unlocked and opened the door, and the three younger siblings toppled into the pharmacy.

"Hello! How are you?" Jonathan gave Julian one of those brotherly handshakes with a quick side hug. This seemed like an improvement from last time.

Jacob helped Jasmine up after she'd tumbled down when they'd pushed themselves in. As soon as she was back on her feet, Jasmine started to sign to Julian. It was too quick and too excited for Rhys to follow, but he could tell she was happy to see Julian. Julian signed something back, but his attention was turned to the door.

"Hello, Julian." Mrs Craft smiled. She seemed nearly as reserved as before but not as outwardly nervous. "We thought we might pop by."

"Why? Did something happen?" Julian looked confused.

"It's the Eve of the Deceased tomorrow, remember?" Mrs Craft said.

"The what?" Julian looked even more confused.

"Where autumn turns to winter, and we remember loved ones recently passed," Rhys recited the common phrase and stood up to greet the Crafts. "People visit graves or set up displays, some families will have a harvest feast or host parties. Back when I was a child we used to go guising, but I don't know if that's done in the city."

He hadn't celebrated in years, but it did bring back a few good memories. It was a shame it was such bad timing; it didn't seem safe to be hosting a family get-together.

"We're here to visit your father's side of the family and your grandfather's grave, and we thought, since it worked out so well the last time, we would—" Mrs Craft was about to suggest it when Julian stopped her.

"I wish you would have contacted me first. I don't mind you coming over for Midwinter, but right now is not a good time." Julian signed it for Jasmine who looked crestfallen.

Hopefully, this business with Hosta would be solved by Midwinter somehow so that they could celebrate it in peace. Victor was working hard trying to locate the headquarters, Rhys planned to continue his nightly interviews with Justin and Julian, and Quin was presumably still following all the leads to gather more information on the Hosta Group. Maybe together they would have figured something out by then.

"Why? Can't you find time for your family? Your sister has been looking forward to this." Mrs Craft milked every last drop of leverage out of Jasmine's disappointment.

"We have some personal business. There's no time."

"We won't get in your way. You won't even notice us here," Mrs Craft promised. "Right, dear?" She turned to her husband. He nodded.

"Perhaps we can even be of assistance? What sort of business are we talking about?"

Rhys could see where all of this was heading.

"I'd rather not involve you in it—" Julian was still trying, but his parents had entered the pharmacy and closed the door. It was getting more and more difficult to be rid of them.

"It's getting cold out there," his mother was saying, "We've come all this way, so, what if we stay for the night and leave in the morning? Surely you're not too busy this evening. You were just about to close up." She let her husband take her coat.

"If it's work-related, you know I could always lend you a hand," Julian's father reminded him.

Julian glanced at Rhys, but Rhys was as much at a loss. It was getting late, but the possibility of them all being in danger did not end at supper time if Hosta had eyes on this building. There was no telling what they might do.

"I, I... I'll have to postpone it." Julian was clearly not happy about the intrusion, but he'd run out of steam trying to ward them off.

"Wonderful! I can help you with supper. Jonathan, Jacob, we know where the kitchen is." Mrs Craft ushered her younger sons to the stairs.

"Do you have something back there you need help with?" Mr Craft, who had previously spent a fair amount of time at the back of the pharmacy doing various experiments and work-related things with his son, seemed eager to do so again, possibly to keep out of the way of his wife and as far away from the kitchen as he could.

"Actually, I was going to balance the till and take inventory here," Julian told his father. He quickly glanced at Rhys, and that brief glance was packed with meaning.

It took Rhys a moment to figure out what that meaning was. When he realised, he slipped into the back room as stealthily as he could and checked up on the remains.

The box was at Julian's desk, and it was precariously half-open. It would have raised some awkward questions, considering whose remains these were, especially since the Crafts hadn't told Julian about his brother, possibly to protect him and to save him from any unnecessary grief.

This was not the time to open that can of worms, not when the subject must have been painful and sensitive for the family.

Rhys tucked the box behind some shelves and added another box on top of it. Then he took a cursory look around the room to check there was nothing else suspicious lying around if Mr Craft came in once they were done with the unintended chores at the front.

V ictor came downstairs just before supper time. He seemed caught off guard by the sudden company, so to make sure they were not missing anything crucial due to his silence, Rhys guided him back upstairs for a chat.

"What are they doing here?" the man asked as soon as they were up and alone in the attic.

"It's the Eve of the Deceased tomorrow. Julian tried to tell them it wasn't a good time but couldn't come up with a good excuse on the spot. It's not like we could tell them about the situation... and I don't even know what would put them more in harm's way: to have them leave or to have them stay here now that they're here."

"This is going to make it tricky to plan or execute anything. I think I've found the right place, but what do we do, and what do we tell them?" Victor gathered some of the excess clutter off his table to give more space for the relevant blueprints.

"They'll hopefully be leaving in the morning. I can probably chat with Justin again tonight. Maybe he'll want to communicate something to his family while they're here. Not sure how I'll pass on anything without it seeming odd, but I'll think of something if it's important enough."

"That's all fine and well, but what bothers me is that these people put their sons into this mess, whatever their reasoning. Something about that doesn't sit right with me." Victor frowned.

"I'd love to pick their brains, but it's probably a delicate family matter. They seem like lovely people, so I don't want to assume they did it know-ingly. Perhaps it's a painful mistake they don't want to be reminded of?"

"They could have information that's valuable. They've contacted Hosta Therapy somehow. Their sons have been in Hosta's 'care'. We're talking about a lengthy relationship spanning over several years by the sound of it. They must know something."

"You're right, but we need to figure out a discreet way about it. I don't want to accuse them of anything without knowing how much they've been lied to. It's possible they're under the impression that they've paid for treatment that's supposed to benefit their sons without realising Hosta has been using them as lab rats for their experiments and making it worse. Imagine what that's like, to find out you've inadvertently caused so much harm to your children."

Rhys was also worried that this would disrupt the already shaky family dynamic. Mrs Craft had been through enough with Julian's anger issues to then add to it by finding out her attempts of getting help had potentially made things worse.

"I also feel like we're grasping at straws. Are we going to gain any new information that's going to be helpful in dealing with Hosta, or just more personal history?" Rhys was intrigued, but a lot of it seemed like private information he wasn't supposed to know and that was nonessential if the aim was to somehow take down Hosta.

"Well, now we know where to look. I suppose the next step is to find out who we're dealing with and what we can do about it." Victor looked distracted for a moment, then added, "Oh, Quin was here when I discovered the spot, so he already knows the address. He seemed on edge to me. May be worth keeping an eye on him, so he doesn't do anything stupid."

"Noted. He's been acting more antsy than usual, but that could just be because he's Quin." Rhys wasn't too worried about it since this was a new environment for the man and the situation itself unusual. Some extra supervision wouldn't hurt, though. "I think I'll go find him and have a little chat, check what's going on with him. Maybe he's found out something new."

"Good. I'm going to see if I can dig up any useful connections to the property. Anyone whose name might come up more than once. I have half a box left here, and, if that yields nothing, I have a friend who still owes me a favour at city hall."

"Any mention of Ballroth in there somewhere?"

"No."

"Too bad. I would have loved to know why he was so interested in buying the building. Maybe he knows something? Should I pretend to want to sell and find out, or would that just be a wild goose chase?"

"If we're still stuck in this impasse a couple of days from now, I'd say go for it, but I hope we find something decent sooner."

"I'll go talk to Quin. Let me know if you find something. Doesn't matter if it's late or I'm asleep, I want to know right away."

"Will do," Victor said.

CHAPTER 28

S ince Quin was not in the lounge, Rhys checked if he'd gone down to see what Julian was doing.

"Have you seen Quin?" Rhys asked. Julian and his father were at the back, tinkering with something mysterious that involved some electrical equipment, glass tubes and liquids. Rhys had seen Julian work before, so these things no longer fazed him.

"No. Wasn't he upstairs?" Julian was busy counting the right amount of drops of something out of a brown bottle and into a beaker. His father was keeping an eye on something else boiling in a flask. The two of them probably wouldn't have noticed had Quin actually been in the room, so Rhys took a quick look around the back as well as the front before he headed back upstairs.

"Have you seen anyone here?" Rhys asked Mrs Craft, who was cleaning in the kitchen while waiting for the supper to cook. Jonathan, Jacob and Jasmine were in the lounge talking amongst themselves. "I'm looking for Quin. He's a friend who's been staying with us."

"Hmm, could he be that tall, rather handsome but shady-looking young gentleman who was here when we came up?" Mrs Craft wondered.

"That's probably him. Is he still here?"

"No, I think he left. I don't want to be rude, but there was something peculiar about him. Are the two of you close?"

"We've known each other for a while. Did he say where he was going?"

"No, but he seemed to be in a hurry."

Mrs Craft's reply was not what Rhys had wanted to hear. Had it been a simple errand, Quin would have said as much.

"What's wrong? Is something the matter?" Mrs Craft asked.

This could be as good a time as any to bring it up, Rhys thought, even if he would have preferred to discuss it with Julian first to confirm the best way to go about it.

"I fear he may be getting himself into trouble."

"Oh dear, does it have something to do with why you didn't want us to stay? Has there been problems with him and my son? Julian used to get himself into trouble with the wrong kinds of people. This Quin, he's not causing trouble like that, is he?" She looked worried.

"No, not like that. We've just had some issues with…" Rhys tried to think of the best way to phrase it. "Some bad people from Julian's past."

"That doesn't sound good."

"We didn't want to worry you, but now that you're here, you're inadvertently involved. We don't know for sure, but being here might have put your family in harm's way."

"Oh, don't worry about us, we're a hardy bunch, isn't that right?" Jonathan and Jacob nodded at her words. "I'm more worried about Julian. What with all that happened, I'm afraid he's fragile." She sighed.

Rhys hoped she'd be more forthcoming on her own, but evidently he'd have to be more intrusive to get her to go into detail.

"What happened exactly? I know it's none of my business, but I feel like we've known each other for a while now, so I would like to know." Rhys hoped this was discreet enough.

"I suppose it's time." She put away her dish cloth to give Rhys her full attention. "Mind you, I'd rather you didn't mention this to Julian."

"I can't promise that," Rhys said, not wanting to lie.

"I'll leave it at your discretion, but I'd rather you didn't. You see, Julian was in treatment for his issues before the incident. It was not a good time in our lives. He," Mrs Craft paused, seemingly to steel herself, "had a brother, Justin. We lost him, unfortunately, to illness. They were both in therapy for years. We tried the best we could, but when Justin died, Julian was devastated. He was beyond help. There was the option to… to erase it from his memory." She could barely force out the words. "We didn't know what else to do. The treatment worked, I think. It's unfortunate that he lost a little more than intended, but looking at him now, it was for the best. He seems much happier for it."

So, they had indeed done it wanting to help? But Hosta had cost them the life of their son and the memory of another.

Mrs Craft did not seem aware of what his son had gone through during that 'therapy', and perhaps that was also for the best. No amount of behaviour problems was bad enough to merit those treatments.

Rhys vowed he would figure out how to make Hosta pay for what they'd done.

W hen Quin was not back for supper, Rhys headed upstairs into the attic to chat with Victor.

"He's not here. Maybe he's running an errand?" One look at Victor confirmed to Rhys they both knew that was probably not the case at this hour. "Why would he go on his own? Is he stupid? He knows it could be dangerous!"

At what point were they supposed to go and try to save Quin, had he gone to the Hosta headquarters on his own? When was it safe to assume that was where he'd headed?

"I hate to bring this up, but he did withhold information from us before when he went to that meeting. This is not the first time he's disappeared without mentioning it to any of us. For all we know, there's something crucial he's not telling us." Victor sat down on his bed. He looked tired.

"Yes, but he did share it eventually. And Justin's folder."

"That almost got us caught. Maybe he brought that up as a distraction? Justin hasn't brought us any closer to our goal. It could be to buy them time."

"You're saying Quin's in on it? With Hosta?"

"I hope he's not, but doesn't it seem like he might? That, or he's really stupid enough to go there on his own, or he's inconsiderately running an errand without mentioning it to anyone. Which do you think is most plausible?"

"I don't like those options, but an errand sounds the least bad. I wish I could think of anywhere he'd need to go this late in the evening. A jog? Why not ask me to go along? He usually wants company."

"I don't like it either, but I fear we may have to prepare ourselves in case it's something worse."

Victor probably wouldn't have been sad if Quin turned out to be untrustworthy. Rhys resented him a little for it.

It seemed more likely that Quin had resorted to idiocy and gone on a solo crusade than that he'd double-crossed everyone, but Rhys hated that he couldn't be absolutely sure.

"I need to tell Julian. I talked to his mother. I don't think they know what sort of place they'd put their sons in. They seem under the impression that those treatments were successful and done for valid reasons. I can't bring myself to correct them. With Quin gone and the Crafts here, I feel like something bad is about to happen soon. It may not be a good idea to sleep tonight without someone keeping watch just in case." Maybe it was silly to stay on guard for the night but Rhys was inclined to trust his instincts.

"We could take turns if it makes you feel better," Victor agreed kindly.

Quin was disappointed in himself. He was on the floor, not sure where, but unable to move or see, helpless. He needed to warn the others, but what could he do?

He tried to determine what they'd used to tie him with and if it was something he could remove somehow. He'd had the foresight to keep his hands spread wide as they'd tied him, but the restraints weren't loose enough to wiggle off. It was possibly a belt. There was little to no give.

The musty, dank air and the tight, cold space hinted he was likely in a cellar. Even if he managed to get his hands loose, the door or hatch was probably locked or latched from the outside. He wouldn't have minded busting a shoulder to break out of here, but since he currently couldn't even move, his willingness to injure himself made no difference.

It was closer to eight with no sign of Quin. Perhaps a quick peek dream-side would reveal something? Rhys had the address of the proposed Hosta headquarters, so venturing there while he was asleep was also a possibility.

Considering that Hosta used Justin for surveillance, it wasn't a stretch to assume they had others similarly connected, keeping watch. Poking around their headquarters would not be without risk, but, with Quin possibly in danger, it seemed a risk worth taking.

Rhys called a quick private meeting with Victor and Julian in the attic so as not to do anything rash without consulting them first. Luckily the Crafts expressed no interest in what they were doing.

"Even if he's got himself caught somewhere, how are we supposed to retrieve him?" Rhys wondered out loud. He was sitting on Victor's bed, while Victor was showing him what to expect based on the building plans, related documents and their discrepancies.

"Concentrate on finding him, and we'll try to sort the rest while you sleep," Julian said. "Are you calm enough to try it on your own, or do you need help?"

"I think I can manage. Keep quiet until I'm out." Rhys made himself comfortable in Victor's bed.

Victor agreed to take the first watch so Julian could spend the rest of the evening with his family. Victor had a fairly good vantage point from up here as he could see the whole street from his dormer window.

There was also a door leading to an alley at the back of the building, but it was locked, and Julian and Victor had moved and filled a huge wardrobe in front of it. It would not budge without a team of men making a whole lot of noise, should any of Hosta's associates decide to pay a surprise visit. The front was more difficult to secure, but it was in view for all the neighbours to see.

As soon as he was asleep, Rhys made haste to find the correct address. As expected, there was nothing on the outside that suggested anything was amiss, but, to Rhys's surprise, it was a residential building rather than a hospital, a treatment centre or some such facility. He was relieved it didn't look at all like where he'd been kept as a child. He wasn't keen on reliving that trauma having to walk those corridors or revisit those rooms.

Rhys searched the house, but whoever resided or worked here was not around. If this was a place of business, regardless of how it looked, it made sense no one was here after working hours, but Rhys had expected round-the-clock dedication.

The only indication that this was the right place was a room on the top floor where Rhys found obscure machinery and the sort of laboratory equipment they'd seen where they'd retrieved Justin's remains from, only more extensive and with some tools scattered on the floor by one of the desks.

Rhys had plenty of time before Victor would wake him up, so he made sure he wasn't missing anything: he spent the full time available picking apart this house in hopes he'd have at least some news to share when he got back.

Quin managed to hook the belt onto something hard on the ground, which made it easier to force it off, even if it felt like he was about to dislocate his thumbs in the process. Some of that determination was fuelled by anger, some of it was sheer desperation.

When he'd read Justin's file and thought he'd stumbled on something big, it had been nothing of this calibre. He also hadn't expected to feel so powerless in the face of it.

Quin had sat in the lounge minding his own business. He'd heard someone come in downstairs, though at this hour, it was presumably not a customer. He hadn't been able to make out what was said, but the conversation had sounded unusual enough to pique his interest, and he'd snuck to the top of the stairs to listen.

Julian's family, he'd determined. Less intrigued by the bunch of them, Quin had returned to his seat. He'd never thought highly of Julian's parents based on what he'd heard from Julian.

He'd been in the process of mustering some civility toward them when she'd walked up the stairs. The sight of her there had made Quin's stomach turn.

"I see," she'd said. "This makes sense. I suppose you'll be making trouble?"

She'd signalled for the two young men behind her to grab a hold of him. Quin had been quick to try to defend himself, but the siblings were capable and efficient and had had him bound up and gagged in no time. He hadn't even had time to call for help.

She'd waited until everyone downstairs had moved into the pharmacy before she'd guided her boys down and to the back.

"If memory serves me, there should be a suitable hole to put him in... Outside, left," she'd instructed.

The specifics of it were lost on Quin, but he'd been quickly dumped down somewhere not very far from the back door.

He was stuck in here, and she was in there with Julian, Rhys and Victor none the wiser.

R hys woke up to Victor shaking his shoulder. It was ten o'clock.

"No sign of Quin?" he asked Victor. Victor shook his head. "Not there either?"

"No. There was no one there. It didn't seem abandoned, but it was empty. Was there a specific reason why you thought this was it? Don't get me wrong, it had Hosta written all over it up in the attic, but it essentially seemed like someone's home, not an underground research facility." Rhys didn't want to doubt Victor's judgement, but something didn't add up.

"I marked all the locations onto this map, and there are only a handful of properties within this centre area of the cluster. The cluster is formed by a certain type of recurring anomaly: a small space less than one room that's on a high floor and within a few kilometres from essential locations such as city hall, the palace or major company buildings. I ruled out the other properties due to access issues. The most telling sign was that it was in a residential area, but the property owner listed was a trust that exists as a name on paper only.

"I had to pull some strings to check all of the property records but found nothing. That shouldn't even be possible. Those records are carefully compiled not only to list ownership but for insurance and liability reasons in case of an emergency. This was all put into place after the fire to ensure property owners were held accountable if their property did not adhere to the newly established code. I'm sure you're at least somewhat aware of the legalities of property ownership in Schadesborough since someone must have explained that to you when you inherited this building."

"Yes, probably..." There had been a lot of paperwork, and Rhys had had a representative take care of most of it. He'd received a pamphlet—something about fire-safety and having to maintain the building to specific standards—but he'd barely skimmed it as inconsequential.

"By the way, where's Julian?"

"He's downstairs at the back, working, trying to stay out of the way."

"Typical. He'd patch things up with his family sooner if he spent more time with them. I thought he would take this opportunity—"

"His father is probably with him. They seem to share an interest in all that scientific stuff."

"Maybe I should go check up on him, do a little dreamside reconnaissance. Are you still good here? Wake me up when you want to rest."

Rhys had no specific need to spy on Julian, but he didn't want to disturb if they were getting along or were busy doing something important. That, and he was tired and wanted to get some rest once he was done with checking the area.

"Will do. I'm sure I'll be fine for a couple more hours." Victor continued his lookout, and Rhys went back to sleep.

Quin banged on what he could only assume was the hatch to his prison. He had no sense of time other than that too much of it must have passed.

What was she doing here? Was it a covert 'family visit' that she didn't want him to ruin, or did she have a specific agenda? Would she be back to dispose of him later?

More than his own safety, Quin was acutely afraid for Julian's. If these people were responsible for Julian's amnesia, they had the means to do it again if they deemed it necessary. They had the means to do the same to Rhys and to Victor as well.

Quin was fairly sure he was already too late. By now, she would have done what she'd come to do. He could ignore the pain but not the multitude of disturbing procedures now coming to mind much too vividly for his liking. He'd studied that list well enough to know it by heart.

The thought of finally busting through, rushing back inside and finding the house empty scared Quin witless, but he continued to jump and ram himself against the door.

He managed to remove the scarf they'd gagged him with, so he was free to shout for help, but wherever he was confined muffled his screams.

The backdoor led to an alley that was seldom used. Quin would have had to be extremely lucky for anyone to pass by this time of night, not to mention close enough to hear. If he couldn't manage to open the hatch himself, he would be at their mercy again when they returned.

Not that it mattered much if she'd already had her way with Julian or with Rhys. If they could no longer remember him, what was the point of any of it? It was irreversible.

Rhys spent a while listening in on Julian and his father, but the subject matter was foreign to him and quickly proved tedious. It was time to get some rest in case this was his only chance for the night.

He settled in where he was and was about to fall into deep sleep when something caught his attention. Right at the cusp of rest, his surroundings usually momentarily became more pronounced as his senses shut down one by one. Usually, the last one left was his hearing, which could be troublesome if he was in a noisy environment.

The sound wasn't loud, but it didn't seem to belong here. As Rhys identified what he was hearing, he was startled back into full awareness with a jolt. Quin. It was Quin's voice.

Sometimes if Rhys was tired enough, he could hear remnants of voices he'd heard throughout the day, but this was different. He most certainly had not heard Quin scream like that perhaps ever. He could recognise it with ease since it was not unlike his crying back at Agnes Point, only it was now much more urgent.

Where? He wasn't far off, but the sound was muffled. Rhys searched the bottom floor, but it was just him, Julian, Julian's father and Justin in here.

"Justin?" Rhys asked. Justin's hands appeared from behind the shelves. "Are you doing that?" The sound of screaming became louder, and Justin started signing firmly but with his hands shaking.

"Danger. Get out. Now. You, Julian, Victor, get out. Danger." Justin repeated this slowly to make sure Rhys understood, but he was clearly frantic enough to want to hurry.

"Where is Quin? Do you know?"

"Yes. Out. NOW."

Rhys hurried into the back alley. There was no one there, but he could just about hear Quin's voice without Justin echoing it.

Justin's hands grasped at his ankles, demanding his attention, so Rhys pulled him all the way out from the void. He looked ghastly. He was oozing black from every orifice.

"Stop that, it's distracting. We need to find Quin. He's in trouble!"

"We need to!" Justin echoed and signed 'LEAVE' over and over again.

Rhys nearly fell to his ass at the sound of wood cracking and the hatch to a coal cellar busting open and into pieces mere metres from where he was standing. Quin climbed out and started scrambling toward the back door.

"He's not going to get in through there. We barricaded that earlier." Rhys frowned. "Why is he this panicked? What's in there?" Rhys peered into the cellar, but it seemed empty. How had he ended up trapped in there, anyway?

"Out here, then?" Rhys tried to see what Quin might be running from.

"NOT, OUT HERE." Justin grabbed Rhys's hand and pointed at something inside.

Quin was trying to open the backdoor but could only move it a finger-length before it hit the wardrobe on the other side.

"Inside?" Rhys began to see the horror unfold.

The banging at the door alerted Julian's father who called in Julian's mother. She grabbed one of her suitcases from the pharmacy, gave some instructions to Jonathan and Jacob and locked herself, Mr Craft, Jasmine and Julian into the back room. Quin was desperately trying to open the backdoor.

There was the option of going around the whole block to the front of the building, but that side was locked and now guarded by Jacob.

Jonathan was heading upstairs. He was hardly a physical match for Victor, but he would have the element of surprise.

"Oh fuck, Victor, please wake me up! Please, for once, why can't I wake up on command?!"

Rhys wasn't sure what all of this meant, but it looked ominous and bone-chilling. Was it mind-control? Were they all being controlled by Hosta somehow?

"H-O-S-T-A." Justin signed and pointed at their mother with no uncertainty. The black smoke was billowing around him, and he shook Rhys's arm in a state of terror.

"There's someone trying to attack us out there!" Mrs Craft was saying to Julian. "We have to defend ourselves." She opened her bag to pull out a device. This made Justin squeeze Rhys's arm hard enough for it to hurt.

The plate at the top of her bag read 'H.A.C.'. The H did not stand for Holly.

"Julian dear, this will seem strange, but I need you to trust me. Hold still."

She took out a needle and a syringe that she filled with a liquid from a small brown bottle. She injected this without Julian so much as voicing an objection.

Rhys felt like he was about to start oozing something black from every orifice himself. Why wasn't Julian questioning it at all? What was she doing? Quin banged the door, fists now bleeding, hysterical.

Mr Craft helped his wife attach Jasmine to the device with some electrodes. She was also injected with the same substance as her brother. After some minutes, Julian was helped down to lie on the table and seemed to lose consciousness. Shortly after, so did Jasmine.

"Good. They are under. We should wipe two years to be safe. He doesn't need to remember any of them. The landlord and the architect are upstairs. When we're done here, we'll take care of them and the one out there. Can you see if you can shift the wardrobe? He'll wake the entire neighbourhood with that noise."

"It's too heavy. I'll send Jacob around to the back," Mr Craft said.

"Thank you, dear. This will be messier than I thought, but as long as it gets done, I'll be happy. He was doing so much better this time. It's a pity. Is Jasmine ready?"

"Yes, dear."

"I'll start the device." She turned some of the knobs. Mr Craft went into the pharmacy to talk to Jacob.

Rhys tried to think. There was nothing he could do here, but if he could reach Julian dreamside, perhaps there would be something there...

"Justin, I need your help!" Just as he was about to follow Justin into the void, he was woken up in the attic.

Jonathan barred the attic door with a piece of wood he wedged between the underside of the door and the floor. When Victor tried to push the door open, he unwittingly jammed it only tighter into place. There was nothing in the attic sturdy enough to pry or smash the door open with, and it would not budge under Victor's full weight no matter how hard he banged or pushed. This was the noise that woke Rhys.

"No, no, no! Not now!" Rhys bolted up. He realised he was stuck in an even worse predicament than before—too anxious to fall back to sleep, and just as, if not more, unable to help.

"Calm down. Stay there and wait. It'll be fine," Jonathan said through the door.

"The hell it will! Your mother will do the same thing to us as she's doing to Julian down there!" Rhys turned his attention to the dormer window. He glanced at Victor. "Does that open? Is there a way down? I need to get back down there."

"It does. There's no ladder, but you might be able to climb down. I should have rope. I could lower you... What will you do alone?"

"Quin is at the back. There's the two of us at least."

Rhys climbed to the windowsill to check the roof. It looked like he might manage it, but unfortunately the gutters would not support Victor's weight. Victor would have to stay and wait to be let out.

"If I can climb up and over to the other side, I'll be able to shout to Quin, I think. Have him meet me at the front." Rhys wasn't worried about Jacob since Quin most certainly would be able to handle him. "Try to keep Jonathan busy, so he doesn't come down to bother us."

"Be careful." Victor gave Rhys the other end of a rope he'd fished from under his bed. Rhys tied it around his waist and climbed out the window.

CHAPTER 29

Julian became aware of Jasmine holding his hand within his sleep. She was smiling.

"Hello, brother," she signed. "Mother wants me to take at least two years. All the preparations are done. She's administered the drug and hooked you onto the device. I am here to ensure the delivery of those chemicals to the correct parts of your brain because she says the guidance apparatus is corrupt. She tells me I've got a knack for it, but I think it's the extensive training. You're in safe hands. Don't worry."

"I'm not worried," Julian signed back.

"Good. We should get started. She's waiting for the data." Jasmine set her hands onto Julian's temples.

Julian wondered how many times something like this had been done to him without him having any knowledge or memory of it. He trusted Jasmine, though. He had no choice but to trust her.

Short clips of memories, visions, sounds, smells and other sensations trickled into his consciousness. It was a steady stream of the past two years, from empty days of busying himself with work, to more interesting moments with Rhys, Victor and even Quin.

A lot had changed.

It was difficult to appreciate what impact these moments had had until they were held up next to his past before he'd moved to Schadesborough.

"Thank you," Jasmine signed. She was still smiling happily. It was a pity she was caught up in all of this, but she seemed to be handling it well. "She'll wake you up soon. She's going to hook herself onto the device to link with me to retrieve the data."

"All right."

"Give her a hug and a kiss from me," Jasmine requested.

"I will," Julian promised. Moments later he woke up.

It took Rhys a while to get Quin's attention from up on the roof.

"Go around to the front!" Rhys shouted and pointed at the end of the alley. Quin started running. Good. Rhys headed to the front and climbed down as quickly and as carefully as he could. He'd be even more useless if he fell to his death.

When he got to ground level by the front door, Quin appeared from behind the corner not far off.

"Jacob should be here somewhere, possibly in the pharmacy..." Rhys tried to look for him.

"He was back there. I rammed him down." Quin wiped his face.

"Is the front door open, then?" Rhys tested it. Yes! Finally some luck. They hurried inside and to the back room door.

"We need to break in. Watch out for Jonathan. Victor is trying to distract him upstairs, but he might turn up." Rhys was of two minds about heading up to free Victor, but chose the door in front of him. There was no time. Julian was on the other side and in grave danger.

"She'll wipe his memory. That's what she's here for. I recognised her from the meeting at Hosta. She's one of them. She's the one I had lunch with in Firth." Quin used his full weight to try to break through the door.

"Quin, hinges." Rhys handed him a sturdy cast-iron poker from the stand next to the log burner. True to expectation, the top hinge popped off with ease. Quin and Rhys lifted the door off the lower hinge and pushed it out of the way.

"Stop!" Rhys yelled just as Julian sat up on the table and his mother was about to lie down in his stead. "Julian, are you all right?"

There was silence as all eyes turned to Julian. Julian looked confused.

"Who is he?" he asked, pointing at Rhys.

In that moment Rhys understood—as close as another person possibly could—how Quin must have felt. The feeling was indescribable. Tears burned at the corners of his eyes.

"No, this is utter garbage! What did you fucking do to him?!" Rhys shrieked. He knew full well what they'd done, but he needed to scream out something.

To hell with trying to set Julian with either Quin or Victor. To hell with worrying about their feelings of jealousy. Fuck! Why hadn't he realised it sooner? He'd been too caught up with his own shit to pay attention, and it was too late now. To hell with anyone else—!

"Grab them," Mrs Craft ordered. Behind him, Jonathan pushed Quin to the ground. As for Rhys, Julian was quick on his feet to do the same.

"Where do you want him?" he asked.

"Tie them up. We'll take care of them next." Mrs Craft smiled, pleased. She started to prepare a syringe.

Julian and Jonathan did as told. Rhys was in too much of a shock to even fight back properly. Perhaps it would be for the best to forget all of this, less painful if nothing else. Quin had said the procedure was irreversible. Slim chance that he'd misunderstood.

"The data," Mr Craft reminded his wife subtly.

"What? Oh, you're right! I must be getting old." She laughed lightly. "I'll try to be quick. Julian dear, could you please prepare the sedative for me?" She pointed at her equipment spread on Julian's desk.

"Yes, Mother," Julian responded. Mr Craft prepared the device.

Rhys tried to shake and wiggle himself loose, but it was useless. Next to him, Quin had apparently dissociated and was staring into nothingness. Rhys wished he could have done the same to not have to watch Julian so obediently administer the sedative.

He and his mother exchanged a few calm words. He gave her a hug and a kiss before she drifted off, and Mr Craft turned to operating the device. There was an excruciating silence as the two of them worked seamlessly to help Mrs Craft retrieve the data. Julian seemed to be in his element.

All of this started to make perfect sense to Rhys. Of course, it wasn't mind-control. How could he have been so stupid, so blind? It was the Guardian damned family business that they never talked about! He'd been at their bloody house earlier that day. Four bedrooms. A private laboratory. This fucking deranged scientist family owned the whole lot of it.

It was no wonder Julian hadn't resisted. His parents hadn't sent him anywhere for therapy or to be fixed. If he or any of his siblings refused or did something inconvenient, all Mrs Craft needed to do was wipe those last memories and start over. They had probably been manipulated and used like this throughout their lives.

Rhys gritted his teeth, frustrated that he could do absolutely nothing to fix it. Something that big seemed beyond fixing.

Julian woke Jasmine up gently.

"Is it done?" he signed. She nodded. She was smiling, but tears pooled and fell across her cheeks. Julian hugged her and stroked her back. "You did well," he mouthed to her. She started to sob. Julian let their father take over comforting her and exhaled like he'd held his breath for a full hour.

"Oh Lord, Rhys, I thought I'd have a heart attack when the two of you burst in!" He looked straight at Rhys. Rhys recoiled. "You were supposed to stay upstairs, safe! Jonathan!" Julian turned to his brother. "What the hell happened?"

"How was I supposed to know he would crawl out the goddamn window?" Jonathan grumbled.

"The window, Rhys? Really? Don't you have *any* sense of self-preservation?" Julian crouched down in front of him and Quin to release them from their ties. "What's wrong with him? Is he all right?" Julian referred to Quin.

"He's in fucking shock because of you!" Finally gaining a rudimentary grasp of the situation, Rhys shoved Julian to vent. "You should have told us you had a plan!"

"I'm sorry. There was no time. My father filled me in after we were done with the inventory," Julian said. "Do I need to do something about that?" He gestured at Quin.

"Maybe he needs a hug, I don't know." Rhys could have used a hug himself but couldn't bring himself to ask. He wasn't sure what he was feeling, but it was like he'd been dragged through some excessively awful and confusing shit and his feelings were yet to catch up.

Julian helped Quin up and gave the man a hug as suggested if for no other reason than to return the favour from before. Quin started to come out of it, so Julian took a step back but then the man's hands caught his attention. He lifted them up for a better look. They were fairly bruised and needed some care, but at least it wasn't urgent.

The plan had been simple but not without risk. They had been lucky that Quin seemed to be the only one with any noticeable injuries.

"The two of you..." Julian mumbled. One would jump out the window and the other bang his fists nearly off trying to save him. It would have been sweet had it not been so incredibly dumb—he, of all people, was not worth risking their lives for. They should have had the common sense to stay safe! This was precisely the reason he'd tried to keep them out of it.

Rhys stood up and dusted himself off as if climbing on the roof and barging into this dangerous situation had been nothing remarkable.

"So, uh, what happened to her?" The boy asked and pointed at Julian's mother.

"She'll wake up and remember none of it," Julian mused. "Right?" He turned to his father.

"Yes. It was getting out of hand. I've been worried for her for a while now. It started innocuous enough, but over the years, she's become more and more consumed by expanding the research and securing the funds. I went along with it because I was hoping she would eventually see her own absurdity, but this latest obsession was the last straw for all of us. She's wanted to shield Julian from everything for so long, she couldn't see the damage she was doing."

"How much is 'none of it'?" Rhys asked.

"I took as much as I could. There's so much I couldn't be very selective. I'm sorry," Jasmine signed.

"It's all right. You did your best, dear. I'll be glad if she remembers me, but, if she doesn't, I will try my best to win her back and do it right this time."

"What will happen to your 'family business'?" Rhys asked.

"She started Hosta Therapy Solutions as a genuine effort to help, but it's grown into a monster since then. It may be difficult to dismantle it completely, but she's the driving force behind the research. I assume it will cease to be sustainable with her no longer at the helm. I'll do what I can to ease that process. I'm hoping we can start over with something less ambitious, if she wants to, but I need to make sure she never gets caught up in it like that again. I'm aware there's nothing we can do to right all the wrongs, but if I can redirect her towards something positive, then perhaps she'll have it in her to make some amends."

"Do you think that will be enough?" Rhys glanced at Julian. Julian shrugged.

"I don't think vengeance would benefit anyone," his father said. "Removing her memories and erasing her research is effectively the same as killing her. At least this way there's a chance that something good might come out of it.

"If she doesn't remember any of you, it's probably for the best if I take her away somewhere for a while. You boys are all adults, I'm going to leave it up to you to choose what you want to do and whether or not you want to have anything to do with her. As for Jasmine," Julian's father turned to his daughter and signed, "you could stay here for a while, if your brother will have you. Right?" He turned to Julian. "I'll come for her once things have settled down, but it would help enormously to know she's here, safe with you."

Julian was surprised by his father's trust in him, but in all honesty, he wasn't sure if he was ready for such a big responsibility.

"Can I?" Jasmine looked hopeful.

Julian sighed. It was going to get even more cramped around here with Quin already hovering around like a horsefly looking for a place to land. "Are you sure that's what you want?" he signed.

"Yes!" She jumped to hug him.

"I trust the two of you won't burn down the house in my absence if you stay at home until you decide to move out?" Julian's father asked his younger sons. Jacob had appeared at the door, and he and Jonathan looked at each other, then at their father, and grinned.

"Sounds good to us," they replied in unison.

"Oh, shit, Victor! He's upstairs!" Rhys exclaimed. "I'm going to go fill him in!" He rushed to the stairs.

Julian felt drained. Once the excitement had worn off, he was really starting to feel the effects of the previous nights' poor sleep and the remnants of the drugs in his system.

"Do you still need me for something?" he asked. Quin looked at him a little worried. "I feel like I haven't slept for ages."

"Sleep-roaming will do that to you if you don't rest," Jasmine signed. She seemed amused. She and Rhys would probably make an insufferable team of taunting amusement and unbridled childish energy, if last Midwinter was anything to go by. Just thinking about it made Julian feel like a cranky and exhausted old man. He needed to go to bed.

Chapter 30

The 31st of October, 04:29.

"There has to be a way to skip this annoying extra step between falling asleep and whatever the hell 'rest' is. No matter what I try, I can't seem to figure out what initiates the transition." Julian had ended up wasting half the night sitting in this stupid bubble narrating his thoughts, while 'rest' happened sporadically, seemingly at random and not nearly often enough to feel like it was doing any good. "It was automatic before, so it must be possible to make it automatic again... I'm so damn tired. I need to rest, but how am I supposed to do that? Do I just close my eyes and wait until something happens?"

"Essentially, yes."

Julian jumped at the unexpected answer to his private musings.

"I told you not to come here!" He stuck his forearm into his mouth.

"Yeah, but I need to talk to you." Rhys sat down next to him.

"I'm exhausted."

"Less chance of you losing your temper then... Don't eat that." Rhys pulled the arm out of Julian's mouth.

"Didn't you say you preferred I tell you things only if I genuinely wanted to? I'm too tired to even try to curb my gibberish today. Can't we do this tomorrow?"

"No." Rhys leaned back and rolled to his side.

"You're always so unreasonable. I sometimes wonder how much more of this I can take—"

"Sorry, bad habits. I'll try not to get on your nerves, but I need to say this. It's important." Rhys sounded earnest. Julian turned to look at him.

"Did you really just say you're sorry, or am I imagining things? What's so important it can't wait? I hope it's nothing complicated…"

"It's not." Rhys pulled Julian's arm out of his mouth again. "Don't eat that. You don't know where it's been."

"Are you trying to be funny?" Julian rolled his eyes.

"I'm nervous. Working up the courage."

"What? What have you got to be nervous about? You're not the one voicing all of your thoughts with no filter. I can't even look at you. It's too distracting. When I look at you, you're all I can think about." Julian turned away. Rhys stopped him from re-inserting the arm.

About to tell Rhys off for interfering, Julian took a hold of Rhys's hand, but instead of gaining a chance to push Rhys away, Rhys pinned both of Julian's hands to the ground.

"What are you doing?"

"Something I should have done a long time ago." Rhys leaned closer.

"Wow, your eyes… Oh, no," Julian realised, "You're not thinking of kissing me, are you?" He panicked. "It's not that I don't want you to, I definitely do! I'm just not ready. Let go of my hands, I need something to stop me from—" He tried to bite his lip to silence himself, but it was no use. "I love you. You're so gorgeous. Oh m-my, your lips are so close! I can't do this. I'm not—" Rhys kissed him. It was such a relief to not be able to speak, Julian relaxed and forgot to raise his guard. He was wholly unprepared when Rhys let go.

"For the love of the Guardian, I want you so m—!" Julian bit his lip to stop the rest, but there was already a faint smile on Rhys's lips.

"I could get addicted to this."

"What?" Julian frowned. "Are you doing this just to tease me? Is that all this is?"

"A bit."

"Please don't. It's not fair. I can't even be mad at you! I want you to kiss me again." Julian felt his face turning red from the embarrassment.

"But only a *wee* bit, though." Rhys fell quiet. As the words sank in, Julian's mind went blank. It took him a fair while to recover.

"Really?" He stared at Rhys. "You mean you're mostly not? You're being serious? How? Why? What happened? What changed?" Could he be this lucky? Was there a chance...?

"I don't know. I had plenty of reasons, but they don't seem important anymore." Rhys shrugged.

"Your eyes are so beautiful." Julian tried to look away, but Rhys's face blocked most of his field of vision. "I can't breathe."

"Oh? I'm sorry. Am I heavy?" Rhys backed away.

"No, it's because you smell so good, but I don't want you to think I'm a complete creep for sniffing you, so I'm trying not to breathe in too deeply. I can't help it. The scent is overwhelming when you are right there."

"What? I smell of something here? That's strange." Rhys tried to smell himself.

"You always smell good, even when you're sweaty. Shit, Rhys, this is embarrassing! I don't want to be telling you this!"

"It's not that bad. You have quirks. I think it's endearing." Rhys smiled. He leaned closer again. "I like hearing what you think."

"You just like to see me flustered."

"It's cute, but not what I'm going for. What I like more is..." Rhys kissed Julian again.

"Please don't stop. Let me have more—!" Julian blurted upon release.

"Hearing how you react to me kissing you." Rhys lowered himself closer but stopped just short and grinned.

"If you keep doing this to me, I swear I will break," Julian warned. "I'm getting arou—" He chomped on his lip and tried to distract himself.

"You're getting what? Aroused? I'd be sad if you didn't." Rhys offered him a finger to bite on. It felt odd at first, but his lip had started to hurt, so he was happy to switch.

"To tell you the truth, I am still afraid that you're expecting something other than what I can give you," Rhys said and added, "That is the only thing holding me back right now." He removed his finger and waited for a response.

"I'll take anything." Julian wanted to give Rhys a coherent reply since it seemed like a legitimate issue for the boy, but coherency proved a challenge. "I'd say anything to have you, but I can't think of the right words. I'm exhausted, confused and a mess. I'm sorry. What was the question?"

"Maybe this isn't the right time..." Rhys looked sad.

"Oh, no. I'm sorry, I'm trying, I don't understand the problem. You need to be more specific!"

It was Rhys's turn to blush. He backed away to sit. Julian followed.

"I don't know what to do with this..." Rhys gestured at his crotch. "If you're looking for what I normally have, that's never going to happen. And as for this stuff..." Rhys again pointed at the appropriate region. "I don't know how these are supposed to go together. How is this going to work?" He included Julian into his gesturing.

"So, it's a minor technical issue?" Julian blurted out, momentarily relieved. "I assumed it was a problem you had with me."

"I need to make sure you don't think I'm going to let you stick that thing into me. It's important!" Rhys reiterated most firmly.

"The thought did cross my mind, and I admit I find it intriguing, but there are other ways to go about it." Julian wasn't an expert, but he could think of quite a few other options. He bit on his arm to save himself from listing them out loud, though.

"Stop biting yourself and tell me! I want to make this work." Rhys pried Julian's arm out of his mouth for what must have been the billionth time.

"I don't want to tell you I suspect I've done most of the stuff I'm thinking about with Quin!" Julian groaned and hid his face behind his hands. "And it's making me want to test it all out with you."

"Oh? Not what I was expecting, but all right. That sounds promising." Rhys seemed to relax a little. There was a hint of a smile as he leaned forward and said, "Let's try this again."

This time, Julian leaned into Rhys's kiss wholeheartedly. Once he'd committed to it, he found himself unable to stop. There was a familiar hum building in his ears, and the very air around him quivered with heat. Rhys's body felt compellingly heavy and warm on top of him. This felt right. It felt firm.

Julian had meant to take it slow, but, just as when he'd been angry, it took mere seconds for him to lose his inhibitions. There was no controlling such immediate, raw lust, but he certainly made an effort to try. With the last shreds of his sanity, Julian forced himself to tilt his head so that their lips parted, but all he could think about was turning back and eating Rhys's face. He was shaking.

"I... I can't. You need to stop me."

"Julian, look at me."

"I can't."

"I want you to look at me. Don't hold back. I want to see it." Rhys nibbled Julian's lip ever so tenderly.

"Ah, I like it when you're being bossy—not... what I meant to say, ignore that, I—I love it!"

"Look at me," Rhys commanded.

As Julian complied, Rhys pressed himself *hard* against Julian's crotch. In this abnormal, volatile state, that pressure and those gorgeous eyes looking right at him were enough to send Julian over the edge.

When he managed to catch his breath, he felt light-headed and almost delirious. What an intense yet mellow sensation; what a ridiculous way to reach an orgasm!

"That has got to be the best, stupidest orgasm I've ever had!" All Julian could do was laugh at himself.

"I can do better," Rhys said.

"I'm sure you can, but I don't know if I could handle it."

"I'll let you rest for a bit, but we should try that again...!"

"I'll try that as many times as you want. In fact, you can do whatever you want, whenever you want. No, wait, that could be dangerous... Ah, screw it." Julian didn't care to try to hold himself back or cover his mouth anymore. He let himself ramble for quite a while about how much he loved Rhys, and what he was feeling, but he was too happy and satisfied to care about the embarrassment or the consequences.

"As much as it pleases me to hear you say these things, I think we should figure out how to fix you. I mean, I don't mind, but I feel like maybe this could be a little dangerous. I'm not sure I can resist teasing you when you're like this."

"I love you."

"Even if we figure it out, please feel free to still tell me that as often as you'd like." Rhys laughed.

Julian woke up in good spirits and feeling more relaxed than he had for a while, regardless of the slim amount of rest he'd been getting. He washed his face, shaved, put on his glasses, got dressed and checked himself in the mirror as he'd always done on a normal day after a normal night's sleep. After everything that had happened the past year, this felt anything but normal. The person looking back at him looked about the same as before, but something felt decidedly different. He hesitated leaving the room.

Quin was in the lounge, still lazying in his temporary guest bed—a mattress on the floor—at the far end of the room. Jasmine had also slept in the lounge, but she'd set aside her mattress and bedding and was putting the kettle on and preparing breakfast for herself. She showed more competence in taking care of herself than most of the rest of her new housemates.

Rhys appeared from his room, joining Quin's degenerate gang of non-morning people. The two of them clambered to the sofa and resumed vegetating in just their underwear and nightshirts.

Julian had assumed this would be more awkward, but seeing Rhys yawn and drool onto a cushion greatly alleviated any concerns he'd had over last night's encounter. He humphed and helped Jasmine with her breakfast before preparing something to serve the hopeless brigade and Victor, who was yet to emerge from his hiding.

When Victor came down the stairs and sat down at the kitchen table, Julian served him some coffee, and the man sat in silence, watching Quin and Rhys try to wake up.

"Father rang earlier this morning to ask whether I needed something from the house," Jasmine signed. "He said to come the sooner the better because he'll be taking mother to Grymswich for a while, and the house will be locked because Jacob and Jonathan will be staying at the school for the rest of the year."

"How about this afternoon?"

"Aren't we going to visit grandpa today?"

"Oh, right. I suppose we can do that afterwards in the evening if you'd like."

"I think I would. I was looking forward to it before father said we had other plans."

"All right. You'll have to excuse me if this is a stupid question, but are there any other traditions you'd like to uphold today? I have no recollection of this Eve of the Deceased."

"Could we light a candle for Mother?" There was a hint of sadness in Jasmine's eyes, though she was persistently smiling.

"Yes, we can do that," Julian promised.

"Ah, good. We should light one for Justin as well." She looked out the window for a moment. Julian checked what she was looking at, but it was a foggy day with low visibility. After a while, she continued, "I wish someone had told me about Justin sooner. I knew it had to be something big. You wouldn't have been so angry for no reason. Usually when I'm angry, it's because deep down I'm overwhelmed by something sad. I can't imagine how awful it must have been for you."

"It's OK, I don't remember it anymore. But yes, I guess we could light a candle for Justin, too." It would take a while to get used to having one more name in that list of siblings, but maybe it would feel more natural sooner if he made an effort. With the root cause of his memory loss no longer a mystery, the worry of spontaneously forgetting everyone had passed. Perhaps it was safe to commit?

"I feel bad that I never cared to ask why you sign like that, but it makes more sense now." Jasmine gave him another smile.

"There's something wrong with how I sign?" Julian hadn't realised.

"No. I understand you just fine, but Mother always complains it's nonstandard, incomprehensible and sloppy." Jasmine chuckled. "You were doing it on purpose, so she couldn't eavesdrop, right?"

"Maybe it's just nonstandard, incomprehensible and sloppy."

"It's not. It was like a quirky secret code you've inadvertently taught to me. I like it." Jasmine patted his hands.

"Well, I'll take that compliment. Thank you very much. I'm glad to have provided my lady with some entertainment." After a moment of thought, Julian added, "There's space upstairs in the attic. Half of it was renovated last year when Victor moved in, but we could ask him if he wouldn't mind fixing the rest of it. He," Julian pointed at Quin, "is not going to leave without a fight—I can already tell. We could split the remaining space into two. You'd have your own room. It's not going to be huge, but if you don't mind—"

"Really?" Jasmine started to ever so slightly bounce up and down from the excitement. She made a valiant effort to contain it by shaking out the shakes from her hands.

"If ever you decide you're unhappy living with a bunch of weirdos, let me know, and we'll think of something else, but you're free to stay for as long as you'd like."

"Thank you, thank you, thank you!" Her hands were a flurry.

The moreish scents of fried bacon, onion, mushrooms and eggs roused Rhys and Quin from their vegetative state on the sofa. They formed a two-person queue to where Julian was plating their breakfast. Not wanting to be left out, Victor gingerly joined the queue.

"I'm starving," Rhys mumbled when Julian handed him the first plate. "Thank you for the cook!" He looked up at Julian with a mischievous grin and gave him a kiss. Reminded of the previous night, Julian felt the hair at the back of his neck perk up.

Both Quin and Victor raised their eyebrows in surprise. Quin glanced at Victor behind him, and as soon as Rhys moved out of the way to sit down at the table, he moved over to retrieve his plate.

Julian was still trying to recover from the first kiss when he realised he was being kissed again. Quin grinned and mouthed his thanks to the cook while his lips were still at touching distance. He ducked away with his plate in case there were repercussions, but Julian merely grumbled under his breath. He glanced at Victor, who was standing a few steps away, his expression getting too complicated to read.

"I suppose you want a share as well?" Julian asked. Victor nodded slowly, eyes firmly fixed at Julian. Julian sighed. "Well, have at it then." He offered Victor the breakfast plate.

Victor took the plate, placed it aside on the table and, without taking his eyes off of Julian, claimed his kiss.

It was not as rough or off-putting as Julian had dreaded, considering Victor was the only one of them to sport a full beard. In fact, it was probably the most delicate and careful kiss of the three.

It was also significantly longer. Long enough for Julian to wonder whether Victor was setting up a house, doing some gardening, gathering the crops and making himself comfortable for the winter. By the end of it, Julian found himself considering this peaceful countryside retirement in earnest. It seemed so naturally soothing.

Victor's face was red and his hands were shaking when he turned to grab his plate and returned to his seat. About five minutes later, he signed an apology to Julian and whispered, "I wanted to make sure I had no regrets if I never get to do that again."

"Don't apologise," Julian signed back. "I heard you."

CHAPTER 31

The 30th of October, 21:22.

James was eager to get to work as soon as he'd brought Hosta back home, but his tasks were interrupted by this nuisance of a late evening phone call.

"After all these years, do you still not trust me?" What had Hosta ever seen in this man, anyway? For the love of the Guardian, he was such a handful! James muffled the telephone transmitter against his chest to allow himself a deep sigh before he continued, "I told you she did not sell the building. She's back there again, right where we want her. I said I would take care of this. Have I ever let you down?"

"You told me you'd take care of it in February."

"It's just a slight delay." James patted his wife's hand. Thankfully, she didn't have to hear any of this. She lay in her bed looking so peaceful, and, after she'd sacrificed herself, yet again, she deserved this moment of undisturbed rest.

"If you haven't delivered her to me by Midwinter, I will personally come and collect her!"

"Yes, yes. Of course. You are more than welcome to, but I assure you I will have sent her back to you by then." James had barely the time to finish his sentence when the line was abruptly disconnected. Ah, finally! He set the receiver on its hook and took her hand into his. "My dear, how did you ever put up with that man? I'll not miss dealing with him when we're done with his wayward daughter." But at least this way he could be sure the past would not come back to haunt Hosta, no matter her supposed debt.

"I hope you forgive me, dear. This is the last time I will act without consulting you." It would weigh on his conscience for a while, but that would ease with time as it always did. "In all fairness, my darling, you are the one to blame for this, aren't you? For insisting on teaching those children so well that we have to resort to extreme measures just to pull some wool over their eyes. And for always getting yourself entangled with such people. With that man. With your offspring. You have to understand I cannot play the second fiddle for all eternity. You did promise yourself to me, did you not? It's time you let them go."

He'd been able to talk her out of her usual precautions by saying they might jeopardise the plan, so he was finally free to take whatever he wanted from that sweet head of hers. All of those ugly memories she'd wanted to preserve. There would be nothing to explain away this time, and no one would care to question why she couldn't remember. It was all so very convenient. He just needed to save the parts he treasured.

"Well, I'll leave Jasmine for you, dear, but the rest of them are not worth your love or the grief." He set her hand back down and started to prepare the treatment.

Finally she would be rid of her unhealthy obsession with her kids and of all the other pesky distractions.

"What about Father?" Justin asked by signing. There shouldn't have been anything left for him to fear, but he was still oozing and frantic, even after his father had taken his mother away on a carriage earlier this evening. Perhaps it was difficult to interpret the situation from his point of view?

"What about him?" Rhys asked.

"Also dangerous," Justin reminded him. "Don't trust."

"Oh? He was the one to help out with your mother, though—"

"Don't trust," Justin repeated.

"What do you want me to do?"

Justin offered his hands to pull Rhys into the void. On his side, he gestured for Rhys to take a seat and started explaining. It seemed to be a rare moment of clarity for him, and the sentences flowed out in less of a disarray than usual.

"Wiping memories is irreversible, but sealing them off is not. Only our father knows how to do the complete memory wipes, and he would never relinquish that kind of power to teach it to Jasmine. She has likely just sealed them. The good news is that if he doesn't hurry to remove the seal, the effect should be the same: the memories will fade until they're gone for good. Snow in the mountains, fancy that—"

"How long will that take?"

"I don't know, but it could be weeks, maybe a month. It depends on the intensity of the memory. She's bound to lose something insignificant, but, if he hurries, he could save most of them. I wish I could see the Northern Sea—"

"What do we do?"

"You might be able to sabotage him since removing the seal isn't as quick as applying it, and he'll need a proper laboratory for the process. Laboratories are stupid. I want my own duck pond with at least a dozen ducks—"

"The process? How long?"

"Imagine spilling something sticky all over your belongings. Spilling it takes mere moments, but cleaning it up can take hours, sometimes days. It probably won't take more than a week. How long does it take to reach Lingslip from here? Do they have ducks?"

"Shit." Rhys would have to make sure Mr Craft did not unseal those memories, but he hadn't the faintest idea on how to go about it.

"Oh, I wonder why he hopes to gain your trust like this. Why not rush in with force and wipe the lot of you if you're a threat or an obstacle? Unless..." Justin cocked his head to the side. "Has she discovered your abilities? If so, when?"

Rhys's neck and back curled with the chills.

"The research always comes first," Justin continued. "Maybe she wants to study you without outside interference first but needs you to lower your guard and go about your business to gain some baseline data? She must have wanted to do that last Midwinter—that's likely why she came here—but you left so suddenly, she lost the opportunity, and when you returned, you were suspicious, creating all sorts of trouble on my behalf. She knows she has to make this convincing to dispel all doubt so that the data she collects through me, or possibly through Jasmine, is reliable. Once she's done, she'll probably want to detain you for more testing."

"Why me?"

"You know why. Me, Julian and Jasmine, we don't roam like you do. You can't see the edge of your bubble or the void from where you are. Maybe your range truly is limitless? For me to leave this confined space and roam further means I need to go through the void. I can withstand it for longer because I'm dead, but she needs to direct me to specific places blind because of my limited perception. Imagine what she could do if she had your range and vision? Imagine all the d—" Justin started to pace back and forth, possibly to keep himself from rambling on about ducks. "She's vulnerable right now. It's probably your only chance to stop her."

"How?"

"Well, maybe Jasmine...?"

"How?" Rhys repeated, confused.

"She's the link between you and our parents. You should find out whether she's in on it knowingly. Considering her age, she probably doesn't know what's at stake. Julian and I were fourteen or fifteen when we started to understand. Before then, it was just how things were done in our family; we didn't question it, and we weren't given the details. We weren't given anything. I wanted a pet d—" Justin huffed. "Never mind. They might have placed Jasmine here as a spy, but my gut says she might be their weakest link. Otherwise, your best and only reasonable option is to run."

Jasmine's bubble was much smaller than Justin's or Julian's and thus a challenge to find. Rhys had had to spend longer in the void than any time before, so, when he finally broke through to the other side, it took him several lengthy moments to catch his breath and calm down. It was enough to alarm Jasmine, who hadn't expected to have any visitors, and most certainly not Rhys, who had already started to turn a sickly bluish tint from his wade.

"Are you all right? Can I do something? Do you need help?" She quickly got up from where she'd been sitting and fussed over Rhys while he steadied himself.

"It's— OK," Rhys gasped between the words, "I— just— need— a moment."

"What are you doing here? You're not supposed to be here. How did you get in?" She seemed to check where Rhys was sleeping. "You don't need to be hooked up to jump?"

Oh, so there was a prerequisite for the members of her family, save for Justin, who was dead? Good. The more limitations they had, the better. All the more reason to not let them gain any new insights from studying his abilities, or there would be more people jumping freely from bubble to bubble, potentially making dreamside much more dangerous than it currently was.

"I'm sorry to barge in like this," Rhys said as soon as he could speak without having to continuously gasp for air out of whatever survival response the void had triggered. "We need to talk."

"I was afraid you might say that," she said. It was then that Rhys realised how strange it was to hear her speak. He eyed her for a moment, pointed at his mouth and raised his eyebrows to form the question.

"I know. I'm sorry. It must seem strange. I'm not deaf. My ears are just in use when Mother needs them. But she's not using them right now, obviously," she explained. "Oh, it was never a complete lie! My hearing isn't great. Mother says it's because of the interference, whatever that means." Jasmine gave him an apologetic smile.

Hosta was incapacitated, so she would not be spying on them personally, but with their habit of collecting data, maybe she or her husband had rigged up something so they'd still be able to hear everything Jasmine heard? Rhys had to think fast.

"Can they still hear?" he signed. He wasn't sure if he could even trust Jasmine—right now *everyone* seemed suspicious—but the fact that she'd even mentioned something as confidential as that meant that she was either incapable of withholding her thoughts like Julian, or she was willing to cooperate with Rhys.

"No, not right now." Jasmine seemed calm and confident. Perhaps she didn't share the same discombobulated rambly trait her brothers had? Still, Rhys could take no chances.

"I'll come to you when I wake up. Don't make noise," he signed. It would be safer that way.

F or once, Rhys managed to wake up before morning if only because he'd been waiting for any small thing that might rouse him.

He got up and snuck into the lounge to wake Jasmine. She woke up and followed Rhys into his bedroom without either of them waking Quin.

"Father said I shouldn't talk to you about family matters while I'm here, but I have a feeling he's keeping things from me. You're my friend, right?" she signed. It was safer to sign and not leave any evidence of their conversation, but Rhys offered Jasmine some paper to fill in the gaps in case there were signs he was unfamiliar with. She wrote down a few of the more difficult words. Rhys nodded. "It's a mess. I don't know who I can trust to tell me the truth, but you wouldn't lie to me, right? You have no reason to..." She looked pained. It seemed she might be maturing faster than her older brothers and was, perhaps, already having some doubts about the family business. "Do you think it's right to deceive others?" It was an easy enough question.

"No," Rhys replied.

"If you were a bad person, I could at least feel like it was justified, but you've been nothing but nice to me. Julian has always been nice to me. Victor has been nice..." She paused and looked uncharacteristically sad. "Haven't I always done as told and been nice? So why do they lie to me? Is it because I'm too young to understand? Don't I deserve to know?" She sighed. "I'm sorry. You had something important you needed to talk to me about. It concerns our parents, doesn't it?"

"Yes, I'm afraid it does."

"They're not very nice people, are they?"

"That seems to be the case, for more reasons than one. It's not right how your mother has been using you and Justin." Rhys wanted to spare Jasmine from the full extent of it, but she needed to understand that he would not be asking if it weren't serious.

"Justin? You mean surveillance unit A7f-2b?"

"No, I mean Justin, your older brother, Julian's twin. But yes, that was the code in his file."

Jasmine shrank back in surprise.

"But A7f-2b isn't a person; it's one of the many surveillance units connected to the *GODS*. I only know of it because Mother likes to call it Justin and uses it a lot from the Bulb—that's the laboratory in our attic," she wrote.

"Justin is Julian's dead twin brother. I'm sorry you had to find out about it like this," Rhys wrote.

"Mother sometimes connects me to it for training, but I never realised... Is that why Julian is so angry with Mother? What happened? I knew Julian had a brother, but no one ever told me the details. How did he die? Why is he used as a surveillance unit?"

"We're not sure, but I suspect it's why they wiped Julian's memory: to cover it up."

"I was told he fell into the wrong crowd and became violent, so Father was forced to intervene." Jasmine pressed her lips together and her jaw was tight. "I'll do my best to help you. I don't want to lie on their behalf anymore."

"Then I need to know where your mother is right now and how to keep your father from removing the seal."

How Jasmine responded to this would tell a lot about the depth of her involvement and what she'd been told about the plan to wipe her mother's memory. Rhys waited as Jasmine thought about it.

"That would mean she would—" she began to write, abruptly stopped and looked at Rhys. "You know?" she signed. "You want my mother to forget everything? For good?" she wrote.

"Yes," Rhys signed. "Are you fine with that?" he wrote.

"Forget me too?" Her signs were slow and deliberate. There was no mistaking it: she looked deeply unhappy. She must have been peeved at them, but they were still her parents. "Is that the only way?"

"I wouldn't ask if I thought there was any other way."

He knew it was an unreasonable request, but this was a desperate situation. He did not want to be turned into their test subject and have the dreamside become some crowded fair or a battlefield like the Crafts' plan seemed to be.

"I understand." For a while, Jasmine eyed the fragments of conversation on the piece of paper and added, "I knew it sounded fishy when Father presented it to me. He said they needed to do this and go away for a while because Mother had made a mistake and things were difficult. A year at most. They needed to make sure you wouldn't ask questions but would take me in for the time being. I knew they were lying through their teeth, but I..." Her shoulders slumped and she breathed a heavy sigh. "Frankly, I've been wanting to get away from them for a while now. He's been in a bad mood lately with something not going his way at work, and I like Julian, so I went along with it."

"Will you help?" Rhys asked.

It would boil down to whether they'd treated her poorly enough, and whether she resented them enough for it. It was not a pleasant feeling to hope that she did.

Jasmine tapped her silver chatelaine pencil on the paper as she wavered. By the time she wrote her answer, all traces of her smile had vanished. "I'll help. I don't want to hurt them, but if I don't have to go back there, it's even better than a temporary holiday. There's a machine at the Bulb. They're probably going to use that to remove the seal. She'll have to be asleep throughout the process, and it's likely to take a day or two. What do you want to do?" She watched him expectantly.

"Destroying the machine or the laboratory seems like a dangerous undertaking. Besides, your father seems savvy enough to fix anything we'd manage to break, or he could just as well move her to another location with similar equipment. I don't think that would delay him enough." Rhys rubbed his chin and tried to come up with alternatives. "Maybe we could apply a mask on your mother like the one Julian had. Do you know what I'm referring to?"

It would keep Hosta from becoming aware dreamside and thus allow Rhys to enter her bubble unbeknownst from a distance whenever he wanted and without her trying to intervene if she was so inclined. With this access, he would likely be able to sabotage the seal removal somehow and delay it for long enough for the memories to be permanently lost.

"A mask? You mean the Automated Rest Facilitator?"

"That sounds about right..."

"I've helped Mother apply it on Jacob a few times when Jacob refused to rest a couple of years ago. It's not complicated, but I'd need to access the settings panel and administer an injection. I've seen Mother do that many times. I've just never done it myself."

"Can you do it?"

"Maybe... but when? Even if my father leaves the house, he'll probably enlist Mr Murray to look after Mother. Mr Murray is his bodyguard. He might let me pass, but there's only so much I can do without raising suspicion. And to be honest, I'd prefer not to see him at all. He's scary."

"Maybe I can scout us an opening dreamside. Don't worry. Even if you do get caught, the chance of you receiving any serious repercussions is fairly low." She had a lot of good, credible excuses to be there. She also knew the place well enough to get in and out without attracting any extra attention. It seemed like this could work so long as her father and the bodyguard left Hosta unattended even for a moment. But didn't it seem just a little too easy? "What about your brothers? Are Jacob and Jonathan going to give us trouble?"

"My guess is that Father will arrange for them to stay at the school dormitory from the first excuse. That's what he always does when they're in the way."

School. Rhys frowned. There had been no mention of Jasmine attending school while staying here. They had enrolled their sons but not her? What a frustrating family.

Unless of course they were grooming Jasmine to enter the family business, and all of this was really an elaborate trap to lure Rhys in...

"Don't worry about them. Even if they're there, I think I can easily outwit them." Jasmine smiled.

Ah, it was probably fine. In what world would such a young girl be capable of such masterful deceit? Perhaps the lack of rest and the anxiety spurred on by the recent events had left him a tad too paranoid.

Once the plan was fleshed out, Rhys urged Jasmine to get some sleep. They would have a busy day ahead of them the next day. The sooner this got done the better, but it wasn't a good idea to rush in exhausted. He gathered the pieces of paper he and Jasmine had scribbled on and destroyed the evidence in the log burner in the lounge before returning to bed.

R hys kicked his duvet aside, too restless to sleep. That smile had been genuine, hadn't it? Something didn't feel right. If this was a trap and he was caught by the Crafts, what did they plan to do with him? Would they lock him in that facility again?

Was it a mistake not telling Julian and the others? But the fewer people knew, the less of a chance something reached the wrong ears.

Maybe it was just the nerves. This would be the last push, and he wouldn't have to worry about it anymore. Just this one more thing, and he'd be done.

Rhys eventually fell asleep, but his restlessness carried over to dream-side. Seeking reassurance or perhaps to distract himself from his nerves, he practised finding the void on his own. If he was caught, perhaps he'd stand a better chance of getting rescued if he could visit Julian in his bubble unassisted. But could he even do it if he had no bubble or edge to pop through like the others had? Maybe, instead of it being an extraordinary gift or a skill, his bubble was *defective*?

Fuelled by desperation after numerous unsuccessful attempts, Rhys decided to change his tactic. He went over to Julian, tried to recall the size of his bubble and shoved his hand through where he assumed the edge was. To his immeasurable relief, the tips of his fingers finally vanished into nothingness.

CHAPTER 32

The 31st of October, 04:29.

Julian was a peculiar sight, lying on the floor and rambling to himself. Rhys watched him for a while before he made his presence known, and sure enough, the man flinched and told him off for the trespass.

Rhys ignored the objections and sat next to Julian.

The conversation that followed was benign, but Julian was adamant to stick his arm into his mouth to the point where it looked painful. Since he wasn't saying anything too embarrassing, the arm seemed to be suffering for nothing.

"Can't we talk about it tomorrow?"

"No." The timing wasn't ideal, but since there was no telling what might happen tomorrow, Rhys wanted to make things clear tonight. No regrets this time.

He leaned back and rolled to his side, trying his hardest to relax. Why was it always so hard to find the right words?

"What have you got to be nervous about? You're not the one voicing all of your thoughts with no filter. I can't even look at you. It's too distracting. When I look at you, you're all I can think about." Julian turned away. Rhys stopped him from re-inserting the arm. He looked like he might soon lose his patience.

Ah, fuck. Words were overrated. When Julian reached for Rhys's hand, Rhys seized the opportunity and pushed him down. It was surprisingly easy.

"What are you doing?"

"Something I should have done a long time ago."

Julian's reaction to the proximity was adorable. The man was practically biting his lip off trying to restrain himself, so, before his lips looked as gruesome as his arms, Rhys kissed him.

When he let go, more words spilled out. He was tempted to keep doing it just to see the reactions, but, if he kept indulging himself like this, it would ultimately be misunderstood.

Rhys bumbled with the words but managed to convey at least some of this sentiment to Julian.

"Really? You mean you're being serious? How? Why? What changed?" Julian stared at him. Those eyes could be uncomfortably sharp while awake but now shone with the eager disbelief of a puppy being shown a new toy. It didn't feel bad to be the centre of his attention.

"I don't know. I had plenty of reasons, but they don't seem all that important anymore." Rhys was sure as hell not going to explain the whole of it to Julian, who would spill the beans immediately if someone else entered his bubble. It wasn't his fault, but he was a liability.

How ironic that, after he'd avoided romantic relationships most of his life, Rhys was this close to potentially entering one, yet he was also right at the cusp of losing it the next day if things went sour—

"So close. I can't breathe."

"Oh? I'm sorry, am I heavy?" Rhys jolted from his thoughts and backed away. Concentrate, concentrate! He'd missed most of what Julian had just said, but it had been something about him smelling nice.

"What? I smell of something here?" Rhys checked himself, fairly sure he wouldn't have been able to tell unless he'd smelled exceptionally bad.

What did Julian smell like? When he leaned closer to check, Rhys caught the familiar medicinal scent with a hint of bergamot. Ah, yes. This. Of course.

"I like hearing what you think," Rhys said, throwing together some last-minute word salad that seemed like it might fit whatever Julian had said a moment before.

"You just like to see me flustered."

"It's cute, but not what I'm going for. What I like more is..." A repeat of the kiss to fully appreciate it this time. Rhys leaned closer and gave his best to stay aware and present in the moment.

When he pulled back, Julian's rambly response was quite something. What was it that made watching the aftermath so much fun? Was it the thrill of having this much influence on another person? Was it because it had been such a good kiss?

Had it been good? Rhys struggled to remember. Had it tasted of something? What had it even felt like?

"...hearing how you react to me kissing you." One more try wouldn't hurt, right? Rhys leaned closer.

"If you keep doing this to me, I swear I will break." Julian's voice sounded different from usual. It was lower and more strained. "I'm getting arou—"

Oh, thank Guardian for that! It would have shattered Rhys's self-esteem had Julian not reacted at all to these kisses. On a whim, he offered his finger to the man to bite on.

It wasn't as if Rhys was completely inexperienced when it came to intimacy, but ever since the first time, he couldn't quite stay focused as it was happening. Like with Quin at Agnes Point. Like with the three kisses he'd just shared with Julian. He knew he wouldn't let it lead to anything. There was no room for a happy ending, so it was best to detach.

The sensation of Julian's warm breath, lips and teeth on his finger was too odd and unexpected to ignore, though.

Realising he was becoming aroused, Rhys had an instant full-blown inner crisis. He was ridiculously late in having one when he'd already kissed Julian thrice, and the man was figuratively and literally wrapped around his finger. Rhys didn't want to stop, but whatever waited for him at the end of this brought chills down his back.

Shit. He'd said he was serious. He'd knowingly allowed himself to be more distracted than usual, to keep himself from backing away as soon as he felt something, so clearly he'd wanted this.

Julian was open and vulnerable in front of him, against his will, and here he was as much of a guarded coward as ever, unable to give anything in return.

Damn it, that needed to stop!

"To tell you the truth, I am still afraid that you're expecting something other than what I can give you. That is the only thing holding me back right now." Rhys forced the words out. He could feel his heart thumping heavily at his throat. Fearing that Julian could tell how nervous he was, and bothered by how it felt, he removed his finger from the man's mouth.

"I'll take anything. I'd say anything to have you, but I can't think of the right words. I'm exhausted, confused and a mess. I'm sorry. What was the question?"

Julian's response was not exactly reassuring. Rhys wanted to trust him. He wanted to trust himself to be able to handle whatever happened. He'd hoped he was ready for this, but the situation felt so rushed...

"Maybe this isn't the right time for this, after all." Granted, he didn't think he'd ever truly be ready.

"I'm sorry, I'm trying, I just don't understand the problem. You need to be more specific," Julian was saying. Rhys backed away to sit, hoping a little distance might help to clear his head, but Julian followed him. There really was no way around it, was there? The only way out was through.

"I don't know what to do with this..." Rhys gestured at his crotch. "If you're looking for what I normally have, that's never going to happen. And as for this stuff," Rhys again pointed at the both of them, "I don't know how these are supposed to go together. How is this going to work?"

"So, it's a minor technical issue? I assumed it was a problem you had with me." Julian seemed relieved.

"I need to make sure you don't think I'm going to let you stick that thing into me. It's important!" Rhys could only hope Julian still had the presence of mind to take it seriously, no matter how ridiculous it might sound to him. It was not a minor technical issue! How could it be when Rhys had spent most of his life avoiding having to face it?

"The thought did cross my mind, and I admit I find it intriguing, but there are other ways to go about it." Julian gnawed his arm with an air of desperation to stop himself from elaborating further.

"Stop biting yourself and tell me. I want to make this work." When Julian refused to cooperate, Rhys was forced to pry that arm out of his mouth again.

"I don't want to tell you I suspect I've done most of the stuff I'm thinking about with Quin! And it's making me want to test it all out with you."

While it didn't require an enormous leap of imagination to understand how unpleasant mentioning someone else's name in this context could be, Rhys found himself unfazed. In fact, he was intrigued. He'd seen them kiss. He'd felt a whole host of feelings. It only now occurred to him what they could mean.

"Not what I was expecting," referring to both Julian's words and his own thoughts, Rhys reached the point where his curiosity outweighed his fears by a fraction of a hair. "But all right. That sounds promising. Let's try this again." He braced himself for another kiss, knowing that he was not going to be able to brush it off this time.

The overwhelming enthusiasm Julian showed next was contagious. For a brief moment, Rhys was confused. He felt like he was wrapped tightly inside a heated blanket. It was at the brink of becoming uncomfortable when Julian tilted his head and their lips parted.

This bubble was his domain. Whatever he was feeling seemed to change their surroundings and spilled over to Rhys.

"I... I can't. You need to stop me," Julian pleaded.

"Julian, look at me."

"I can't."

"I want you to look at me. Don't hold back. I want to see it." Rhys nibbled Julian's lip, hoping to bridge the gap to find out how far he could go.

"Ah... I like it when you're being bossy—not... what I meant to say, ignore that, I—I love it!"

"Look at me." Rhys was getting impatient. He pressed his body against Julian's for another taste of that almost excruciating heat from moments before. As he did, everything around him became just a little bit too bright, a little bit too sharp, too heavy and too hot for comfort. Then, as soon as it had passed, Rhys felt almost disgustingly mellow and relaxed throughout his body, as if he was drunk out of his mind.

Julian started to laugh, and Rhys felt an urge to join him.

"That has got to be the best, stupidest orgasm I've ever had!"

This declaration was bittersweet. Rhys was left feeling vaguely unsatisfied by the brevity while still being relieved and vicariously happy for Julian.

"I can do better," Rhys declared, hoping to resume.

"I'm sure you can, but I don't know if I could handle it."

"I'll let you rest for a bit, but we should try that again…!" Rhys tried not to sound too eager or impatient but was fairly sure he was failing. Julian would have promised him anything in the state he was in, and though Rhys enjoyed listening to him rambling, he did wish the man would stop for a moment to realise he'd left Rhys hanging.

"As much as it pleases me to hear you say these things, I think we should figure out how to fix you." It seemed the more feasible option since Rhys had no intention of ever dealing with his issues while awake. "I mean, I don't mind, but I feel like maybe this could be a little dangerous. I'm not sure I can resist teasing you when you're like this." A few excuses to make it less glaringly obvious that he wanted to help for purely selfish reasons.

"I love you," Julian said.

It was sweet of him to say, but probably unfounded. That didn't stop Rhys from wanting to hear it again.

"Even if we figure it out, please feel free to still tell me that as often as you'd like." He hoped at least one of those times he'd be able to receive it in earnest.

Victor had returned to his room in the attic, but he hadn't been able to sleep, so he spread some blueprints onto his desk and inspected them again.

The situation seemed to have resolved itself, but something about it bothered Victor. Would the vast expanse of it really crumble with Hosta out of the picture? Was there something he could do that was within his expertise that might speed up that process? All he'd done so far was stare at blueprints and run around checking different archives for crumbs of information that didn't seem to lead anywhere.

Victor turned to the dormer window. The weather outside was ghastly: cold and rainy with strong gusts of wind. Just the type of weather one would want to avoid going out in.

The blueprint he'd spread out was for an address just a five-minute walk away. It was an old three-storey building with an abnormally large cellar space that spanned under the neighbouring building. It was much larger than most of the spaces Victor had spotted.

There was an underground spring in the area. The buildings were old stock from a time when the ground surveys hadn't been as thorough as they were today. The foundations were simple, but adequate, save for one improbable scenario.

What was one more nightmare going to matter anyway, if it came to it? Victor rubbed the bridge of his nose. The thought had crossed his mind a few times in the past few days, but he'd suppressed it as too dangerous. He was fairly sure it would not be life-threatening, but there was no guarantee.

He packed his bag. Once he was sure everyone else was asleep, he grabbed his umbrella and left the house.

Approximately a month later, the building was condemned as irreparable due to subsidence caused by a change in the groundwater level. No one quite knew why. It was torn down.

After a few such ventures, Victor got into the swing of things. Some misplaced roof tiles here or a leaky pipe there, some heavy rain over a weekend, and, depending on the material, floors and ceilings would collapse in a matter of weeks if not days.

He had access to insects and fungi that could wreak havoc on most building materials, although the damage would take a year or two to be significant enough to discover. By that time, it would be beyond easy repairs. Add moisture and saltpetre and that process could be sped along somewhat.

Introducing the right components to the right locations took a bit of imagination but ultimately wasn't difficult. Some of the building code violations were begging for an accident to happen. A leaky gas pipe, poorly constructed chimney flue... It didn't take much to trigger immediate effects.

In addition to property damage, the equipment within the locations was susceptible to moisture and the sharp teeth of some conveniently placed and quickly reproducing rodents that happened to appear as if from thin air. But the city was full of vermin, and this was just an especially bad year.

Victor paced himself and picked locations and times to avoid a traceable pattern. Slower methods for places that weren't critical, quick ones for what he wanted unusable before Midwinter Fest.

Someone would undoubtedly take notice once the results of the quicker methods rolled in, but so long as they were not going to survey each location thoroughly, they would not know the full extent until it was too late.

Because they likely wanted to keep their spaces out of the public eye, they could not start any official police investigations and would have to rely on whatever information they could dig up privately. Victor made sure there wasn't much to find.

Since his cellar test run, Victor had targeted as many of the tiny spaces as he could without it becoming too obvious. He made sure to ruin those spots from a distance whenever possible as they seemed to form the backbone of Hosta's surveillance network and hence would be something they were likely to keep an exceptionally close eye on.

Most of them were unmanned during the night, though, so Victor didn't have to worry about casualties. And so far he'd seen no indication of anyone or anything tracking his visits.

He did run into some rotten cadavers or mummified remains at a large number of those locations. He carefully picked them up and buried them in various locations as far off as he had time to carry them without wasting the whole night. After all, he needed his sleep to do his regular work during the day.

On occasions where the posts had been manned by corpses, Victor had been lucky that the machines had been switched off. Perhaps the dead were not as useful during the night?

He hoped those poor souls would find peace once they were no longer forced to work as spies. Perhaps later on, he could find out who they were and whether they'd had any last wishes they'd wanted fulfilled. He'd ask Rhys if the situation ever seemed stable enough for something like that.

Victor wasn't naïve enough to think that mere sabotage was enough to stop something as big as the Hosta Group, but if they had to relocate and rebuild, it would be money diverted away from other activities and their research.

Monetary losses. Downtime. Disgruntled customers refusing to pay. Considering their client base, problems with delivery might lead to other kinds of trouble.

The amount of effort Victor was putting in was very small compared to the possible benefits, so he was highly motivated to continue for as long as he could while the risks were still minimal. It was an engaging little game he enjoyed, and it made him feel better about having been so useless when Julian and Rhys had needed help in the past.

CHAPTER 33

An errant swipe and Theodore slid over the edge of the desk, smashed into pieces and spilled cold coffee across the floor.

Dr Vesper turned to look. A mess. She rubbed her brow and suppressed her yawn. Could she ask someone else to clean that up, or...? Damn it.

She got up to pick up the pieces and to wipe what she could with her handkerchief. The rest would have to wait. She was too tired.

There was no getting around it, it seemed. She'd got her hands on every piece of information about subject one, as well as the Guardian, but no matter how many times she pored over it, there was always something missing.

"Why do I bother," she mumbled to herself. She didn't even know where Vincent was, and Vincent himself didn't seem to care.

Yet, it didn't feel right to give up on it. There had to be a way to reverse Vincent's condition.

Dr Vesper had dug up one of Hosta's private research notebooks from the depths of the archives, and it had all but confirmed as much. It just hadn't mentioned the method.

Maybe there was a way to ask her about it without it seeming suspicious? Or wring it out of her by force if necessary? Dr Vesper was certainly tired enough to no longer care about the consequences. She'd been at this for what must have been weeks, and she did not do well with this much pressure coupled with such little sleep.

She picked up the receiver and requested the operator to put her through to Hosta's office. Her secretary picked up the call.

"I'm sorry. She's not in at the moment. She has taken some personal time off for the Day of the Deceased."

"Did she say when she'd be back?"

"The day after tomorrow, but she did leave me a number in case of an emergency."

This likely did not count as an emergency, but Dr Vesper figured she would risk it. After obtaining the number, she asked the operator to connect her to it.

"The Craft Pharmacy, Julian Craft speaking. How may I help you?"

Dr Vesper froze as her tired head ambled to catch up.

"Hello, Julian. Sorry, I didn't expect this to be your number..." She collected her scattered thoughts.

"Excuse me, miss. Who am I speaking to?"

"Oh, pardon me. It's Vera. Dr Vesper. I meant to call after Hosta Aelia..."

"I'm sorry. My mother is not available right now. Can I take a message?"

Your mother? Your *mother*?! They were—? That was—? Well, they did seem a little alike to think of it. There was a certain sharpness to the features.

"Dr Vesper, are you there? Are you working for her? Was it something important you needed her for?" Julian asked.

"No... Well, yes. It was work-related. I'll just ask her when she gets back—"

"I hope it isn't anything too pressing. She might not be returning to work."

"What do you mean? Is she unwell?"

"I'm assuming my father will explain the details when it's time, but I would suggest looking for alternative employment. My parents may have to close the business."

Well, that didn't sound good. What about all the work they were doing? What was so bad it could cause Hosta to abandon this research so suddenly?

But even if she did retire, so long as she was still alive, there might be a chance to talk to her about subject one and how to reverse whatever she'd done to him.

"Have you heard anything about Vincent?" Dr Vesper thought to ask for no other reason than 'while she was at it'.

"No, not since he left. But Rhys said he was heading to Làirig Áir with Ren for the winter, so I suppose he won't be back until spring."

Làirig Áir? That imbecile couldn't have run off much further without leaving the damn continent. Dr Vesper clenched the receiver in her hand. Hopefully Ren would keep him out of trouble.

"All right. Well, if Rhys sends him a message, tell him to add that he needs to get his butt back here for the treatment as soon as possib—!" Dr Vesper bit her tongue, exasperated. What the hell was she even saying?

"I'll relay your message."

No, no, please don't. She shielded her tired eyes with her forearm and leaned back in her chair.

"Thank you. Well, say hello to everyone from me." Guardian help her for being such a fool to reduce herself to this every time she so much as had a stray thought about Vincent.

"Will do."

Dr Vesper said something resembling a goodbye and hung up the phone.

Why was it always such bad news? Things had all been going downhill ever since she'd bumped into Vincent at the Sleepy Leighs.

She reached to take a sip out of Theodore to realise that he, too, had abandoned her.

Men were always so troublesome and dramatic with their exits! The corner of her eye twitched.

Rhys left the house with Jasmine after breakfast with the pretence of taking her out for some shopping now that she would be staying at the pharmacy for a while.

Jasmine knew her neighbourhood in the Ear of the City, so finding a quiet, secluded place for some shut-eye proved easy. There was a courtyard with a fenced off garden only a few streets away from the house, and she said hardly anyone ever used it.

Rhys made himself as comfortable as one could on an old wooden bench that was much too short for him, at the far end of the garden. Jasmine waited and kept watch. She was to wake Rhys after a quarter of an hour to hear if the coast was clear.

Not knowing if Mr Craft and his bodyguard Mr Murray would even leave the house that day was making the both of them nervous, but Jasmine seemed sure her father would head out at least once before noon since that was what he always did. Hopefully, the situation with his wife did not merit a deviation from his routines and that he wouldn't leave Mr Murray behind.

Rhys entered the building dreamside. While he couldn't be sure that no one was able to detect his arrival, according to Jasmine, there was no round-the-clock surveillance. Rhys remained on edge regardless, even when, after ten or so minutes of going through the house, nothing unexpected had happened.

Hosta lay unconscious in a bed in the laboratory, hooked to an impressive array of machinery. Mr Craft or the bodyguard were nowhere to be seen. There was no sign of either Jonathan or Jacob.

Jasmine woke Rhys as planned. From then on, it was all up to her. To ease his paranoia, Rhys relocated after she'd left. They'd estimated it would take at least half an hour for her to manage everything, so Rhys spent that time walking at a nearby park, admiring an old stave church, trying not to appear shifty despite the constant urge to peek over his shoulders.

When he returned, he could see Jasmine from a distance, sitting on the bench alone, looking rather miserable to have been so cruelly abandoned. As soon as she saw him, she looked relieved and happy. She did not even ask where he'd been but, instead, reported her success with enthusiasm. The first stage of their plan had gone without a hitch.

S ince time was of the essence, Rhys needed to re-enter dreamside posthaste. Reluctant to stay at the same place, he hurried to the park where he'd been only moments earlier. There were several benches, but the area was popular this time of day, and the benches were exposed right next to pathways. Rhys was forced to make do with one by the pond, a little to the side, with some trees and bushes blocking at least some of the view. There was enough space for Jasmine to sit this time, and so, from where people passed them, it looked like she was there feeding the ducks alone.

Rhys fell asleep easily. He headed straight for the Crafts' house and up into the laboratory. He was not particularly confident about finding his way into Hosta's bubble because he had no idea of its size, but hopefully, it would be about the same size as her sons'.

Handling this without having to enlist help was much faster, safer and more convenient than trying to find a way to bring either Justin or Jasmine close enough to pull Rhys into the void at a safe distance from Hosta. It had nothing to do with the nagging feeling someone might double-cross him if he asked for their help.

Finding the receiving edge was much more comfortable as well, as he could pop right over without most of the nastiness of going through the void. There was plenty of motivation, even when it felt like a hopeless task.

Rhys found the edge after ten or so long and frustrating minutes of shoving and poking. According to Jasmine, he had over a half an hour from when she'd administered the drug, so he was still well within the time frame. Even had he been a little late, it would have been trickier but not impossible.

He entered fully expecting this to be a trap.

At the centre of the bubble, back towards Rhys, there sat a slender young woman not at all what Mrs Craft looked like at present. She had pale skin, dark, almost black hair all the way down to her hips, and she wore a simple white shift that made her look much like the archetypal ghost.

She turned to look at Rhys.

"Who's there? Who are you?" Her having to ask was promising. "Where am I?" Her second question was even better. If she could not tell where she was, her memory must have still been mostly sealed.

"I'm here to help you." Rhys felt guilt over the lie, but he'd gladly live with a bit of guilt for this cause.

He knelt down next to Hosta and set his palms over her head as Jasmine had instructed. All the while, he felt nauseated from the nerves and the expectation that someone was about to stab him if or when he let his guard down.

"Where's my baby?" Hosta asked but did not resist. She sat there waiting for Rhys to do whatever he was doing without questioning any of it.

Too easy. For the full thirty minutes that Rhys spent making sure the drug Jasmine had administered was spread evenly across Hosta's brain, she sat there without saying anything other than occasionally asking about a baby, and Rhys fought against his nerves and the urge to run off. What baby? She seemed much too young to be referring to Julian.

When Rhys was done, he was relieved, but at the back of his mind he was already dreading having to come back to make sure Mr Craft hadn't noticed or tried to remove the ARF mask. The saving grace was that when she would next fall to rest, she was unlikely to become aware again and would instead stay resting indefinitely until the mask was removed.

CHAPTER 34

Dr Vesper was called into Mr Craft's office. The office mirrored the grandeur of the ReM Clinic's stave church-like entrance, although it was smaller in scale.

"It's the old chapel," Mr Craft noted when Dr Vesper examined some of the detailed religious carvings on the staves themselves. "Please, take a seat." He directed her to a chair. "I know you only just transferred here, and this may be sudden, but my wife has named you one of her most trusted employees. There is something I would like your help with."

"What is it, sir?"

"In this line of work, it is difficult to survive without making some enemies. My wife has sacrificed herself to ensure the integrity of our research. It may cost her memories if we do not reverse what was done to her. Seeing as you are part of her sleep cleanliness research team, I would be grateful for your help." He presented her with what was presumably Hosta's diagnostic data. "As you can see, if this persists, there will be irreversible consequences. Luckily, we have researched these underhanded techniques in preparation for an occasion such as this. Unfortunately, the reversal process seems to be slower than anticipated. I need your help in determining why that is."

"I cannot promise anything, but I will take a look." Perhaps aiding Hosta in this way would make it easier to persuade her to reveal how to deal with Vincent's problem.

"Good." Mr Craft seemed relieved. "There is one more thing I would like you to consider."

"Yes, sir?" As long as it was within her expertise. The more they trusted her and were indebted, the better her chances.

"My wife is understandably not in a condition to resume her research or her administrative duties, and I have my hands full with the business and marketing. I know this is a lot to ask, but could you assume her role for the time being?"

A lot to ask?

"I couldn't possibly…"

A lot? This was huge.

"She has named you for this position herself, so she must have great faith in you."

"And that is an honour, sir, but—" There was no way she would be able to handle all of that. She had no training. She was essentially a bookworm with a single special interest.

"Please. In all honesty, it would be greatly advantageous since you have not been with us at the ReM Clinic for long enough to become entangled in the office politics. I shouldn't be saying this, but my hands are effectively tied. If I choose any other person here, I will be accused of favouritism and cause major discontent that will disrupt the research."

It was ultimately going to be an unfavourable career move, but since Dr Vesper wasn't feeling excessively optimistic about her career at present anyway, it wouldn't necessarily make much of a difference. If nothing else, she might be able to wring a recommendation letter out of Mr Craft at the end of it and find herself another job somewhere else.

"I'm not sure I'm qualified."

"That's fine. I will guide you through it. And you will be able to return to your research as soon as my wife has recovered and is able to resume her work." Mr Craft offered her a set of keys and a badge. "I will have my lawyer go through the contract with you later today, and here is the address to our private laboratory. If you could join us this afternoon to start the treatment without delay." He handed her a card with the address on it.

"I will do my best." Dr Vesper frowned at the keys, the badge and the card. The keys looked promising and might grant her access to a few of the previously restricted places. Perhaps she'd find something so useful she wouldn't even have to ask Hosta about subject one.

The items in her hand felt incredibly heavy. This freedom no doubt carried a price the size of which was difficult to foresee.

Dr Vesper had been momentarily tempted to take Hosta up on her offer of conveniently forgetting some of the less enjoyable aspects of her research, but tackling what had been done to Hosta to seal her memories made her glad she'd decided against it.

Trying to manipulate the output back to normal was like cleaning treacle from a thick, high-pile rya with her bare hands. She could remove a lot of the proverbial gunk, but a sticky layer still remained at the end of the day, and a new, thicker layer would appear out of nowhere the next day.

It felt like she wasn't making any headway, and the lack of progress was worrisome. If she couldn't salvage this, how would Mr Craft react? He didn't seem like an unkind man, but something suggested he wouldn't be as understanding as the initial impression led on.

Back at the ReM Clinic, Dr Vesper's research into the restricted areas she'd gained access to hadn't borne much fruit. It had been educational, for sure, but it hadn't been the sort of information she'd wanted to find. There was a whole seedy underbelly to the Hosta Group Dr Vesper would have preferred to leave undiscovered. It certainly wasn't helping her sleep her nights any better.

A person capable of shouldering these responsibilities must have either been rotten to the core or driven by something to the point of absolute blindness. Whatever the reason Hosta and her husband were doing this for must have been extremely corruptive, important, or both, for them to be able to ignore the collateral damage.

Dr Vesper scoured through research notes for any clues as to why Hosta's condition was not improving despite the treatment, when a colleague of hers knocked on the door to her office.

"Excuse me, Dr Vesper, there's a visitor here for you," she informed her from the door.

"Who is it?"

"I'm sorry. I didn't think to ask, but I was told they are waiting upstairs in the nave."

Dr Vesper thanked her and left the office. There weren't many people who knew where she worked, and the few who did wouldn't have turned up unannounced. She was rightly taken aback by the sight of Ren's hunched figure near the main entrance.

"Dr Vera!" She looked up, face smudged by some dirt and possibly tears.

"What's wrong?" Dr Vesper hurried over to her to check that she was unharmed. With nothing visible the matter with her, it must have been Vincent. Her heart sank.

"It's..." Ren pressed her lips together and wrinkled her brow from the effort. "Vincent," she whispered.

"Where is he? What's wrong?" Weren't they supposed to be halfway across the continent?

"We're staying at a boarding house on Codtrough Street." Ren looked ready to cry, so Dr Vesper instinctively gave her a hug.

"Is it the cold?" she asked, kneeling next to the girl. Running around in such chilly, wet weather may have easily made Vincent's condition life-threatening. Knowing how stubborn he could be about accepting help and knowing that Ren would not have turned up if the situation weren't dire, Dr Vesper didn't bother with an overcoat. "I'll come at once." She took Ren by the hand and headed out.

"I'm sorry I lashed out at you before. I know you were only trying to help," Ren peeped as they hurried across the yard.

"It's all forgotten. Don't worry about it." It wasn't personal. Dr Vesper had always known as much. "Codtrough Street, that's west from here, right?" She remembered passing it on her way to work. To think that they had been almost next door to her all this time.

"Yes. It seemed like a good area. Homey, he said."

"How did you find me?" Dr Vesper thought to ask. She wasn't surprised by Ren's resourcefulness, but the details intrigued her.

"I saw you."

"When?"

"A few times the past few days. We've been here for a while. I wanted to come sooner, but—" She stopped walking. Dr Vesper turned to look. "I thought you'd be mad. And he's not been himself."

Oh, right. Dr Vesper paused to think about it. Yes, that was right. She was upset. That damn scoundrel. From her perspective, leaving without a trace sounded exactly like something he would do.

What was she doing, dropping everything and going after him again, when it was likely unwanted attention? Why not just call a doctor and stay out of it? Never mind that she'd been exhausting herself with research for weeks just to get a step closer to figuring out how to reverse his condition. Maybe this was supposed to be a wake-up call for her to get her life back on track and stop wasting time on this pointless side quest.

"Look, Ren, maybe I should—" She was yanked forward by the girl now in front of her.

"You need to come with me." Ren didn't look back, just pulled Dr Vesper along with the determination of an oxe. With so little distance to Codtrough Street left, Dr Vesper effectively ran out of time to object, and, already pulled into the building, she was too exhausted to put up a fight.

Ren led her up the stairs to similar but more modest accommodations than her own just a few streets down from here.

"Here." The girl opened the door and pushed Dr Vesper in. To her surprise, the door was shut behind her, and she could hear the sound of the lock being turned.

"Ren?" What on earth? She tried the handle to confirm the door was locked. When she turned around, Vincent sat on the bed at the other end of the room, probably equally perplexed, but looking just about as healthy as he could for someone so severely, chronically sleep-deprived.

"I'm sorry, what? Why are you here?" Vincent frowned.

Ren, the little snake. When had she learnt to be so cunning?

"Ren! Could you open the door, please?" Dr Vesper peeked through the keyhole, but the corridor on the other side was empty. What did she expect her to do? If it wasn't for a life-threatening illness, was she supposed to talk Vincent back into treatment for his sleeping issues?

"Did she lock us in here?" Vincent walked to her at the door. His height always caught her off guard. "Ren?" He tried to open the door.

"I'm sorry, I didn't mean to disturb..." Why was she having to feel like an intruder in a situation she'd been forcefully pushed into?

"No, I'm sorry. I don't know what's got into her." Vincent turned to a desk and pulled out a spare key from one of the drawers. "My apologies for wasting your time like this. I'll have a talk with her to make sure it doesn't happen again." He opened the door.

"It's fine..." What was this feeling she struggled to identify? Exhaustion?

"I trust you know your way out. Please excuse me."

Vincent left Dr Vesper standing alone in the room. The door inched its way back shut.

Did this count? Was this the third time?

It had to be exhaustion. She took a few steps back and sat on the bed, feeling absolutely drained. Really, she should have kept a distance since the first time, but she was too tired even to scold herself. What good did it do when she never seemed to learn anything from it? Was she doomed to repeat the same mistake? And moreover, how did Vincent deal with this level of exhaustion day in and out? It was brutal.

The door opened. No one entered for the first few seconds, but, by the time Dr Vesper thought to look up, Vincent peeked through the crack.

"I'll deal with her later. I'm sorry." He stepped in and closed the door.

She was too tired to think of anything to say, so she watched him there, somehow less sure of himself than usual. What was he sorry for? Ren? Were his hands shaking, or was she imagining things? Vincent always seemed so confident and experienced, like he'd seen so much he wasn't rattled about anything. Was this, then, a physical symptom of something? Malnutrition? A muscle tremor from weakness after his illness? Simple fatigue?

"I'm sorry I left you like that. I'm a coward," he said. "I know it was inexcusable, and I don't expect you to forgive me, but I feel like I owe you an explanation should you want one."

Dr Vesper searched for the words, but when the right ones eluded her, she contended with a nod.

"The truth is, I-I find you delightful company. I'm— I, I think you're unendingly fascinating, and I would very much like to spend all my time in your company, but I... I don't have much to offer to you in terms of, ah, intellectual conversation or, or, or companionship. I'm afraid I am so flawed I cannot imagine myself being much more than a burden to you.

And I suppose, for this reason, my instinct is to withdraw before I hurt myself or cause you more trouble than I already have. I am deeply sorry for my cowardly, rude behaviour before. Rest assured, it was no reflection on you."

Oh, my Lord, my Guardian, my Saviour, Dr Vesper thought she might just faint. He wanted to spend *all* his time in her company? How the hell did Vincent deal with never being sure whether he was asleep or awake when she couldn't cope with these few minutes of feeling like she was hallucinating from being so tired?

"Please say something..." He crouched down in front of her as she sat on his bed. "It would be easier if you told me if you wanted me to leave."

"I don't want you to leave." She swallowed.

"Really?" He set his hand on hers.

"When have I ever said I wanted you to leave?"

"Not in so many words, but I thought..."

"You thought what? Why did you leave? What did I do to make you feel anything but wanted?" He'd said it wasn't her fault, but she'd spent so many years trying to figure out what she'd done wrong, there had to have been something.

His eyebrows crashed into a quivering caterpillar trainwreck. Watching them at it usually brought Dr Vesper a fair bit of joy, but she feared this time it meant he was about to say something difficult that she didn't want to hear.

"You did call out... Ah, never mind."

"What? I called out what?" She leaned a little closer to hear better.

"I'm sorry, I thought I heard you call out someone else's name, but it was probably a hallucination brought on by my insecurities or this damned condition. You probably did no such thing, but I was so afraid of rejection, I thought I would sabotage everything and make it even worse for the both of us." He squeezed her hands.

"What name? When?"

"It doesn't matter, I don't even remember. Maybe Harold... Or Jeremy?"

Dr Vesper blushed all the way to her ears. With nowhere to go, she leaned forward and hid her face in his shirt.

"Are you all right? What is it?" He tried to move her hair aside to see.

"It was Gerard," she said. Whatever had possessed her to name some-thing at that precise moment, as if it were hers to own, she could not bring herself to even think about.

"Ah, right..." He sounded disappointed.

It was frightfully embarrassing, but this seemed like a misunderstanding she would have to clear up, regardless of how much it made her cheeks burn.

She closed her eyes and moved closer to his ear to say it as quietly as she could with him still able to hear her. As soon as she'd said it, Vincent coughed and cleared his throat.

"That... That's a little too flattering for... That's a..."

"I thought it was fitting." She heard herself let out a nervous giggle. With her nerves finally easing, she felt like she might fall asleep where she sat.

"Are you sure you're all right?" Vincent's voice sounded distant.

"I don't know how you can bear this."

"What do you mean?"

"I haven't been sleeping... Can I just sleep here for a moment?" She didn't want to move.

"Yes, of course." He stroked her hair.

"You're not going to leave while I'm asleep, are you?"

"No, not if you don't want me to."

"You'd better not, or I won't forgive you." She clutched at his shirt. "Not for at least a week."

CHAPTER 35

Rhys helped Victor work on the attic, and, with occasional help from Quin, they added insulation to the roof, put up partition walls and did the rendering.

Jasmine picked out a lovely floral wallpaper for her room, and Quin painted his walls rich, dark green. There was talk about adding some panelling come summer, but these finishing touches could wait. The two rooms were now ready to move in. They hauled in the essential furniture a few days before Midwinter Fest.

The Fest, of course, wouldn't be the same as the previous year's, but Rhys had promised Jasmine a tree, some decorations and lights and that they'd go visit the market square.

A card arrived from Jasmine's father, wishing them happy holidays, and it seemed this was going to be Jasmine's first Midwinter Fest without her parents. Rhys vowed to do his best to make it as good as it could be for her under the circumstances.

Julian and Jasmine were in charge of food with Rhys helping out with a few choice items familiar to him. The selection was not going to be as varied and fancy as before, but they took a stab at as many of the traditional dishes as was feasible. Rhys had asked the neighbours for some recipes to try, and on top of the recipes, some of them came by with offerings of pudding, mulled wine and ginger cakes.

Despite them having been away most of the year, the neighbours were supportive and welcoming, and Julian's customer base was growing steadily. People had also been inquiring after Rhys's services, but between everything he'd crammed into his days—the workouts, the signing, trying to figure out how to help fix Julian dreamside and dealing with Hosta—he'd had to cut back somewhere.

There was a lot to be thankful for, even if it had been a difficult year.

Quin had transferred a portion of his wealth over to Julian, explaining that it was his fair share of what he'd helped to build. This meant that Julian was free to no longer work, but he kept the pharmacy running mostly as a hobby and a charity for some of his less wealthy customers.

Victor was doing well, steadily selling some of his paintings or doing carpentry jobs. On top of the renovations on the attic, he'd had time to carve and paint a set of Midwinter-themed woodland creatures for decorating the wreaths and the tree to complement the glass baubles that Rhys had bought from a little shop down the street. He'd also fixed the gutters to make them sturdier. For his contributions, he'd received a formidable rent decrease, so he was also not struggling financially.

If not for feeling like he was stretched thin into multiple directions, Rhys was feeling good about the upcoming holidays.

Julian was lost in his thoughts at his work desk, periodically forgetting what he was doing. He'd meant to wrap up and draw a bath for himself, but he was sitting there with his things scattered, unable to concentrate for long enough to put them away.

It hadn't been an easy decision to relinquish sleep-roaming when it had become clear he wasn't able to initiate sufficient rest in his corrupted state. He'd enjoyed Rhys's company, but the lack of inhibition had got much worse the more rest-deprived he'd become, and in just a few short days, he'd been genuinely afraid something terrible might happen if they didn't do something to fix him.

Good thing, then, that Jasmine had known about the ARF procedure, and they'd been able to reapply the mask that helped him rest. Unfortunately, he was too reserved, too self-conscious, and too much of a wimp, even, to approach Rhys with anything intimate while awake, so their relationship had consequently come to a frustrating standstill. He kept himself busy with work to avoid the issue, but if this persisted, Rhys would, with good reason, think he was no longer interested.

Midwinter was almost here, and Julian still had no idea what to give Rhys. He'd found gifts for Quin, Victor and Jasmine, but nothing seemed meaningful enough to give to Rhys. At this rate he'd end up having nothing to give, which was frankly, a disaster. He was keenly aware that he was running out of time, but that was admittedly the only thing he was keenly aware of.

It had been a long night. Rhys was exhausted. He dragged himself into the lounge as always, although this morning he really wasn't in the mood to finish off the Midwinter preparations.

The food that could be prepared in advance had been prepared, he had decorated the lounge the day before, and the top floors were all cleaned and ready for what was ahead. There wasn't much left to do; just a few details here and there, but he was tired and regretting his level of commitment.

Julian was up early as per usual.

"Once you have eaten, if you can spare a moment, I have a surprise for you," he said.

"Really? What is it?" Rhys tried to engage with curiosity and excitement but couldn't resist a yawn.

"It's a surprise."

Rhys sat down at the table and hoped sustenance would help him gather some more enthusiasm. He had no appetite, so he spent a quarter of an hour forcing down a few bites and poking the rest with his fork before he gave up.

He got dressed and ready to go, even though he wondered in passing whether today was going to be the day Julian double-crossed him and took him somewhere to be prodded on like a lab animal.

He'd had a bad feeling throughout last night—well, throughout the past week—that something bad was bound to happen soon. He didn't know what, but it was bound to be something awful.

Julian abruptly realised that Rhys was acting moodier than usual this morning. Had he missed something important and angered the boy? Had Rhys reached the end of his patience? This added worry did not help Julian's insecurity over the gift he'd chosen.

It had been a little at the last minute, but, having the ease of ample finances, Julian had managed to secure the appointment. Rhys trailed after him, looking less than pleased, but it was to be expected for dragging him out here with no forewarning.

Having seen the full rotation of Rhys's wardrobe, Julian was aware of the dismal state of it. Most of his clothes seemed like something he'd purchased second-hand without bothering with fittings or alterations.

It didn't matter much in the case of informal wear, and, in truth, most of what Rhys wore was casual these days. But there were a handful of occasions that required a properly fitted full formal dress or at least something neater to wear. Rhys had nothing that would fit that description—especially after all the hard work he'd put in this year. He probably hadn't noticed it himself, but most of his shirts were tight around the chest and shoulders, and his trousers looked short for being too small where they clung to his newly gained leg muscles.

When they arrived at a small but reasonably well-known tailor's shop a walking distance from the pharmacy, Julian opened the door for Rhys, and he entered, suspicious, as if he were led to slaughter.

"What did you have in mind?" he asked, eyeing some gloves on display.

"I was thinking of a full dress: coat, waistcoat, shirt, tie, trousers, socks, boots, hat, gloves; everything." Possibly also some shirts and trousers for more frequent use.

"What?" Rhys stared at him. "I thought maybe a pocket square..."

Julian glanced at the saleswoman, who had let the tailor know they had arrived. She smiled at him.

"Mr Craft, I presume?" She welcomed them and offered to take their coats to hang aside. The tailor appeared from the back shortly after.

"My apologies for keeping you waiting, good sirs. I trust you are well. Shall we begin? Is this the gentleman we will be serving today?" The tailor turned to Rhys, who was clearly in a more dire need of it. Rhys seemed to be in a state of shock.

"A full dress, are you insane? That's *expensive*," he whispered to Julian.

"You know that's not an issue."

"It's an issue for me. You can't be spending that much money on me!"

"Why not?"

"It's not— it's— I don't know, it feels *wrong*. It's too much."

"What's the use of having this wealth if I can't spend it on something that makes me happy?"

Julian hoped that emphasising he was doing it for his own sake would help Rhys come to terms with the price. It seemed it might have done the trick since Rhys was only mildly cringing when they discussed the cloth, style and trim options with the tailor. He looked pale but did not resist when the tailor guided him to a corner of the room to take the measurements.

"I will have the informal wear for you by the end of the week. Expedited, the dress will be six to eight weeks depending on when you are available for fittings, sir."

The tailor was swift to take the measurements, but there were a lot of measurements to take, so it did take him a while.

The full dress was going to be completely bespoke, but the informal shirts were pre-made according to the tailor's own standard patterns. Rhys needed to try on the different sizes to see which was the closest fit and what alterations needed to be made. He stood through the measuring and the fitting, looking somewhat mortified, like he was trying to calculate how expensive all of this would be.

"Don't worry about it. I want you to feel comfortable in clothes that fit properly," Julian tried to assure him.

"I appreciate it." Rhys seemed to have given up on the objections. "It's just a little overwhelming." He sighed heavily.

"Also, if there's anything else here you'd like, let me know. A scarf maybe?" Julian perused the fine woollen scarves in muted patterns and shades of brown, green, burgundy and blue. "How's this?" He suggested one that complemented the coat Rhys was currently wearing. Rhys did not seem impressed but, by the looks of it, deemed the material soft and pleasant enough to touch.

"I did get you a present, but I'm starting to feel like it's nowhere near enough." Rhys looked increasingly worried when Julian set the scarf onto the counter as something he was going to buy and moved onto the gloves.

"I want to show my appreciation. There's no need for you to match it." Julian picked out a pair with lining similar to the scarf. "How do these fit?"

Rhys sighed but took the gloves and put them on. They were much too large for him, and, while they would have kept his fingers warm, he didn't seem like he'd be able to do much with them on. Julian offered him a smaller pair. He put them on, and they fit just fine, but he looked tortured.

"What is it? Are they not to your liking?"

"They're a little stiff..." He moved his fingers, and they barely moved. Out of the men's glove selection, these two seemed like the only two pairs that might fit him and even remotely match the scarf, so Julian was at a loss.

Then he remembered the pair Rhys had looked at when they had walked in. They were an unusually dark pair of women's 4-button kid leather gloves with small flower-shaped brass buttons. They were obviously women's gloves when on display, but, with sleeves covering the buttons, no one would know the difference when worn. Bringing them up seemed like it might upset Rhys, so Julian kept his mouth shut and sat down while he waited for the tailor to be done.

Julian had mentioned Rhys's unconventional proportions in advance to avoid as much of the discomfort the fitting might cause the boy. The tailor was an experienced professional. He made no unnecessary remarks and took extra care to make the shirt fit Rhys's slender figure in a way that would be the most flattering. Rhys still looked uncomfortable having to strip in front of a stranger, but he was wearing his binding undershirt, and there was nothing markedly unusual or revealing about the process.

As the tailor pinned the last seams into place, Julian was taken aback by how big a difference a mere properly fitted shirt could make. Instead of an adolescent boy, Rhys finally looked like an adult man.

The tailor took a step back to take in the full view. He adjusted one more pin before he was satisfied and then turned to Julian.

"He is in need of trousers as well, isn't he?" The trousers Rhys was wearing looked especially bad now that the shirt fit. "I think I have something in the back in his approximate size. I could alter them so he has something to go with the shirts until I can make him his own pair."

The tailor gestured for Rhys to take off his trousers while he hurried to the back. Rhys heaved another massive sigh once the man was out of sight but did as he was told and removed his trousers.

"Should I get something for the others as well?" Julian had made some acquisitions prior to this, but, since he was here and satisfied with the quality and designs available, it seemed like an easy addition.

There was a pretty light blue shawl that Jasmine might like and slippers in sizes large enough to fit Victor. Quin seemed like he already had everything he needed but probably wouldn't mind another scarf. Perhaps one that was thinner than the woollen winter scarves...

At a glance, Rhys looked like he was suffering.

"Are you going to empty the whole shop?" he asked.

"No. Just this shelf."

Julian picked out the ones he liked and stacked them onto the counter. The women's gloves were still weighing on his mind, so he picked them up to take a better look of the shape and size. If it weren't for the buttons, he wouldn't have hesitated.

"For Jasmine?" Rhys had noticed him with the gloves.

"No..." Julian admitted. Rhys looked at him about as disappointed and upset as could be expected but said nothing. Julian decided to push it just a tiny bit. "Would it hurt to try them on?"

Still no reply.

Julian sat back down and watched Rhys finger the hem of the shirt he was wearing. After a minute or two, he reached to grab the gloves from the counter, put them on and showed them to Julian.

Something about his eyes seemed as if challenging Julian to a fight. The gloves fit perfectly, and they looked good on him. They were a solid pair of gloves.

"Well, say something," Rhys finally said.

"They look fine to me, but what matters is whether you're comfortable wearing them."

The tailor returned with the trousers. He glanced at the gloves Rhys was wearing and then at him.

"Would you like us to replace the buttons with something else, sir?" he asked.

Rhys traced his finger along the row of them with a difficult to interpret expression on his face.

"Would it seem off if I didn't?"

The tailor shrugged.

"Truth be told, that design is one of my favourites. I have these same buttons on a waistcoat I'm especially fond of. Would you like them on yours, sir?"

Rhys nodded, put the gloves back on the counter with the rest of Julian's intended purchases and returned for the trouser fitting.

The trousers were too long for him but otherwise a near-to-perfect fit. Once the trouser legs were pinned to the correct length, all that was missing was a less scruffy looking coat. Rhys's patience appeared to be at its limit for the day, so there was no sense in prolonging his torment. There would be time to talk him into it later.

"It's an improvement, certainly." The tailor sounded somewhat more critical than Julian. "But there are some more fashionable, flattering options."

Neither Julian nor Rhys had paid much attention to what was fashionable, but, so long as it was practical, reasonably comfortable and didn't look like a shapeless burlap sack, Julian was happy to trust the tailor's expertise.

"You can change back to your own clothes now, sir," the tailor said to Rhys while scribbling down some notes onto a piece of paper.

Rhys responded with a series of yawns.

Julian turned to discuss the details of the final order with the tailor and paid for the stack of gifts. He was about to give Rhys the scarf and the gloves when he heard a loud thump behind him.

The tailor looked up and a quick glance of the man's startled face hastened Julian to spin around to see what had happened. Rhys was on the floor unconscious. A wave of nausea flushed over Julian.

"What happened? Are you all right?" the tailor asked before Julian could react. Once he'd shaken off his initial shock, Julian knelt down to check. The pulse was fine. No fever. Rhys was cool and clammy to touch.

Had he just fainted? The under-shirt was a little tighter than what one normally would wear but not by much.

"Did he faint?" the tailor asked. "I've seen my share of people fainting during long fittings, but they are usually women."

Julian prayed Rhys had not heard this comment as he was regaining consciousness. Thankfully, he was starting to come out of it on his own. That was a good sign.

"What happened? Where am I?" Rhys closed his eyes and rubbed his creased forehead.

"You fainted. We're at the tailor's shop," Julian replied. "How do you feel?"

"Fainted? No, I was— No, don't touch me." He looked confused. Then he looked at the tailor and seemed to remember. "Oh, right. I could have sworn I was..." He looked around himself.

"It's all right. You ate next to nothing for breakfast this morning, and I assume you didn't sleep too well. You've had to stay on your feet for quite a while. It happens."

"This is a dream, right?" Rhys scrambled back up to stand. He refused Julian's help and steadied himself by leaning on the back of a chair behind him instead.

"No, we're awake," Julian corrected him.

"Really?" Rhys scratched his head. "That can't be right."

"I think you're just tired. You looked more frazzled than usual this morning."

To think of it, Rhys had seemed fatigued for a while now. Julian figured it was probably because he'd been busy with the renovations, his hobbies and the Midwinter preparations. Perhaps this was a sign he needed to take it easy for a while?

"No, this is a dream. I need to wake up. How do I wake up?"

"You're awake."

"No," Rhys insisted.

The tailor eyed the both of them worriedly. "Perhaps he hit his head when he fell?" the man suggested.

"I will take him to see the doctor. We were done here, right? We'll be back for the fittings later." Julian helped Rhys put on his coat, although this was met with some resistance. He managed to pack everything up and push Rhys out the door before the situation could escalate. Once outside, Rhys stared at his shaky hands and took furtive glances at his surroundings, still seeming highly doubtful about being awake.

"You're awake. You fainted for a minute or two," Julian reminded him, concerned that he hadn't yet snapped out of it. He'd never seen Rhys confused like this before.

"I don't trust you."

"Does your head hurt? Did you really hit it?" Julian tried to check, but Rhys wouldn't let him any nearer.

"I need to wake up. Why can't I wake up?"

"Even if you were asleep, which you are not, you've never been able to wake up on command. Why would you be able to do it now?"

"The more you try to convince me, the more suspicious this seems."

Rhys started to walk down the street, heading the wrong way. Julian grabbed him by the hand to stop him, but he shook his hand off and looked frightened. Whatever the reason, Rhys seemed to be losing his grip on reality. Unsure what to do about it in the middle of the street and afraid that the boy might dash off, Julian hurried to consider his options.

"Let's go home and sort this out, all right?"

If he grabbed Rhys and carried him home, he would probably put up a fight and attract a lot of attention. Having to chase Rhys, if he decided to make a run for it, seemed worse, though. Maybe if he waited, it would pass?

"I need to wake up; this isn't real." Rhys blinked repeatedly. "No, is it real? Why doesn't it seem real?" He frowned. "What was that just now?" He glanced back at the tailor's shop.

"You passed out. Maybe we really should go see a doctor."

"No, I'm fine. I just thought..." Rhys wiggled his fingers. "Am I really awake? I feel... sick." He seemed a little out of breath as well, and pale to boot. "What time is it? I need to go back."

"It's ten past eleven. You have something you need to do?"

"Yes, I— no, that was... did that happen? Fuck, I can't tell."

He looked Julian in the eye, absolutely terrified.

CHAPTER 36

It took Julian some time and persuasion to get Rhys to follow him home. Quin was tending to the heater downstairs in the pharmacy when they arrived. He greeted them, finished what he was doing and turned to Julian.

"What's wrong with him? He looks about ready to faint."

"Upstairs, I'll explain it once we're seated." Julian hoped sitting in the lounge would calm Rhys down. He was still not himself, though he was more subdued and compliant than some moments prior.

Quin led the way and the three of them sat down in the lounge, Rhys and Quin on the sofa and Julian on the armchair across from them. Rhys leaned back and massaged his brow.

"How much did you sleep last night?" Julian asked to begin to diagnose the problem.

"I'm not sure," Rhys replied.

"Let me rephrase that. When did you last have some rest?"

"I don't know."

"Do you know what happened? Can you describe it to Quin here?"

"I... was asleep, and then I dreamt I was out with you, and I woke up briefly, but now I can't wake up. How is Quin here?" Rhys frowned.

"You're awake," Julian reminded the boy. To Quin, he explained, "When I served him breakfast this morning, he seemed fine. We went to a tailor, and, as we were about to leave, he fainted. He's been like this since then."

"But I don't... that's not—I wouldn't make that sort of a mistake." Rhys stared at Quin. Quin waved his hand as a greeting. "I must be dreaming again. I meant to rest, I think."

"No, you're definitely awake. Unless..." Quin glanced at Julian. "Is he sleepwalking?"

"What?" Rhys was still staring, but his stare slowly morphed into a squint.

"You look like you're awake and you're chatting with us, but if you think you're asleep, I don't know what else it could be." Quin shrugged. "What makes you think you're asleep?"

"I can tell. There's a difference. I know there's a difference... I can't remember what that is right now." Rhys looked ready to burst into hysterics again.

"Do you have something you normally do to check? I can't read or tell the time properly if I'm dreaming." Quin was trying to help, but Rhys looked all the more frustrated.

"I don't understand what you mean. I'm always able to read and tell the time. Why wouldn't I be? I don't check anything, I just know. At least I know most of the time... Sometimes my dreams can be very realistic, like this one, but this is definitely a dream. I need to stop dreaming. I'm out there somewhere right now, in danger! You need to help me. Hosta... Hosta is watching me, testing me." Rhys paused. "Or was that a nightmare? No, that really happened. I know I was supposed to rest. I need to... I need to go there tonight. What day is it? What time?" As Rhys was searching for a clock, Jasmine came downstairs from the attic.

"What's wrong?" She signed her question to Julian.

"There's something wrong with Rhys, and we're trying to figure out what," Julian signed back to her.

"She's a spy!" Rhys exclaimed and pointed at Jasmine.

"Spy...? Did he say spy? Me?" She looked rightfully upset. "What happened? Is he all right?"

"He may have hit his head. I didn't see what happened. I had my back turned when it did, but he fainted," Julian explained.

"He looks delirious from lack of rest," Jasmine pointed out. "Like Jacob a few years ago. It's important to rest, very important!"

"How can we help? What do we do?"

"If he's lost sense of it, he might not be able to do much about it on his own. Mother had to use ARF on Jacob to fix it, and it took months before he was himself again." Jasmine looked apologetic.

"What's she saying?" Quin asked.

"He may have overexerted himself. But why did you stop resting properly?" Julian turned to Rhys. Rhys frowned.

"I'm not sure. I think I was busy? No, I woke up in the middle of it. I wake up before I can... no, I start to dream. It was the nightmares? No, I was with Hosta, and then I fell asleep, but when—?" Rhys started to stare at his hands again as if they held the answer to what was confusing him. "It doesn't feel real. Nothing feels real... but usually everything feels real, so how can this be?"

"Oh, I think I may know what happened." Jasmine hurried over to Rhys and took him by the hands. "Is she still there? It's not done yet?" She said this out loud, and, though her voice was weak from disuse, it was clear enough to understand. Rhys seemed to be processing the words.

"She's there when I close my... no, open my eyes?" Rhys was signing it to Jasmine. "She was asleep before, but I'm not sure if that was a dream."

"Rhys, concentrate. Did you go there last night, in any form, dream or otherwise?"

"Yesterday... yes. I checked and readjusted the memory seal. At least, I think I did." Rhys messed up most of his signs, but Jasmine seemed to understand what he was getting at.

"So, father is still at it? The memories haven't faded yet?" Jasmine signed this so that Julian could see.

"I don't know. I also talked to her, and she..." Rhys shuddered. "She strapped me onto that thing..."

"That's not possible. You've been here for at least since the day before yesterday." Jasmine turned to Julian to confirm.

"He hasn't left the house since last Tuesday," Julian said. "What is he talking about? Is he mistaking his dreams for reality?"

"No, the first part was correct. He's been guarding our mother to make sure the memories fade before Father can remove my seal. Did he not mention this to you?" Jasmine frowned. Julian felt a chill creep down his spine.

"What do you mean? Why does she need guarding?"

"I only sealed her memories. Father is the only one who knows how to wipe them, and he never taught me. We blocked Mother from accessing dreamside, so Rhys could go in and make sure Father cannot remove my seal. The memories should have faded by now! It's been weeks. I thought it would take a few days at most."

"That sounds familiar. It wasn't a dream then? Or it was a dream, and you're referring to it in my dream?"

"So wait, is that where he's supposed to be? He said something about needing to go back somewhere. If he doesn't, will Hosta regain her memories?" Julian wasn't sure which was worse: having to deal with Hosta all over again or seeing Rhys this messed up from trying to fix it.

"I need to, uh, I need to go." Rhys slumped like he was about to pass out.

"What do we do? Can any of us meet him on the other side to see if he's any more coherent there? Will he be able to do anything about Hosta in this condition? How long does he need to rest to be coherent again?"

"I'm not sure he can. Jacob stopped being able to. That's why Mother had to apply the ARF. But a few hours won't be enough. He'd need to rest for weeks for this to pass."

"Days or weeks, we'll still need to apply that mask for him to rest, correct? Can you do it?" It was a lot of weight to put on such a young girl, but she was the most experienced after Rhys.

"I can't cross the void without help. At least, I don't think I can. Mother always hooks me up first to make sure it's safe. I've never done it without Mother. I'm not supposed to..." Jasmine looked miserable.

"Rhys? Can you do it yourself?" Julian asked, though Rhys seemed only barely conscious. "Can we trust him to do anything at this point?"

"What?" Rhys looked confused.

"If you fall asleep now, can you go meet Jasmine or me dreamside or ask Justin for help to apply the ARF mask on yourself?" Julian asked.

"I don't understand. Why?"

"You need to rest." Julian sighed and looked at Jasmine.

"No, I can't. I'm not done. I need to go."

"Justin!" Julian realised. "If we can communicate with Justin somehow, wouldn't he be able to jump over to Rhys? He's done it before. Would he be able to apply the mask for us?" Julian asked Jasmine.

"Ah, that might work if we had a way to communicate with him... I know Mother sometimes connects to him, but I don't know where he is."

"He's downstairs." Julian realised Justin was perhaps not in a presentable state, and hauling him up in his box might be a bit disturbing for a twelve-year-old. "How squeamish are you?"

Jasmine paused and bit her lip. "I don't have much experience, so I don't know," she signed.

"Maybe we can keep the lid closed."

"It might be enough that he's in the same room with me."

"We'll give it a try. Quin, could you go get the box?"

Quin nodded and left.

"If our father is still trying to save our mother's memories, that means they staged quite the play for us," Julian signed to Jasmine. "Were you aware?"

"Yes, but they lied to me about why they were doing it. That's why I agreed to help Rhys fix it. I'm sorry. I thought he told you." Jasmine looked like she was going to cry but was making a good effort not to. "I would have told you."

"Does that mean they can still use Justin to listen in on us?" Julian tried to keep his annoyance in check since this was not the time for emotional outbursts, but the situation was definitely beginning to trigger some of his more unruly feelings.

"Yes, I suppose. But as far as I'm aware, if Father is working on removing the seal, that means Mother has to be unconscious to receive the treatment. Father doesn't normally check the incoming data. He might not even know how."

"Let's hope that's the case, or else we'll all be in trouble."

"My ears work, so he's not listening through me right now," Jasmine signed. "I keep signing out of habit," she said out loud.

"Would that, then, also mean that if Justin can hear us, they're not listening through him either?" Julian wondered.

"Probably," Jasmine signed.

"Let's hope he can hear us, then. For Rhys's sake." Julian glanced at Rhys, who was stubbornly refusing to sleep, but was in a near-to catatonic state, staring into empty air. "What do we do with him in the meantime? I'm worried he might do something stupid in the state he's in."

Quin returned with the box and set it on the floor between the chair and the sofa. Jasmine reached over to take a look, but Julian closed the lid to prevent her from seeing what was inside.

"Trust me, you don't want to see him," Julian said.

"He's really in there? How does he fit?" Jasmine signed.

"I suppose we need to prepare Rhys. I should have some of the solution left over from before... I'm going to go get it. Jasmine, if you could start by explaining the procedure. Quin, keep an eye on him, will you? So he doesn't do anything stupid."

CHAPTER 37

Rhys had stared at something for a while now, but he was too tired to understand what it was. His eyelids? Phosphenes? Hallucinations within his dream? One thing was for sure, he'd never been this tired in his life.

He caught fragments of conversation, but the hands were moving much too fast to understand. He knew he needed to concentrate because he was supposed to be doing something, but his short-term memory was significantly impaired, and he was frequently interrupted by the feeling of either falling asleep or waking up. Not sure which was which, he went between the states sometimes quicker than he could realise. It was impossible to keep track.

He was startled by one of these shifts. He was transported somewhere where he was restrained and lying down, then yanked straight back to sit on the sofa in the lounge. Neither of these seemed like where he was supposed to be.

Lifting his hands felt like he was wading through lukewarm water; a strange, soft feeling of resistance that made his body parts feel heavier than usual. He slapped himself a few times. If he couldn't pull himself together, someone else would have to deal with Hosta, and none of them had that sort of range. It was dangerous.

Rhys realised they were preparing for something. The box of remains, Justin, an injection? Rhys had meant to resist but was too slow to react in his current state.

No, they were going to ARF him? Shit. Fuck. No. He needed to do something... what was it? He fumbled but managed to grasp the situation again, momentarily.

Hosta.

His daily check was due! He closed his eyes and was surprised to find himself where he was supposed to be: the entrance. He was definitely asleep now, probably. No, definitely.

He aimed at the address he'd been visiting regularly for almost a month now. Even if this was just a dream, he needed to at least try his best despite the confusion. He vowed to rest once he was done.

Hosta was in her usual state. Being able to see this amidst all the chaos was oddly comforting. He worked as fast as he could, and he was fairly sure he was done when Hosta sat up and smiled at him.

"Hello, Rhys," she said. She was beautiful here, but her smile chilled Rhys to the core. There was an injection. Rhys screamed not so much from the pain but from the fright. He was falling down deeper into the darkness.

"Don't worry, you'll be all right." It was a female voice, but Rhys could no longer see anyone or anything. He was not in pain, but didn't this feel somehow worse? He'd experienced a lot of things, but this level of confusion and lack of control was unparalleled. There was nothing he could do. He was at their mercy.

"Is he out?" Quin asked. He was behind the sofa, holding Rhys down by the shoulders.

"He's out," Julian confirmed and woke up Jasmine. "How did it go?"

"It's done. Apparently he ran off, but Justin managed to bring him back and apply the ARF mask, as per my instructions. At least, I think that's what he was trying to say."

"All right. Let's hope that's enough." They moved Rhys to lie on the sofa, and Julian turned his attention to the next problem. "With him out of commission, we need to figure out what to do about Hosta. Any suggestions?"

"We could start by reinforcing the seal, but I can't jump through the void. Justin is the only one of us capable of it right now, so maybe I could try to explain it to him." Jasmine sat down in the armchair and dozed off to give it a go. She seemed even better at falling asleep on command than Rhys, but no doubt she'd had plenty of practice.

"Perhaps we should figure out what to do about our father to at least keep him preoccupied, so he stops meddling with the seal. We may need to go on site." Julian removed his glasses and rubbed the bridge of his nose.

"Should we involve Victor? Some extra muscle might be useful in a pinch," Quin suggested.

"Yes, if he's willing. If we're lucky, they haven't foreseen a need for extra security, so we might have an advantage. I just don't understand why they've gone through all this trouble."

"I have an idea." It was Victor. He looked like he'd been standing at the stairs for who knew how long, but at least Quin looked as surprised as Julian. "It's for Rhys. And I think Rhys knows it. I hope he's just tired and stressed out and that these symptoms aren't something they've already done to him somehow. You saw how intrigued Dr Vesper was hearing just a hint of Rhys's abilities. I think she might be involved."

"You might be right about that. She rang the pharmacy back in November, asking for our mother. She's probably been working for her all this time." Julian sighed.

The woman had hovered around Rhys and Rhys's brother, poking and prodding, but she had seemed friendly, so no one had expected anything untoward from her.

"And yes, for the record, I am willing to help and come with you. We need to sort this out before it gets any worse. This needs to *end* once and for all." Victor looked grim.

"Jasmine." Julian nudged her shoulder to wake her up gently. "How's it going with Justin? We're about to leave the house for a moment."

"He says it would help to be closer because he can't see and doesn't know where he's going."

"That can be arranged. Now, all we need is a plan."

Victor spread the blueprint of the Craft's house onto the dining table. Julian and Quin studied it with interest.

"Rhys mentioned the laboratory is here." Victor turned to Jasmine for confirmation. Jasmine nodded. Almost the whole top floor was used to house Hosta's home experiments. "For whatever reason, they haven't added any security detail, so there's only one guard that comes according to a sparse schedule." One of the locations he'd sabotaged had happened to be Mr Craft's personal office with a convenient abundance of employment records, contracts and schedules. Victor was a quick study.

"That's Mr Murray," Jasmine said. "He's my father's personal bodyguard. He has a scary temper. A very big man, even bigger than you." She pointed at Victor.

"Yes. He has a patient file as thick as a thumb. Considering everything they've done to him to improve his performance, we'd best steer clear of him. My vote is we go through the roof," Victor said.

"What about access? I don't see any windows." Julian frowned.

"I mean literally through the roof." Victor pointed at a separate, smaller room on the other side of the staircase. "There's space here, presumably for a water tank. It is separate from the rest of the space. We can remove the slates, push through the batten and the rafters at the underside of the purlin here and enter this space without attracting too much attention. I should have the right tools. It might take some time, but I'm fairly sure I can do it without too much noise. The weather should be on our side as it looks like it will be a windy, rough night tonight. That's access sorted, but what do you want to do once we're there?"

These were Julian and Jasmine's parents and not some random strangers. It was hardly polite to assume murder was on the agenda.

"I suppose we should try to avoid killing them." Julian glanced at Jasmine. Jasmine didn't seem shocked to hear this was one of the options, but she did look sad.

"That means we need to do something about his memory as well as hers. We can't detain him for weeks on end. He will be missed if he doesn't turn up for work, and who knows what types that will attract our way. It will have to be a proper, immediate memory wipe, and we need to be out of there without leaving evidence of ourselves as soon as possible," Victor said.

"I only know how to seal," Jasmine reminded him, looking miserable.

"I know. And it's all right, we might have a way. Your father doesn't sleep-roam, am I right?"

"Yes. Mother is also not very good at it. She knows a lot of theory but can't do much herself. That's why they have me."

"That means that even I could do the wipe, if I had access to the right equipment and knew how to do it." Victor knew it had been a good call to spend a little more time poking around Mr Craft's office when he'd found it. "Luckily we have both," he said and grinned inwardly.

This garnered quite a lot of blinking and surprised looks from his audience.

"What have you been up to behind our backs? How long have you known?" Quin's expression was peculiar.

"I haven't been sitting on this information for very long if that's what you're wondering. I found out a couple of days ago while doing some research."

"I like it! You've just become my favourite person!" Quin patted Victor's back with some enthusiasm, causing Victor to blush.

"Let's not get carried away," he mumbled and cleared his throat before continuing. "We'll need to restrain him and make sure neither of them raise an alarm or get away. For that, we need manpower. Rhys is out, obviously." They all turned to look at Rhys, who lay unconscious on the sofa.

"We'll need someone to babysit him, so it might be for the best if she stays here," Quin pointed at Jasmine, "while the three of us go. The numbers are in our favour, but your father may have unexpected tricks up his sleeves. Also, if we happen to attract Mr Murray's attention, it may become too close to call."

"What about Justin? Do we still need to lug him along if the wipes can be done without sleep-roaming?" Julian asked.

"He can hear us chat if we're nearby, right? It'd be good to have some options for what we can do dreamside. We only need to bring him somewhere close, find a good spot to store him out of the way safely... A better box might be a good call, for courtesy."

Victor was fairly confident that he'd be able to perform the wipe, but if he failed, having Justin there to at least seal Mr Craft until they could figure things out would take some of the pressure off.

"What else do we need? What's the plan?" Quin looked at Victor for the answers. Victor hadn't taken the lead on any projects since the incident and avoided that sort of responsibility like the plague. He was far from ready for it, but there wasn't much choice.

In terms of having the necessary information, clarity of mind and skills, he realised he needed to gather his confidence and step up for the challenge.

Fine. It seemed likely this whole thing would go to shit, but anyone else at the helm would face the same dismal odds with less to work with.

He'd shoulder the blame.

It's just one more nightmare, he reminded himself. "Here's what we need to do."

CHAPTER 38

It got dark around four in the afternoon. Delaying it any more than that was out of the question, but they would need the cover of darkness to avoid drawing any inconvenient attention.

After depositing Justin in a safe spot under the stairs of a covered staircase at the side of the building, Victor, Julian and Quin made their way to the east wall.

There was a pull-down ladder leading to stairs that took them to the second floor, but the remainder of the way up to the roof was going to be trickier.

Victor led the way. He was agile for someone his size, and something suggested he'd done this before.

Julian let Quin go second since the two of them seemed like the more proficient climbers. He was not confident about his climbing prowess, and, if he happened to slip, he'd rather not fall on Quin's face.

The weather was indeed atrocious and bitterly cold, and, having dressed accordingly, Julian felt especially encumbered and clumsy. It was impossible to secure a proper grip with his thick leather gloves, so he stuffed them hastily into his pocket.

It became a race against the chill. The last metres to the top were a struggle, but Julian did eventually manage to haul himself, with a few scrapes and scratches, up to where Victor and Quin were already removing the roof tiles.

"What took you so long?" Quin asked as he lowered the tiles that Victor was handing over to him into a pile to one side. Julian cast him a sour look, put his gloves back on and rubbed his hands together to warm up.

"We're almost done here." Victor shoved the slate ripper under the last remaining slate.

Once that was loose and removed, the opening was large enough. There was the matter of dealing with the batten, but Victor had come prepared: he pulled a thin-bladed pull saw from his bag, and, with just a few quick pulls, formed a man-sized hole all the way through. What little noise he'd made was easily drowned by the wind.

The trio entered the dark room on the other side of the staircase. There was a water tank there, as expected. It took up most of the space.

Not knowing whether the door would make a sound when opened, Quin took a peek through the keyhole. It was no use, but he had more luck crouching down and peering under the door.

"He's in there," Quin whispered. "Back left corner."

The most important part was to subdue Mr Craft. They had the element of surprise on their side. Once that was accomplished, the rest would be easy.

R hys woke up. Though there had been times that had come close, he'd never felt so relieved to wake up in his life.

Not having any control over his sleep was terrifying. Being trapped in the middle of his worst nightmares, unable to do anything about it, whilst confused whether it even was a dream... He shuddered. At least he had a slightly better understanding of reality now that he was fairly sure he was in it.

Jasmine sat in the armchair across from the sofa, reading a book. She lifted her gaze when Rhys sat up.

"Oh shit, Jasmine—!" Rhys exclaimed as he realised it, "I need to check on Hosta! How do I do that?"

"It's OK, your friends are on it," Jasmine replied, sounding calm. The sound of her voice was still novel, even if she'd been speaking more as of late.

"What? How?" Rhys frowned.

"They went to settle it. Victor said he knows what to do."

"Victor?"

"They told me to stay behind to keep an eye on you. You're not going to give me trouble, are you?" Jasmine set the bookmark and put her book down. "It's best if you rest some more. You've been skipping it lately, haven't you? That's dangerous. Say what you will about my mother, she always made sure we know just how important rest is. You need your rest."

"I don't doubt that, but how can I rest when they might be in danger?"

Truth be told, Rhys did not want to sleep at all. If he was truly awake right now, he wanted to remain that way until he could at least calm his nerves enough to not return to the same exact nightmares.

He was also not in the best of positions to be making smart decisions. He could vaguely tell there was something wrong with him, but the experiences from this past day had been so awful, the last thing he wanted to do was sleep. Sitting still and waiting for news did not suit him either.

"Are they aware of Mr Murray?" Rhys had caught some glimpses of the bodyguard, although the giant had been out of the house most times he'd visited.

"Yes, don't worry."

"He could be there right now. He seems extremely dangerous!"

"Victor said as much. Don't worry, I'm sure they have it under control."

Rhys wanted to trust Jasmine, but her assurances made her seem all the more suspicious. Maybe she'd guided them right into a trap! If they'd even left voluntarily. Rhys needed to see it for himself.

"I need to go!" He jumped off the sofa and into the stairs before Jasmine could do anything to stop him.

"No, Rhys!"

What could she even do? Rhys had just enough presence of mind to grab his coat and mittens before he headed out the door.

Jasmine did not pursue him past the door, thankfully. She wouldn't have been able to keep up anyway, and on the off chance she was being truthful, she would be safer left behind.

Quin slammed open the door to the laboratory. He and Victor rushed to detain Mr Craft, and Julian headed over to his mother to unhook her from the machine. Since she was currently less of a threat out of the two, they would deal with her later. First, they needed to take care of Mr Craft's memory wipe.

Victor secured Mr Craft, who quickly realised how much stronger Victor was, and stopped struggling. To prevent him from alerting Mr Murray, Victor gagged him with a scarf. Quin went back to the door to keep an eye on the staircase, regardless.

So far, things were running smoothly.

"Keep an eye on her." Julian dragged his mother across the floor, closer to Quin. Quin nodded.

Victor tied up Mr Craft to have his hands free to set up the machine. He had been as thorough as possible and brought everything he might possibly need and could carry without a problem, as well as notes he could follow so as not to make mistakes.

Julian had contributed with some of his offerings to be sure they would not be short on any of the chemical components. The only thing none of them had accounted for was that Hosta would start screaming before she'd even opened her eyes.

"Shit, this woman—!" Quin cupped her mouth with his hand, but she'd definitely been too loud to dismiss. "This is going to get hairy." He grabbed Hosta to tie and gag her, checking back at the door all the while. He could hear the footsteps.

When Mr Murray appeared, chills ran down Quin's spine. The man was massive and counterintuitively fast for his size.

"Victor, look out!" Quin yelled.

In that same instance, Mr Murray grabbed the slate ripper from the floor and struck Victor with it. Victor stumbled backwards and tried to counter any following strikes barehanded. The best he could do was try to back out of the way.

When he found himself backed to a corner, Mr Murray sunk the slate ripper into Victor's thigh. He pulled it right out by taking a good hold of the tool and pushing Victor off. Victor let out a growl as he fell backwards, and deep red blood started to gush steadily out of the wound. He hurried to press it but was given the parting gift of a couple of nasty blows in the head, although thankfully not with the slate ripper.

With Hosta struggling against her restraints so forcefully, Quin had yet to do anything to help, but realising Victor was going to bleed to death, he abandoned the woman and rushed to suppress the bleeding.

"Thank you," Mr Craft said to Mr Murray as the man released him. "Take her to safety. I can manage."

Mr Murray was free to take Hosta for now, since, if her memories were still mostly sealed, she would not regain them without treatment. All they had to do was make sure Mr Craft wouldn't be available to do the treatment.

The situation was dire, but all was not lost just yet.

While still catching his breath from running, Rhys wandered around the building and spotted the hole in the roof. Grateful that he'd noticed it before heading in through the front door and possibly bumping into Mr Murray, he hurried up the ladder and the stairs.

He could hear sounds of struggle from inside. Heart thumping too hard for comfort, he threw away his mittens, wiped off the sweat on his hands and climbed the rest of the way like his life depended on it.

Since he hadn't thought to bring a weapon, Rhys gravitated towards the pile of slates, but upon testing their weight they were much too heavy for him to throw. Was there something else here he could use? Anything? There had to be something!

Julian dropped what he was doing to assess the situation. Mr Murray grabbed Hosta and carried her out the door. There was no sense trying to stop them, but his father was another matter. Julian quickly placed himself between the man and the door to block the way.

"Move aside!" Mr Craft snapped at him, vexed.

"No, this has gone on for long enough."

"What happened to staying out of our sight? You used to be so good at that."

"And I would have kept being excellent at it if you hadn't stirred up shit that's impossible to ignore."

"I said I would take care of her! All you needed to do was keep your meddling paws off it."

"It's not just her I have to worry about, is it? Am I supposed to sit back and watch the two of you ruin lives collecting data from Rhys and selling them to the highest bidder, regardless of the consequences?"

"Don't you start with the lecture on morals! You know nothing about the realities of this business or what she's set out to do. You don't even know what you put your mother through! Let me pass!"

Julian did not back down. Whatever he'd done in the past did not change the fact that the two of them were responsible for ruining countless lives for profit or personal satisfaction.

"Look at you, all high and mighty. You don't still seriously think you can save the world by opposing us?" His father laughed. "You really haven't learned anything."

"Maybe. But I will stop you this time or die trying," Julian replied coldly.

"Then why don't you?!" His father glared at him and charged at his throat. In a fit of rage, his attack was so forceful, it made Julian take some steps back until he hit the wall behind him. He fought back, but his father's hands remained at his throat. "You should have died alongside your brother! Your mother took pity on you. You should be thanking her!"

"For what exactly?" Julian managed to thrust his father back with enough force to get loose, before the man charged at him again and landed a few of his punches. They stung, but Julian fought to keep calm.

"Ungrateful brat! You don't even realise how much your mother loves you, worries about you!" his father roared.

"What good is that?" Julian snarled between clenched teeth, tasting blood but trying not to be sucked into a similar fury as his father's.

"You do not deserve her!" His father took a jab at him, but this time Julian dodged successfully and seized the opportunity to return the favour. Once his father recovered, he leapt at Julian again.

"Are you jealous?" Julian said, purely out of spite. He seemed to have hit the nail on its head. The hands that reached at his throat tightened their grip.

"You shut your mouth, you drug-munching sodomite piece of trash!" With that, his hold was so tight, Julian could no longer respond. "She is mine! I'm tired of sharing her with you ungrateful assholes! You do not deserve her!"

Who else was included in that plural? Jonathan? Jacob? Where were they? Julian could do nothing but stare at his father in shock, realising that no matter how much he tried to fight back, this time the hold persisted without fail. The pressure in his head became painful.

Curiously enough, just before he passed out from the lack of oxygen, he wondered if this was so familiar because it was a skill he'd learned from his father.

How many times had he done it before?

Quin reached for the scarf he'd used to gag Mr Craft and tied it around Victor's thigh. Victor was regaining consciousness.

"Press this, *hard*, or you'll bleed to death!" Quin guided Victor's hands to make sure he would do as told. Julian was in trouble. There was no time to lose. "This goddamn shit show..."

Quin got up to beat the shit out of Mr Craft, but, just as he was about to let the man have it, the door behind the two of them opened with a bam.

Julian's father stood up from where his son lay on the floor to see who was at the door. Rhys's single-syllable name was too long to utter before the boy had moved forth and swung his weapon.

The saw-teeth sunk into Mr Craft's throat with ease. There was the unsettling sound of the saw being pulled through cartilage. A bright spray of blood surged out in several successive violent spurts until it subsided, and Mr Craft fell down to his knees. The saw-cut spread open wide as the head hit the floor and rolled unnaturally to one side.

Rhys breathed raggedly, drenched in blood.

Quin could say nothing. The sound of footsteps from the staircase alerted him into action. He rushed past Rhys and to the top landing before Mr Murray could reach the attic.

"Victor is bleeding. Take care of them. Keep this door shut until you're sure the coast is clear, and get them the fuck out of here!"

He'd make sure to delay the giant for as long as he could to give them a decent chance to retreat.

CHAPTER 39

R hys had stood behind the door long enough to hear the conversation. When Julian had no longer responded, he'd had enough imagination to guess what was happening. It was so much worse than any of his nightmares.

He hadn't had much time to think it over; he'd just grabbed the first thing he could find in the dark and barged through the door. With very little thought to the consequences, he'd started with a side sweep, going in with all he had, knowing that his lack of strength was his worst weakness.

When his weapon had met resistance, his instinct was to pull harder to free it so that he would have something to defend himself with in case his attack was unsuccessful. The force of the shower of blood took him by surprise. In fact, he hadn't expected to draw blood at all. The smell of it was ghastly, the sensation against his skin sickening.

Quin brushed past him as he stood there in shock, trying to take in what had just happened.

Was he really awake?

He dropped the saw, and it fell with a clank. Julian lay on the floor, motionless. Victor was covered in blood at the other end of the room. Rhys looked at his hands like he'd already done so many times that day, but this time they were covered in blood.

"Take care of them," Quin's words echoed in his mind.

He knelt to check for Julian's pulse. Had he been too late, again? He could feel the tears fall down across his cheeks, but his mind was too numb to understand what they were for. His fingers were slippery from the blood. It was difficult to find the right spot. Giving up on the search, he shook Julian's shoulder, hoping to wake him up.

"You need to wake up, please wake up, please..." If only he hadn't slept for so long. If he'd just hurried more and run faster! "Oh God, please!"

He turned Julian over, shook him as hard as he dared and started to bawl. From the blood and the tears, he almost missed it, but Julian drew a breath. Relieved to the point of sobbing, Rhys made an effort to calm down, but, as so many times before, his body would not listen to him. Julian propped himself to sit, alarmed by the sight of Rhys.

"Are you all right? What happened? Whose blood is this?" He rushed to check if and where Rhys was hurt.

"I'm fine, I'm fine, I'm fine..." Rhys repeated. He was still shaking. "It's all his, it's him, it's his." Rhys pointed at the bled out carcass behind Julian. Julian turned to look. "I'm sorry... I didn't mean to... I... I... F-fuck, f-fucking hell..."

A little less would have been enough, surely. He'd gone and literally nearly sawed a person's head off. How was that not excessive? How...?

Victor limped over from his end of the room. He inspected the carnage for a moment and said in no uncertain tone, "Pardon my language, but the asshole probably deserved it."

He helped both Julian and Rhys up to stand, and his words helped Rhys overcome the worst of his shock—at least enough to be alerted to the sounds coming from the other side of the door, in the staircase.

"Oh shit, Quin!"

Not in any shape or form ready to retreat and leave Quin behind, Rhys opened the door and jumped straight down the stairs. The lower end of the railing was missing. There were pieces of broken furniture and wood strewn across the lower landing and blood splatter and stains on the walls and floor.

One floor lower, Quin was still alive, trying to keep a distance from Mr Murray, but considerably less agile or graceful than his usual self. He looked like he'd been tossed around the room like a sack of potatoes, bruised and battered, but at least he was still breathing.

Quin looked up. Ah, for fuck's sake. He was glad to see Rhys and Julian, but not here and not now.

"You were supposed to leave!" he yelled at them. "Get Victor and get the fuck out of here!"

"Not without you!" Rhys threw the leg of a chair at Mr Murray.

"You idiot!" Quin tried to draw the giant's attention back to himself.

What was he doing? As if he could do anything against this monster borne from Hosta's scientific experiments. All Quin could manage was to not get immediately mauled to death. Even with the three of them, they were no match for Mr Murray's insane destructive capabilities.

Rhys charged at the man by throwing debris at him with fierce speed. He did look quite terrifying in his current state, but he was absolutely tiny compared to Mr Murray, who used his hefty forearms to deflect what was thrown at him. It did provide enough of a distraction to allow Quin to circle around to the stairs, though.

"Back up! Now!" Quin shouted right at Rhys's face to get him to comply.

Mr Murray wasted no time to charge at them when he noticed Quin had moved. Julian pulled Rhys along and started climbing back up the stairs.

Quin tried to stall as best he could without getting himself killed. He had a piece of railing to swing at the bodyguard, but Mr Murray took a hold of it by the third swing and snapped it in half with ease. It was no wonder Mr Craft had thought just one Mr Murray was enough.

The next floor up, there was a sitting room connected to a library and some bedrooms to the side. Rhys ran across to find something he could arm himself with. There wasn't much available, so he had to make do with a floor lamp.

Quin was too out of breath to do anything but try to keep out of the way for a while. Between Rhys and Julian, the two of them managed to keep Mr Murray entertained so that Quin was at least allowed a breather and a moment to think.

They would not be able to beat Mr Murray with brute force since the man was practically a golem. Evidently Julian was still trying, and to his credit, he did manage to connect some punches and ram the man with a table, right at the level of his privates. He used that moment of distraction to break a vase the breadth of his chest on Mr Murray's head, though even this was not enough to stop the man. It did leave him momentarily confused and bleeding so that Rhys, Julian and Quin could escape yet another floor up.

Victor let them into the laboratory and closed the door. Shortly after, Mr Murray was banging it on the other side. It would not hold for long. Julian pushed a desk in front of it to slow him down, but that would only buy them minutes.

Rhys vomited. He must have been in too much of a shock to do it sooner, but it seemed the sight of Mr Craft's nearly severed head proved something he wasn't prepared to get reacquainted with. Either that, or he had a concussion from his share of the generous blows Mr Murray had been dealing. He looked miserable as he clutched to the floor lamp.

Julian wiped blood and sweat from his brow. He paced around the room, looking for something useful, then pushed another piece of furniture in front of the door.

"Time," he pointed out, "should be on our side." If he had a plan, this was certainly the time Quin wanted to hear it.

Victor lowered himself down on the floor. He looked exhausted. No doubt he'd lost a decent amount of blood before they'd managed to stop the bleeding. He was lucky that, instead of an artery, the slate ripper had only grazed a vein. It was his thigh, so blood had oozed out with some force, but if they could get out of here without him losing much more, he might still make it.

Quin checked that the scarf was still tight enough. He removed his belt to add more pressure and to keep everything securely in place. Victor seemed appreciative, though it was clearly painful for him. Quin turned back to Julian.

"What's the plan?"

Julian took out his kit from his pocket. The needle and syringe were in another pocket. He refilled it.

"He's huge, so one dose may not be enough, but it should at least slow him down in a couple more minutes. Try to distract him again, so I can jab him with the rest. Then it's a matter of keeping him away from Victor and trying not to get smashed into pulp before it kicks in."

"Yes, all right, that sounds good." Quin was immensely relieved Julian actually had a plan. The rest was a matter of whether he had the stamina to dodge another round of blows.

Mr Murray broke through the door. Julian hid the needle and syringe behind his back and moved to one side. Quin and Rhys made their way to the other.

"Can you help Victor to the back of the room?" Rhys suggested. Quin did as told. Mr Murray ripped planks of wood off the door to gain access.

"He's already dead. What good does it do to kill us?" Julian tried to reason with him.

"I have my orders. The Crafts have told me to catch any intruders by all means necessary, and that is what I will do."

The man kicked the door, and it cracked so that he could lift it out of his way. The furniture he pushed off until he could walk past. He rammed Julian to the ground, but at least before he did, Julian managed to toss the needle and syringe to Rhys, who caught it and stabbed Mr Murray in the back with it. He hadn't the chance to inject all of its contents when Mr Murray retaliated, but it was stuck there until Julian could finish the job some moments later.

Rhys was on the floor and scooted his butt to back away. Julian made use of everything breakable the laboratory had to offer and threw as many beakers, pots, bottles and petri dishes he could get his hands on. They were mostly too small to do any significant damage but kept Mr Murray busy chasing after him so that Rhys could get well out of the way, grab the floor lamp and start whacking the man with it.

"How long?" Rhys asked between whacks. He was out of breath and struggling but tenacious enough to persist past what must have already been his limit.

"Fifteen minutes. Ten if we're lucky!" Julian shouted before he received the right hook of the deranged bodyguard. It might have been considerably worse had the first dose not have started to take effect, but even so, it was a direct hit to the side of his face and hard enough to knock him out.

Mr Murray blinked and swayed erratically but aimed at Rhys next with reasonable accuracy. Rhys ducked under the row of work desks and crawled away as quickly as the space allowed. Mr Murray bashed the desks and threw some of them aside like they were made of paper.

Having had a chance to rest, Quin jumped and smashed a heavy piece of machinery on the bodyguard's neck. He'd hoped to hit the head, but the thing had been too heavy to manoeuvre properly. As luck had it, hitting the neck proved almost as effective. For once, Mr Murray wavered and fell down to one knee.

Rhys picked up a chair and used that next. They were running out of furniture and things to throw, but at least there was a time limit to this madness.

Surely it would be enough? Rhys fell back onto his ass. He looked ready to pass out from exhaustion. Quin could relate. There wasn't enough adrenaline to keep him going for much longer, but he couldn't stop now. With Julian still out, Victor severely wounded and Rhys at his limit, who else was there to keep at it until the monster finally succumbed to whatever Julian had given him?

Quin ran across the room and wielded Rhys's floor lamp with nothing better at hand. It was enough to coax Mr Murray to follow him and leave the others alone. The lamp was, however, not in any shape to be useful. Mr Murray yanked it out of Quin's hands, bent it out of shape and tossed it aside. He took a hold of Quin's arm and sent him flying like a ragdoll over the remaining desks, beat up furniture, shards of glass, blood and debris on the floor.

Barely hanging onto consciousness, Quin could see Julian get up, but the bodyguard threw him aside just as easily. He was heading for Rhys.

"Rhys, run!"

Rhys panted where he sat, arms limp at his sides, probably too spent to even move. It was not going to be enough, was it?

Quin tried to crawl to help, though he knew he could only buy perhaps seconds of distraction before the inevitable. Rhys did nothing but stared as Mr Murray approached him. Quin closed his eyes. He didn't want to see it. At least he could save himself from having to watch, even if he couldn't cover his ears and was forced to hear.

There was a heavy thump, and he could feel the floor shaking. A moment of silence where Quin would have expected at least some sort of scream. He opened his eyes. Mr Murray was on the floor. Rhys's feet were trapped under him. By the looks of it, he'd used the last of his energy to trip the man and even succeeded, but Mr Murray was already getting up again.

For a moment there, Quin had dared to hope that the drug had kicked in in the nick of time. As his heart sank, he was interrupted by a swoosh and a muted thud, then a ghastly, low growl that was followed by another such thud and a gurgling sound.

From his perspective on the floor, he couldn't understand what the sounds were from. When he pulled himself up to sit, he could see Victor leaning over Mr Murray, in his hands the slate ripper with its other end sunk into the bodyguard's back and presumably all the way through to explain the thuds.

Victor looked over at Quin, but neither of them knew what to say. When the bodyguard seemed to try to move, Victor pulled out the slate ripper and impaled him once more. Then he sat back to take a deep breath.

CHAPTER 40

The connection between the attic laboratory and *the Guardian Observation and Diagnostics System* was abruptly severed. Aurora was amidst retrieving some more extensive diagnostics data from Vincent, whom she'd persuaded to give the treatment one more try now that she had access to more modern equipment. She'd Hosta remotely in the meanwhile to determine what was causing her condition to worsen, but so far she'd had no luck.

"That's odd." She asked to connect a call to the attic laboratory, but there was no response from Mr Craft. He was often busy with other things—especially after someone had broken in and trashed his office some days ago—so she didn't think much of it. She tried the system service hall, where the equipment supporting the GODS was housed. "It's Dr Vesper. Could you—"

"Dr Vesper? Please excuse my impertinence, but we currently have our hands full—"

"I'm frightfully sorry to disturb you, but could you tell me what happened? I have lost connection to the Bulb. Is it a temporary pause in operations? For how long?"

"We don't know. As you're aware, we've been losing contact points across the city for weeks now. Just a single one here and there but totalling well over two dozen. We have the team investigating the causes, but so far the issues surfacing seem to have been unrelated and down to bad luck. But it keeps happening. And now with the Bulb as well, but we're running out of personnel to send out. The system itself is stable as always. It's just the contact points... I don't know how long it will take to restore everything, but it's not a matter of mere hours. I'm so sorry."

What an unfortunate timing to be having trouble with the system alongside with Hosta's health issues.

"Well, thank you, and forgive my interruption. Please keep me informed of the situation at your earliest convenience."

The last few minutes of data showed nothing abnormal in Hosta's condition, so Aurora decided to prioritise Vincent and retrieve the rest of his data first. She would peruse it later this evening after she'd gone to the attic laboratory herself to see what had caused the connection to fail and to make sure Hosta was doing all right.

"I'm sorry, Aurora. Was I supposed to be sleeping right now?" Vincent's voice carried through the speaking tube from the next room.

"Ah, darn. Yes, one moment, please."

She'd missed the spike in arousal caused by a cycle shift, and it had been enough for Vincent to pop out of sleep. He was so dagnabbit sensitive about any fluctuations, it seemed his brain wasn't meant to stay asleep at all. Even with such a precise cocktail and carefully timed doses, it was looking for any excuse to wake up. What in the world had Hosta done to him to make him this way?

Aurora prepared another dose of the sedative-hormone mixture and rushed into the other room to administer it. She had plenty of supplies here and enough stock for a fair amount of diagnostics tests, but the sad truth was that she needed other means to help Vincent sleep. The current method was too costly for both his health and finances to be sustainable in the long run.

"Is something wrong?" Vincent asked, stopping her before she gave him the shot. "You seem upset."

"There's trouble with the GODS. I have a lot of things going on right now, but it's nothing you need to worry about." She lifted up the needle. He stopped her again.

"I had the most peculiar dream," Vincent said and sat up.

"Oh?" Aurora was usually open to dream-tellings, but she was too stressed out to be in the mood for one now. She couldn't come up with a polite way to decline on the spot, though. Maybe it would be something short and sweet? Vincent hadn't been asleep for very long.

"As much as I'd like to get back to it, ah, could you please put this aside for a moment? I want to tell you something." He was referring to the needle. Aurora sighed but set it aside on an instrument tray. Please don't be a long-winded story about losing teeth, falling from a high place or public indecency. She'd heard enough of those to last a lifetime.

"I had a dream about you."

It wasn't the first time someone had reported having dreams about her, but the way his hand lingered on top of hers hinted it hadn't been as mundane as the ones she was used to hearing from her other patients. Any other time, the details would have intrigued her.

"Vincent..." She had too many things on her plate to be emotionally ready for... whatever this was going to be.

"It was a mistake to ever leave you," he said.

Despite having yearned to hear these words, she would have never been ready to actually hear them. For a moment, she wasn't sure how to breathe or think. She tried to redirect herself back to what she was supposed to be doing, but the needle looked foreign, the diagnostic equipment... She'd meant to— what had she meant to do?

"Vincent, I—"

Vincent squeezed her hand.

"May I kiss you?" he asked.

Over the course of these past however many years, she'd imagined this plenty of times in more romantic settings, then cursed herself for forgiving him each of those times. What was he doing, asking her at such an awful, stressful, horrible moment?

She found herself wondering what sort of kiss it was going to be. A gentle, polite one? Something short to test it out? He was reserved and sensible by nature, so it probably wouldn't be more than a curious, tentative peck, much like the one he'd given her before. Or maybe something akin to the very first one years ago, when he'd been almost frustratingly timid and slow? In either case, she felt safe with him.

She nodded and watched Vincent's worried expression turn into a smile. He expelled some air through his nose, as if letting out a near-to-silent nervous laugh, and leaned closer.

Ah, yes, these lips felt familiar. She relaxed and closed her eyes. Her mother would have had a fit had she known she was letting a boy kiss her. She chuckled. She hadn't put much weight on her mother's words for years now, but this brought her right back to that time.

Except something was not the same. She opened her eyes to him watching her. The rug was pulled from right under her when she realised it wasn't the same at all. What was this? What was his mouth doing? Sweet, righteous Guardian have mercy—! She almost fell down from the side of the bed she was sitting on. As she scrambled, Vincent took a hold of her to give her support.

"Are you all right?" he whispered. Whatever his mouth had just done felt wholly indecent but left her insides simmering. His low voice and kind concern were only stirring the broth.

"Yes, I'm—" He interrupted her by nibbling and kissing the side of her mouth. "Oh, my word. What sort of a dream was it...?"

"A good one, but this is better."

Well, clearly, but—

"Excuse me, Dr Vesper. Are you in here?" a most inconvenient, highly errant individual asked from the door.

"What? Who is it?" she was startled and backed away from Vincent.

"It's Assistant Cockscomb from the system service hall. I tried to call your office but there was no answer. You said to report back at our earliest convenience."

"Yes, right, of course. What is it?" She patted and straightened her clothes, as if that could do something about the lingering sensation of Vincent's tongue in her mouth, and hurried to the door.

The system service hall was packed with people trying to finish their work to go home for Midwinter, delayed because of the issues with the GODS, now demanding answers.

Without Hosta's no-nonsense aura at the helm, the sleep research department had descended into an unwieldy chaos of yelling and shouting.

Assistant Cockscomb showed Aurora the cluster of devices responsible for monitoring the Bulb. The output had seemed normal all the way to the cut-off point, and the assistant was kindly trying to explain something about the details, but it was nigh impossible to hear anything from the noise.

Aurora had about two minutes worth of patience left for any of it, and once that was up, she lifted up her badge and shrieked on top of the hubbub.

"Will each and every one of you shut up this instant!" She didn't have much of a voice and wouldn't raise it often, so it could have stood to be stronger, but it thankfully did its job. The room fell quiet. "Service technicians, over there. The rest of you, form a queue here!" She directed them.

Approximately thirty-odd bobbing heads formed a line in front of her, and the dozen or so technicians huddled to one side. "The rest of you keep your mouths shut for now, and I'll see what we can do about your issues."

There were some murmurs, but the mass of disgruntled people was surprisingly docile. Aurora received a general briefing from the technicians and started to go over the demands, mapping their priorities. This seemed like it would take a while, so she tried to delegate some of it to Assistant Cockscomb.

It would be this, then Hosta, then finishing up with Vincent... Oh, dear sweet Guardian have mercy and help her get through all this.

CHAPTER 41

Julian didn't want to move but was compelled to check if Rhys, Quin and Victor were still alive. He got up and staggered over to Quin, who was badly beaten up but sitting. Victor was helping Rhys free himself from under Mr Murray, who was pinned to the floor with the slate ripper.

"We're all still alive?" he asked, unsure whether to believe it.

"I don't know, am I?" Rhys looked ready to faint. Victor helped him up, but, hobbling on one foot, he didn't look much better off than Rhys. Quin got up on his own, but he was leaning heavily on the only desk in the room that remained unscathed.

"Now what do we do?" Quin asked. "Do we have to do something, or can we go home?"

"I don't even know anymore," Julian admitted.

The house was a bloody mess, evidence pointing every which way, but at least it could be said Rhys had made sure Julian's father would not voice a complaint or bother anyone again.

As for his mother, they could not be sure how much remained once her sealed memories had fully been lost, but with her husband gone, she would not be doing much any time soon. The machinery in this laboratory was destroyed, but if it turned out that there was indeed need, finding the suitable equipment to wipe Hosta's memory for good would probably not be too difficult. It did not seem like a pressing concern for now.

"Considering where we are, I doubt there will be an investigation," Victor said. Julian agreed.

Whatever anyone made of it, it probably wouldn't make much difference. The types that were affiliated with the Hosta Group would probably not be interested in vengeance but rather gather like scavengers feeding on carrion to grab what they could for themselves. It would have been better to destroy all the research to prevent anything like Mr Murray surfacing from it again, but since that didn't seem possible, at least, with the driving force now gone, there would be no more of it.

"We may need to clean this mess at some point, but I'm sure as hell not doing it now," Julian noted. "Can you walk? Let's just go home and worry about it later."

He helped Victor, who had trouble staying upright. Quin was ambitious enough to offer to carry Rhys but looked relieved when he didn't have to. Rhys was unsteady on his feet but managed on his own.

Halfway down the stairs, Julian noticed his reflection in the mirror across the hall and realised what he looked like. What they all pretty much looked like.

"Wait," he stopped them as they reached the ground floor. "It's maybe not the best idea to march out there looking like this... There may not be as many people out there as there will be tomorrow and the day after, but there's still bound to be people." He reached to open the door to a washroom.

Sprawled on the washroom floor, his mother whimpered in fear. She turned to look at him and screamed. Alarmed by this, Julian covered her mouth and tried to sound as kind as he could, telling her to shut up. She was sobbing and shaking. He pulled her up and out of the washroom.

"Who are you? What do you want from me?" she asked between sobs. She didn't seem to remember enough to remember any of them. "Where's my baby?"

"It could be an act," Quin noted.

"True." Julian frowned. "I suppose we should make sure somehow. Victor, any ideas?"

Victor looked around the room. There were packed bags near the door—either left there when they'd come back from seeing Julian or for heading out. Victor limped over to the luggage and opened it up.

"Well, we have one of the devices here, and we have Justin."

With these words, all four of them eyed each other, no doubt equally reluctant to go out and walk the extra steps to get the box with the remains. They were in a wordless consensus, however, that retrieving the box to have it close by would be better than merely waiting to see if Justin would realise he was needed for something on his own.

"Fine, I'll go." Quin was about to leave. Julian stopped him.

"No, I'll go."

Quin looked incredibly relieved. By the looks of him, he'd been roughed up, possibly taken a tumble down the stairs and cracked some ribs. With each breath, he winced from the pain. Having him try to carry a box in his condition would be an unjust punishment, but it had been brave of him to volunteer.

Julian felt a strange, queasy feeling looking at Quin. It took him a moment to realise what it was. Damn it. "Make sure she's restrained and doesn't escape. I'll be right back." Wasn't it already enough that he was forced to worry this much over Rhys?

"Don't worry, I won't make the same mistake twice," Quin assured him.

Victor started setting up the device, and Julian watched him for a moment, distracted. Damn it. It was all three of them now, making him feel like this? He hurried out the door.

W hen Julian returned, his mother had been tied up in such a fashion there wasn't even a pinky left for her to move, and she'd been gagged to reduce the noise. She looked calmer than before but by no means unafraid.

For a passing moment, Julian felt odd doing this to his own mother, but looking at her did not elicit the appropriate emotional response like the three banged up doofuses did. She wasn't a complete stranger anymore, but she wasn't any different from a woman living down the street that he'd seen a couple of times. To top it off, she'd threatened the wellbeing of the people he actually cared about.

Julian supposed he was lucky to not have to feel a particular sense of loss.

His father lay dead in the attic, and, while it was uncomfortable to be in the presence of death, the only thing Julian could think of mourning was the concept of having a father. With this, the possibility, however theoretical, of ever having loving parents was taken from him, but it wasn't as if he didn't still have a family.

Victor had finished with the preparations. Wiping all of Hosta's memories would have been better, but the machinery required for it was in pieces up in the attic. Sealing as much as possible with no one around to reverse the seal seemed a good enough alternative.

It had taken Jasmine approximately fifteen minutes, so they gave Justin a leisurely half an hour while they washed themselves. If it wasn't enough for Justin, they'd get back to it at a later date.

Even after the wash, Rhys looked like death itself with gunk stuck in his wet hair, clothes stained and expression tired and glum. He sat down and said nothing, just stared ahead.

Watching him in that state was much worse than witnessing what had happened to his parents. Julian had to look away because his heart hurt. Rhys hadn't deserved any of this.

"It's as good as it's going to get," Victor said. "We should get going."

"Yes." Julian lifted Justin's box.

It had snowed a decent amount in the past few hours, so the streets were covered by an unusually thick layer of the stuff.

Julian had borrowed a sledge he'd found by the door—presumably Jasmine's—when he'd fetched Justin. He placed Justin into it again and packed and added Hosta's device next to the box.

"In case we need it," he said to Victor.

Victor nodded. He'd finished penning a short note for Hosta for when she would wake up.

He said it was something to lead her out of the house and to give her a chance to escape in case any of her seedier associates turned up and found her defenceless without her memories—a small act of kindness she probably didn't deserve, but leaving her with absolutely nothing felt the same as outright killing her, and two deaths for one night was already quite enough.

It was up to her to save herself.

Chapter 42

Aurora dismissed the nonessential employees, so they could go home to their families and get back to problem-solving after the holidays. The remaining handful concentrated on the contact point at the Bulb and some of the other more pressing locations.

"Has anyone reached Mr Craft?" Aurora's question prompted some looks and a few headshakes from the people left behind. "As soon as we get someone returning from the field, can you tell them to check on the Bulb in person? I need to head back to my office."

She'd left an assistant to take care of the rest of Vincent's diagnostics data, but she needed to go through it as soon as possible, and it was getting late.

With her hands full of paperwork, she wasn't sure she would even get to it today. She'd inadvertently promised Ren to spend time with her and Vincent for Midwinter, and she wasn't sure whether they preferred to celebrate on the Eve or the day itself.

She'd hoped to wrap up the last of her work today, but, since she'd been put in charge of everything and with no word from Mr Craft, it seemed likely she would have to hold the fort through the next few days.

Her office was empty and quiet. She stood by the door, took a deep breath and closed her eyes. She needed to get through this, take care of Hosta, make the woman help fix Vincent and quit this awful place.

A noise from somewhere above caught her attention. There was a layer of snow blocking the skylight up to the garden, so she couldn't see whether someone was up there, but it sounded like footsteps.

The glass of the skylight made an ominous yet soft creak as it gave in under the pressure of someone walking on top of it. Whoever was up in the garden must have not known about its existence and didn't realise they might fall down through it if they kept walking over it.

Aurora moved aside and waited for a moment. When it happened again, she decided to check whether the small door she'd seen in the break room next door could be opened. It seemed like it might lead up to the garden above.

The door was old and in somewhat of a disrepair from not being used, but she was able to push it open just enough to fit through. There were indeed some steps up to the garden, and, curiously enough, fresh footprints in the snow all the way down to the door and back up.

No one had opened the door to come in, but they had definitely been down here for something.

Aurora stepped up to the garden to see who was there. It was dark, but she could see several trails of footprints criss-crossing the yard. A hunched figure stood a little ways from where Aurora estimated her skylight was.

"Excuse me?" She pulled her cardigan a little closer to her skin and headed for the figure. The closer she came, the clearer it became who it was, even if she did not seem herself the way she crouched and cowered. "Hosta? What are you doing here?"

The outfit she was wearing was tattered and dirty and grossly unsuited for this weather.

"You know me?" She looked up. Her hair was usually done up, so Aurora hadn't realised how long and thick it was. It was now a clumped mess over her shoulders.

"What on earth has happened to you?" Aurora rushed closer and wrapped her cardigan over Hosta's shoulders.

"I don't know. There was a note." She offered Aurora a piece of paper. It was too dark to read what it said.

"Let's get you inside before you freeze. Where's Mr Craft?"

"Who?"

Ah, the seal was still firmly in place, and the memory loss seemed extensive. Aurora guided Hosta to the door and down into the break room. In better light, the stains on her clothes looked worryingly much like blood.

"Was there a man with you when you woke up? What happened to him? What do you remember? How old are you?"

"There were several." She tried offering the piece of paper again. "But it seems like it might have been a dream. I dreamt I had a baby... but I'm only sixteen."

Aurora read the note but became not much wiser. Had someone actually attacked the Bulb? That seemed like something that would not happen in real life. Not in Aurora's reality, at least. Then again, a woman in her fifties believing she was forty years younger also seemed unusual. Sixteen was far too far back for Hosta to remember what she'd done to Vincent.

"I'd like to help you remember everything." Aurora offered her a cup of tea to build trust.

She seemed skittish and ready to bolt, and Aurora did not want to run out in the snow after her if she did.

"How do I know it wasn't you that caused me to grow this old?"

"I can do a lot, but that is out of my scope."

"How do I know I can trust you?" She pulled out a knife and pushed Aurora to the wall. The teacup fell on the floor and shattered. The blade was pressed uncomfortably close to Aurora's throat. Feisty woman.

The knife was a bit of a worry, but it was small and slapping it to the ground didn't seem all too difficult. Aurora played along, for now.

"Would it help if I gave you a solid reason for my help? One that is not some bullshit about doing it from the goodness of my heart?"

Hosta pulled back the knife somewhat.

"What is it?"

"There's a piece of information I need, and it's in there somewhere, sealed away inside your head. That's all I want. I'll help you in whatever way you choose so long as you let me retrieve that. Deal?"

"You could do that? You can help?" She still seemed sceptical.

"They've put a nasty seal in there. I'll help you remove it. What you do beyond that is your business, but I need you to promise me you'll tell me what you did to Vincent and how to reverse it."

"I don't even know anyone by that name."

"It might be stored as subject one in there, and, if you think you're sixteen, it hasn't happened to you yet.

"I know. I'm not stupid."

"In any case, you know I wouldn't hurt you because you have what I need. How about you give me the knife?"

"And be left completely defenceless? Are you crazy?"

Perhaps it was fair to let her have it for now. Aurora moved the knife blade aside and started collecting the mess of a teacup off the floor.

"You seem confident and trustworthy, but you don't know what we are dealing with. There were corpses in that house! They'd fought over something. I need to figure out what that was and why I was there. Judging by that note, I may be in grave danger." Hosta seemed to be searching through the break room for something. "Do you have a mirror somewhere?"

"I may have one in my office."

"What's your name? What do I call you?" She took off Aurora's cardigan and used it to dry her hair.

"I'm Vera." Aurora set the shards of the teacup on the table and took the cardigan Hosta gave back to her. It was smeared with blood. "Follow me."

She headed for her office.

After some persuasion, Hosta allowed Aurora to inject her with the preparative mixture.

With the Bulb out of commission, Aurora had requested an alternative contact point to use to connect to the Guardian. The one she was given was slightly less reliable, but the data it provided from Hosta were just as hopeless as from the Bulb.

The sludge was there, thick as ever, but this time Aurora decided to try to remove as much of it as possible, even if it took her the whole night. She'd wasted precious time juggling her work and her responsibilities. It was high time and possibly her last chance to do this before those memories disappeared forever.

CHAPTER 43

Rhys seemed to be freezing by the time they reached the pharmacy. Jasmine was at the door, waiting, even though the heater had long since cooled and the front room was getting chilly. Victor was about to restart the heater when Quin kindly guided him to the stairs with Julian and Rhys and took care of it instead.

Rhys could barely walk up the stairs, stiff from the cold. He'd tried to wash his hair and turned his coat inside out to look less conspicuous, and, without a hat or mittens, he'd been at the mercy of the icy winds.

Julian wasn't faring that much better himself, but since he'd had to carry Rhys some of the way, he was warmed by the exercise.

"Let's take a look at Victor's leg first and see what we can do." He directed Victor to take a seat and carefully removed the belt and the scarf.

That side of Victor's trousers was soaked with blood, but the wound no longer bled. He'd been extremely lucky with it. A venous bleed could be significantly more serious than this, but the slate ripper had only just nicked the vein.

"It needs to be kept clean, and you should take it easy for a while. You can and should keep moving to prevent blood clots but be careful with it."

Julian cleaned and dressed the wound. "And thank you." He set his hand on Victor's hand and looked him in the eyes.

"Uh, what for?" Victor blushed and frowned slightly.

"We'd be dead without you."

"I did what I had to." Victor swallowed and looked away, abashed.

"Don't be modest," Quin joined in. "You were great!"

"I killed a man. It's hardly something to celebrate."

"He would have killed all of us if you hadn't. But that's not what I meant. It was thanks to your careful research and planning that we managed to stop them."

"It was a fiasco, though," Victor reminded him.

"That was on me. I should have gagged her right away. I'm so sorry!" Quin bowed his head.

"You don't have to—" Victor tried to stop him. Julian interrupted them.

"I think I need to take care of him." He gestured at Rhys, who seemed to be struggling to stay upright. "But I'll check on you after, all right? Take it easy until then," he told Quin.

Jasmine offered to warm up something for them to eat, and Julian guided Rhys into the bathroom.

R hys let Julian take off his coat. With his fingers clumsy and shaking from the cold, it would have otherwise taken ages to undo the buttons.

"Take it all off. We'll use it as fuel for the fire once it's dry." Julian started to undress himself.

Once he'd taken off his own coat and shirt, he helped Rhys with his shirt buttons. Rhys was too tired to object. He only stopped Julian when he was about to take off the undershirt.

"Don't think about it. I want to help you wash and warm up. That's all," Julian said.

At this point, modesty seemed arbitrary, but Rhys wished he could have skipped having to feel his self-loathing resurface.

"Trousers," Julian said and opened the front. Rhys pushed them down and sat on the side of the bathtub so that Julian could pull them off. All that was left were the drawers. Was this really the moment he had to face humiliation as well? On top of everything?

"Turn around and take them off. I won't look," Julian told him gently. "Get in the tub. I'll help you wash. Once that's done, you can soak in the warm bath until you feel better. Let me know if it's too warm or you start to feel dizzy."

Oh, so Julian was worried he might faint? In all honesty, that seemed warranted.

Rhys removed his drawers and climbed into the tub. He sat with his back turned towards Julian, covered himself with his hands and let Julian wash him.

The water felt painfully hot on his cold skin, but there was something very enjoyable about the pain. The small cuts all over his body stung. Absent-minded, he inspected his hands for shards of glass. Miraculously, he could only find one. He showed the hand to Julian and said nothing. Julian took a look.

"It's glass? Want me to remove it for you?"

Rhys nodded. He wasn't going to be able to do it on his own with his hands trembling.

Julian searched for the tweezers in the little cabinet by the basin. He was so careful with them, Rhys could hardly feel him remove the shard.

"It's out. I wonder how many of these we'll have to dig out between the four of us." Julian rinsed Rhys's hand. "Do you mind if I wash myself before you bathe? Are you still cold?" He offered Rhys a robe.

Rhys took the robe and wrapped it tightly around himself. He sat up on the side of the tub and stared at his feet in silence while Julian washed himself.

"Ah, shit, this hurts so bad," Julian voiced a rare, voluble complaint.

Rhys glanced at him to see what he was talking about. He had similar small cuts all over his body but also some rather hideous looking bruises that were so purple they neared black. He looked less gruesome once he'd managed to rinse off the blood but not by much.

"Is there something on my back?" He turned his back to Rhys and squatted down awkwardly.

Rhys leaned closer to look. There was a piece of glass the size of a coin embedded into his shoulder. It hadn't sunk in deep, so Rhys removed it without a problem. There were a few smaller ones, but he dropped the tweezers before he could even try removing them.

"Sorry," he forced himself to whisper. Julian turned to look.

"It's OK, I'll ask Quin or Victor to do it," he said.

Rhys started to cry. He wasn't sure why this was the moment to do so, but it was probably out of frustration.

"Sorry," he repeated and tried to wipe his tears and stop.

"Don't worry about it. Let's draw that bath for you so you can warm up and get some sleep."

"No..."

Julian raised his brow.

"You don't want a bath?"

"No." Rhys sighed. "I mean yes. But I'm not going to sleep."

"But you do want a bath?" Julian confirmed.

"Yes." Rhys lowered himself back into the tub and tossed the robe over the side. Julian turned the taps and adjusted the temperature for him.

"That seems fine to me. Is it good?" Julian asked. Rhys wasn't sure, so he nodded and left it up to Julian.

"I'm going to go get dressed and find something for you to wear. I'll be right back. Don't fall asleep in there."

"I won't."

Rhys waited for the water level to slowly rise high enough to ease the chill in his bones. As he was finally relieved from that discomfort, he started to cry again. He wiped off the silent flow of tears with the back of his hand. He was safe at home, wasn't he? They'd made it home, it was over, so what was there to cry about?

When the water level was up to his neck, he turned off the taps and leaned back to watch the ceiling. He was not going to wake up and realise that this had been a dream, right? Not after all that.

Yet, the feeling of it being unreal still persisted. Surely this was one of his nightmares, and he hadn't just killed a man?

What an exhausting nightmare. When he woke up from this, he did not want to sleep again for a very long time.

He held his breath and sank into the water but continued to watch the ceiling through the ripples. This way, it didn't matter if he cried.

Shortly after, his view was obstructed by Julian's startled face, and he was pulled up from the water.

"For the love of— Rhys! What did I just tell you?!"

"Don't fall asleep?" Rhys tried to recall if there was something else. "I didn't, did I? Or...?"

He sat in the bathtub, but this was within a dream, wasn't it? But when—? And why was he told to not fall asleep if he was already asleep?

He looked at his hands and realised they weren't going to reveal anything. He needed to look elsewhere to be sure which one this was.

He looked down.

No amount of protective silence could save Rhys from understanding what that meant. He scrambled backwards with enough speed to slide up from the curved end of the tub. The sound he made was unrecognisable.

For a while there, he'd allowed himself to believe that no matter what signs indicated otherwise, he must have been dreaming. It had certainly been similar enough to a lot of his recent nightmares—if considerably worse.

In a split second, he was brought back to the moment the saw blade touched Mr Craft's throat and the sensation of resistance that followed. His expression. The blood. All of it. In his head, he knew the man had said and done some awful things. He'd been about to murder his own son—! But Rhys hadn't actually *seen* any of it, and the Mr Craft that had stared at him in horror had been the one he'd only ever seen mild-mannered and kind.

As he gasped for breath after worthless breath, Rhys's clammy back was pressed hard against the wall. He'd killed a man.

Julian had received quite the fright when he returned to the bathroom and seen Rhys submerged. He'd only been away for a few minutes! And then once he'd pulled Rhys up and scolded him, he'd almost had a heart attack from the noise that Rhys had made when he'd jolted himself violently out of the water.

"What is it? What's the matter?!" Julian hurried to grab him by the shoulders to stop him from hurting himself.

"I— I—" He was unable to say it from his ragged breaths, but at least he was trying to explain.

"You're all right. You're sleep-deprived. It's been a rough day," Julian tried to calm him down.

"I can't!" Rhys started to bawl hysterically. It was a surprise he even had it in him, what with how spent he seemed.

Julian grabbed the towel and wrapped him in it since the noise he was making was sure to soon attract an audience. Then he held Rhys as firmly as he dared. Rhys seemed so fragile, Julian feared he might break.

"Everything is fine, we're fine, it'll all be all right." He repeated these words a few times and felt Rhys grasp at his shirt to hold on. "Let's get you dressed, all right?" Despite still crying against Julian's chest, Rhys managed to nod. Quin appeared at the bathroom door.

"Is everything all right? We heard the most dreadful scream..."

"It's fine, I think, I'm not sure. Probably." Julian shrugged but kept holding Rhys in his arms protectively, afraid to let go in case something happened again.

"That looks a little suspect," Quin pointed out. Julian gave him an acrid look. Quin turned back to Victor, who had stayed behind. "It's fine. He just made Rhys cry."

"I did no such thing!" Julian exclaimed before he realised he was being made fun of.

Quin grinned at him, then levelled his expression back to normal to ask, "Are you sure he's fine? He needs rest, right?"

"It's been a shitty day for him. Frankly, I'm surprised he's lasted this long without breaking down. I'd probably had a fit long since."

Julian hadn't forgotten how he'd felt when he'd been unable to rest. That experience had brought a lot of perspective and context to some of Rhys's idiosyncrasies. He felt a little guilty about having simply been impressed by how well Rhys could manage everything dreamside without realising it could come at a cost.

Julian shooed Quin for some privacy before handing Rhys some clean flannel long underwear and a robe. He dried Rhys's hair and helped again with the buttons. By the time he was done, Rhys had calmed down enough to stop crying.

"That was dramatic, I'm sorry..." He swallowed audibly.

"Don't worry about it." Julian gave him another hug, but in truth, it was more to calm his own nerves than to assure Rhys. "You need some sleep."

"No..."

"I know you don't want to, but you need to."

"No."

"Well, get a bite to eat first and see how you feel about it after." Julian led him into the lounge. "Give him something to eat, I need to change my shirt." The sleeves were wet and starting to get cold.

Rhys felt better, but the difference was marginal. He sat on the sofa hugging his knees when Julian returned from changing his shirt.

Julian brought him a plate Jasmine had so kindly prepared, but he had no appetite, even if the food did look delicious. It was a small selection of the feast meant for Midwinter Fest, and there was a glass of mulled wine to go along with it.

Rhys ignored the food and watched Julian check Quin's injuries. He splinted Quin's sprained wrist, determined the severity of his rib fractures, pulled out some debris from under his skin, cleaned up and dressed the deepest cuts and lacerations and periodically forgot himself watching Quin. He was probably unaware he was doing it. Quin, in turn, took care of Julian's back.

"Oh, I gave Victor some of your laudanum for the pain. I hope you don't mind," Quin noted. Victor was dozing off in the armchair.

"How much?" Julian eyed Quin.

"He's a big man, but I gave him the standard dose, don't worry. He's just tired. I'm sure we all are."

"Do you need something?"

"I wouldn't mind, to be honest. I didn't dare to take anything before you had a chance to check me over... It hurts like that time I fell off the cliff on the way to Agnes Point." When Quin spoke, he was trying to do it with as little air as possible.

"All right. Maybe go up to your room before you take it. I cannot carry you."

"I don't want to move." Quin was sitting on the floor, leaning against the wall.

"Well, you can't stay there all night."

"Can't you bring me a mattress?" Quin sounded even whinier than usual. Julian sighed.

"I'll get it," Jasmine offered. "I can manage a mattress. Which one? From upstairs, or?"

"There's a spare one in Rhys's room. It's closer," Julian said. "Could you bring Rhys's duvet as well?"

This sounded promising to Rhys, who had previously followed the conversation with half an ear. The more warmth, the better.

Julian sat down next to him on the sofa. "You should eat something." The man picked up the untouched plate of food and started feeding Rhys.

Well, of course he would, Rhys thought, while reluctantly chewing a piece of the pie. He glanced at Quin, who was chuckling at them.

"I never thought I'd see the day," Quin said to himself, then turned to Julian. "Can you feed me too?"

"Haven't you eaten yet?" Julian's gaze was stern. Quin looked guilty. There was an empty plate next to him.

"I could always go for seconds!"

Jasmine returned first with the mattress and then with Rhys's duvet. Rhys wrapped it around himself and let Julian feed him, but if they thought they were going to fool him into sleeping because he was comfortable, they were grossly mistaken.

"He really should sleep," Jasmine said to Julian. She looked worried.

"I know."

"Jacob stayed up for six days because he refused to go to sleep. He was delirious by the end of it. It was horrible."

"I'm not going to sleep," Rhys told her, no longer sure why he was so dead against it or why the prospect felt so inherently terrifying.

"Don't worry, I'll make sure he does," Julian said. "It's getting late. Maybe you should go to bed as well?"

"I suppose." Jasmine seemed reluctant.

"I know we said we'd take you to see the lights, but, as you can probably tell, we might not be fit for the walk tomorrow. We should all get some rest, though. Who knows..."

"I understand. I'm just happy you came back."

"I'll take you to see the lights." Rhys was determined to keep his promise.

"Then you're going to have to sleep," Julian reminded him.

"No..."

"You're not taking my sister anywhere without first getting some sleep." Julian offered Rhys the last piece of pie and handed him the rest of the mulled wine. Rhys swallowed the pie and emptied the glass to quickly retort, "Who's going to stop me?"

It was silly to argue over it. He knew as much but didn't want to give in. Julian ignored him and turned to Jasmine.

"I'll settle this here, don't worry. You go to bed. Either way, we'll have a decent day tomorrow, all right?"

"All right. Sleep well!" She smiled before she headed upstairs.

"How are you feeling?" Julian asked Rhys. With some delay, Rhys managed to answer.

"Fine." He fell over to lie on the sofa with Julian's lap as his pillow. "Dirty... dirty trick." He'd been right to not trust any of them!

"What did you give him?" Quin asked.

"Just a little something to ease the process," Julian replied.

"You piece of sh— I'm not goin' to sleep." Rhys felt a deceptive calm come over him. It was actually very pleasant and not painful at all. He watched Julian, forgetting why he was supposed to be angry. "You're pretty."

"Can I have what he's having?" Quin laughed.

"That's what I just gave you," Julian noted.

"Oh, how come I'm not having as much fun?"

"Because I gave you less so you don't break yourself."

"Stupid ribs," Quin huffed, then wailed.

"Very pretty..." Rhys turned to look at Quin on the floor. "I love you. All of you. You're the best." This felt like an incredibly important thing to say. "I'm sorry, about everything."

"It's all right, just go to sleep."

"Nooo..." Rhys struggled to keep his eyes open.

"What's so bad about going to sleep?"

"Hmmmm, what if I wake up?"

"You're awake right now," Julian reminded him very, very patiently.

"Oh, right! I am! But if I sleep, will I have nightmares again?"

"It's possible, but they can't hurt you. They'll be normal nightmares."

"How can you cope with not being able to control it?"

"What choice do I have? Just ride it out."

"But it feels so awful to slide from rest to a dream and back again!"

"The quicker you get to sleep and have enough rest, the quicker we can let you control it again."

"I know..." Rhys wasn't stupid. It just felt so awful, unpredictable and foreign to him, like not being able to breathe when he needed to. It felt worse every time it happened. "I'm scared."

"I'll be right here," Julian assured him.

"Please don't leave."

"I won't." Julian's voice was kind but confident. Rhys let go.

V incent knocked on the door to Aurora's office.

"I'm sorry to disturb you. That lady you left me with finished the diagnostics thing a half an hour ago, and she seemed tired, so I sent her home. I rang our lodgings, and they've made sure Ren has eaten supper and gone to bed on time. I'm not in a hurry to leave, but I was wondering if you still needed me for something."

Things had felt promising earlier this afternoon, but when she'd retreated with such haste, the nerves were back. Aurora seemed hesitant over something. Had he been too enthusiastic?

"I'm sorry, I think I'll be stuck here all night," she said.

"Ah, I understand. Ren is looking forward to spending Midwinter with you. Do you think you'll be able to make it tomorrow, or the day after, or should I tell her we can celebrate together sometime later?"

"I don't know. I'd better not promise anything..."

Was she really busy with work or trying to turn him down gently? The latter seemed more likely. He knew he should have behaved himself, but he was overcome by such strange energetic optimism after these brief spells of sleep, he'd dared to hope that maybe she might respond favourably. Unfortunately, the 'better not' seemed like a recurring theme.

"Well, we're probably going to spend tomorrow with Rhys at the pharmacy, but you're free to join us if you have time. I'm sure he won't mind, and Ren would be delighted."

He wished he'd had the courage to say it was him who would be delighted, but she was avoiding even looking at him through a barely cracked-open door. There was something she kept checking behind her, as if she wanted to be rid of him to get back to it.

"I should get back to—"

"It's me, I'd be delighted if you joined us." He'd rather have her reject him openly than keep skirting around it. It was only going to hurt once.

She opened the door a bit wider and turned to look at him, finally.

"It's not that I don't want to. I really am busy here with something that can't wait."

"You can tell me if you've changed your mind. I apologise if I came on too strong earlier—"

She placed her fingers onto his lips to stop him from speaking and opened the door to let him in.

There was a woman asleep on the sofa in her office with electrodes attached to her head like the ones Aurora had used on him.

"A patient?" Vincent whispered. "Why are you treating her in your office?"

The place was full of examination rooms with various medical equipment, and this was just an office, even if it was rather spacious.

"No. This is my boss. It's Julian's mother. Something awful has happened to her, and I'm trying to help her. I don't know who's behind it, so I thought I would try to lie low until we figure it out."

"Does Mr Craft, I mean Julian, know?"

"I don't know. I haven't told anyone. I don't know who to trust here. I wanted to avoid making noise, as someone could be listening."

"Is that blood? Wait... Do I know this woman?" There was something familiar about her. It could be because of the resemblance to the pharmacist, but he had a strange feeling they both looked familiar for the same reason.

"It's possible." Aurora reached over to her desk for a thick folder and handed it to him. He opened it to see what it contained.

"Subject one?" It seemed like an old patient file for a very young child.

"I think this may be you."

"What? How?" Vincent looked at it again. There was a picture of the child, but most tiny humans looked like chubby little sausage rolls at that age, so he struggled to see the similarity. Women were quite remarkable to be able to tell something like that!

"I couldn't tell from the picture, silly." Evidently Aurora had noticed him pause at it. "I inferred it from the diagnostics data. It aligns so well with yours. The more I compare, the more obvious it becomes. The symptoms, everything."

"'Type seven pattern? Restorative impact negligible?'"

"There are eight different patterns that have been detected so far in our research. The first three are the most common ones. People tend to fall into one of these three and have very few problems with their sleep. The fourth and fifth patterns usually indicate simple issues with falling asleep or staying asleep. Those are most common for the people who sought our help at the Sleepy Leighs. The sixth is a fairly difficult combination of symptoms where the patient spontaneously falls asleep even without realising. The seventh pattern is the near-to complete inability to fall asleep, stay asleep or the subject reaching only a form of sleep where they fail to connect to or disengage from the Guardian without an unrelated health anomaly, usually fever, somehow mitigating the process. We do not know what causes it, and it is extremely rare."

"And that's what I have?"

"Yes. It seems so."

"And it's rare enough for you to think this 'subject one' might be me?"

"Yes, in fact, I don't know any other cases. I've only ever read about it from her work." Aurora gestured at the woman asleep on the sofa.

"What about number eight?"

"That's a catch-all for anything that doesn't fall in any of the other categories."

"What is this Guardian I'm supposed to be connecting to or disengaging from?" That sounded like something he'd never thought to do when going to sleep. How was he supposed to connect to something he hadn't even known existed?

"We're still researching that, but it seems like an apparatus or a system created by the ancients that manages our health when we sleep."

"And that's where you're connecting me to with the injections?"

"Yes, we alter your brain chemistry so that the Guardian is able to pick you up, so to speak. We don't know how it happens, but after years of analysing the data we get from the system via the contact points, we've been able to discover a multitude of compounds that seem to have something to do with it."

"That sounds incredible."

"I say we, but I've only worked here for a few weeks. It's mostly all her research." Aurora seemed dejected. "I fear that, for whatever reason—convenience perhaps—she has used you for this research to gain new insight on the Guardian and what it can do, and it has left you with this type seven pattern. She's had her memory tampered by someone, I don't know who, but I'm trying to recover it before it's lost, so I can find out what she's done and reverse it for you."

"You're doing this for me?" He'd known she'd been fairly dedicated to treating him, but he'd assumed she was driven by curiosity and finding him a fascinating research subject. Working towards fixing the abnormality seemed counterintuitive if it were mere scientific interest. Unless he was reading too much into this?

"Who else would I be doing it for? I'm trying to help you have a better life. What I've read about your condition, it sounds horrendous."

"It's not that bad..."

She gave him a stern look.

"Can I help you with it somehow?" he offered. Maybe there was something he could do to speed up the process.

"Actually, there might be." She hurried over to her desk. "When I help you sleep and you connect to the Guardian, what's it like?"

"Rhys asked me something like this once. I didn't even understand the question back then, but now... I enter a bubble, and I stay there for the duration of it. Is that the Guardian?"

"Can you do something in there, or does it cycle you through the stages unprompted?"

"I can walk around freely and do things, but if I relax enough, things seem to happen on their own."

"But you have to do something for it to happen?"

"Yes, well, if I chat with the hands, nothing else happens. It's when I relax that it takes over. How so? Is that not how it's supposed to work?" He watched her shuffle through her notes for something.

"It's promising. It sounds a lot like how your brother described it. Maybe you can help me help her. I need another set." She rushed out of the room.

Vincent glanced at the folder still in his hand. The discrepancies that had plagued him about the files he'd received from Mr Benton and the matron of the workhouse had been a trail of crumbs trying to lead him to this.

Was this what Aster had tried to keep from him?

There were pages upon pages of notes about experiments in this file. Reading some of the descriptions, Aster's words about some things being better left unknown seemed to make more sense. The thought of her—with her kind sensibilities—reading any of this made Vincent feel ill in the stomach. He wished she'd never had to know any of it and that she'd at least been spared the details.

Aurora returned, pushing a cart with another device.

"We'll connect you to it and see if we can find a way for you to jump over to her bubble. I can only show you the same passages I've read, and you'll have to figure it out yourself. If it doesn't work, no harm done. I'll continue with what I was doing before. But I feel like this would be faster with someone on the inside, and unfortunately that's where I fall short."

"All right, point me to it, and I'll do my best."

CHAPTER 45

It was nearing seven in the morning. The output of the device seemed encouraging, so Aurora decided to wake Vincent.

"Coffee? Tea?" she asked him.

Despite sleeping through the night, without rest, he was probably feeling as exhausted as she was. His side of the monitoring equipment had shown alarming spikes throughout the night, and she'd ended up spending most of her time trying to keep him asleep.

Whatever he'd done, though, had cleared Hosta's output much faster than anything Aurora had managed to do remotely.

"Whichever you have in that pot," Vincent replied and suppressed a yawn. "Did it help? If that was her, it was easier than I thought to find her. She looked much younger there, though. She seemed like she was covered in something, so I tried removing it, but I have no idea whether that did anything."

"The numbers look promising, but we won't know until she wakes up." Aurora poured the last of the coffee into a cup and pushed it across the desk. "I'm sorry, the coffee is probably cold. I don't have milk or cream, but there's sugar if you prefer."

"That's all right. I don't enjoy it either way." He took a healthy swig and winced.

"I could have made you some tea." There was a stove in the break room next door. She'd brewed the coffee there some hours ago. Boiling water would only have taken a moment.

"This is fine." He finished the cup and put it aside.

Hosta sat up on the sofa behind him.

"Excuse me. Who are you?" she asked.

"Vincent Swifty, nice to meet you." Vincent offered her his hand without hesitation. "I could have sworn we've met, but unfortunately I don't remember where."

She took her time to evaluate him from head to toe but eventually stood up to shake his hand.

"The feeling is mutual, it seems," she said. "But apparently there's a lot I do not remember."

"Did it get any better since yesterday?" Aurora asked. Just a couple of more years was all she needed.

"Difficult to say. Yesterday is the easiest to recall. Everything else feels like it has happened to someone else a long time ago. This place is no more familiar, and I do not remember either of you two. I suppose this is the Vincent you're hoping to fix?"

"Yes. I have his file here, in case that might refresh your memory." Aurora handed her the folder.

"I'm a research assistant, so I don't know what good I will do, but I'll take a look. Oh, is this my handwriting?"

She seemed perfectly calm up to the point of opening the folder. The creases on her face deepened as her jaw, and her grip of the folder tightened. She looked up from the file and straight at Aurora, her eyes piercing dark and lips quivering.

"Where is my baby? What have you done with my baby?" She charged forward, but with the desk between them, she did not reach a target with the knife she'd pulled. Vincent was quick to grab the knife and restrain her.

"That file is from over three decades ago!" Aurora reminded her. She glanced at Vincent. Was it not Vincent's file? Were there others with type seven patterns out there? Was this Hosta's baby? Had she done these things to her own child?!

Hosta backed away and looked at her hands and arms, seeming to confirm she was no longer a young woman, but when she looked at the files now scattered on the floor and Aurora behind the desk, she was shaking.

"I remember having him. I remember he was in my arms. He was crying. I remember he was crying so much, and I couldn't get him to settle..." She knelt to pick up the photograph. "My baby. Where is he?"

"We don't know. I thought..." Aurora struggled to read Vincent's expression. He was holding his hand where the knife had nicked him, but it didn't look serious. Between him and Hosta, the resemblances were few. It was possible that they were related but not apparent beyond a doubt.

"The restorative index was always so low..." Hosta's hostile exterior crumbled as she picked up the papers one by one off the floor and started to cry. "I feared he was going to die. He was so sickly. I tried to— I tried everything."

"Do you remember what happened?" Aurora knelt next to her. Maybe there was a chance she would recall something she'd done... Although, it was starting to look likelier that this baby, whether he was Vincent or not, had been fussy because he'd been this way from birth. If that was the case, what was there to reverse?

"I couldn't get him to stop crying. I was alone. He couldn't sleep. I couldn't sleep. I was so tired, I had to do something. The nanny—" She clenched her teeth. "That wretched piece of—" She turned to look at Vincent, something seemed to twist inside of her, and she charged at him instead. "You! You vile cockroach, you disgust me!"

Vincent backed away, startled, but could only back away some steps before hitting a wall. Hosta was considerably shorter than him but grabbed the lapels of his shirt and shoved him as if size made no difference at all.

"Not you. You are not him." She doubled back. Still seething, she looked elsewhere for her target. "Where is that treacherous, cheating maggot?!"

"There's no one here but us. I'm not sure who you're referring to." Aurora tried to keep her voice steady, hoping to guide her back to her senses.

"Who else? Walter, my husband, that good-for-nothing whoremonger!" Hosta trod over the papers on the floor as she paced back and forth in a state of continuous agitation.

"I'm sorry. I haven't heard from your husband since—" Aurora stopped to think. "The day before yesterday."

She could have sworn Mr Craft's given name had started with the letter J.

With Hosta this volatile and aggressive, having Vincent there was a relief. Aurora glanced at Vincent, hoping he would intervene. He stood where he'd been pushed and looked to be shaking.

"Vincent?" Aurora's question also made Hosta return her attention to Vincent.

"You're his son, aren't you? You're that rat's offspring! I bet you are as disgusting as the treacherous demon that sired you. You look just like him!" she snarled and spat at him. He looked like a timid street dog receiving a beating and made no move to defend himself.

Aurora was about to tell Hosta off for her unhinged behaviour when the woman grabbed the coffee cup and saucer from the desk and threw them at him. Because he made no effort to deflect, they hit him across the chest. He did, however, crouch down to shield himself after the fact.

Hosta stormed out of the room, which was frankly both a relief and a convenience. Aurora hurried over to Vincent.

"Are you all right?"

He seemed to be struggling to breathe. How hard had she thrown that cup...?

No, it wasn't the cup. Was it the words that had knocked him so hard out of his senses? He was breathing much too fast to be sensible. By this rate, he might make himself faint from it.

"Follow my lead and breathe as I breathe." Aurora gently turned his face to look at herself and exaggerated each deliberate, slow breath until Vincent was following. He looked at her as if frightened out of his mind, but at least he was making an effort.

"M-mother," he mouthed, his lips trembling. He was trying to say something more, but Aurora couldn't make out what it was.

"I don't understand. Take it slow. She left. You're safe."

"I-I'm not a d-demon child." He looked at her like he was pleading for understanding and mercy, as if afraid she would take any of those words to heart.

"I know. She was entirely mistaken. You're a sweet, gentle, considerate man. I know you wouldn't knowingly hurt a soul." That was why she'd always felt so confused by him leaving without a word those years ago.

It made more sense now that she knew of his issues and a little of his background, but it also hurt worse to know she was so powerless to help him.

"I'm sorry, I'm useless. I only wanted to help," he said.

"Oh, Vincent. Me too. That's what I wanted to say." She hugged him so that he wouldn't have to see her cry.

None of the religious texts she'd pored over had described his condition. None of the research notes had revealed a cure. If Hosta hadn't caused this, and if she hadn't figured it out, then what chance would any of them have? He was likely doomed to live his whole life in this miserable between-state, always exhausted and breaking down, unable to heal from his trauma.

She would do her best to give him as much rest as possible, but for how much longer would she have access to the equipment and the drugs needed? A few good nights seemed insignificant when he would have deserved to sleep properly for the rest of what was left to him.

These months of effort had been for nothing, yet she would have done it all again for a chance to cure him.

R hys woke up to the distant sound of bells ringing. Head still resting on Julian's lap, he opened his eyes to a view of the man's sleeping face leaning awkwardly on the backrest of the sofa above him. Julian looked like how Rhys was feeling: like he'd fallen off Vincent's speeder and rolled a hundred metres across rocky terrain.

Rhys stayed still to determine that Julian was indeed breathing and hadn't died during the night. The hand on his chest was warm to his relief.

He turned his head to see Victor sleeping in the chair and Quin on a mattress on the floor. They were both also breathing. Suffering from a lingering tinge of paranoia, Rhys checked that he was breathing himself and hadn't become like Justin without realising it.

No. He seemed fine.

To think of it, yesterday had felt confusingly similar to a dream, but today was somewhat more solid. Last night's sleep hadn't been enjoyable, but he'd survived and was better for it. Now, if he could will himself to move and get some sustenance...

"Fucking ssshit, f-fuck! Ffff—!" He pushed himself up and continued to mutter the litany of expletives until he was sitting upright. Even then, every part of his body was screaming in pain. Quin made a nagging, whining sound on the floor.

"You're up? I'm sorry, did I wake you?" It was Jasmine's voice from the kitchen area.

"Shit, sorry!" Rhys apologised for the language. "Didn't mean to—didn't realise you were—"

"Those words are not new to me, don't worry." She laughed softly. "Do you want something to eat?"

"Yes, please!" Rhys was starving. He lowered his legs carefully to the floor. If he was in this much pain, then what was it like for Julian, Victor and Quin?

"I'm never going to move again," Quin whispered with his eyes closed. His breathing was slow and deliberate. Out of the four, he had probably been roughed up the worst, having faced Mr Murray on his own.

"Julian?" Rhys had intended to wake Julian gently, but the man bolted up to sit and consequently visibly regretted the choice. He even uttered a few very strong and surprisingly nuanced curse words.

"Sorry... uh, Julian?"

"Yes?" Julian lowered himself slowly back to the backrest.

"Quin's pretty sore; can you give him something?"

There was a pitiful wail coming from the floor.

"I don't want to move," Julian mumbled.

"I see. This is going to be a fun day." Rhys ventured to try a one-syllable laugh. "Jasmine, could you help out? I'd do it, but I feel like it would take me about an hour."

"What do you need?" The newly appointed resident pharmacist asked.

"My kit." Julian paused. "It's on the dining table, I think."

Jasmine retrieved it. The two of them discussed dosages, and Jasmine diligently measured them accordingly.

"You seem like you might have a knack for this. How about becoming my apprentice?" Julian suggested. She brushed him off at first. "I'm serious."

Jasmine gave Quin the medicine and stopped to think.

"Do I get paid?"

"Yes."

"Please teach me well!" She rejoiced and handed Rhys his dose.

Rhys looked at it as if it were poison. If he didn't move at all, the pain wasn't so bad... He was about to set it aside.

"It's acetylsalicylic acid," Julian said.

"Sounds ominous."

"It's made from the salicylic acid present in meadowsweet and willow."

"Oh."

"I wouldn't over-medicate you first thing in the morning unless you were wailing in pain, on the floor unable to move like a certain someone over there, and even he's getting just enough to get by."

"Stingy bastard," Quin muttered, face twisted from the pain. "I don't want to live."

"It'll kick in soon enough." Julian stretched himself ever so carefully. The side of his face was a curious purplish colour and slightly swollen. Jasmine offered him a fresh cool cloth to hold against it.

"Shit, I promised you a tree, didn't I?" Rhys realised.

All the other decorations and food were sorted, but he'd meant to get the tree this morning. He had a moment of internal agony trying to decide which was worse: letting Jasmine down or going out to get the tree.

He'd offed her father. The least he could do was get a tree... That thought was so off-putting, he felt nauseated.

"Are you going to have a panic attack over the thing?" Julian asked. Rhys felt like he might, so he nodded.

"I don't need it; it's fine," Jasmine assured him.

"I— I... I'm sorry, I should at least..." At least try to breathe normally, you idiot, Rhys thought. It was just impossible to remain calm once he'd thought the thought. The feeling of guilt was crushing. "At least..." A stupid tree was not going to make up for it. Clearly.

He looked at Julian, seeking his help but unable to put into words what he needed. Mr Craft had been a monster, right? Right? Things were never that black and white, but surely just this once...?

"Calm down. It's not the end of the world." Julian's tone suggested he didn't mean to belittle how Rhys was feeling but was genuinely trying to help. It just wasn't very helpful. Rhys bent over where he sat.

"I can't—" It felt like something he'd tried to say before. Julian massaged his back lightly. "I can't pretend like it didn't happen..."

"What's he talking about?" Jasmine asked.

"This is maybe not the best time," Julian said. "We'll talk about it tomorrow."

"What is it?" Jasmine knelt next to Rhys. "What happened? I don't care about the tree. I'm just glad you're all right. That's the best Midwinter gift I could have, really." Her words were making it worse.

"I'm so sorry. I didn't mean to…" It was so selfish of him to be losing his shit over it, but he'd never killed a man before. It wasn't as if he had any experience in how to deal with it.

Julian cleared his throat. His hand moved away from Rhys's back when he stood up. He guided Jasmine to sit down next to Rhys on the sofa and sat on his haunches in front of her.

After a moment of silence, he told her in no uncertain terms what had happened. He left out the worst of the details but made sure Jasmine understood it was an immediate lethal injury.

Jasmine listened to him in silence, tears streaming down her face. Rhys wiped his own, feeling like it was disrespectful for him to be crying, too. When she glanced at him, it made him want to die.

"Rhys—" She swallowed to contain each of her sobs, but she was just a little girl wrestling with an unfair burden of grief. It seemed like her petite frame might just buckle under it. "Oh, Rhys." After what seemed like ages of having to watch her cry, she turned to give Rhys a hug. "Thank you for saving my brother." She squeezed Rhys so tight her strength took him by surprise.

"But—"

"No, Rhys. I know my father. He was kind to me most of the time, but he must have had it coming." She wiped her face. "Mr Murray didn't live with us for nothing. If it hadn't been you, it would have been somebody else. And I might not have Julian anymore."

Was she trying to make him feel better? She, who'd just heard her father was dead. And him, who was responsible for that death.

"I'm sorry. I'll get you the tree. I'll get you a thousand trees. Anything you want," Rhys promised.

"You really don't have to."

"I need to do something!"

"You saved Julian, and all of you came back safe. I'm going to be grateful for that, and that's the end of it! I'll be sad, but I'll try to enjoy today, and

I'll cry whenever I want to and however much I feel like crying, but I'm not going to blame you for this! I don't have very many friends. I don't want to lose you, too."

Rhys tried to pull himself together.

"I'm going to get you the f—ing tree, and we're going to decorate it together, all right?" He got up, stormed off into his room to put on some clothes and then down the stairs. In truth, he needed a moment to sort himself out, but it was an added bonus to suffer at least some form of punishment for what he'd done.

T he room was quiet for a while after Rhys had stomped off.

"Where's he going to get the tree?" Quin broke the silence.

"I suppose he knows someone?" Julian suggested.

"I can't believe he actually went."

"Who? Rhys?" Victor woke up. He looked confused, but it was a confusing situation to wake up to.

"I would have given him a hand, but frankly I think *no*." Quin tried to turn onto his side to see better but quickly gave up.

"What's going on? Where did Rhys go? Why's she crying?" Victor frowned.

"I told her about yesterday. Rhys went to go get a tree," Julian informed him.

"How's a tree going to help?" Victor straightened himself in the chair.

"Who knows." Julian shrugged.

"Was he delirious again?"

"No, I don't think so." Julian considered it. "Maybe. I'm not sure."

"Somebody should probably go after him," Victor pointed out.

"Not me," Quin mumbled. "Uh..." He promptly passed out.

"I'll go. Can you keep Jasmine some company for a bit?" Julian asked Victor.

"Of course."

"I'll be right back."

Julian got dressed, followed Rhys downstairs and grabbed Rhys's new gloves, scarf and hat before heading out.

Julian caught up with Rhys at the other end of the street. He was perusing a row of conifers spread out in front of a cart. There weren't very many left.

Julian was caught slightly off guard by the sight. He'd forgotten the tree wasn't figurative. It blew his mind that it was customary to bring an actual full-grown tree into the house. Who had decided this was a good idea, and how had they talked everyone else into it?

"Julian?" Rhys noticed him. "Help me with this, will you?" He was going for the biggest one.

"Does it have to be that big?" Where was that even going to fit? Julian hoped he'd arrived in time to talk some sense into Rhys, but alas, this was not the case.

"It's the only one that's the right shape and in good condition. Look at the smaller ones. This one is bare from the back. That's way too small. The third is already yellowing from the bottom—"

"We could put the first one next to the wall. Who's going to see the back of it? No one. And it'll take less space."

"But it's puny. The branches will bend down from the weight of the ornaments."

The tree Rhys had selected was taller than him by half his height. How was he going to reach up there to decorate, and more importantly, what did he mean to decorate it with? Something heavy? That seemed like an accident waiting to happen.

At least the tree-seller had set up shop closer than what Julian had expected, so they wouldn't have to haul the tree back more than a few hundred metres. Granted, something that size and covered in prickly needles would not be fun to carry regardless of the distance. Good thing he'd brought gloves.

"Can we at least cut it shorter from the bottom?" Julian suggested. Rhys stopped to stare at the tree for a while and looked pale.

"Yes, but how?" he asked slowly.

"Victor probably has— oh."

Yes, Victor was likely to have more than one saw, but he'd inadvertently reminded Rhys of something he shouldn't have.

"All right, you're right, it's too big for us..." Rhys took a deep breath and moved aside to calm himself down.

"I'll take care of it. It'll be fine. We should have a proper tree while we're at it." Julian paid for the big tree and urged Rhys to grab one end of it. He was not looking forward to moving the thing, but he was willing to humour Rhys, if there was a chance it might cheer him up. Rhys looked especially appreciative when Julian handed him his gloves.

Halfway back to the pharmacy, Rhys's hold slipped, and his end of the tree fell to the ground.

"I can't get it out of my mind," he said quietly. Julian waited. "Maybe he wasn't going to kill you. Maybe he was angry but about to stop when I barged in... I keep reliving that moment over and over. Did I miss something? I should have checked what I was holding before I—" He swallowed.

"He definitely intended to kill me." Julian couldn't read minds, but he was fairly sure he'd felt the intent. His father would not have stopped unless someone had interrupted him. "I'm afraid he might have already done something to Jonathan and Jacob. I contacted their school, and I was told they've gone missing. The person I spoke with assured me they would contact the police and investigate, but I'm yet to hear anything back." He almost didn't want to know. The Greater Schades Police Department wasn't exactly renowned for their efficiency, but even had they known where to look, neither Julian, Rhys, Quin nor Victor were in any condition to go on a search themselves. The only upside to not knowing for sure was that Julian didn't have to give Jasmine more awful news just yet. "Let's try to enjoy today as best we can."

"I'm sorry," Rhys said.

"For what?"

"For being such a handful."

"You're not a handful; you're human. I'd be worried if you'd brushed it off like it was nothing. I feel like an absolute asshole, being so fine with it." Julian sighed. Despite everything, shouldn't it have made him feel at least a little bit more *something?*

"If you ever want to talk about it, I'll be he—"

"Hah," Julian interrupted him. "I appreciate the offer, but if I ever start offloading on you, you'll start crying, and I'll be the one feeling awful and trying to console you."

Rhys gave Julian an annoyed look.

"If anything, I should be thanking you for saving my life, more than once, as well as apologising that you had to go through all that, largely because of me. I'm thankful, and I'm sorry. You can do whatever you need to do to feel better. It's all fine with me. Let's move this tree out of the way first though, right? I'm getting cold, and that means you're probably freezing."

CHAPTER 47

Vincent grappled with the remnants of the inexplicable fear that had come over him at the sound of that woman's voice. Having Aurora there was both useful and inconvenient. She'd helped him calm himself more quickly, but it meant she'd been there to see him stumble through all of it.

"Do you hear that?" Aurora backed away to listen. "I don't care where she shuffled off to or what she means to do with that rage she's brewing, but what is that noise? I thought I'd sent everyone home. Who could she have run into?"

The stinging in his palm distracted Vincent from the words. He realised there was a shallow cut across the fleshy part of his thumb. It was no longer bleeding, but his hand was smeared by sticky, half-dried blood. Such a small cut let out a surprising amount of blood.

He shuddered.

Lucky that the woman had been slow with the knife. She may not have intended to stab Aurora, but charging forth like that had spurred Vincent straight into action. The thought of that knife hitting its target uninterrupted was much worse than any abruptly stirred childhood trauma that came after.

"I'm going to go check what that is. Will you wait here?" Aurora asked.

"No, I'll come." Far from ready, Vincent braced himself and scrambled up. He would process his crap during or after, but there was no way he was going to let Aurora go out there alone.

Indeed, once they'd left the room, a heated conversation between two voices was easily audible in the corridor.

Vincent followed Aurora towards the stairs. When they reached the bottom, he could see that woman standing at the top, talking to someone. A man's voice responded to her.

"I gave you until Midwinter to cure my daughter. Where is she?"

Vincent closed his eyes and exhaled to distance himself from the immediate surge of anger at the sound of that voice.

"I know nothing of any filthy crotchlings you may have begotten. Did you make some with her? Were they as faulty as the one you forced upon me?" The woman at the top of the stairs glanced down as she said it, and their eyes met.

"You will not speak another word about my daughter, or I will rip that depraved tongue right out of your mouth!" These words made Vincent want to rip the man's face apart and feed it to the dogs, but the poor dogs would not have deserved such an ill-tasting meal.

"Who is that? Someone she knows?" Aurora whispered.

"Sounds like a typical Wakefield family reunion," Vincent muttered back.

"I have held my end of our agreement. I've honoured your husband's outrageous demands and stayed out of your way all these years when you've been messing around, trying to fix your half-witted progeny. I've even given you a more than courteous chance to study my daughter, so long as you make sure she has no memory of it when you return her to me. I will not repeat this again. Where is she? Where did you stash my daughter?"

"Get it through to your thick skull, Walter, I wouldn never have any interest in something that's originated from your shrivelled, scabby ball sac!"

"Your face is not as smooth as my scrotum, woman. A preposterously pustular hag like you should consider herself lucky to have a man so much as lay his finger on you. I'm surprised your husband doesn't heave at the sight of you!" The man lowered his tone when he continued, "I should have known the two of you weren't to be trusted. She is not here, is she? I swear to the Guardian you're going to pay for this." He came into view as he leaned in closer to shake his fist at her.

"It's true I have no vapid wench here to gift you, but you can take your defective excuse of a son if you please!"

"I have no son!"

The man was thrown into a full fit of rage and grabbed a hold of her. She seemed unruffled in the face of the aggression, and merely laughed and pointed at Vincent. There was nowhere to step away and hide, so Vincent stood still and met their eyes.

Vincent watched Walter Wakefield shove Hosta Craft aside. She fell to the floor but kept on laughing in hysterics. The now unrecognisable caricature of a man at the top of the stairs let out a guttural growl and turned to glare at Vincent, seemingly readying himself to charge down.

"You p—!" A mighty whack cut his words short before he could make another move, and his body fell down the stairs as dead weight.

When it came to a stop just short of the landing, Vincent looked up to see a woman holding the ceremonial torch of the Guardian, lifted off of the giant statue in the chancel. Hosta had stopped laughing and looked at her with one raised eyebrow.

"But I do. I have a son. You bastard," Mrs Wakefield said.

Beyond that one brave swing, the torch proved too heavy for her to carry, so the other end of it fell with a heavy thunk, spilling the rest of the embers in its cup onto the floor. She looked at Vincent but didn't seem too surprised it wasn't Rhys that had prompted her husband's fury.

"You're worth saving, too," she said, then turned to Hosta. "As for you, I did you a favour. Then and now."

"I'm about to return that favour. We need to leave!" Hosta pushed Mrs Wakefield to the stairs.

Vincent caught the scent of smoke. The chancel above bathed in an eerie orange glow.

"Why down? The door—" Mrs Wakefield pointed behind her, but Hosta pulled her along down the stairs.

"Do you want to be blamed for this?"

"No."

"Then you'd better not run out the front door in broad daylight!" She turned to Aurora. "You know this place. Where was that door we used yesterday?"

"This way." Aurora obliged.

Vincent climbed up a few steps and confirmed that the tapestries and wooden structures of the chancel were soon to be engulfed by the flames, started by the rain of embers from the torch's cup when Mrs Wakefield had swung it.

"Vincent! Hurry up," Aurora yelled from the corridor. Vincent stepped back down and past his father's lifeless body.

As a last sign of mercy, he checked that the man was dead and would not wake up to being burnt alive.

There was no pulse. He'd received a death quicker than he'd perhaps deserved... But it was not up to Vincent to judge. Feeling both relief and guilt over his relief, he limped after the women as fast as his injured knee allowed.

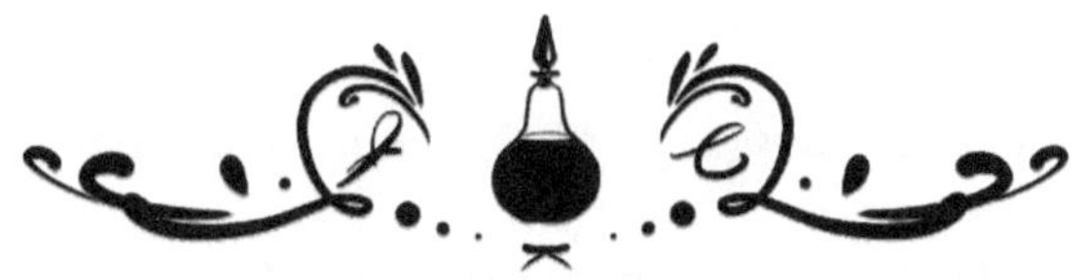

Julian kicked the snow off of his boots and held the door open to push the tree the rest of the way into the pharmacy.

"I'll go get the, ah..." Rhys let go of the tree and took off his gloves. "The, ah..."

"I can do it." Julian removed his boots and was about to head upstairs when he realised Victor was standing at the last step with a saw in his hand.

"I thought you might need this," he said and handed it to Rhys, who in turn passed it on to Julian as if it were hot coal.

"I'll go get the decorations." Rhys excused himself and disappeared into the storage at the back.

"Do you need help?" Victor offered and hobbled closer to inspect the tree.

"I might need an extra hand. How's the thigh?" Julian asked.

"Fine." Victor used his commendable arm-span to take some rough measurements of the tree presumably to determine how much of it would fit to stand in the lounge. Then he looked up at Julian and gave him the signs for 'dizzy' and 'tired'.

"Don't forget to drink fluids, all right?" Julian snapped off some of the thinner, drier branches near the bottom and sawed off the ones that were too tough to remove by hand. Victor showed him where best to cut the bottom off and held the tree still while Julian sawed.

"How are you holding up?" the man asked once Julian was done sawing.

Julian tossed the bottom stump closer to the log burner and put the saw down to rest against the counter.

"Well." He paused to think. "I'm fine. A little worried about my sister, you, Rhys and Quin, but other than that, I'm just looking forward to a quiet evening."

"All right."

He said 'all right' but sounded like he was just humouring an obvious lie.

"Don't worry about me. It's really not an issue. There's nothing boiling under the surface. I don't feel anything." He pruned off a few split and dried leaves. Victor grabbed a stool from behind the counter, planted his healthier bottom half on it and waited. "I don't know what to tell you. Maybe it hasn't caught up to me yet?" The question was whether it ever would.

"It could take a while." Victor rubbed his beard and leaned on the counter.

"I guess, but I suppose it's for the best." Julian shrugged. Victor frowned. "Well, you know. The timing would be bad for me to start raging just as it's the most difficult for them." Julian nudged his head toward the staircase, referring to Rhys and Jasmine. Victor's forehead remained creased. Julian's followed suit. "I really don't have enough rage in me to cause a scene. It's all in the past now."

"That's not what I'm worried about."

Julian looked at him and waited for further clarification. Nothing.

"Can you be a little less cryptic about it?" He crossed his arms and exhaled to release the rapidly mounting annoyance.

"You're welcome to cause a scene."

"I won't. I'm not angry." He probably would have sounded more credible had his voice not been as strained by the usual irritation caused by Victor's waffling. But that was different...!

"But if you were." Victor shrugged.

"Are you up for carrying this thing upstairs? I can do it myself if you're feeling too dizzy." Julian searched for the best place to grab the trunk for a good hold. When he looked up, Victor looked apologetic. He was probably not feeling great after the blood he'd lost. It was already unexpected that he'd ventured down the stairs today considering he'd have to climb them back up again. Julian braced himself to carry the tree up by himself.

"No, wait. I'll help you." Victor stood up.

"It's not that heavy. Just awkward to carry."

"Sorry."

"Don't worry about it."

CHAPTER 48

The door in the break room was jammed by nearly half a metre of snow. It hadn't snowed as much, but the wind had carried it into the recessed entrance and failed to carry it out.

Vincent pushed the door with all his might but could only crack it open enough to fit a hand. It was not enough to dig away the snow behind the door.

"It's no use." He'd attempted to go through many enough snow-jammed doors to know when to give up. "Why the hell do they always have to open outwards?"

"Fire safety." Aurora checked the corridor. "It sounds like the fire might be spreading down here. There's smoke."

"Are there any other doors?"

"Probably, but I don't know the place well enough to know where."

"Anything to break the door with? An axe?"

"No," Aurora paused to think, "but there's a skylight in my office next door."

They returned into the corridor where a thin veil of smoke crawled across the ceiling. The ladies crouched down, and Vincent did the same, but because of his knee injury and his height, he had difficulty crouching down low enough, and with his barely healed lungs, it didn't take much for him to start coughing. Thankfully, the smoke hadn't yet reached the office.

"Move aside and face away." Vincent grabbed the desk lamp and used its marble leg and weighty base to crack the skylight. It didn't require much of a tap for the glass to break, although he needed to repeat the process a few times for the bulk of it to crash down, along with a flurry of snow.

The current of air drew in a thick cloud of smoke from the corridor, and it soon filled the office, worsening Vincent's cough.

"Let's move the desk." Aurora was ready in position to move it under the newly opened escape route, but it was too heavy for her on her own.

Vincent supposed he wouldn't have been able to make it budge on his own either, but the four of them managed to push it across the room.

"Watch out for the glass." Vincent helped the older ladies up onto the desk, and he and Aurora gave them a boost so they could climb out. They helped pull Aurora up in turn with Vincent giving her a push. As soon as she was out of harm's way, he heaved a figurative sigh of relief. The smoke was too thick for him to breathe, much less sigh.

"Give me your hand!"

The knee was not doing too great. Vincent had been doing his best to ignore it, but it was really making itself known now.

"Vincent! Give me your hand!" Aurora was stretching out her hand to him. He felt dizzy. He lifted his arm up. A drop of blood fell on his face, and he shielded himself out of instinct.

This seemed like a dream. The edge of the bubble was always right there, even when he wasn't sure he was seeing it.

Oh, he was dreaming? It was a nightmare? He coughed. The house was on fire?

The cat! He needed to save the cat! He couldn't leave without saving Swifty!

Aurora grabbed him by the forearm.

"Up! Now!" She tried to get a proper grip. The two women beside her couldn't quite reach, but they were trying, bless them.

"I need to save the cat." Vincent wasn't entirely sure if this was a sane notion, but he was tired of watching his words.

"The cat is with Ren!"

Oh God, Ren! Where was Ren? He looked around in panic. Was she supposed to be here? Where? He couldn't breathe. He tried to breathe faster, draw in more air, but there was so much smoke it made his throat and lungs burn.

"The cat is safe with Ren! Give me your hand, and we'll pull you up!"

He crouched down in search of fresher air. The damn knee felt like it was being stabbed with barbed skewers.

"Vincent, for the love of the Guardian, give me your hands!"

Aurora fought to maintain her grip on Vincent's wrist, afraid he would give in and crouch down again if she let go. His hand and forearm were slippery with blood. He felt hopelessly heavy to pull up alone, and the women next to her had no room or purchase to reach down close enough to get a proper hold, barely grasping at his sleeves.

Even Hosta was biting her teeth together, grunting and growling to heave Vincent up every chance she managed to grab a hold of something but to no avail. They would lift his feet off the desk, but there seemed no way they'd be able to pull him all the way up without using leverage, and there was nothing like that visible at the snow-covered yard.

"It's no good. We're wasting time," Hosta said and let go.

"You can't say that! What kind of a mother are you?!" Aurora screamed at her.

"A bad one! But I'm not stupid." She backed away from the skylight. "Drop him down before he suffocates!"

The other woman turned to look at Hosta, hesitated for a moment but let go. Aurora glared at them, tears and smoke stinging in her eyes.

Hosta ran off.

When Aurora realised she wasn't running away, she let go of Vincent's hands.

"Crouch! Crouch!" She yelled at him. He seemed confused but looked up at her. "Go back down! Into the break room!"

Hosta was clawing off the snow in the recessed entrance when Aurora waded her way to the door.

"Who knows what's in the smoke in there, so crouch as low down as you can, and try not to breathe it in," Aurora reminded her and helped Hosta dig.

It seemed to take ages to force the door to open enough to squeeze back inside.

There was no sign of Vincent in the break room. Either he'd never left the office, or he'd got lost on the way.

Aurora debated whether to close the door or leave it open, and, with the snow coming down so heavily, she opted to leave it open. The draught was already pulling more black smoke into the room, but she hoped they would be in and out quickly enough for it to not make a difference. It would be worse if the door was sealed shut again with them inside. She did, however, have the foresight to close the break room door as they left it.

The corridor was considerably hotter than it had been when they'd last run through it. The smoke was thick, visibility zero. Aurora almost missed the door to her office.

"Vincent!"

He was lying on his side on the floor beside the desk but turned to look and made an effort to crawl towards her.

"What are you doing here? Is it a dream after a—?" He wheezed and coughed.

"No, we need to go." She pulled him to his feet, Hosta and the other woman giving support to keep him from falling back down. He dragged his injured leg, veering out of balance, half crawling and half having to be carried.

Aurora realised she wouldn't have stood a chance without the two other women, who so far hadn't voiced complaints or hesitated to risk their lives for him. This seemed especially peculiar after the vile words and attitude Hosta had shown towards Vincent mere moments ago.

Hosta was sweating, face covered in soot and dirt, jaw taut, pulling Vincent along like her life depended on it. With something either collapsing, exploding or both nearby and the ground shaking by the impact, she was right to hurry.

The foundations creaked and moaned around them. Tufts of thick, black smoke and heat rushed into the break room. The air was heavy with the putrid stench of chemicals. Aurora had a fairly educated hunch this soup of gases was not far from exploding into an inferno that might have burnt most of the city had the weather not been on their side.

"You! Ram it! More! Open it wider," Hosta ordered the other woman, so she could force Vincent through the door and into the fresh, cold air. Aurora pulled him under his armpits and up the stairs with Hosta dragging him by his clothes from the side.

Vincent stared at the plump clusters of snowflakes forming vast schools, like fish swimming across his field of vision. He was only barely aware of the pain. His skin no longer burned from the heat. Everything felt distant and muffled around him. The edges of the bubble faded in and out of view.

Was he dying? Was he dead?

Cold.

It felt almost as if he was about to start shivering.

So, not numb, and thus presumably not dead. Not yet, anyway.

But this feeling at the edge of it was like meeting an old friend.

With no sign of colourful tail whisks, the sky was dull grey and overcast. Not a worthy time to die, then, he chuckled.

Aurora's beautiful face blocked the lacklustre view. Her hair—normally like thousands of fine, wavy strands of copper wire—stuck together, dark and wet, having escaped from whatever usually kept it in place behind her head. The map of freckles across her nose and cheeks was barely visible. Her eyes were watering, and she wiped them with her least soot-smeared fingers.

Imagine, if he hadn't been fished out of the sea, if he'd given up somewhere along the way. If he'd decided to take his life when things were miserable, he wouldn't have been here, realising how happy he was to see her face.

"Are you cold?" Aurora asked.

"I've been colder. This is nothing." He could feel his teeth clattering, and the absurdity was making him want to laugh.

"Is he delirious?" someone asked.

Perhaps, but that was hardly newsworthy. The edge of the bubble faded away, though, as he took a few more careful breaths of fresh air.

"Has someone called the firemen?"

"Yes, I saw at least two fire engines arrive. There were men pumping water and locals moving more snow to keep it contained. It looks like it's all going to burn, but it might not take anything else along with it."

"All of that research, all of the precious texts, gone in an instant." Aurora looked sad. Vincent raised his hand to cradle her cheek, and she looked at him. "It's heartbreaking, but it's not the end of the world. Let's get you somewhere inside."

"All right." He pushed himself up to sit. Sweet all-mighty Guardian! The knee reported its opinions on his recent activities with some new-found vigour. He was definitely alive and awake now.

"I'd advise against going in there. It was not a pretty sight yesterday, and I can't imagine a day has done it any good. Besides, not exactly where you want to be if you want to stay out of trouble with the law."

Vincent turned toward the voice to see the woman supposedly his mother and, next to her, the woman who looked more like how he'd imagined his mother would look like. Neither of them were his mother, though. His mother had done her best to protect him from the mess of them.

"Thank you for pulling me out," he said. For that, he was truly grateful. "Ren is probably waiting with the cat. Right?" Still not feeling quite up to speed, he confirmed this from Aurora.

"Yes. We should head over there, but first..." She scooped some snow to help wipe the blood off his face. "It looks like I have nowhere to be this Midwinter's Eve, so if the offer is still valid..."

"Of course it is!"

CHAPTER 49

"Oh, my ever-loving Guardian, Vincent! What in the world has happened to you?" Ren rushed to hover around Vincent.

"It's fine, it's fine." Vincent cleared his throat—an action ill-advised after the amount of hacking and coughing he'd been doing. Ren gave him a pointed look. "It hurts, and I think my knee will hate me for a while, but I'll survive. Be easy on me."

"That's better." She turned to Aurora. "What about you? Are you all right? Who are they?" Ren's attention turned to the two women waiting in the doorway. She did an awkward curtsy and offered Mrs Wakefield her hand.

"Lillian Wakefield. Nice to meet you." Mrs Wakefield shook the hand offered and smiled.

"Ren Swifty. Are you related to Uncle Rhys?"

"Yes, he is my son."

"Wow! Really? We're going to go see him today. Will you be joining us?"

"If you'll have me..." Mrs Wakefield turned to Vincent, seeming uncertain but clearly wanting to come.

"I think Rhys would like that," Vincent said.

"And you, missus?" Ren turned to Hosta.

Her question hung in the air for a while as the present company stood in silence. With no answer within the usual timeframe, Ren turned to Vincent. Vincent looked at Hosta, and their eyes met.

Throughout the morning, she'd been headstrong and assertive. Her grief and rage had seemed frighteningly intense to Vincent. Now that she stood at the doorway, her hair dishevelled, clothes tattered and expression level but decidedly tired, she seemed no larger than her actual size.

"My name is Hosta Aelia." She paused, eyes still fixed on Vincent's. "I believe I gave birth to a boy, whom I loved dearly, but who was too much for my young selfish self to handle. He got caught in the middle of my war with the world and had to pay a price that wasn't his to pay. It doesn't weigh much in the scheme of things, but should it bring you any consolation, I am truly sorry. I don't remember what I've done all these years or whether it was something irredeemable. I certainly do not expect to be forgiven. But I want you to know that from where I'm standing and what I know right now, I feel like I would have done *everything* in my power to help you."

"Everything?" Vincent wondered, not meaning to say it out loud.

"Yes. Seeing as you are still struggling, I must have failed. Tell me, are you unhappy with your life? It may be too late for me to get caught up with the research to start again, and you don't have to have anything to do with me if you so wish, but would you want me to do that? Try to fix it while I have life in me, I mean."

"Why did you give me up if you meant to do everything to help me?"

The things she was saying were all fine and good, and, if he ignored what had actually happened, it would have warmed his heart to know she felt this way. But she'd sent him into a bloody workhouse!

"You fell gravely ill after your father left. I was consumed with work, trying to find something that would improve your sleep enough to help you recover, but none of my relatives agreed to keep you for longer than a week. They said you were disrupting their lives too much. In the end, no one would take you. I wish I could have kept you close to me, but at least I knew where you were at all times. Until... until..." She rubbed her temples. "I can't remember. I think they must have placed you without my knowledge. The matron was always so suspicious when I came to give you your treatments and take the latest data. I told her you wouldn't remember any of it, no matter how unpleasant those experimental treatments may have seemed, but she must have not believed me. I don't remember much beyond that, but I would assume I did everything in my power to get them to return you to me. If that didn't happen, I'm so sorry, I must have failed you."

If she'd been as fierce about it as she'd been toward her ex-husband today, it would have stood to reason Mr Foxwick-Benton had become suspicious and wanted to keep Vincent out of harm's way. The blessing in all of this was that he'd eventually ended up with the Brambles.

"To answer your question, no, I'm not unhappy. I can't say it has always been a pleasure, but right now I'm ready to go spend Midwinter's Eve with my brother and our loved ones—" As he said it, another piece fell into place, and he turned to Aurora. "Didn't you say she was Julian's—?" He gestured at Hosta, struggling to finish the sentence. Aurora seemed to make the connection and opened her mouth in similar surprise.

"How many—?" Vincent tried to recall any and all occasions when the Crafts had come up in conversation with Rhys. He couldn't quite recall the details, but he was fairly sure there were several siblings. Julian, at the very least. And the hands! The voiceless. What was his name? Justin? "Do they all start with J? Now I feel left out."

As a counterbalance to his sudden enthusiasm, Vincent felt an overwhelming urge to sulk.

"What are you talking about?" Hosta frowned.

"Ah, come inside and close the door. I guess there are a few more things we need to talk about as we get ourselves cleaned up. Ren, could you fetch us some more towels? And Aurora, would you happen to know how to find these ladies something fresh to wear at this strange hour, on the Eve of Midwinter?" The lot of them reeked of smoke and sweat, but besides his own clothes, they only had something in Ren's size.

"I might have something," Aurora said. "And if I don't, I'm sure the building manager, Mr Chatbury, will be able to assist. Perhaps I should take the ladies to my apartment to freshen up and meet with you after?"

"That might be more practical, considering we only have these two rooms, and there's not much space in the washroom," Vincent agreed. "Ren, could you be a dear and fetch a towel just for me, then?"

"Sure. You should sit down and keep off of that knee, anyway." She ushered him to take a seat on the bed.

"What time is it? Almost noon? How about we come back here at three o'clock and head to Rhys's together?" Aurora suggested.

"We...?" Hosta seemed hesitant.

"Unless you have somewhere else to be? If there's someone after you, you'd probably be safest with us for now until you figure out what you want to do. Unless that had something to do with Mr Wakefield?"

"No, I don't know who those people were. If it's not too imposing, I will take you up on your offer."

"Then it's settled."

As soon as Julian had hauled the tree upstairs, Jasmine admired it with her eyes wide and gleaming like she'd never seen a spruce before. Rhys brought her the box of glass baubles, ribbons, decorative sweets and paper ornaments, and she spent several hours placing them in just the right order.

The tree was large enough to fit everything with still room for more, so Rhys showed Jasmine how to make colourful paper baskets for nuts, fruit and berries. Busied in this way seemed to work well to keep their minds off of the events of the recent past. Julian watched the two of them at it, feeling as old as ever but not as annoyed about it. The mulled wine he was sipping might have had something to do with it.

Quin woke up in the afternoon. He was feeling well enough to sit up without making as much noise and even ventured to stand and stretch his legs. Since Julian dragging and setting up the tree hadn't roused him from his slumber, he was fittingly perplexed and impressed when he noticed it had appeared as if by magic to the corner of the lounge.

"Wow, you really did get a tree! And you got Julian to carry it here?"

Julian raised a brow at the question. Quin chuckled.

"Yes, yes, I know you've changed. It'll never cease to amaze me how much! I had to fight you over getting one of those small, tree-shaped table ornaments back in the day. You said they were for kids, and you completely refused to celebrate in any other way save for getting drunk and—" Quin coughed. Julian rolled his eyes, covered his face with his hand and shook his head.

"I was probably happy about the ornament," he admitted begrudgingly. He had a feeling he'd just been young and stupid. Why else would he feel so sceptical about the purpose of the tree, yet, when it was there, enjoy watching it?

"Once the kids have gone to bed, want to engage in some Midwinter traditions with me?" Quin flashed him a mischievous grin.

"Your ribs are broken," Julian reminded him. This only made Quin smile more brightly. "Now what? What did I do?"

"You're saying you would have, had they not been?" Quin looked like he might have jumped up and down from joy had he not been so sore.

Julian re-rolled his eyes and sighed. In all honesty, had Rhys approved, he might have... but there wasn't enough mulled wine in this building to get him drunk enough to admit that to Quin.

"What did you say to him? He looks like he's been opening presents early." Rhys had finished placing the gifts under the tree and sat down next to Julian on the sofa. Quin lowered himself back onto the mattress. It looked as painful as before, but he was beaming happily.

"I may have unwittingly said something encouraging," Julian said.

"I think I can guess what it was."

"Please don't."

"I don't mind if you want to."

"You don't know what you're saying." Julian snorted.

After chuckling over it inwardly for a moment, he glanced back at Rhys and froze. Surely he didn't? He hadn't actually heard the conversation, had he? Rhys smiled at him. Nah, it had to be a coincidence. Why would he bother asking if he'd heard...

"Heh," Rhys heh'ed deliberately and kept on watching him with a subtle smile lingering on his lips. Something about this made Julian blush.

"Is your brother coming today?" he asked to deflect.

"Yes, he rang an hour ago and said they'd be here by four. That's in," Rhys checked the clock, "oh, any minute now, actually."

Good, that'll get the two of you busy and off my back, Julian thought.

Rhys jumped and rushed downstairs at the sound of someone knocking on the door.

"Vincent, it's open! Come on in!" he yelled from the landing. "Joyful Midwinter!"

"Joyful Midwinter to you as well... oh dear, what's happened to you?" Vincent leaned on the door frame and stepped in.

"An accident... wait— you're the one to talk! What did you do to your hand?" It was wrapped in a bandage, and, that aside, he was standing suspiciously lopsided. "Did you take a tumble?"

"No, there was a fire at the clinic. I'll tell you about it later. It's freezing out there." He held the door open for Ren and Vera as well as Hosta. The latter was about to enter when one look at Rhys made her stop in her tracks.

"It's you!" she exclaimed.

"What's she doing here?" Rhys had been looking forward to a superbly uneventful evening, and the sight of her brought back the sickening sensation of blood sprayed on his skin.

"She said someone was out to get her, so we brought her over with us," Vincent explained.

"That was us! She wanted to erase Julian's memory and use me as a test subject in one of her deranged experiments—who knows why! She's in charge of a Guardian-damned criminal organisation! We almost got ourselves killed trying to stop her and her husband yesterday!"

"What?" Vincent turned to look at Hosta. "When you said 'everything', you don't mean going as far as pestering and poking my brother without his consent to try to further the research?"

Hosta seemed to be right in the middle of either blowing up or cowering back.

"Well, I don't know! Is he type eight? Does he have something I could use to help the Guardian pick up your corrupt signature?"

"Wait," Rhys interjected. "You were trying to help him? How do you know Vincent? Why didn't you just tell me you wanted to study me to help Vincent?"

"I don't know, I don't know who you are! But people usually respond poorly to my proposals, and trying to find willing research subjects is such a pain..." As Hosta was saying this, Vera nodded in sympathy, presumably realised who she was agreeing with and abruptly stopped nodding. "As for him, I think he might be my son. At least, I'm fairly sure that's him, even if he does look disturbingly like his depraved, treacherous rogue of a f—"

"Hold up!" Rhys cut her off. "You're *her*?" He'd known his father must have had someone before his mother for Vincent to exist, but this seemed like an outrageous connection. "Justin was right! There was one starting with a V!"

"Look, I don't want to interrupt or ruin your Midwinter. I only came here because Vera said there are some people I should meet, but if I'm not wanted, I'll be on my way."

She didn't appear to have the means or the urge to wipe anyone's memory nor abuse Rhys for his abilities in the name of science or profit, so in most respects it seemed harmless to let her in.

"I don't mind having you here, but I think we should ask the others whether they want to share their Eve with you—" Rhys noticed there was still someone standing behind Hosta at the door. "Pardon me, I didn't realise... Come in. Are you cold?"

When Hosta moved aside and he saw who it was, Rhys understood the significance of her presence.

"Is he dead?" He felt the proverbial lump swell in his throat and swallowed. His mother nodded. "But you're fine? You're not hurt?"

She nodded again.

An immense sense of relief washed over Rhys, and he jumped to hug his mother.

"We're free?" he whispered to her.

"I'm so sorry, Rhys. I was such a coward. I should have done something sooner!" She squeezed him.

Rhys wanted to cry. Ah, why fight it? She was safe! "This is the best Midwinter's gift. I've missed you so much!" he said between his sobs.

She hugged him until he calmed down somewhat, then pushed him back a little to take a good look at him. "I can't believe how much you've grown. I wanted to say this the last time we saw each other, but there was no time. You look so grown up, confident and handsome."

"I'm bawling my eyes out, Ma." Rhys laughed at her comment.

"Can't a mother be proud of her son? I'm so glad you look more at peace with yourself. Although, please forgive me for saying this, you did look ever so charming in that blue dress, the laced choker and your great aunt's earr—"

"Ma!" Rhys huffed.

"They're perhaps out of fashion now, but you used to spend ages watching those earrings dangle from her ears as a baby. Maybe you would like to gift them to someone special one day?"

It had been a pretty pair for sure, but Vincent had said... Rhys shot Vincent a scathing look.

"What?" Vincent blinked.

"If you still have them, I'd like you to bring them next time you come and see me," Rhys said to his mother.

The thought of giving a pair of earrings to Julian, Quin or Victor was ridiculous, and Rhys couldn't think of anyone more special to him than his tenants. Ren didn't seem the type to ever want to wear earrings, so there was no sense saving them for her. Jasmine seemed like the only one who might have worn them out of courtesy, even though they weren't her style.

In all honesty, Rhys didn't even feel too keen to part with them. He found himself entertaining the thought that sometime in the not-too-distant future he might, perhaps, be ready to challenge Victor on his resolve to never question his gender, regardless of his outfit decisions. It felt like ages since Victor had said those words, and though Rhys had appreciated them at the time, he'd never thought he'd dare to actually test their validity.

Quin often wore an earring and other jewellery. The floral buttons Rhys had liked on his new gloves were the same the tailor himself wore proudly on his favourite waistcoat. Maybe these small things would eventually give him courage to be himself and to finally enjoy *all* the things he wanted to enjoy?

Out of instinct, he pawed for the little bird whistle necklace in his trouser pocket. What better way to ease himself into it? He fished it out, tied it around his neck and left it hanging on top of his shirt. Something about it made him smile, now, without having to force it.

"I'm sorry. Where are my manners? Take off your coats, and let's get you settled. All of you." Rhys glanced at Hosta. "I'm sure in the spirit of Midwinter we'll fit under the same roof."

"Why is she here?" Quin commented on that wretched woman coming up the stairs to the lounge behind Rhys, Rhys's brother, Dr Vesper, the little girl with the cat carrier and another woman Quin did not recognise.

"Do you mind if she joins us? She's not here to cause trouble." Rhys turned to Hosta. "Right?"

"I'm not sure what trouble I could cause you. I don't know who you are. Except, he looks familiar..." She pointed at Julian. "Are you my son? You're Julian, right?"

"Yes. You seem to have retained more of your memories than expected. Do you remember Justin too, or did he slip your mind?" Julian sat up on the sofa. Something about him seemed off, but her presence could have soured anyone's mood, so perhaps this was to be expected.

"Oh, right. There were two of you." The woman appeared to have to strain to remember.

"Yes, indeed. A spare if you will. It must have been convenient to have one that's expendable." Julian was definitely in a crabby mood.

"What do you mean?"

"You don't suppose you recall what you and Father meant to do with Jonathan and Jacob? The two of them have disappeared from the face of the earth. Were they no longer useful to you?"

"Jonathan? Jacob?" She seemed confused.

"Did you care about any of us? Or was it always just about the research?!"

Ah, that enraged timbre always brought such pleasant chills down Quin's back.

"Have you been drinking?" Expression ashen, Hosta seemed to be looking for the bottle. "How much?" She asked this from Rhys and Quin, but Rhys merely shrugged, and Quin never had objections to Julian's drinking, so he had no reason to pay much attention to it. The rage was often a hint more vibrant and delicious when he was drunk, though, so he'd probably enjoyed more than a glass of the mulled wine.

"So what if I have?" Julian snarled back at her. "Is it inconvenient for you?"

"Mother?" Julian's sister came down the stairs from the attic. "Julian? What happened? Why are you so upset?"

Julian signed something to her.

"No, I'm not going back upstairs. What's Mother doing here? Will she be staying with us?"

"No! I will not have her in this house! I—!" Victor interrupted Julian by taking him by the arm. This warded off Julian's anger temporarily, even if Victor wasn't in a condition to stand up to him. "Sit down before you hurt yourself!" Julian barked back.

For a moment, it looked like Victor might do as told, but then he opened his mouth and raised his voice to an impressive volume instead.

"No. This is your chance to deal with it! You're feeling something *now*, right? Don't chase her out the second it catches up with you!" Whatever that meant, Julian seemed to pause to take it in. "If it feels like you can't contain it, and you want to break something, you should go downstairs and scream at a wall until it passes, but you deal with it!"

Quin raised his hand sheepishly. "Can I go downstairs to deal with it with him?"

"You stay out of this! I'm not going anywhere!" Julian turned to roar at his face. Like old times! Quin smiled.

Hosta stared at them in a state of obvious horror and looked ready to bolt.

"Why are you egging him on?" she peeped.

Rhys was on top of the situation. "Jasmine, dear, could you do me a favour and show Ren your room? Take the cat up there with you as well. He doesn't seem to appreciate the noise. I'll call you down when we're ready to eat," he said.

Jasmine nodded and guided the little girl and the cat away and up to the attic. Good thinking.

"Ma, would you mind warming up the supper for us? It's mostly ready. I'd do it myself, but they may need a mediator, and this might take a while."

Oh, she was Rhys's mother? She seemed glad to move aside with something to do. But this was no time to be distracted. Julian was steaming and raving at Quin, who watched his stupidly handsome face twist in its typical, lovely expression of fury.

"How much did you let him drink? Has he lost his senses completely?" That woman already had one foot on the first step down the stairs.

Julian grabbed Quin by the cheeks and held his grinning face up in a vice-like grip. This dance was just one short step away from its first kiss. Too bad the new Julian couldn't remember the steps.

"It's best to let him blow off some steam when he gets riled up like this. I'll intervene if they start making out," Rhys said.

"Please don't!" Quin requested.

"Then go downstairs with your bloody foreplay!" Rhys snapped at them. Julian turned to look at him and immediately let go of Quin's face.

"I'm sorry. Not sure what came over me," he said. He glanced at his mother with some lingering discontent, sighed and sat back down on the sofa. Quin sat down next to him and leaned back, fanning his flustered cheeks with his hand.

"Look, if it helps any, I don't think of anyone as a spare." Hosta bit her lip. Was she trying to elicit sympathy? "My memory is hazy, but I know none of you are a spare or extra or expendable." Her lip quivered no matter how she was biting it. "Least of all Justin. I tried to help him. I was getting so close, but I ran out of time." She seemed to make some effort to not burst into tears, but the weeping was likely just part of her theatrics. "I'm sorry... I'm so sorry. I tried to protect you. I didn't know what else to do."

"You hooked me to a machine and used me to spy on people across the city for what, for funding?" Julian's voice was unrelenting and cold.

Something about that statement hadn't sounded quite right.

"That was to keep you active so you wouldn't—!" Hosta choked, fell to her knees and started sobbing. It was quite the act. Dr Vesper knelt next to her to comfort her.

"Wouldn't what? Cause you more grief?" Julian wasn't drunk enough to fall for it. He watched her, none the kinder.

"Die off completely! I may have an ugly temper, but I'm not a complete monster!" She wiped her eyes and nose to a handkerchief Dr Vesper offered her. "I remember enough to know I'm far from perfect, but I wouldn't knowingly hurt any of you."

It was all fairly convincing. Just the right amount of emotion. She sounded almost sincere.

"You could have at least let me have the duck, for Guardian's sake!" Julian stood back up to berate her mercilessly.

What duck? What?

"I'm sorry, Justin, but you were *allergic*!" Hosta was swallowing tears, but her eyes were sharp. Quin struggled to keep up. What on earth were they talking about?

"What did it matter? I was dying anyway!"

"Well, I didn't know that for sure!" She stopped to take notice of the rest of the people in the room now staring at her. "They sometimes connect through the Guardian when he's drunk. It's Justin."

Julian's face distorted into something nearly unrecognisable. It was a mix between pain and fury, and he seemed about to explode.

"Oh, no." Hosta raised her hands in an apparent effort to placate him. Gripped with inexplicable fear, Quin glanced at Rhys. Rhys looked equally unsettled. What the hell was happening? Had she broken Julian somehow?!

Hosta had looked ready to retreat down the stairs ever since she'd come up, but this time she stepped forth. Instead of them butting heads with sparks and brimstone, Julian let out a tortured noise, and she wrapped her arms around him.

"Justin…" Julian wheezed and looked like he'd been punched in the gut. Quin could not remember Julian ever looking like that, but there was something horribly, gut-wrenchingly familiar about the deep sorrow shadowing in his eyes.

"There, there. I'm sorry. It's OK. He's still there."

"Don't you try to soothe me, woman!" Julian shrieked at her but let her hold him while he cried.

"Do you want me to take away the pain? I'll take away the pain..." She hugged him and rubbed his back protectively. "You shouldn't drink, right? It's not good for you."

"Shut up, you hag!" He was still actively raging at her but made no effort to move out of her reach. "I should destroy you..."

"I know. I'm sorry." She held him all the same.

"Quin...?" Julian suddenly looked up from his mother's shoulder. Tears streamed down his face, but it was instantly recognisable: it had been years since he'd looked at Quin like that. Even if it was just a brief moment of recognition, and even if he'd never remember everything, that look was enough.

Quin thought his heart might just stop beating from him being so happy.

"I'm sorry. Excuse me," Aurora interrupted them gently. "This seems important, but we're probably all tired and hungry and not in our best frames of mind. Perhaps it might be wise to rest and have a bite to eat before you resume this?" She turned around. "And for heaven's sake, Vincent, sit down!"

Vincent flinched. He'd been standing on his healthier leg all the while but was starting to feel the strain.

He tottered over to one of the dining chairs and sat down as told. But the knee already throbbed like the distended gular pouch of a frigatebird desperate to attract a mate, and it was worse now that he'd lost the benefit of the distractions. He rubbed it despite knowing it wouldn't help any.

"Does it hurt? Ah, you'll open the wound on your palm if you keep doing that." Aurora walked over to him to check. "It's swollen. You should be more careful, or you'll have to go see Dr Skinpitt again."

"Please don't say such awful things..." Vincent tried to joke, but his clenched teeth and tight voice foiled the attempt.

"Ah, Julian? Would it be possible to get something for his knee?"

"Of course. I'd hesitate to give him laudanum considering that cough, though." Julian seemed to have returned to his senses even if he sounded suspiciously nasally.

"Camphor liniment, then? Or acetylsalicylic acid?"

"Yes, although their efficacy for such severe pain may be limited..."

There they were at it again with their fancy medical talk. Vincent sighed. Maybe it wasn't that fancy this time, but he was feeling too tired to follow words with more than one Y or two C's in them.

"The food is ready," Mrs Wakefield announced.

She had set the table in front of Vincent, so at least he didn't have to move anywhere. Aurora finished spreading something on his knee, and Julian mixed him a dose of white powder into a half a glass of water.

And here he was, wallowing in self-pity over his envy, when they were clearly busy with problems of their own but still showed such kindness to him.

"What's wrong?" Aurora pulled down the leg of his trousers and turned to look at him.

Would it hurt to tell the truth without belittling it or pretending to be fine about it? He'd already said so many things, so why not the thing that worried him the most?

The others had gathered around the table to either take a seat or stuff food on their plates to eat wherever there was space to sit.

"I'm tired," he said. Aurora took his hand in hers. "I'm tired of myself, for feeling stupid, useless and confused more often than not, and even though you're here regardless of all that, I can't help but wonder how long it will take for you to tire and give up on me.

"I'm trying my best to be dependable and not an annoyance or a burden. Most of the time I'm genuinely fine with being like this because I know I'm doing my best with something that's no fault of my own. But I do get tired of having to be me sometimes."

The others had stopped what they were doing and watched him in silence.

"Vincent…" Aurora leaned in closer and set her hand by his ear. "You don't have to worry about that. You're more than enough just as you are." She gave him a kiss on the cheek. "Try to enjoy the evening as best you can, but if you don't feel well, it's all right. I've brought some of your medicine with me to help you get to sleep. I don't have anything here to monitor your sleep with, but it should give you an hour or two and hopefully make you feel better. Can you make it through supper? We haven't eaten much today, so you should probably eat something."

"I've been tired for thirty-seven years. I can manage through one supper."

Vincent chuckled. He was glad to realise it wasn't out of his usual habit of making light of the situation. He was actually feeling a wee bit better with her looking at him.

"Aurora."

"Hmm?"

"I'm going to say this even if I'm not proud of it."

"Yes?"

"I get horribly jealous when you're chatting with Julian."

"What?"

"I'd like to think it's envy over the two of you being able to sustain conversations I'm too exhausted to follow and too stupid to understand, but it's really just me feeling insecure and fearing you'll prefer him over me."

There. He'd said it. He closed his eyes to avoid seeing her face.

"Vincent, my love," he heard her say. "You really don't have to ever worry about that. I'm head over heels for your gorgeous self."

Vincent opened his eyes. She was blushing, but she was wearing the most beautiful, kind smile and looking straight at him. He cupped her face and gave her a tender kiss.

"All right, the pair of you," Rhys interrupted one gracious but short moment later. "You're no doubt keeping warm, basking in the warmth of your love, but the food is not as lucky, and it's getting cold." He was holding up a heavy pot of mash so his mother could reach and add a serving on the plate she was filling.

Once she was done adding everything, she handed the plate over to Vincent and started filling Aurora's, but she'd hardly taken one scoop of the mash before she turned back. "Oh, goodness me. I put peas on yours. Should I remove them for you?"

"Huh?" Vincent frowned and looked at the peas. It was true he wasn't a huge fan, but he'd long since learnt to appreciate whatever was given to him.

"Truth be told, I was always most cross that the deceitful maggot took you along with him." Hosta glanced at Mrs Wakefield. "Never mind him, but you were so particular with the details and took such good care of my boy, I wish I could have kept you when I threw my husband's foul fundament out the door."

"The peas are fine..." Vincent noted.

"You have to believe me, none of it was ever up to me," Mrs Wakefield said and offered to pour mulled wine into Hosta's glass. "The only reason I asked him if we could take Vincent along was because I was worried you wouldn't have time for him."

"I know. I think I've always known. It's just that the thought of his repulsive face makes me want to break things, sours my mood and ruins my appetite. Let's not talk about it. It's all in the past." Hosta tasted a forkful of the casserole and looked surprised. "This is delicious. Whose is it?"

Mrs Wakefield pointed at Rhys and smiled happily. "It's a family recipe."

Their conversation was cut short by the sound of the telephone ringing.

"I'll get it," Jasmine offered and hurried downstairs to answer it.

"Who could it be, at this hour on the Eve?" Mrs Wakefield voiced what must have been on everyone's mind.

They waited in silence until Jasmine finally returned.

"Who was it?" Julian asked.

"It was Jonathan wishing us a Joyous Midwinter. He and Jacob are up in Grymswich visiting Aunt and Uncle, but he said it was really because Jacob has met a girl he fancies. He said to thank Rhys for the excellent advice last Midwinter. They would have got in touch much sooner but said the telephone lines were cut because of the exceptionally rough weather. He hopes you're not too cross with them for leaving without explaining."

"Well, I suppose that puts my mind at ease." Julian emptied his glass of mulled wine. Hosta glanced at him worriedly but then turned to her own glass.

Vincent tasted the peas. Yes. They were definitely not a favourite but posed no issue with a bit of gravy. He glanced at Aurora, hoping to steal it unnoticed, but she was looking at him while she ate.

He gave her an awkward smile, which made her blush and hide behind her hands, smiling. She was so fascinating, so sweet, just watching her eat made Vincent's heart flutter. The supper was delicious, but it could have been paper and tasted the same when she was there sharing it with him. He was so glad to be reminded of this feeling.

F inished with the food, Vincent retired to the sofa with Aurora taking a seat next to him.

Rhys, Julian, Justin, Hosta and Mrs Wakefield remained chatting at the table, clearing their grievances. Mr Hart and Mr Quin sat in their respective armchairs, Mr Quin making idle conversation with Mr Hart as if old friends. The girls had retreated back upstairs in the attic.

Swifty emerged from under the dining table and stretched lazily. He seemed well-fed and satisfied. Aurora called him to her, and he jumped on her lap and watched Vincent without a word. Somehow Vincent could still imagine what he was saying.

"Come on then. It's not hurting as bad right now," he told the cat. Swifty curled up on his lap and started purring. Vincent relaxed.

"I'd like to start my own clinic to continue where she left off but without any of the shady excess," Aurora said.

That sounded nice.

"Would you be horribly against travelling with me in search of more of those ancient texts? I'd like to learn everything I can about the Guardian, to help you, but also to help all the others suffering in similar ways."

"I would love to take you," Vincent mumbled. He was exhausted, but listening to Aurora's soft voice by his ear while sleepless wasn't so bad.

"I wouldn't mind starting a family," she said. "But I might have my hands full with the research..."

"Whatever you want, I'll do my best to support you."

"Really?"

"I already get no sleep. It's fine." Vincent chuckled tiredly. "But I should warn you, the child might turn out like me."

"Good. That's what I'm hoping for."

"You'll have your work cut out for you." Vincent smiled and closed his eyes.

"I know." She kissed him. "Should I get the medicine for you?"

"It's fine. I want to enjoy this moment for a while longer." It wasn't sleep, but it was so pleasant it was difficult to say which was better. There was no sign of the bubble, no pesky fever. He was just tired. "Can you kiss me again? That was nice..."

She let out a subdued laugh and gave him another kiss.

He couldn't see the bubble, but it did seem to be there all the same. Maybe if he used his imagination and concentrated on where his instincts told him it was... It might come into view again.

After a while, it was indeed there. How curious.

Aurora fingered Vincent's slightly curled, overgrown sideburn, absent-minded. It was sad to see him so tired, but, despite not being able to sleep, he looked content.

"We'd still have time to go see the lights. Anyone up for it?" Rhys asked.

"Maybe," Mr Quin responded.

"I'll stay with Vincent. It's best he rests his knee," Aurora said. "Right?" She turned to Vincent.

Vincent said nothing.

Aurora frowned.

"Vincent?"

"Is something wrong?" Rhys asked.

Aurora had time to feel the cold sweat of dread at the back of her neck before she realised Vincent was breathing just fine.

She turned to Rhys and lifted her finger to her lips to shush him.

"What is it?" Rhys whispered and inched closer.

"I think he's asleep."

Glossary

May contain spoilers!

ARF mask, the (the Automated Rest Facilitator) A mask applied to a person to stop them from sleep-roaming and interfering with the Guardian's automated rest procedures.

Batten in this case a strip of wood used in constructing a roof.

Bubble the confined space within which a person sleeps dreamside.

Bulb, the the private attic laboratory at the Craft's house.

Chancel the part of the church nearest to the altar.

Contact points Surveillance units out in the field that form a network connected to the Guardian. Also, any unmanned devices facilitating that network.

Crook of the Ear, a region named after its location on the cat-shaped continent of Furuyan.

Ear of the City an affluent area of Schadesborough with a distinct style in architecture and a lot of immigrants from the North.

Earemoss one of the two expanses of land that made up the cat's ear. Earemoss is lush, green and mountainous.

Furuyan, the name of the continent where this story takes place.

Guardian, supposedly a widely worshipped deity on Furuyan, second only to the god of another monotheist religion similar to Christianity. More accurately, an apparatus used for analysing, diagnosing, preventing and curing health issues related to, or through, sleep.

GODS, the (the Guardian Observation and Diagnostics System) as the name suggests, a system used at the ReM Clinic to observe and diagnose the Guardian.

Healia Healthcare the entity that Dr Vesper works for.

Kid leather not made of or for children, it's a type of soft, thin leather typically used for gloves.

Maury, (Holy Maury, Mother of the Sea and Weaver of the Waves) the deity most revered by the fisher communities in the Arctic regions of Furuyan.

Memory seal a seal to keep a person from accessing their memories until they fade from disuse. This usually happens more quickly than forgetting something normally because the brain will treat those memories as gone and will consequently overwrite them with new information. The Guardian has several memory-enhancing features that mitigate this process as it routinely accesses and organises the memories of everyone connected to it.

Midwinter, a time of celebration during the winter solstice.

Nave the central part of a church.

Purlin a horizontal beam used for structural support, in a roof.

Rest the restorative stages of sleep. This is not one specific stage but a combination of processes often aided and automated by the Guardian that make a person feel refreshed and well-rested in the morning.

RI Index, the, (the Restorative Impact Index) an index used to measure the restorative impact of a person's sleep.

Rood screen an ornate partition separating the chancel and the nave.

Rya a thick, knotted high-pile cloth, usually a rug, sometimes used as bedding.

Sleep-roaming being aware of dreamside while you sleep.

Surveillance Unit a machine connected to the remains of a person who was capable of sleep-roaming.

System service hall the space at the ReM Clinic where the GODS is housed.

Tribal guardians supposedly people, who take care of the wellbeing of their tribe via the Guardian.

Void the unwelcoming space between the bubbles.

Whitskersey, the Island of the White Skerries, a small island in the Arctic, near the Crook of the Ear.

Yaveleng one of the two expanses of land that made up the cat's ear. Yaveleng was arid and flat.

Cast of Characters

May contain spoilers!

Abelia, Nurse a nurse at the Sleepy Leighs Treatment Centre.

Ballroth, Winston an off-putting rich man who tries to buy Rhys's building.

Barffmouth, Dr a doctor at the Sleepy Leighs Treatment Centre.

Bramble, Aster Celandine's sister, Vincent's guardian.

Buttercup, Celandine Aster's sister, Vincent's guardian.

Catherine Dr Vesper's croton.

Cobbs, Russ 'Rusty' Quin's ill-tempered associate.

Corkbottom. Dr a doctor at the Sleepy Leighs Treatment Centre.

Craft, James Julian's father.

Craft, H.A. Julian's mother.

Craft, Jacob Julian's younger brother.

Craft, Jasmine Julian's younger sister.

Craft, Jonathan Julian's younger brother.

Craft, Julian Rhys's pharmacist tenant.

Craft, Justin Julian's twin brother.

Florence Dr Vesper's fountain pen.

Hargrave, Mrs Rhys's great aunt. Remarried.

Hart, Victor Rhys's attic tenant.

Hughes Quin's butler.

Jarvis Dr Vesper's journal.

Jenkins, Jon 'Two-Face' (Jon-Jon) Quin's foul-mouthed associate.

Larkspur, Ms a receptionist at the Sleepy Leighs Treatment Centre.

Limpqvist, Dr A professor at the Grovestead School for Boys.

Lobelia, Ms an assistant at the ReM Clinic.

Quin, Adair Julian's former partner in crime.

Skinpitt, Dr a doctor at the Sleepy Leighs Treatment Centre.

Swifty, Ren Vincent's ward. Bryony and Marcus's daughter.

Swifty, Sir Vincent's trusty feline companion.

Swifty, Vincent the title character of book one. Ren's guardian.

Theodore Dr Vesper's teacup.

Vesper, A.L. (Vera) a doctor specialising in sleep science at the Sleepy Leighs Treatment Centre. The title character of this book.

Wakefield, Dahlia Rhys's great aunt.

Wakefield, Lillian Rhys's mother.

Wakefield, Rhys M. our building-owning protagonist.

Wakefield, Walter Rhys's father. Vincent's father.

Williams, Mr Julian's archaeologist friend.

About the Author

J.B. Thwaite is the author of dozens of best-selling books that only exist in her dreams. She lives in the darkest, most inhospitable depths of Southern Finland with her spouse, scion and feline companion. She has discovered fire and re-invented the wheel in exactly the same form as before but better. With an incredibly busy schedule, she uses her scarce free time to nap, sleep and doomscroll on social media. She is also a connoisseur of the highest quality Asian homoerotic literature and a bit too neurodivergent to enjoy long walks on the beach.

Also by

The Catnap Ramblers:
Vincent and the Cat (2023)
Rhys and the Voiceless (2023)
Aurora and the Guardian (2023)

Novellas:
Private Afterwords (~2024)
Solicitous Missteps (~2024)

Other books in the works:
Pandion (~2024)
Fingers and Thumbs (~2024)